For Heidi

PRAISE FOR *RAFT OF STARS*

'One of the finest debut novels to emerge so far in 2021'
Sunday Post

'A poignant coming-of-age adventure'
Candis

'Absolutely wonderful. Beautifully written, characters that will
stay with me. I didn't want it to end'
Jo Spain

'A powerful, gripping, coming-of-age novel about friendship,
parenting, violence and beauty'
Platinum, Book of the Month

'An engrossing, large-hearted debut novel'
New York Times

'Graff writes exquisitely about the wilderness ... A gripping
adventure tale'
Washington Post

'A rugged outdoors adventure with a warm heart, intense
thrills and some genuinely beautiful writing'
Paul Finch

'The best book I've read all year!'
Anita Frank

'This a book for our times and in it lies a truth about man,
nature and the strength of love'
Sally Gardner

'A coming of age tale that any adult who has ever felt a little
lost can identify with. A beautiful book that will stay with me'
Louise Hare

Andrew J. Graff is the author of novel *Raft of Stars*. His fiction and essays have appeared in *Image* and *Dappled Things*. Andrew grew up fishing, hiking, and hunting in Wisconsin's Northwoods. After a tour of duty in Afghanistan, Graff earned an MFA from the Iowa Writers' Workshop. He lives in Ohio and teaches at Wittenberg University.

RAFT OF STARS

Andrew J. Graff

ONE PLACE. MANY STORIES

HQ
An imprint of HarperCollins*Publishers* Ltd
1 London Bridge Street
London SE1 9GF

www.harpercollins.co.uk

HarperCollins*Publishers*
1st Floor, Watermarque Building, Ringsend Road
Dublin 4, Ireland

This paperback edition 2022

1

First published in Great Britain by
HQ, an imprint of HarperCollins*Publishers* Ltd 2021

Copyright © Andrew J. Graff 2021

Andrew J. Graff asserts the moral right to be
identified as the author of this work.
A catalogue record for this book is
available from the British Library.

ISBN: 978-0-00-845362-6

MIX
Paper from
responsible sources

FSC
www.fsc.org **FSC™ C007454**

This book is produced from independently certified FSC™ paper
to ensure responsible forest management.

For more information visit: www.harpercollins.co.uk/green

Printed and Bound in the UK using 100% Renewable Electricity at
CPI Group (UK) Ltd

PROLOGUE

To: Fish's Grandpa

Fish had me put this note on your fridge to tell you we are running away.

He says we're going to find his dad. We will mail you money for the sack of food we took from your cupboard, and the jack-knife, and the two cups, and the pack of matches. Fish says to tell his mom don't worry. We have my old man's gun and five bullets. We have our bikes and fish poles, and a tarp, and also a pouch of your tobacco, and will send money for that too.

Please tell the sheriff that Fish didn't want to shoot my old man. My old man is dead in my kitchen, on the floor by the table.

From: Dale Breadwin

ONE

THE BABY TURTLES THE BOYS CARRIED IN THE FRONT OF THEIR shirts were the size of half-dollars. Fish stopped on the asphalt and looked down into his shirt as he crossed the road from the field to the marsh for the fifth time. It was early June and the sun was hot, and the turtles looked bothered and parched as they clawed in a pile. The turtles were *tenacious,* which meant "persisting in existence." That was a word Fish knew from fifth grade.

Fish's friend, Bread, clawed up from the ditch clover, its lazy bees, and caught up with Fish on the road. A redwing blackbird clung to one of last year's dried cattail stalks.

"You know these are snappers we're saving," said Bread. "See them bony shells? We're saving snappers."

The boys feared grown snappers like they feared Bread's old man. If there was one thing that could stop the boys in their tracks, it was the discovery of a full-grown snapper, how the thing reared up and hissed in that way that didn't seem right for a turtle to do. Turtles and dads weren't supposed to rear up and hiss.

Fish looked down into his own shirt and shrugged. "They don't look mean yet," he said.

The asphalt road they stood on was quiet and old and bleached nearly white by the sun. It cut through marshes and drained marshes that had been long ago tilled into cornfields. The rooftops of the town of Claypot rose up from the fields a half mile away. The two sagging roofs of Bread's old man's house and mechanic shop butted up against the fields to the south. Fish hated that house and shop.

"But they'll get mean once they grow up," said Bread.

Fish looked at the turtles again. It didn't seem right to judge them this early in life, the way they were nearly dried up and only just hatched. Poor damn things. That's something his grandfather often said when a calf was born a runt and couldn't eat, or a baby bird had fallen from its nest for the cats to find. The world was full of poor damn things. Sometimes Fish's grandfather looked at Bread with the same kind of pity in his eyes, but then he'd seem to catch himself and say something about how grateful he was for Bread's hard work that day, and how he hoped Bread would be back the next. Fish had seen the same looks of pity in the eyes of other grown-ups when they got around Bread. He'd seen it in the eyes of the sheriff when he came around, and even the gas station clerk, when Bread trudged up to the counter in his ragged sneakers to buy a candy bar with money Fish's grandpa had given him. There was pity, but also wariness, like they were just waiting for Bread to turn out like his dad, waiting for him to pocket the candy and bolt. Bread was poor, and his dad was mean, but Fish disliked the way grown-ups looked at his friend. He didn't like what it did in his heart, how it made his friendship bear some sort of shame.

"I want to save 'em," said Fish.

Bread nodded and grinned. "Me too," he said.

The boys had been walking their bikes toward Claypot when they found the turtles. The overwintered snappers emerged from a dried culvert ditch—the tracks were evident—but instead of clawing their way through the culvert and into the marsh, they clawed their way into the dry dirt of the tilled-up cornfield. They wouldn't find water if they went that way. And in another week they'd get beaten up by the planters. There were hundreds of them, like little round stones pushed up by a thaw. The boys leaned on their handlebars, watching all the doomed turtles. It had been a good day until then, and doom would ruin it. Before they found the turtles, they sat in the pine trees behind Fish's grandpa's barn, and before that they lit off firecrackers in the barn's silos. Fish loved lighting off firecrackers in silos. The way the air was so dank and still. The way the match flared and the fuse sparked and you covered your ears and squinted your eyes because the darkness was about to become so filled with noise and light. Lighting firecrackers always made Fish feel as if something big was about to happen, big enough to change a regular day. You just had to wait for the fuse, and then the noise and smoke would take you somewhere. And when things got quiet and dark again, you could always light off more firecrackers as long as you had more matches. It was a lot like Fish's friendship with Bread these last three summers he spent at his grandpa's farm. Fish was a fuse and Bread was the match, or maybe it was the other way around. Either way, summer was too tame if you had one without the other. Once school let out, his mom would drive him up from town to drop him off, and Fish's grandpa would be waiting on the porch, and Fish would hug his mom and bolt from the car with his duffel packed for weeks of fields and trees and rivers.

Both boys were covered in cornfield dust up to their armpits from gathering the turtles, and the turtles themselves were white with it, like they'd been shook up in a bag of frying flour Fish's mom used to batter chicken halves. It was a dry spring. The tractors that dragged the soil smooth last week raised dust clouds that hung in the air for hours. A frigid winter with too much snow, and now a spring without rain. The winter was hard on the wildlife. When what snow there was first melted, the boys found three deer lying dead in the woods beneath a cedar tree, eyes milky and open. It looked as if the animals had grown too tired of the cold and decided to lie down for a while, amazed that a winter so cold could exist even this far north. "Poor damn things," Fish had said, after hesitantly prodding one with a stick to prove death didn't bother him.

On the opposite side of the asphalt road, the ditch met marsh water. The water was cold and dark with silt, and the wet bank seeped into the toes of the boys' shoes as they squatted down to free the snappers. As they lowered each leathery creature into the water, the turtles seemed awakened by it. The way the dust washed away. The suddenness of submersion. The turtles craned their little heads forward and waved their legs and swam away into the silt and water. They were like pigeons taking flight in pairs from the roof of Fish's grandpa's barn, aimless and erratic, surprised.

"Last one," said Fish, holding a kicking turtle over the water. Bread had already emptied his shirt and now washed his hands in the marsh. He sat back on his heels looking very satisfied as Fish freed the baby snapper. If Fish could pray the way his mom prayed, which was without ceasing and for everything, he would say a prayer for these turtles. He felt happy for them, or at least happy with himself, but he worried too. They were so small to be out in the marsh. They were each of them alone out there. Fish couldn't decide whether to admire or mourn them.

"Good luck," he said in a whisper, rubbing his palms together in the water and then looking up at the position of the sun. It was about to sink toward the treetops of Claypot. His smile faded as he saw the town again, saw the rusted tin roof of Bread's old man's house.

"What are you going to say?" asked Fish.

"To the turtles?" Bread asked. The boys watched the surface of the marsh water as if waiting for the tiny heads to pop back up. They never came. After their dry march through the unplanted field, they wanted to stay buried in the silt for a good long while.

"To your dad, I meant," said Fish, and then regretted saying it at all.

Bread looked up from the water. His neck tightened. "Oh," he said, and looked back at the marsh.

The water's surface was filled with light. On the banks, last year's grass lay brown and matted, but a good six inches of new growth poked through. Fish picked a flat blade of marsh grass, ran his fingers against its coarse grain, pretended to be interested in it. Then inspiration struck. There was a chance.

"My grandpa has more work for me to do tomorrow," said Fish. "You could help again if you want." He paused and gauged Bread's reaction, and then he purposefully brightened his voice as if he just came up with what he was really trying to say. "Why don't you not go home at all? You can come spend the night again. My grandpa can call."

Bread shook his head. "My old man said to get home," he said, standing up and swatting dust from the knees of his jeans. "He meant yesterday."

SOME DAYS THE BOYS MADE A GAME OF DREAMING UP WAYS TO RID Bread of his old man. They sunk the man in the marsh once. Another time they tied him up in raspberry bushes and let black bears get him. They ran him down with countless trucks and tractors, and they once buried him up to his neck in an anthill they found behind the barn. The game was a way of deadening the blows of Bread's real life. Bread would come out to Fish's grandpa's for a few days at a time. He'd arrive with stories about falling down steps or crashing his bike, and his face and neck would get so red with shame that the bruises seemed to fade. Always, though, by the time he left the farm the bruises had more or less yellowed. It wasn't every time. But it happened.

One evening when Bread spent the night, Fish overheard his

grandpa talking with Bread on the porch, asking him how bad it was at home. Bread hardly answered him, until Grandpa offered to go and talk to his old man, which Bread quickly refused. Fish overheard the talk from inside the kitchen where he filled a glass with water. He tiptoed to the porch door and leaned close to the screen.

"He just gets mad," said Bread. "He's usually always mad."

"He drink every night?" asked Grandpa, and after a pause, "He ever mess with them guns when he's drunk? Hmm."

Fish could smell the dust in the screen and felt a bad sort of envy about his friend. Fish's grandpa spoke to Bread as if he were an equal. Fish hadn't experienced that. Ever since Fish started spending summers at his grandpa's farm, he sensed his grandpa was somehow ill at ease around him. His grandpa was strong and gentle and good, but there was a certain distance between them that never allowed them to talk about real things, big things. They could talk easily about baseball players, or truck tires, or what needed doing around the place. But if Fish found himself crying in the hayloft—as he did often enough his first summer out, terrified by his new life without his father in it—he knew he was on his own. So he'd stop crying, finish his chores, wipe his face with his shirt, and stride toward the house to announce his hunger for dinner. It once occurred to Fish that maybe his grandpa's distance was a kindness as well, a lesson from a man to a boy about how not to dwell too much on things. Fish couldn't tell. It made him feel the way he did when he tried not to cry in front of boys at school. It was good not to cry. It was also awful.

"Look here, Dale," said Grandpa. "I don't mean to get in your business. But just so you know how I know, my old man used to push me and my sisters around too."

There was a pause. A heavy june bug attached itself to the screen near Fish's face and nearly caused Fish to reveal his presence. Fish's grandpa stood, reached for his pouch of tobacco.

"And I know how it goes if other people poke around in it, how it can make it all so much worse. So. But if you ever need a place to go, ever, you come right straight here. You run straight through the corn if you got to. Understand?"

"Yes sir."

"Good."

The three of them sat in the quiet, Fish on one side of the screen and his grandpa and Bread on the porch. The sun was all the way down now, and the fireflies were starting to lift out of the grass and float past the apple trees, speaking silently about whatever it is fireflies have to say to one another.

"None of it means you can't grow up good, Dale, a hell of a lot better than your old man. You're going to be a good one, you and Fischer are both going to be good." He stood now, walked across the porch boards, spat chew over the railing, and adjusted the green fatigue cap that always sat on the back of his head, its stout brim skyward. Fish was pretty sure he got the hat in Korea, but he never asked. It never left his head unless he slept, or used it to wipe sweat from his brow. "You boys are good, and strong enough to make it. You just keep going. Do you understand?"

"Yes sir."

In the distance, a pack of coyotes announced their hunt. The yipping howls lifted into the night and fell away just as quickly.

"Plenty of coyotes this year," he heard his grandpa say, to change the subject. "Plenty of hungry coyotes."

Fish joined his grandpa and friend on the porch, where he drank his water and watched the stars emerge in the new sort of silence. The stars hummed. Fish's blood hummed. The bad envy was gone, and a new light emerged. At Fischer's mom's church, congregants often "spoke over" one another. It's how they talked—*spoken over, spoken to, words from the Lord, for a brother.* Fish never minded it, but now he seemed to understand it. Bread and Fish had just been spoken over. His grandfather knew that all was not well in the world, that it was a *choice* to bear it quietly, and something grave and peaceful rose like a moon in Fish's heart.

THE SIDE STREET LEADING TO BREAD'S HOUSE WAS GRAVEL; THE town tore it up the previous summer to fix some pipes and never got around to repaving it. Bread said his math teacher said the roads and lots of other things would change for the better now that President Clinton was in office. All Fish knew about President Clinton was that he seemed to smile a lot and played a saxophone on the TV. Fish didn't know how much help a smiling man with a saxophone would be about a gravel road in Claypot. Fish's grandpa didn't know either.

Bread's house was the last on the left, and while none of them were nice, Bread's house was the worst. It had peeling paint like the rest, but it seemed to peel back in a meaner sort of way. The siding curled away in places, revealing bits of pink foamboard and blackened wood, like lips peeled back from bad gums and teeth. The grass was cut only when Bread was there to cut it, and even then, only when there was enough gas to run the smoking mower. Overgrown lilacs grew against the windowpanes. His dad's shop sat adjacent to the house. The two buildings were separated by a weedy patch of gravel, stained black where his dad dumped oil pans. Halves of car transmissions and rusted motor blocks leaned against the cinderblock shop. A flat-bottomed duckboat lay hull-up across bald tires.

The boys stopped walking their bikes as they approached. The house was silent. Dusk was coming. A few bats flew anxious circles between trees overhead. Fish gripped his handlebars a little tighter as he paused, listening. Bread shivered, even though it wasn't very cool. He did that sometimes when he got around his dad, or when his dad spoke to him. It was a visible rattling Fish pretended to ignore. It reminded Fish of the way a calf looks when it gets too bothered by flies on too hot a day. He hated it, for Bread's sake, he told himself.

"Maybe we can trap some coyotes," whispered Fish, "and we can loose 'em in your house."

Bread shrugged. "Maybe," he stammered.

"We could starve 'em first."

Two weekends ago, the boys found one of Grandpa's calves lying dead inside its own fence. The coyotes typically hunted rabbits and fawns, but after hard winters like the last one, the rabbits were picked thin and fawns scarce, and the coyotes were forced to go after larger prey. The coyotes peeled back the calf's hide and ate most of what they could. Grandpa got his deer rifle out of his closet. Killing coyotes wasn't a thing he wanted to do. The coyotes have pups to feed too. But there's a tipping point, and when calves start getting killed, and right near the barns too, things have damn well tipped, he explained. Fish had helped birth that calf. He remembered the way it stood up for the first moment, all tipsy and bowlegged in the straw. Fish felt anger in his jaw and stomach when he saw that calf half eaten in the mud, paw prints all over it. It felt righteous to him that night, going out in the fields with a spotlight and rifle in his grandpa's truck to kill coyotes.

"I suppose I'll get in there now," said Bread. His shakes had nearly stopped. "Seems quiet."

"Okay," said Fish. He felt himself swallow.

They were always awkward about parting when Bread had to go home. It was as if they were strangers, unable to do much besides formally shake hands and bid the other farewell. They shook hands now and nodded, and Fish wiped his hands on his jeans and swung a leg over his bike. Bread laid his bike in the weeds and stepped up the concrete porch. He looked small and dried up, like those turtles looked, bowlegged and weak like that calf was. And Fish felt dried up and weak for abandoning him again. He hated it. The world was too full of coyotes and calves. Something had to change. Something firecracker big. Fish's mom said the most powerful thing a person can do in this life is to pray, that ours was a "God of well-timed miracles." Fish believed that was true, or wanted to. But always after waiting for what seemed long enough, he'd stop believing, like so many other people seemed to do but never talked about.

The door to Bread's house rattled tight, and Fish pedaled as hard as he could down the gravel street. Every time he left Bread, he'd race his bike back to his grandpa's farm, trying to pray for help, or trying not to, until the quiet of the fields and fireflies offered its solace again. This time, though, something different happened inside him. This time, from somewhere or something, a reply seemed to come from all that stillness and sky. He couldn't hear it, but it was spoken somehow, this crystalline understanding. Fish *was* the change being sent. It was loud enough to make him lock up his coaster brake in the gravel. Stars aligned overhead. The moon and crickets waited.

Fish clenched his fists on his handlebar tape. He wasn't going to leave Bread this time, and the bravery of that thought seemed so foreign to him it was almost as if it belonged to someone else. But it didn't. It belonged to him. Maybe it was because he'd known Bread for three summers, and Bread had become more like a brother than a friend. Maybe it was because Fish was ten years old now, and would turn eleven by fall, and there was a very big difference between the heart of a boy turning ten and one turning eleven. Maybe it was because he'd overheard his grandfather, a good and strong man, declare him good and strong. Something deep in his gut, something bright and dangerous and match-like, made him stop on that road. And it felt right and made his heart hammer like it did when he rode out with his grandpa to kill coyotes.

Fish looked out toward the marshes. Then he looked back at Bread's house. The moon witnessed the decision. Fish turned his bike around.

TWO

THE DOOR OF THE SIT & GO GAS STATION TWO MILES NORTH OF Claypot swung open, and two men walked in from the purple dusk—one a thickset farmer wearing dirt-caked coveralls, a John Deere ball cap, and incredibly thick glasses, the other a man in his early thirties, tall and wearing a vest with a badge, a radio and pistol on his belt, a cowboy hat on his head.

Tiffany Robins looked up from where she leaned behind the counter. Her eyes brightened at the sight of the taller man. She'd been reading her latest library loan, a book of poems by Emily Dickinson, one about the author's life compared to a loaded gun, a thing so latent and potent, ready to be lifted from its corner and fill the hills with echoes. Tiffany tried to imagine herself as a gun, even a great big shotgun like Dickinson seemed to do, but the best Tiffany could muster was an image of a beat-up rabbit rifle, her dad's .22, the only gun she'd ever really handled, and that before her parents divorced. Upon spotting the sheriff, Tiffany hid the book and stood to pull her dark green sweater down to the hips of her jeans. She smiled and tucked her purple hair behind her ears. Last night, out of boredom, she dyed a few highlights in her bathroom. She regretted it even as she was dyeing it, just as she did the time before that, and she regretted it even more now that the sheriff was here. She didn't need the man, but she did wonder about him and had for some time. She reminded herself that she'd proved her independence last year, during a hungry summer spent alone in a tent, but she remained unconvinced.

"Hey, Sheriff Cal," she said, trying not to sound overeager, looking forward to hearing him say her name. She loved his Texan voice, the way it carried hints of sweet tea and rattlesnakes and desolate places. This close to Wisconsin's northern border, a man from Texas was downright exotic.

"Hey, Tiff," said the sheriff, in midconversation with the older man. The smell of leather and sweat and manure swept inside with the men. "I've told you ten times, Burt, I've got no authority to tell game wardens to back off. If they don't want you shooting coyotes on public land, they *don't* want you shooting coyotes on public land!" The sheriff didn't stop to face the other man when he spoke, but moved with purpose toward the coffee carafes. The farmer's lips pursed together as he followed. He seemed to boil a bit before he popped. Tiffany had seen it happen many times. She herself had caused Burt Akinson to erupt once or twice. She took pride in it. It was a game the two played.

"You know as well as I do, Sheriff—hey there, Tiff."

"Hey, Burt," she said.

"You know as well as I do them wardens is working according to state numbers and don't know local needs. They think with their fancy charts since there's no coyotes in Milwaukee, there ain't no coyotes in Claypot, so we're the ones have to get into that forest and push them packs of bastards off farms." Burt said the word *coyotes* like *oats*—no *coyoats* in Claypot—and as he did, he held his hands in the air and threw them forward as if holding gnats at bay. Tiff shook her head and put together a fresh filter of coffee behind the lotto tickets. Burt threw his hands forward again. "Gotta push 'em back into them woods or they'll keep coming after calves."

Sheriff Cal plucked a cup from the stack and turned toward the older man. "Burt, I know you got cattle, and on your own land you can shoot all the coyotes you want."

"Sheriff Cal?" said Tiff.

He didn't hear her. "And I don't care about state or county numbers or anything else."

"Sheriff Cal," said Tiff. "There's no coffee in that one."

"But I do care that when the wardens find dead coyotes on state land, they start asking me questions." Cal pushed the dispenser and the carafe sputtered. "Tiff, there's no coffee in this carafe."

"Fresh pot's coming," she said.

"Thanks."

Burt wagged his head. "We call 'em *cows* here, Texas Ranger. *Cow* farming, not *cattle* ranching. And those parklands sit right up against my farm," he complained. "You know when I was a boy, them parklands belonged to my—"

"I'm making light roast, Sheriff. Do you like light roast?"

"That's just fine, Tiff. And when wardens start asking me questions, Burt, and I tell them I don't know who's shooting coyotes, it makes me look like the only fool in this town who doesn't."

Burt wrinkled his face. "Nobody knows it's me shooting them coyotes. And they're bad this year, too many of 'em. I'm doing folks a favor, before the coyotes run out of calves to eat and start picking off children."

The sheriff closed his eyes a moment, left them shut. "Tiff," he asked, "would you please tell Burt who people say has been shooting coyotes?"

"Everyone knows Burt's been shooting coyotes."

The sheriff lifted his eyebrows.

Burt raised his hands and boiled. "Oh, bah," he said, and left his hands in the air this time, as if overwhelmed by the gnats. "She knows because she just heard you talking all about it!"

"People know, Burt," said Tiffany, and she frowned. "And who ever heard of coyotes eating children?"

"Shows what both of you know, then," said Burt.

Sheriff Cal set his empty cup on the counter. "Shoot all the coyotes you want. Just shoot them on your own side of the fence."

"But that land used to belong to my—"

"On your own land, Burt."

There was deep frustration in Burt's pinched eyes. He was killing coyotes with his pupils, and maybe game wardens too, blowing them out his nostrils.

"What's the missus going to say," asked Cal, "when you've got to sell off that new tractor to pay for shooting coyotes?"

"What's my tractor got to do with it?"

"What's she going to say, Burt? You got a rig so big and shiny your whole farm's got to be leveraged on it. And how are you gonna pay a fifty-thousand-dollar fine?"

"Fifty thousand!" Burt's eyes got wide. "For poppin' coyotes?"

Tiffany frowned at him again, shook her head in exaggerated pity. "Missus is gonna snip your balls off, Burt." She lifted her fingers in the air, made two neat snips, and grinned at him. Burt was a friend, and Tiffany knew how to talk to him. He used to let her parade his prize hogs at the fair when she was a girl in 4-H. Now that she'd grown, they'd often cross paths and tease each other in the Sunrise Café. Last year, during her hungry summer, Burt was kind enough to pretend he didn't notice that she was squatting on the back forty of his property in a Coleman tent for four months, bathing in the creek, and helping herself to a few of his chickens' eggs once a week. In late fall after the apples had all dropped, she stole a whole chicken. Burt's wife noticed, and Burt had to drive his truck back there over the corn stubble and say something. He asked Tiffany through the wall of her zipped tent if she needed help. She told him if she needed help she'd have asked for it, and she'd thank him for minding his own business. When he told her she might get a boyfriend who'd take care of her if she'd only stop scrunching her face so much, she leapt out of her tent in her long underwear and dragged the whole works fifty yards onto state land—which was illegal without permits, but she wasn't about to pay the money she was saving for an apartment on a corner of brambles no one ever looked at. Burt liked banter. It was his first language. And Tiffany's work at the gas station made her well suited to it, although it never felt entirely natural to her, never her true self telling the jokes, blocking the jabs, smiling so long.

The coffee pot gurgled and hissed, and Tiffany filled the sheriff's cup before pouring the rest into the empty carafe.

Burt took a step backward. He'd completely ignored Tiffany's remark. "Sheriff, I—" He swallowed. "I had no idea they could do that to a man, for varmints?" His face reddened, then grew white, and then couldn't decide which color to turn, so it just stayed mottled. He wiped his stout fingers on the chest pockets of his coveralls, then spoke in a conspiratorial voice. "You think they know it's me that's been shooting?"

"Wardens don't know yet," said the sheriff, "but people do. So stop doing it."

Burt reached his hand out to shake the sheriff's. "I'll do that, Sheriff. Thank you. You're a good man, Sheriff, that's what we all said since you come here. *He's a good one, Sheriff Cal. A bit inexperienced, but cares for people.* I had no idea they could bring that kind of hurt down on a man, for varmints?"

Cal dropped the handshake and winced at the floor. "It's all right," he said.

Burt had his John Deere cap off his head now. He wrung it in his hands. Thin, matted hair crossed his forehead above his glasses. Then anger flashed in his eyes.

"I'm gonna go sit out by my field tonight and shoot at every set of eyeballs I can shine. Bears. Coyotes. Porkies. I figure I'm gonna pretty much shoot at everything." He smiled a bit, like the declaration had allowed him to regain a piece of himself, remedy some wrong. Burt nodded and made his way toward the door. He stopped. "Oh, by the way, Tiff, I seen a hawk pick up a year-old puppy once, dropped it right on a barn roof."

Tiff and Cal just looked at him, waiting.

"So there ain't no saying what coyotes will get after—calves, children—if a hawk can pick up a dog. Nature's a hell of a thing when it's hungry." He shook his head at the floor. "Fifty thousand!"

"See you, Burt."

"See you," he said, and he got a mischievous gleam in his eye. "Say, Tiff, you found a boyfriend to kiss on yet?"

Tiff raised her eyes at him like a teacher would, a warning for silence.

"I'd give that Texas Ranger a smooch if I was a lonely girl like you," and then Burt pushed through the door, muttering about damning game wardens and all of Milwaukee as he went.

Tiffany wiped some spilled sugar from the countertop with a napkin. "Could wardens really fine him that much?"

Cal smiled as he watched Burt walk off toward his truck under the station lights. Burt's truck was a big diesel with a spotlight attached to the driver's side mirror. He used it for shining, which Cal learned was a pastime for many of the men in the county. They'd drive the back roads with a case of beer and shine for deer, not to poach but just to see what was out there, see whose fields had the biggest bucks. Cal had had a lot to learn in the past year. People didn't go shining for deer in Houston.

"I have no idea, Tiff. I just figured if I threatened his tractor, he'd stop causing me trouble."

Tiff smiled as she placed the empty pot back on the rack. She tucked her purple hair behind her ears and stole a glance at the sheriff's pistol. It was a beautiful firearm, not plastic and soulless like the guns they carried on cop shows. Cal's was made of brushed steel, buckled to his waist by a thick leather belt. The gun had checkered rosewood grips—she loved rosewood—and black sights and a black hammer. At least she thought that was what it was called, a hammer. It was the kind of gun a person could write a poem about.

"So when are you gonna take me shooting like you said you would, Sheriff?"

"What's that, Tiff?"

"You promised to take me shooting at the range last month. You haven't."

The sheriff's face immediately colored a bit red. Tiffany didn't know how to read him. Was it frustration? When she was a girl, her dad's face used to get red when he was frustrated. She didn't want to frustrate Cal and regretted bringing it up. She turned back toward the carafes and pretended to straighten a stack of lids. Beer coolers hummed in the quiet. The sheriff was ten years older than she was, but that didn't matter to her at all, and it wouldn't matter to him either, once he got to know her. He was thirty-five. Tiffany learned his age from the captain of the women's bowling team when the woman stopped in for cigarettes on her way to a tournament. The sheriff was outside pumping gas. The woman called him a tall drink, too young for herself—but now Tiffany, on the other hand. Cal was friendly, from what Tiffany knew of him from the gas station, and he had something reluctant or reserved about him that made her want to know him more. She had that too, that reluctance to enter into others' lives. The good thing was that Marigamie County was a big county, and the sheriff had to fill his tank nearly every night at her station before heading home. She knew he lived in a cabin by Shannon Lake just past the North Star Bar, and that hers was the nearest gas station, but she hoped there was more to it, that he chose her, nightly, in some real way. Truth was, independence wasn't all it was cracked up to be.

Tiffany didn't just read poetry. She wrote it too and had done so ever since childhood. It was her way of thinking things out, naming them, knowing them. One year prior to her hungry summer, Tiffany's poetry became preoccupied with all the lost hopes of living alone in a small town, the slow march of writing checks to banks and utility companies, the banality of daily life. Last winter, not long after she saved enough to get back indoors, she realized she'd convinced herself too completely of the enormity of her hopelessness. It frightened her, and she woke one night and rose quickly and burned with the electric oven-top all the poems she'd written in the last two years. Since then, she's made an effort to name beauty or gladness wherever she found it—the sound of carrots being cut against a countertop, the oddly comforting smell of blankets in need of washing. Hope was a work in progress. The sheriff's arrival didn't hurt. Fall came, the leaves dropped, the old sheriff died, and suddenly there was Cal.

Tiffany picked a coffee lid off the stack. She set it down again. She just had to be bold.

"I'm off this Tuesday," she said, turning to him. Her eyes came level with the square line of his jaw, his neck in his collar. "If you want to—" she began, but was interrupted by the radio on Cal's belt crackling to life.

He plucked it off. "This is Rover," he said. "Go ahead."

"—take me shooting," finished Tiff, as quietly as she could.

A woman's voice came loudly from the radio, and Cal turned it down a notch. "We've got a call for a disturbance on Bell Street. Neighbors heard gunfire coming from Breadwin's Auto. Address is, hold on a second, okay, three-one-two East Bell."

"What's the time?" Cal asked.

There was a pause. Marge was working the Marigamie County dispatch, and she always held down the radio button too long. Hurried conversation came through the radio, quieter now, and Cal had to turn the volume up again.

"He said he wants the time," said Marge's voice.

"What does he want?" asked a man's.

"The time, Bobby."

"The time for what?"

The sheriff made a painful face, closed his eyes. "Dispatch, Rover," he said into his radio, but he couldn't get through because Marge continued to jam the airwaves.

"Did you tell him there were gunshots as Jack's place?" asked the man.

There was irritation in the woman's voice now. "Bobby, you heard me tell him that."

"Tell him again, this don't make sense."

"ROVER, DISPATCH!" Both Cal and Tiffany recoiled from the noise.

"I copy the call, okay! I copy the call," Cal said, turning the radio all the way down. "I copy, it's fine."

The sheriff placed his radio back on his belt, steadied himself with a breath or two, and adjusted the brim of his hat. He sighed.

"Well, I'll see you, Tiff," he said, turning to go.

"Just a sec," she said. "Your coffee."

She placed it in his hand and her fingertips touched his wrist. He looked at them, and then at her, and then she swore his face colored a tiny bit before he nodded and made for the door. He never gave her an answer about the shooting range. Should she ask again? Should she invite him for dinner? She could do spaghetti and canned sauce, an iceberg salad, buy bread. Not tonight, she thought, and a part of her wilted. There was time tomorrow, and the next day, she thought. There was nothing but time in Claypot.

Cal thanked her for the coffee, and on his way out he turned back. "I like the purple, Tiff," he said, and touched his coffee to the brim of his hat, and Tiffany lifted her chin and smiled as the door closed behind him. She watched him climb into the driver's seat of his truck. His black and white dog moved over to make room in the cab. She hadn't met his dog yet. The animal seemed happy, though, wagging its tail.

"And I like you," she said, hoping for hope again amid the humming coolers and racks of candy bars and jerky. The sky outside had turned from purple to silver. She could feel it in her gut and her hands. Change was coming. God, let change come. Tonight she would write a poem about a coyote, a female, silver-furred, sprinting like fire through pine.

THE TWO BOYS RAN WITH THEIR BIKES BENEATH EMERGING STARS through the plowed field. The earth was uneven and perilous, and sometimes one of the boys would tumble and take a mouthful of dirt, and the other would have to stop and untangle him. They reached a fence line between fields and collapsed for a moment's rest.

"We're almost there," said Fish, heavily winded, panicked. Bread just panted and nodded in the moonlight, still unable to speak. Mud stuck to his cheeks, his eyes. They were crossing the fence line onto Blind Burt Akinson's land now, which meant they were one farm away from Fish's grandpa's. Crossing Blind Burt's fields was always a gamble. Last fall, Burt nearly ran them over with his new tractor, steaming on by with his thick glasses blazing in the midday sun. He hadn't even seen them. But it was nighttime now, and the fields were empty of crops. Fish wished for a field filled thick with corn to hide in, but there was only bare earth, a bright moon, everything silver and exposed.

"Come on," said Fish. "I'll hold the wire."

Bread dropped his bike over the barbed wire and slipped beneath it. Fish handed his bike over to Bread. The air was growing cool already. Fish's lungs burned from running. Overhead, the stars brightened, and Fish's pounding heart made them blaze with accusation. The sky had eyes, and it had seen what Fish had done.

Fish needed a plan. He needed to think. He couldn't. So he just ran again, all lung and heart and foot.

When they shot the coyotes that killed the calf, Fish's grandpa had a plan. He got the deer rifle out of the bedroom, a .243 with a walnut stock and a Bushnell scope. The .243 shot flat and straight, and didn't recoil as badly as the thirty-aught-six Fish's grandpa used for deer in November. "Plenty of gun for coyotes," his grandpa said, rummaging around in a crate he pulled down from the closet shelf. Bread was over that night and stood by the lighted doorway. Grandpa waved him in. "Dale, come carry a few boxes of these shells," he said. The boys did everything they were told. The older man knew what to do. They only had to follow.

Over the course of the last three summers at the farm, Fish's grandpa taught Fish to shoot. He started him out on tuna cans with a BB gun, and after a week or two of that, moved him up to a .22 rimfire, then a .410 shotgun. By the end of that first summer, Fish was helping his grandfather sight-in the aught-six for deer season. The recoil of the aught-six was incredible, as was the report and muzzle flash. When his grandpa shot it, Fish felt it in his shoes and lungs. Fish remembered shouldering the rifle for the first time, placing his grandpa's folded Army cap over its buttstock for extra padding, then sliding the bolt forward to chamber the largest brass cartridge he'd ever handled. It scared him, but it was his first summer with his grandpa. Fish hadn't spent a great deal of time with the man prior to that and wanted dearly to please him. Fish made one good shot with the aught-six. It hurt his shoulder, but not badly enough to make him stop. He chambered another round, aimed, grimaced, and the second shot missed the target completely. After the third miss, his grandpa moved him back down to the .243. "No sense in developing a flinch," he said. They'd work back up to the aught-six, his grandpa assured him, and then slapped him on the back and smiled a bit, his eyes shining in the bright fall field.

The three of them rode to the fields in the cab of Grandpa's truck. Fish would do the shooting. Bread was in charge of running the spotlight. They drove back along a drainage ditch. The stars were clouded over to the west, a bank of clouds closed in on the moon. As Bread swept the spotlight along the edge of the woods, there came into focus a field of stars, the reflective eyes of a pack of coyotes. "All right," his grandpa said, putting the truck in park. "Fischer, get as many as you can."

It was the first time Fish had ever placed crosshairs on a live animal, unless he counted the roosting pigeons he shot with the pellet gun in the granary. But that was different. These coyotes had thoughtful eyes, full and alive and knowing. The rifle rested on the open window of the truck. Fish knew where to shoot at a coyote, or a deer for that matter, just behind the front shoulder where the lungs were, where the heart was. Fish could hear Bread breathing next to him in the cab, holding the light out over his shoulder.

"Easy, Fischer," his grandpa said. "No different than targets."

Fish nestled his cheek against the smooth stock and took aim. The coyotes stood with stiff tails and alert ears, what looked to be twenty of them, smallish dogs staring into the light. Fish placed the crosshairs behind the shoulder of one of the larger ones. He felt a pang of pity, but then he remembered the calf, mud-strewn and torn. There were tipping points. Things had tipped. Poor damn things. Fish rested his finger against the trigger. He exhaled and squeezed. Boom and flash filled the truck cab. Instinctively, just as he'd been taught, Fish drew the bolt back and chambered another round as his eyes readjusted. He looked through the scope. One coyote lay dead, and the others had repositioned themselves, some nervously circling their fallen chief, some looking back into the light. Fish felt a surge of fear and triumph course through his body. His pulse and breathing quickened. He placed his finger against the trigger again.

"Steady," whispered his grandpa.

Fish tightened his lips in the darkness. He had killed his first coyote. And now he was going to kill another. He thought again of the calf. Slowly. Smoothly. Exhale. Another round. The coyotes fell like cordwood. They didn't run. They just stood, circled each other. By the time Fish had finished, the sun was nearly rising. Grandpa took them back to the house and put on coffee and set three mugs on the counter. Bread and Fish sat at the table, feeling as if they'd crossed over into some new threshold of life. They had. They sat and tried not to grin as they sipped black coffee, which was awful, while they listened to Grandpa tell them how they could skin out the coyotes after breakfast and sell the pelts for cash. "But first let me make you men some toast," he said.

But that was then. Now, panic was in the stars. They had crossed about fifty yards of Blind Burt Akinson's fields. They just had to run. They had to stay off the roads, keep away from headlights, and people, and the stars, and the sheriff. Without thinking about it, the boys ran instinctively toward Fish's grandpa. He, of all men, could sort out this kind of thing. The web of Fish's hand still hurt from the recoil of Bread's old man's revolver, which Bread now carried in a cloth sack next to his handlebars. The boys once examined it in a lilac hedge when Bread's dad was passed out in a lawn chair. It was a Smith & Wesson .44 Magnum, a massive handgun, the same kind Dirty Harry used. Bread pointed it out of the lilacs at a calico cat on a fence post and asked the cat in a gravelly voice how lucky it felt. The cat licked itself. The boys chuckled. The revolver's thick, blunt-nosed bullets were the size of color crayons. It was a pistol used out west for protection from bears, and it was Bread's old man's constant companion. His dad didn't carry it holstered to his belt. He carried it around the house and shop in his hand like a heavy wrench and set it wherever he planned on being for the next hour or so. It was lying on the kitchen counter when Fish burst through the door this evening.

Fish had no plan when he turned back to Bread's house, only bravery, but was met in the kitchen with the sight of Bread's dad twisting up the collar of Bread's shirt in his fist. Fish froze when the door banged shut behind him. All three of them did. Bread was on his knees and looking back at his friend. His face was bright red. His eyes were wild with horror and his face was tear-stained. Fish knew it happened, but he'd never seen it, not like this. His friend was so helpless in the blackened hands of his father. Bread looked incredibly small, his father so unbelievably large. Fish's head thrummed. Everything in that kitchen seemed unreal and washed out, the way colors in dreams seem scrubbed over. Fish remembered Bread's dad saying only one word—*Who?*—which seemed to carry all the accusation of hell inside its single syllable. He had awful eyes, which made Fish turn away toward the kitchen counter, where the revolver lay. The next few seconds moved so slowly, so automatically, the way Fish's hand closed on the grip of the revolver, the way Bread drifted noiselessly to the floor, his father floating across the kitchen, the weightlessness as Fish lifted the stainless barrel into the quiet, yellow light. Fish remembered frogs chirping outside the open window. He remembered smelling lilacs, and then he drew back the hammer and fired.

Bread stopped running. "Fish, there's a light coming!" he said in a frantic whisper. From the far side of the field, a spotlight shone from a truck parked in the driveway of Blind Burt Akinson's place. It swept along the fence line to the boys' right, casting shadows across dirt clods. The truck was well over three hundred yards from where they stood.

They're already coming for us, thought Fish, his breath blocking his throat. Soon there would be dogs. Sheriffs. Helicopters. Channel 13. Fish felt a deep pang of shame as he pictured his grandfather in his TV chair, his ball game interrupted by a special announcement, his grandson Fischer lit up by floodlights, lifting his hands to shield his eyes from the glare.

The spotlight by Akinson's place swept closer. The beam froze when it reached them. Bread, standing in front of Fish, became a silhouette.

I didn't have a choice, Fish would tell them. He stared into the light, wondering if his eyes looked like that coyote's—guilty, murdering, frightened. Bread tried to step free of the light and stumbled over his bike. Fish moved forward to pick him up, along with the sack holding the gun. He could see the spotlight quivering as it held on them. Anger rose in Fish's heart. *Cowards,* he would tell them. *You are all cowards!* And then he felt like crying. He thought again of the way that Magnum filled the kitchen so full of noise, and then silence. How Bread's father fell forward, midstride, in so unnatural a way. He fell facedown on top of his own arms, and he didn't stir from the discomfort of lying there like that.

Fish raised his hands in the spotlight, that Magnum in its sack. He began to cry, and stepped forward. And then a rifle shot rang out in the dark. The round ripped through the air overhead. Fish heard it impact the tree line behind him. Another shot rang out, another round zipped past them. And another.

The boys bolted, and moments later were panting on their stomachs, forehead to forehead in the tall brown grass of a drainage ditch. Bread stared at Fish with wild eyes. He was shaking the way he did sometimes, trying to swallow between breaths. A memory came to Fish, at that very moment. It was a memory of his mother, staring at him with wild red eyes on the worst night of Fish's life, three years ago, late spring of the first year he started going out to his grandfather's farm. His mother sat on her legs in the kitchen, trying to breathe with the cord of the phone wrapped in her fists.

He is not coming back, she said.

THREE

SHERIFF CAL KNOCKED ON THE ALUMINUM SCREEN DOOR OF THE Breadwin home. The door had been left ajar. Not much of a place, he knew. He'd been here before. Jack Breadwin was known around Claypot for being good with his hands. He was a natural mechanic when he was sober, and a natural fistfighter when he wasn't. Sheriff Cal had dragged Jack home from bars enough times to know Jack was a lone father. His wife died years before. Some folks said he was mean to that boy, and Cal made it a point to keep a closer eye on things, but he knew the boy spent the majority of his summers out at the Branson farm, and Teddy Branson was a good man, grandfather to that boy Fischer. Those boys seemed happy enough, tearing all over town on their Huffys.

Cal knew from experience it was no good for a cop to push too far into other people's business. You get too wrapped up, too tangled, and things fall apart. Familiarity destroys authority. People don't fear a friend. These were the sorts of things his chief in Houston had tried to teach him. And while Cal had no desire to be feared—it wasn't who he was—he did appreciate the need to have a presence and bearing that made people move, or get back inside, or sit down and shut up at his word. He was the one who needed to be able to silence a tavern with his presence. A cop had to be in the world, but not of it. That's what his chief in Houston had told him, said it was in the King James, someplace.

"Anybody home?" Cal rapped his knuckles on the door once more and peered inside. "Sheriff's department. Jack, you home?" The kitchen light was on, and Cal noticed an overturned chair on the kitchen floor. Then he saw a pair of boots sticking out from behind the counter. Cal's immediate thought was *Drunken fool,* but as he pushed his way in the door, a coppery smell lingered in the air. He smelled blood, clear as the lilacs.

With one hand on the door, he unsnapped his holster with the other. He slipped into the kitchen, pressing the web of his hand against the familiar checkered back-strap of his Colt 1911. It was a bad habit, resting his hand on his firearm when things felt off. The guys in the department back in Houston nearly broke him of it, but now that he was a lone sheriff in a desolate county, the habit returned. He liked the way the 1911 fit in his hand. It was an outdated style of handgun, and Cal knew it, but loved it anyway. Most of the cops in Houston had switched over to the new Glocks, the polymer pistols with superior capacity and reliability, lighter weight too, they said. Cal remembered when the first guy in his department showed off a Glock in the locker room. Men gathered around with towels draped over their shoulders, the younger ones whistling praise, the older ones wrinkling their noses. Cal thought the pistol seemed soulless, utilitarian only, like a TV remote. He'd never had to shoot anyone, and feared he probably couldn't if the need arose, so he chose his sidearm based on his attraction to it, the way a person might choose a dog. The oiled metal and checkered wood even smelled good. It was a pleasure to shoot, and shoot well. Cal enjoyed fieldstripping it, wiping down the internals. It was an emotional connection, exactly the kind of sentimentality and attachment his chief tried to warn him against. Don't get close to them. Don't stop by for a drink. Don't go in.

Cal listened, took a step inside, listened again. When he reached the far side of the kitchen counter and saw the entirety of Jack Bread-win, he stopped in his tracks.

"Jesus," he said.

THE BOYS RUMMAGED IN THE DARK GARAGE FOR A TARP AND SOME fish poles. Fish pocketed a barlow knife he found on the work-bench, along with a piece of flint he knew was in the top drawer of his grandpa's toolbox. The packing went quickly.

They made such lists before, planning for battle or escape. They once climbed into the hayloft of the barn and spent an afternoon planning in case the Iraqis ever attacked Claypot. Fish's dad had been a tanker in Desert Storm, so the boys knew all about fighting Iraqis. They spent hours deliberating over the list. A radio would be good to have, but they decided it was better to be battery-free, to prepare to survive with bare essentials. They would escape into the Mishicot Forest—a wilderness that stretched for more than a hundred miles through Marigamie County's northern region. The southern edge of the forest stopped at the fields of Fish's grandpa's farm, and Burt Akinson's too. They would need fish poles, and pocketknives, and a flint, and tarps, just like the mountain men, the kind of men who could walk into a wilderness and not walk out until they were good and ready. "Mountain men usually have a sack of pemmican," suggested Bread one summer afternoon. In school, he'd learned how Indians made a paste of meat and spices and then pounded it flat to dry. The boys tried making pemmican, drying a baking pan of bacon and hamburger meat in the sun on top of the milkshed roof, but it turned green in two days, and neither boy could lift it to his mouth. "We'll pack Slim Jims if we ever need to take to the woods," Fish said, scraping the pan into the weeds. "Slim Jims are as good as pemmican."

Tonight, their planning paid off. They knew what to gather before they arrived. As they crept along the fence line behind the barn, they saw Fish's grandpa's truck pull out of the driveway. The taillights turned onto the asphalt and sped off toward Claypot. The tires chirped as they left the gravel.

"He's in a hurry," said Bread, who had stopped shaking enough to speak again. "He knows, doesn't he?"

A cow stirred in the stable behind the barn and stamped its hoof in the dirt. It huffed through its nose. Fish saw its startled eyes glimmer in the moonlight. "Easy, girl," he said. "Easy." During the three years Fish had come to know his grandpa, the man had never left for town after dark. He was a man who retired in the evening, on the porch or on the sofa, a wedge of Red Man in his cheek, with a newspaper or a ball game on the TV. As the taillights faded into the darkness, Fish knew that his grandpa knew, which only confirmed his need to flee, even more than the gunshots in Akinson's field. To stay here would be worse. His grandpa would try to hide him, and would never turn him over. There would probably be a standoff like the one Fish once saw on Channel 13, down in Texas, in Waco. No, it was up to Bread and Fish. They had to get away and survive, alone, somehow.

"We're in a hurry too," said Fish in a quiet voice. "Come on."

As the boys loaded backpacks, Bread started asking questions about where they were going. It was obvious to both boys that they would take to the forest. But it wasn't obvious what they would do once they got in there, where they would go, or how far. Fish had an idea forming in his mind, but knew it'd be wrong to lie at a time like this.

Bread poked through an open tackle box, handpicking the better fishing lures. When he stopped and turned to face Fish in the moonlit garage, Fish stopped packing too. Bread stood still, a crankbait dangling in his fingers, the way a boy stands still when he feels tears coming on in front of his friends.

"Do you think he hurt?" Bread's whisper filled the garage, the night itself.

Fish swallowed.

"My old man," said Bread, "when you shot him?"

Fish couldn't tell what the answer to that should be, or what Bread would most want to hear. Bread's old man was awful, but he was still his dad. For the first time that evening, Fish realized how quiet the night was. He heard a pigeon flap its wings on the roof of the granary. A mouse scurried along the wall of the garage. The panic that carried him at first was all but spent. Fish had killed a man. He shot him in the head. And now Fish felt dreamy and puppetlike, as if his hands weren't really his hands, his mouth trying to move a tongue that wasn't his tongue. It reminded Fish— reminded him in his gut—of the night he spent on the kitchen floor with his mom, waiting for the sun to rise. He knew how long the sun could take to rise, what the dark felt like.

"Look," said Fish, "maybe one of us should go inside and leave a note for my grandpa."

Bread didn't move.

"I mean, it doesn't feel right leaving without a note. Does it?"

His friend needed something. They both did. They needed a destination, a point of aim, no matter how improbable. Even after all their preparations for a moment like this, it was clear that it wasn't enough to simply survive. Survive for what, or to do what? That was the question they never planned for. And so Fish spoke the half-formed lie that had been in his mind.

"We're going to the National Guard armory, Bread." Fish paused here, and then he cursed himself even as the words were leaving his mouth. "We're going to see my dad. He'll know what to do."

Bread shifted on his feet. "Do you think he'll help us?" Bread's tone had changed. There was a whisper of hope in his voice. A small light in his eyes. Fish's lie worked.

"My dad will keep us safe."

Bread nodded in the darkness, zipped the fishing lure into the pocket of his bag. "I'll leave a note if you tell me what it should say," he said.

Bread went inside, and Fish's throat felt dry as he stood alone in the darkness. Bread had asked so many times when he'd get to meet Fish's dad—*Bear, the famous tank driver of Desert Storm*—about whom Fish told so many stories. Bread asked each August if Fish's dad was going to pick him up instead of his mom. Fish usually told a lie, something like how his dad was planning to come, in uniform too, but had to go back to the desert at the last minute. Desert Storm was over, but there was still a rotation of troops in a place called Saudi. Fish cursed himself. He could have chosen any other destination, like his mom's house, or the train tracks south of town, or California, anything. Now, if they ever made it to the armory, he'd have to tell more lies. The armory was in Ironsford, on the other side of Mishicot Forest. Fish hadn't been to the armory since he was six years old. His dad wasn't there. His dad wasn't anywhere anymore.

THE AMBULANCE HAD ALREADY PULLED AWAY FROM JACK BREAD-win's house by the time Teddy Branson knocked on the door. By dumb luck, an ambulance crew was nearby when Cal made the call, for which he was especially thankful. He hated death. When he discovered Jack's body, he quickly cleared the rest of the home, and then attempted to assess the victim. When he stooped to check for a pulse, he slipped in Jack's blood, and that got his own heart racing so badly that he couldn't bring himself to touch the body. The man was headshot, gray and bled out, damn it. That was assessed enough. Cal stood and washed his shaking hands in the sink and made the call. He hadn't seen this in a while, he reminded himself, not since Houston. He was okay. It was okay. He poured himself a glass of cold water, but it wasn't much help.

Cal excused himself while the ambulance crew did its work, and he didn't enter the house again until after they left. He stood in the shadows by the passenger door of his truck, spoke soothingly to his dog. When his hands wouldn't stop trembling, he took a drink or two of whiskey from the bottle he kept behind the seat. It helped, unfortunately.

The house was silent now. Cal opened another window. Lilacs mixed with the copper. A knock on the door gave him a start.

"Sheriff?" Teddy stepped into the kitchen, then stopped. Cal knew that Teddy knew the smell of blood as well as he did. Teddy knew it from Korea, and from slaughtering hogs.

"Teddy. Thanks for coming." Cal put on his best sheriff voice, as if the night hadn't shaken him. He busied his hands by tapping a pen on his notepad, his radio lying next to it on the kitchen table.

"Where are the boys?" asked Teddy. He moved farther into the room and pulled the green cap from his head. When he reached the far side of the kitchen counter, he stopped and moved a step backward. Blood pooled along the linoleum from the counter to the table.

The sheriff looked up from his notes. "I was going to ask you the same. They're not here."

The deep lines in the older man's face relaxed, and then furrowed. "They'll probably turn up at my place," said Ted. "I should get back over there."

"Maybe not," said Cal, tapping a final dot onto his notepad before folding it into the pocket of his vest. His radio came to life as he picked it up off the table.

"Sheriff, Dispatch," said the voice in the radio.

"Dispatch, go ahead."

"We've got another call," said Marge, worry in her voice.

Cal waited, and kept waiting, and then he closed his eyes. This wasn't Houston. He'd reminded himself of that so many times over the last eight months. He keyed his radio, lifted it to his mouth.

"A call for what?" he said.

"Mrs. Meyers said she heard *more* gunshots coming from over by Burt Akinson's farm, and it's too late for hunting, so she's worried and wants you to go over to Burt's place."

Teddy took a step closer. "What do you mean, *Maybe not?*" he said.

Cal felt his neck tense up. He didn't move from Houston to take on this type of thing, he had left precisely to avoid it. Four years as a young cop in the city burnt him out. His nerves weren't built for it, nor was his bleeding heart, and it eventually became clear that it was either move and start over in a place less stressful or find a new line of work. He was capable—his chief had told him that much—*but the drinking, Cal,* the drinking had become too much, and then the situation with the mother and that kid and the father. Everyone knew the next morning what Cal had done to that man, and quietly loved him for it, though they all said it was bad form. The chief even set him up with the sheriff's position on the very morning he was forced to suspend him. It was in a place called Claypot, Wisconsin, population 1,999, county seat of Marigamie County, a sprawling, forested county, sparsely populated. Cal's chief said it was the kind of place a cop could spend the rest of his days drinking coffee with his dog, painting up a cabin on a lake, dragging the occasional drunk out of a country bar if things got too stale. Cal immediately rejected the idea—he'd have to run for the position anyway—but the chief assured him that he knew some folks, had a cousin up there on a town board, said the last sheriff died two weeks earlier, sitting in a chair. A place like Claypot would gladly take him on as interim until an election took place. Don't miss the opportunity, his chief said. It was now or nothing. Cal stood on the old carpet in front of the chief's desk, rubbing the scab where he'd split the skin on that kid's father's jaw. He tried to picture his hand holding a paintbrush, a snow shovel, a match in a fireplace. Cal had never been north of Missouri. Never been in the woods either, except for Boy Scouts, which he wouldn't have joined had his father not shamed him into it. He'd never had a dog, although he used to want one as a kid. The reality was, his chief reminded him, that as of the altercation with that kid's father, Cal's options in Houston or Dallas or anywhere else in God's Own Country were gone. He'd do his best to avoid a paperwork trail, but word gets around, and no department wants to take on a young cop who beats up parolees in his free time. This was a chance to start again, brand new.

Teddy eyeballed him, made himself larger. "I said, what do you mean, *Maybe not?*"

Cal remembered himself. "Because, Ted, those boys are—"

"Sheriff Cal, Dispatch. Do you copy the call? Mrs. Meyers said she—"

Cal lifted the radio to his mouth but Teddy stepped forward and swatted it away. He was an old man, but not a small man, and Cal knew he still unloaded hay wagons by himself when his grandson wasn't around.

"Never mind that damn call about Burt's place," said Teddy. "I stopped at Burt's on the way over here to ask if he's seen Fischer." He shook his head in frustration. "All he's been shooting at are coyotes in his field. Now say what you were saying about the boys."

Cal backed one step away from the older man and raised his radio to his mouth. Teddy Branson had fear in his eyes, and anger too. Cal considered Teddy a friend in this town, but Cal also knew better than to stand too close to anger, his own or anyone else's. And he didn't appreciate having his radio nearly cuffed from his hand. He was sheriff, after all, even if he was young, even if he always felt like a fake. He took a metered breath.

"I copy the call," he said, and added, "It's just Burt, shooting coyotes."

"Dispatch copies. Oh, and Bobby wants you to know he'll be right there for the ambulance call once he gets out of the bathroom." Bobby was the county constable, the closest thing Cal had to a deputy. Bobby was a seventy-year-old, plump retiree with bad knees. He could be found most often sitting at Dispatch, a package of cookies and a blanket on his lap. Cal liked him well enough, when he stayed put. The last time he accompanied Cal on a lost person call, it took Cal an hour and a half to help Bobby back up a hill to his car.

"That's a negative, Dispatch. I repeat, that is a negative." Cal paused a moment. "Tell Bobby to stay where he is. Please. I'll call if I need him."

Cal turned the radio off. "What I was saying, Ted, is that those boys might be in bad trouble."

"Why?"

"Because Bread's dad was headshot."

Cal was deliberate in using the word *was*. It implied a shooter other than the victim. He saw Teddy swallow, and knew his point wasn't lost on the man.

Teddy frowned, annoyed. "Jack probably did it to his damn self," he said, as hopefully as a person can say that sort of thing. "He messed with that gun when he was drunk."

The sheriff shook his head.

Teddy waited.

"There ain't a gun here, Ted," said the sheriff. "If he shot himself, there'd be a gun."

A bat attached itself to the window screen, rattled its wings, and dropped away. Both men looked out at the square of darkness, standing still in the quiet kitchen, blood still soaking along the lines of linoleum, the smell of lilacs in the air.

"We gotta find them boys," said Teddy. "Right now."

The sheriff nodded. "That's why I called you," he said, and then looked at the floor and then back into Teddy's eyes. "I need help."

FIVE MILES AWAY IN TEDDY'S BACK FIELD, BREAD AND FISH LEANED on their bikes, which were loaded like pack animals. The white pines at the edge of Mishicot Forest towered into the stars and galaxy. Fish looked into the depths of the trees, the sky. He knew the trail that would take them as far as the river. He and Bread had taken it before, but they never went by it at night. There was something that changed a forest at night, something awful about it. Bread put his finger on it last August, after the boys spent the first hours of moonlight scaring themselves by running as far into the trees as they could muster, and then tearing out into the corn again, breathless. "The scary thing about the woods at night," he said, panting, "is that you just can't *see*." Fish thought that about summed it up.

Silence came from that darkness now. And silence came from the sky overhead. Fish's fingers tingled. He made a fist a few times. He looked at Bread, and Bread's eyes looked like that cow's eyes had—all starlit and startled. Fish knew he looked the same.

"So we got everything, then?" asked Fish. The darkness seemed to swallow his words.

"Yeah," said Bread.

"Okay, then," said Fish.

"Okay," said Bread.

FOUR

"**C**AN YOU TELL ME ABOUT THE ARMY AGAIN?" ASKED BREAD IN a hushed voice. The boys pushed their bikes along a ridge trail overlooking a moonlit river. The trail was soft with pine needles where it wasn't riddled with rocks. The air smelled green, like ferns and cedar. About forty feet below, to the boys' left, the river sparkled blackly as it coursed and spilled through its beds and eddies. Last spring, when the water was high and powerful, Fish heard the river moving rocks. He remembered it sounding like marbles teased together. He thought about the rocks tearing loose, tumbling in that frigid current.

Bread tried again. "Tell me about your dad. Will he let us drive the tanks?"

Fish pushed his bike up and over a downed tree blocking the path. They needed to gain distance from Claypot tonight, and their progress had been slower than he would have liked. The darkness and footing forced them to shuffle amid the trees and stones. Every so often a branch would snap off in the darkness, or an animal would bolt through the underbrush, and the boys would either freeze or start walking faster. As difficult as it was, Fish was thankful for the distraction offered by the slow deliberateness of walking the trail.

"Maybe we should stay quiet a little longer," said Fish. "Until we get where we're going for the night."

Bread pushed his bike up and over the same downed tree. Its chain clanked. "Where *are* we going to stop for the night?" he asked.

"Shh," whispered Fish. "Lantern Rock, I figure."

Fish waited for a response, but when none came he took the silence for consent. Lantern Rock was a place the boys named themselves. It was six miles into the forest, where the trail crossed the river at a series of islands and shallow rapids. A split boulder of granite jutted out from a rise near shore. The rock had a good lookout, a flat spot on its top about fifteen feet high. The split itself was three feet wide with a cedar growing out of it. It made a good fort, what with the lookout and hideout and access to skipping stones and crayfish.

The rock got its name when the boys once saw a lantern out on one of the nearby islands. They had played too long and let dusk catch them, and as darkness fell a light snapped on and hovered in the darkness in the trees across the channel. It looked to them like a spirit. The boys bolted. They sprinted the rocky trails and crashed through hedges of ferns to make it out of the forest before moonlight. *Probably just a coon hunter,* Fish's grandpa had said when they arrived breathlessly back at the farm. But it wasn't a coon hunter. Coon hunters were noisy. They had dogs. This lantern, this light, it just sparked to life, swayed in the quiet.

It bothered Fish, the way his grandpa seemed unable to get caught up in the excitement of things. It was his constant reluctance. Fish learned early on how his grandpa liked rhythms in life. Daily, the man woke without an alarm, drank his coffee standing in the kitchen, placed his milk pail on the same wooden block in the barn, said the same things to the same cows. *How's Rocket this morning, attagirl, and Pipe, out you go, all done.* Fish's mom said he'd been like that for as long as she'd known him, but Fish's grandma said he'd been like that only since he came back from the war. Before he left—she'd laugh as she said it—he was pure gasoline. When he returned, he demanded peace. He wouldn't stand an argument, or emotions in general, would walk away from it all. Spontaneity made him uncomfortable. He didn't like a mess. He hated loose ends, and bills, so he mailed payments the day they arrived, handed them directly to the postmaster on his way to the feed mill. The man oiled his work boots every Friday, watching the alfalfa field from the porch while rubbing his thumbs into the leather. *But he's better than most,* Fish's grandma said. He'd overheard her saying such things enough times to learn that providing an explanation for her husband was a refrain in her life. *Some of 'em came back mean. Some of 'em angry. Teddy came back quiet.* Fish's memories of his grandma always had her with something in her lap—some knitting if she was indoors, a bowl of peas if she was on the porch. *He never did expand the farm,* she said of her once-ambitious husband returned from war. She spoke such things when Fish was old enough to understand, but still young enough that adults felt they could speak freely around him. *He's like a river that's been dammed up,* she said. *The river is there, buried, but there.* And then she'd sigh and shell her bowl of peas.

Fish often wondered if his grandpa didn't treat him with an extra dose of such restraint. When Fish told of a snake behind the barn, a tree branch that snapped with him on it, or a porcupine in the hayloft, his grandpa would just smooth the air over with his hands, as if washing it all, and then he'd wave Fish back to the dinner table, or the milkshed, or whatever he was busy with.

This need to smooth over disturbance reminded Fish of his own father, the sorts of things he would say before leaving for another deployment. Fish hated deployment, but knew it was shameful to say so. His dad would kneel down next to his packed duffel bags. *It's no big deal,* he'd say. *I'll be back before you know it.* But it was a big deal, and he wouldn't be back for months. And no amount of hand-waving could smooth over his father's long absence. Fish idolized the man. It wasn't just that his dad was a sergeant in the National Guard. It wasn't the way he folded those exotic desert uniforms into his green canvas bags. Instead, it was the simple presence Fish missed most—the way his dad's whiskers covered the sink after he shaved, the shape of his jaw, the way his father used to smile and wink at Fish when his mom chided him too much. With that wink Fish always felt he'd been offered the keys to manhood, and all other hidden knowledge in the universe. Don't worry about it, that wink seemed to say. Just keep busy. I *know*.

Fish's dad's buddies called him Bear. He was of medium build but solid strong. And it pleased Fish to no end when his mom or his grandma said he was turning out to be the spitting image of his father. Fish would stare in the mirror and try to see it. The blue eyes. The high cheekbones. Fish prayed for whiskers. On weekends, his dad often took him to the armory, to sit on the tanks, or to the machine shop, where he worked when the Army didn't need him. They'd drive in his Ford truck, stop for Cokes, and then pull into the shop and talk with machinists on the Saturday shift. Fish used to watch the metal shavings spool from the lathes while the men pushed and pulled and adjusted the machines in a way that seemed a mystery to him. Fish got to start a tank motor once. Another time, he watched his dad walk in a Labor Day parade. Fish needed nothing in life.

But then it all changed. Channel 13 brought news from overseas that began to absorb the adults, and the armory started calling on the phone more often. Not long after, Fish heard words at home that he couldn't piece together, other than that they made his mom cry quietly and his father's smile seem strange. *Kuwait* and *oil fields. Iraq. Jordan. Saudi.*

Dad's first deployment took him away for part of the winter. Fish watched the news on TV when his mom allowed it. Scud missiles. Naval rockets. And Republican Guard tanks, retreating. When his dad came home from the war one month early, the town of Ironsford had a parade, and Fish got to eat an entire bag of cotton candy and sit on his dad's shoulders, straddling the man's sun-burned neck. That summer, the neighborhood boys played war amid creeks and leaf piles, arguing over who got to be General Powell, President Bush, or better yet, Schwarzkopf. Fish always used the name Bear. In late fall, when the trees were naked and the leaf piles gone, Fish's dad deployed again, to the peacekeeping force in Saudi.

The floors seemed colder that winter. At night the wind blew through the frozen tines of the maple outside Fish's window, and Fish would close his eyes and picture his dad walking across some desert dune, leaning into the wind and shielding his eyes, looking always homeward. In Fish's mind, the desert was frozen too, and he often wanted to go there, bring a blanket, offer his father warmth, wipe the sand from the corners of his eyes. When his dad came home this time, there was no parade. It was as if the town and the boys had tired of it all, forgotten about it all. The war was over, and yet Fish's father still deployed. Fish's dad didn't take him to the armory anymore, though he seemed to spend more time there. The house stayed quiet even when the Ford was in the driveway. Fish would sit at the table and watch his father chew his food. The man looked older, unfamiliar somehow, a foreign visitor. Dad would sometimes turn the TV on during supper, pause midbite, look at the fork in his hand, and get up from the table and go outside. Mom would point her fork at Fish's plate. "Eat, please," she'd say, and then she'd make her way out to the kitchen and stand by the screen door.

On a school night in spring, when the buds on the maple hadn't opened yet, the phone rang late and Fish heard his father answer in the kitchen. Fish was in bed. His mom walked softly downstairs. There was talking and then silence, and then Fish heard his mom say, "Tell them you won't go."

His father uttered a muffled response.

Fish heard nothing for a time.

"We can't do this again. Tell them you won't go back."

His father's voice became louder.

"Fischer and I are alone!" yelled his mother.

"I said," his father bellowed, giving every syllable its own breath, "this is not my choice!"

Mom started crying. Fish stopped breathing. His father boomed. His mom moaned. A glass shattered. The whole house stood still on its bones. Crickets went quiet. This was wrong. This was dead wrong. Fish's parents didn't fight. They didn't yell. Fish's dad was a smiling, Ford-driving tanker. He worked at Bryce Machine Tool. His mom packed his father sandwiches for lunch, and made Fish sandwiches too, and washed Fish's hair in the sink before school. Their house had never known this. Fish felt a gap of great danger open beneath the home. Fear seeped up through it. He bit his blanket.

"Don't leave," cried his mother. "Don't go."

The door opened and shut. Mom wept. Fish sat up on his elbow and listened as his dad's truck started, and then he watched out the window as it pulled out of the driveway beneath the maple tree. It paused there with its glaring brake lights, and Fish willed it to stay, but it turned onto the road and was gone.

Taillights hovering in tree limbs—that is the image that sticks in Fish's mind whenever he thinks of his father. It wasn't for keeps that night. Fish's dad would be in and out for the two weeks before he deployed again. He fixed a gutter on the house. He bought flowers for Mom. But that night did mark the beginning of the end, the crack that widened until it swallowed life. Fish often imagined a braver version of himself, a version that bolted from bed rather than stared out the window, that sprinted barefoot down the stairs and across the cold gravel to beat on the door of the truck. *Don't you leave, Dad,* said that braver version of himself. *Don't go.*

Fish learned of fragility during those last two weeks. Even his grandfather's. When his mom begged Fish's grandpa to talk to her husband, to persuade him to give up the war and stay home, Fish watched his grandpa's face spark heat, and he took his green cap from his head and wrung it in his hands, and then he waved his hands in the air to wash himself of it all as he retreated across the gravel driveway. His grandpa took the Lord's name in vain, slammed shut the door of his truck, while Fish's mom bit her lip on the porch and closed her eyes. Fish knew nobody was supposed to take the Lord's name in vain. His mom told him as much. But there was something about the way his grandpa spat the words that made them seem *not* in vain. It was as if he was invoking the Lord's name, calling upon it, actually asking God to damn some thing, some act or thought, something buried and about to tear loose.

LANTERN ROCK ROSE UP IN THE STARLIGHT. THE MILKY WAY PRO- vided enough light for them to reach the riverbank, hide their bikes in a patch of ferns, and hunker down in the crevasse. The air was cool, but the large split in the boulder held heat.

Fish sat on his heels and leaned against the smooth rock, letting the warmth seep into his back. He looked up at the sky, the way the cedar tree rose into it like a black spire, and how above it the bright smear of the Milky Way looked like sunlight spilling through a very old blanket hung to dry. The stars seemed so near, as if Fish could reach up with a hand and stir them. He knew it was an illusion, a trick. He used to feel so safe in the world, peace felt so permanent. He thought of Bread, how only hours ago he was busy releasing turtles into marsh water. Now everything felt like darkness in the woods feels. A person just can't *see*.

Fish heard a crinkling sound and turned to find Bread rummaging through a pocket on his backpack. His hand came out with a Slim Jim. The boy peeled the wrapper, bit the beef stick in its middle, and handed half to Fish while he chewed.

"I figure we might eat supper," whispered Bread.

Fish took it, and his eyes welled up. He wanted so badly to go home, and not only to his grandpa's but to his mom's. He wanted to sit down, have supper with her, and listen to her talk. He wanted his dad back. Fish knew if he tried to speak right now his voice would crack, so he just nodded and took a bite of the Slim Jim.

The two boys sat on their heels and chewed their dinner. They knew each other well enough to know when the other was about to cry. Bread was good enough to not ask him questions.

"Pretty good Slim Jim," he said, and pulled his knees up inside his arms.

Fish nodded.

"We're going to make it, Fish." Fish knew Bread was trying to cheer him. Bread took an exaggerated bite of his beef stick. "Yes sir," he said, his mouth full, "we're going to make it, and we're going to follow this river, and we're going to build a raft too, and we ain't gonna get caught." Bread paused and looked out at the river, then at the cedar towering overhead. "Fish, how big a raft you think we need to carry us and our bikes?"

Fish didn't answer.

"I bet we need at least five or six cedars, and then we need to find some vine or something to bind 'em together like the Indians did." He gave Fish a poke with his elbow. "I bet you I'm going to use cedar bark for rope. You think that'd make a good rope, Fish? Fishy? Fish Face? Fischer?"

"You can't make good rope out of cedar bark," said Fish.

"Says who?"

"You gotta make rope out of roots. That's the way the Indians did it."

Bread nodded.

"So which one of us is gonna dig roots, and which one of us is gonna chop trees?"

Fish hadn't thought about making a raft, but it was a good idea. The river pushed right up through all that forest, right toward Ironsford. And he liked the thought of building it. It made the sky seem more ordered. Just keep busy, the stars seemed to say. We *know.*

"You figure we could sleep on the raft too?" Fish asked. "Anchor it somehow?"

Bread grinned in the starlight, nodding. "We're gonna make beds from cedar branches," he said. "And we're going to be cocaptains, equal pay and duties." He patted the trunk of the cedar tree. "I'm gonna cut this one down first thing tomorrow."

The two boys looked up at the cedar tree, at the warm blanket of stars. They'd never built a raft before. Not like this one. Fish allowed himself the beginnings of a smile. Something sparked to life in his gut. They didn't have fathers. But they had each other. They had a plan. Fish tried to put his finger on the spark rising inside him.

"Can we name our raft *Hope*?" said Fish, and the stars shone.

"That's a good name for a raft," said Bread.

"The *Hope of Lantern Rock,*" said Fish.

"That's even better," said Bread.

The boys exhaled and watched the sky awhile. It was stunning, the way it hung and spun.

"Thank you, Bread," said Fish.

"For what?"

Fish didn't answer. He was already twisting root ropes in his mind, already diving from their raft into the deep black river, drying himself in sunlight, eating catfish caught with cane poles. He was no longer afraid, the terror of the night washed away in river sounds.

"Well," said Bread, making himself comfortable against his backpack, "I got more Slim Jims, if you want another one."

FIVE

S HERIFF CAL PULLED HIMSELF INTO HIS TRUCK. HIS DOG, JACKS, moved over on the bench seat, circled, and settled onto his haunches, panting and grinning. Jacks was a young blue heeler Cal picked up from a barn litter for thirty-five dollars. *Thirty dollars is how much the worm shots cost me,* said the old woman, wiping her hands on her apron as Cal lifted the puppy up by its armpits to examine him more closely. The pup had one blue eye and one brown, a white patch of fur on his belly. Cal asked if the puppy had a name, and also why the extra five dollars. *That one's name is Jacks, and he's been a pain in my ass, that's why—he escapes—and you ain't from here, are you, I can tell from how you talk.* She said it all without pause, which made Cal smile and the puppy squirm. Cal decided to rescue the dog—he imagined the woman cussing after it with a broom—paid the woman, and placed the puppy in his truck on top of an old sweatshirt. *Where you from,* the woman asked him. *Texas,* Cal told her, *I'm the new sheriff, pleasure to meet you.* The woman widened her eyes at him, shook his hand like a man does. *Uh-huh* is all she said. On the drive home, the puppy chewed through a seat belt and put teeth marks in the armrest but didn't try to escape. He seemed pleased to be sitting somewhere other than that woman's garage. Cal never could train Jacks to do very much, and frankly, he didn't want to. Jacks had an independent mind, considered himself an equal. Cal didn't argue.

"All right, Jacks," said Cal, sliding his key into the ignition.

The dog panted and swallowed.

"We're in it now," said Cal. "We are in it."

The truck's motor came to life and the heater fans blew cold air into the cab. The digital clock said it was a quarter past three in the morning. Teddy and Cal planned to leave at first light. Cal closed his eyes a moment, rubbed his face with his hands, and put the truck in gear. He needed to get to the station, pack up some gear and two or three days' worth of food. He needed a place for Jacks to stay too, and he needed sleep but knew there wasn't time. The boys hadn't shown up at Teddy's like Cal hoped, or at least not in the way he had hoped. They had been there all right. They just didn't stay. Cal and Teddy had spent a good two hours turning the farm upside down—the machine sheds and barn, the silos, the ditches by the pasture—and then they met back in Teddy's kitchen. Cal unfolded a plat of the county on the table. Teddy worked on making a pot of black coffee, then phoned his daughter.

"Miranda," he said in a quiet voice, "you ain't heard from Fischer, have you?" It was prayerful, the way Teddy seemed to speak those words. There was fear and hope in his voice. Cal had always known Teddy as a capable man, quiet, who kept to himself. But he had fire in him too, beneath the surface. Teddy once helped Cal pull a farmer's body out of a tiller. The man had fallen backward while dragging a field, and the tractor raked up its driver and found its way into a marsh, stuck on its oil pan with its tires churning the mud like a riverboat. Cal was no farmer, never drove a tractor in his life, and ended up flagging down Teddy from the road to help him shut down the machine. Cal played it cool like a sheriff should but was amazed at the way Ted gathered up the pieces as calmly as if he were lifting sacks of grain. *That's all of him,* Ted said, stooping to wash his hands in the marsh water. And then something seemed to rise in him, an anger so instant and shaking and hot it was more surprising than frightening. Cal had no time to react. Ted stood from the marsh and poked a trembling finger into Cal's chest, told him to do his own work from then on, called him something awful, cursed the fields and the morning and drove away. The next day Ted called Cal's office and apologized, cool as could be. It was a mystery, the thing that ignited him so. It wasn't just the sight of the body. Something seemed to scare Teddy out there. Something in himself after partaking of the recovery.

Tonight, Ted's hands shook as he poured Cal a cup of coffee. Ted had had trouble finding matches to light the oven-top, and he couldn't find his two coffee mugs either. Cal watched him turn on his heel several times, as if he didn't know his way around his own kitchen, and then Teddy hastily dug out a half stack of paper cups from a lower cupboard. Teddy's voice quavered now as he spoke on the phone.

"Miranda," he said. "No. Don't come just yet. I know. I know it is." Cal watched Ted's fingers twist the cord in his free hand, squeeze it as if to break a bird's neck, then loosen to decide against it. "I'll call you soon as I know something. Okay? Stay put. The sheriff thinks the boys might call. Goodbye. I will."

There had been no initial sign of the boys in Claypot, but eventually Jacks sniffed out a pair of bike tracks and footprints that led through the soft dirt in the fields adjoining the Breadwin home. Jacks was a natural tracker, self-taught. It's an interest he chose for himself. Cal could just say, "Find it, find 'em," and his piebald dog would trot around with his nose to the dirt until he found something. Sometimes it was a skunk, sometimes a rabbit, this time the footprints of two ten-year-old boys. The boys' tracks led across the plowed fields into marsh grass. They were headed in the general direction of Burt Akinson's farm. The men backtracked, searched the fields with spotlights. There was nothing there. Not even coyotes. They got in their trucks and drove to Teddy's.

Ted hung up the phone and paced the kitchen while Cal tapped the antenna of his radio against the map.

"Where," Teddy asked himself, "did those *mugs* go?"

The sheriff pretended to study the map, but really he was studying Teddy. Cal had noticed over the years the way calm people could break down when problems became personal. He knew a trauma nurse who couldn't watch her son get stitches after a spill on his bike. Maybe Cal was wrong to involve Ted in all of this. Cal *did* have a deputy, after all, and maybe Bobby would have to do. Maybe Teddy needed to stay home.

"And my matches," Teddy said. "I swear I had a full book of matches in this jar right here." He hefted the jar in his hand as if he wanted to smash it, then let it rattle to the counter. His face was red. "Something ain't right."

Cal decided it—he was on his own. He'd bother Teddy for a cup of coffee and that would be it. Cal studied the map again. Claypot was backed up to the north by a massive swath of forest. The few towns large enough to have their own police force were all a forty-minute drive to the south, where the soil was better and the farming communities had a chance to grow. Only two primary tracks cut through the county's northern territory, the river and the highway. Both wove through just under ten thousand square miles of forest. Cal knew a few of the unmarked logging roads that snaked through the place. They were often washed out and grown over and hardly roads at all. The closest town on the north side of the forest was Ironsford, a paper town with a Guard armory. It was just within Cal's jurisdiction, so he made it up that way from time to time. The drive was a lonely one, about ninety miles of pine and poplar trees, the occasional trailer home with woodsmoke coming from it, a sheet of plywood nailed up over a window. Every now and then the highway ran parallel to the river for a quarter mile or so, just close enough for the water to sparkle through the trees. Hunting cabins stood along the river. As did methamphetamine operations. A few families lived lonely sorts of lives out there, at least that's the way they looked to Cal—a woman hanging handkerchiefs on a line, a small boy chasing a dog around a rotted garden fence. If a person got off the river or the highway, he could walk for days through cedar swamps and poplar stands and black flies and bear tracks and never feel as if he'd moved ten feet. To Cal, the forest had only one look to it, only one way of being. It was impassable, except for that river and that road. Cal once had to track a group of poachers into that forest along with some game wardens. Jacks was by his side, and Cal was thankful for the company. Though he and the wardens never separated more than one hundred yards as they traversed the swamps, the way that forest closed in made Cal feel lost in the first twenty steps. It was a difficult thing to bear for a man raised in Houston's suburbs. He liked the southern part of Marigamie County much better, with its neat rows of corn, its bigger towns and gas stations, sidewalks and people. When the wardens eventually called off that particular search, Cal found himself walking quickly through the brambles and pine branches as if racing the sunlight, whispering, *Find it, Jacks, find the truck.*

Cal traced the expanse of forest on the map. If he had just killed a man and—God forbid it—kidnapped two boys, that great erasure of forest is where he would head. Cal shuddered at the thought of those boys bouncing around in the back of a truck on one of those awful logging roads, nothing but the scrape of tree limbs, the glow of brake lights. If the boys were out there, it would be hell to find them. Cal looked hopefully to the south of Claypot. Teddy said his daughter, Fischer's mom, lived in Cedar, one of the farming towns thirty miles south where the cornfields didn't have a cedar left in them. If the boys *were* on their own, if they were just scared and running, maybe they would be headed that way. But then why wouldn't they have run here, to Teddy's place?

"Sheriff," said Teddy.

Cal answered him but didn't look up. It wouldn't be any easier finding the boys if they'd taken off to the south. An eighty-acre cornfield could be just as disorienting as any cedar swamp. And who knows if those boys would stay on the roads or even near them. Kids could take off when they were afraid. Cal had seen it happen. They could run in circles. In the academy in Texas, Cal once assisted a search for a lost child that lasted two rain-soaked days and covered five ranches. The child was found, safe but cold, wrinkled as a prune, hunkered beneath a willow tree less than five hundred yards from his own front door. The child hadn't answered anyone's call. He just hid. Cal decided he would have Bobby continually check both properties, Ted's and Breadwin's, in case the thing resolved itself in such a way.

"Sheriff," Teddy said again.

Cal looked up.

"I know where them mugs went."

Cal tried not to reveal his certainty that Teddy was losing his grasp. Teddy stood in the corner of the kitchen, holding a sheet of notepaper in his hands.

Cal forced a smile and looked back at his map. "That's real good, Ted." This confirmed his decision to exclude Ted from the search. It wasn't just fire, it was confusion. He'd give the old man something to do at home to keep him occupied, something important-sounding, like manning an old radio.

"They're in the forest."

Cal looked up again, concealing nothing this time.

"Your mugs are in the forest?"

Ted held up the piece of paper he found. There was writing on it.

"The boys left a note. They stopped here for supplies. They're headed north through the forest, to the armory."

Cal stood straight up. "To Ironsford?"

Teddy nodded. "It's where Fish's dad served."

Cal swallowed, looked at the floor. The thought of two boys trying to cross ninety miles of woods was unthinkable. It made Cal nervous, and the search just got a whole lot worse. Gone was any hope of cornfields or sidewalks or civilization.

"I know where they'll go first," Teddy said. "There's a path they frequent that goes as far as the river. After that, we'll need horses. I got horses."

Ted was back in the plan. He had to be. If Teddy knew how to get to those boys before they got too deep into the forest, Cal was all for it. There are bad things in those woods, both two- and four-legged. Cal felt like cussing, despite his relief.

"At least this means they're on their own, that they haven't been—taken." Cal paused on the word. "But they must have seen something, seen who it was shot Breadwin."

Teddy shook his head, his mouth tight in disagreement.

"What?"

"There's more," said Teddy. He stopped and held out the note for Cal to read. Cal stepped forward to take it. Teddy's eyes glistened in the dim kitchen light.

Cal straightened the wrinkled note, began reading aloud: "Fish had me put this note on your fridge to tell you we are running away." He stopped and skimmed the rest and pushed his lips together, swallowed.

When he looked up, Teddy's eyes were red-rimmed and wet, but then a different sort of question rose in his expression. Ted held his nose in the air a bit, as if he'd smelled something. Cal had forgotten about the whiskey in his stomach and stepped immediately back across the kitchen.

"This is all right, Teddy," he said. "This is okay. We know where they are and where they're headed."

"There's more to it," said Teddy, and Cal heard the deep reluctance in the words.

Cal waited. Looked at him. The question was gone from Teddy's face. There were more important things to worry about than why the young sheriff has whiskey on his breath. Maybe Teddy hadn't smelled it at all.

Teddy closed his eyes as he spoke. "The note says they're off to meet Fish's dad at the armory."

"Makes sense. It's a person to run toward."

Teddy shook his head. He took off his cap and wiped back his gray hair.

"Fish's father is dead." The kitchen fell silent. "It's why Fischer's mom sends him up here to stay with me during summers."

"But the note says—"

"Bread wrote the note." There was impatience in Teddy's voice now. "Fischer must never have told him the truth."

Cal stared at the note. Something turned deep in his gut, a memory of some old familiar sensation.

"Those boys," Teddy spoke slowly, "are running through the woods toward something that ain't there." He took a rattling breath.

Cal folded his map. "I'll be back here at dawn, Ted. I'm gonna wake up Bobby. Be ready to leave."

Teddy remained slumped back against the kitchen counter. He stared at the floor.

"Teddy, you all right for this? You don't have to come." Few locals knew the woods better than Teddy Branson—except maybe Burt Akinson, who was not Cal's first choice of guides—but he also didn't want to drag a man into a search if he wasn't clear-headed.

Teddy stood up straight, pulled his cap down tightly on his head. He took a breath. "Can you ride a horse, Sheriff?"

"I was planning on taking my truck."

Teddy shook his head. "The boys are on foot. We will be too. I'll saddle my mare for you. All roads end at that river."

As the door closed behind him, Cal cussed under his breath.

In his truck he took out his whiskey bottle, held it almost to his lips, and then he cussed at it and capped it and drove away.

CAL WALKED UP THE STEPS OF A SMALL GREEN HOUSE NORTH OF Claypot and looked for a doorbell in the starlight. Jacks stood by his side, sniffing the concrete steps. Weeds grew up alongside the porch, but so did lilies and some kind of good-smelling shrub that pricked his finger when he touched it. Cal straightened his vest, quietly cleared his throat. He had almost knocked on this door once before, or at least planned to, but he never made it up the porch steps, never got out of his car in fact. But now necessity brought him here, at four in the morning. Jacks needed a place to stay. He and Teddy would be traveling on horseback, and Cal had seen how fast horses ran in the Westerns, and he didn't like the thought of Jacks bursting his heart trying to keep up. Cal cleared his throat again. The sky to the east was beginning to color. Cal rapped his knuckles on the aluminum screen door, gently at first, then a bit louder. He looked out at the yard. His truck sat idling in the driveway next to a cherry-red Ford Fiesta with a dent in its front quarter panel, the car usually parked outside the Sit & Go gas station. Cal turned to knock again, but as he did, a porch light blinded him.

"I'll call the cops!" threatened a woman's voice from within. The sheriff couldn't see through the screen into the dark house. Jacks barked and growled. Cal held his hands up.

"Tiff?" he said.

"Sheriff Cal?"

"Yeah."

Silence came from within.

Cal shifted his weight on his feet, squinted his eyes. "Tiff, you ain't pointing a gun at me, are you?"

A light came on inside, and Tiffany Robins appeared. She carried a baseball bat in her hand and wore a T-shirt that came down about midthigh. She leaned the bat against the wall and tucked her hair behind her ears, unlocked the screen door.

"Sheriff," she said sleepily. "Hey."

Cal lowered his hands. Jacks grumbled, but Cal reached down and smoothed the fur on his back. "Relax, boy."

"Sorry for the bat," she said.

Cal wagged his chin. "Sorry for waking you up."

The two stood on the porch for a moment, and Cal actually forgot what he came to say. Tiffany was pretty, there was no denying it. Cal always thought so. And she looked even prettier now, half asleep. Her legs flowed out of her shirt toward smooth bare feet. Cal didn't know where to look at her. He tried her eyes, but the sleepiness in them felt somehow as intimate as her legs. He nearly turned to walk away.

"You want some coffee?" she asked.

"No, Tiff, I didn't want to bother you. I just—"

"Come in," she said, already turning inside, her voice waking up. "It's cold. Your dog can come. Come in. Give me a sec." She turned on the kitchen light and then disappeared into a darkened hallway. Cal stepped into the kitchen, took off his hat. There was a Formica table with two chrome-legged chairs in the center of the room. He wasn't asked to sit down, so he didn't, but he placed his hat on the table next to a few bills and a pen or two. He looked closer and saw writing on all the papers, just words, rhyming words, lines scribbled out. *Silver furred, musk and haunch.* And on an unopened utility bill: *She is den born, moon born, speed and fire and bristle.* Cal rubbed his eyes and face. He was in need of a shave. He must have looked like an absolute fool out there on the porch, barely able to speak. He shook his head. *Useless.* It gave him the same sensation he'd felt in Teddy's kitchen when Teddy mentioned Fischer's sustained lie about his dad. Cal didn't think he had to think about that anymore. He blew the thought away. He would leave if he wasn't already standing in the kitchen. Jacks sniffed at something under the table, found a spot to lie down.

A thud came from the darkened hallway. Then Cal heard what sounded like coat hangers being pushed rapidly aside. A muffled *Dang it* came from within.

The sheriff opened his mouth to ask if she was okay, but closed it again. A coffee pot sat on the counter. He knew Tiffany well enough to know she wouldn't let him leave without making him a cup. Maybe he could help things along. "Tiff," he called out, "you want me to start the coffee?"

More drawers, and now a running sink. "What's that, Sheriff?" she called out.

"The coffee, do you want me to make it?"

He couldn't be sure, but Cal thought he heard a blow-dryer come briefly to life.

"Just a sec," she called back.

The sheriff decided to sit down on one of the chairs, just in time to stand up again. Jacks stood and barked. Tiffany appeared wearing tight-fitting blue jeans and a gray V-neck sweater. Her hair was pulled back in a ponytail. Her purple bangs framed her eyes. Because of his frequent coffee stops at the Sit & Go, she was the closest thing he had to a friend in town. Being a sheriff was kind of like being a pastor or a doctor. One gets to know the most intimate things without ever really becoming close to anybody. There was something uncomfortably paternal about it all. Cal couldn't have real conversations with most of the people he knew, let alone ask one out on a date. He once drove thirty miles, from his cabin to Claypot, to ask Tiffany out, offer to take her to see *Jurassic Park,* which people said was pretty great. That's how he'd planned to say it, *People say it's pretty great, the dinosaurs, and I was wondering if,* but he couldn't get the thing right in his mouth. When he got there, he drove right past her house. He didn't even tap the brake.

She wouldn't be interested, and he'd be a fool. People would get the wrong idea if she said yes. A sheriff needed to remain aloof. He thought he would have learned that by now, given what had happened back home. Home. Texas. Why was he here in this awful North?

"Tiff, I really don't have much time. Me and Ted, we—"

She smiled at him as he spoke, and turned to the cupboard to make some coffee. Cal caught a glimpse of a pack of spaghetti noodles and a bag of rice. There were two cans of soup, one of peaches, a jar of olives. It reminded Cal of camping food, the sort of thing that can be opened and heated. It reminded him of his own cooking. Beyond the few canned items, the cupboards were empty. There was fruit on the counter, a loaf of bread. Tiffany moved quickly with her back to him, scooping coffee as he told her why he'd come. He explained about the boys, and how he and Teddy were headed after them. "Into the woods," he said. Her spoon paused only once, when he mentioned the shooting, and then Cal paused too when he remembered the sight of Jack Breadwin in that kitchen. He stopped talking, his thoughts turning to the forest, the enormity of it, the task at hand. Tiffany wrung a kitchen rag beneath the faucet and wiped the counter clean, twice. The coffee pot sputtered and finished brewing. The kitchen felt warm, with the pot of coffee full and black. He looked at her back, her waist, the belt loops of her jeans. He couldn't help imagining coming home to her and embracing her waist, smelling her, saying hello, a woman smiling back at him. He forced his eyes to the floor.

"Tiff, I just stopped by to ask if you would please watch my dog."

Tiffany nodded and began pouring two mugs of coffee. Cal stood and took a step toward her to receive one. Without hearing him, Tiffany turned flat up against him, nearly spilling the coffee held up between their faces. She was shorter than he was, but not by much. Cal forgot himself. Tiffany smelled like flowers, or candy. Cal couldn't put his finger on it. She had a beautiful face. Cal swallowed and took the dripping mugs by their rims and set them on the table.

"So, can you watch him, then?" Cal asked, the words dry in his mouth as he wiped a small spill with his sleeve.

"Sure," she said. "Cal?"

He looked at her.

She looked at him, and then shook her head.

"It's good to have you over," she said. "I'll take good care of your dog."

Cal thanked her and told Jacks to stay and walked to the door. The light outside was purple now. Soon it'd be pink, and the sun would rise above the brown fields surrounding Claypot. Cal felt Tiffany's hand inside his elbow. She handed him a mug.

"Take it with you," she said. "Do good."

"Thanks," he said, and smiled at her. "And thanks for the coffee." He walked down the steps and called back from his truck, "And thanks for watching Jacks!" She grinned and waved at him, crossed her arms over her chest, and then she stooped to snatch Jacks' collar to keep him inside.

As Cal drove back to Teddy's, he found his mind still in that small kitchen. The smell of coffee, the smell of a woman, and then it came to him. Lavender. Tiffany Robins smells like lavender. He smiled at the pink light over the fields and woods. Drove with his hands loose on the wheel. He rubbed his eyes and face and cursed himself, sat upright in his cab. He was sheriff again. Two scared boys about to lose themselves in a forest were having a very bad time.

"Sit tight, fellas," Cal said, pushing the wheel through a gravel turn. "Don't run."

SIX

"**T**HIS IS KIND OF A GOOD TIME!" SAID BREAD. HE AND FISH knelt in the morning sun next to the riverbank with their supplies laid out on a tarp. The dew on the grass soaked the knees of Fish's jeans, but it didn't bother him. It couldn't. They'd need to get used to discomforts from here on out—the damp and dirt, maybe hunger too—they were in the wild. It surprised Fish how unshaken Bread seemed this morning after what happened the night before. But then, Fish felt less shaken too. Here they were at their favorite spot on the river, a whole mess of bushcrafting supplies before them, and they were going to build a raft and name it and take it downriver with poles. The water slid between islands and toppled over boulders. A finch sat in a tree and watched, cocked its small eye toward the boys. Yesterday was a dream. Today was a good time. They could do this.

"Okay," said Fish, "which of us is going to carry the barlow?"

Bread pursed his lips and studied the pocketknife. In their rush to leave last night, their gear became what Fish's grandpa would have called lopsided. First on the agenda this morning, after waking amid boulders and stumbling to the river to pee in the rapids, was fixing that lopsidedness. It's something Fish's grandpa used to do when he took him hunting or fishing in these forests. When one of them lost too many lures or ate up his reserves of jerky, his grandpa would take a break on a stump somewhere and lay his vest and pack on the ground. *Last thing you want in the bush,* he'd say, pushing back the brim of his green cap, *is lopsided supplies.* Fish enjoyed the process. It meant a break from hiking. It meant he could take the brass cartridges out of his rifle, count them, and put them back in again. It usually meant he'd get more of his grandpa's jerky. *It's poor form,* his grandpa explained, *for one guy to have all of one thing and the other to have all of another thing. If one guy has all the jerky and loses his pack, then nobody has any jerky. Gotta divvy it up, and re-divvy it. Same with lures and matches and shot shells. How many you got left?*

The boys had already divided the matches. They each had ten, and even tore the striker in half to share it. They each had two fishing lures, red and white bobbers, collapsible poles, two Slim Jims, one can of Bumble Bee tuna, two mugs, and half a pouch of Red Man chewing tobacco. They didn't want to tear the tobacco pouch and ruin its seal, so Fish took a moist handful of the sticky black leaves, packed it like a snowball, and put it in the chest pocket of his flannel shirt. All that remained on the tarp were two Ninja Turtles—Donatello and Michelangelo, and Fish already knew Donatello belonged to Bread—the barlow knife and sharpening stone, a thumb-sized piece of flint, and the revolver with five rounds in it.

"I think you should carry the barlow knife," said Bread. "You know how to sharpen it better than me."

"You sure?"

Bread nodded. Fish did know how to sharpen a knife well. He'd been a quick study. His grandpa had taught him how to tell if a blade was dull by looking at its edge in the sunlight. If the cutting edge reflected light, it wasn't thin enough and needed touching up.

Fish learned how to slice the blade across the stone until he raised a burr on one side of the edge. Once that burr was raised, he'd flip it and slice the other way. It took a while before he got the feel of when a blade became sharp against the stone. The sensation was a lack of friction, but then again, there seemed something spiritual to it as well, like divining water with a stick or sensing when a person was about to cry. It wasn't science, it was knowledge. Fish's grandpa had given him knowledge.

Fish picked up the barlow knife, opened it, studied its edge in the sunlight, and folded it closed. The knife felt reassuring in his hand. The blade was a clip-point style, which meant it was good for dressing game. It had jigged bone handles riveted in place. The nickel bolster that held the blade's hinge was engraved with the letters *TBB*. Teddy Branson's Barlow. Fish felt a pang of guilt for taking it without asking. But he was sure his grandpa would want him to have such a knife in the bush. It was one of the essentials. His grandpa told him that. *A man can make it in the bush until he loses his knife,* his grandpa said. *The knife and the flint. Don't ever lose those.*

"You should carry the flint," said Fish. "I'll carry the blade to strike it. Together we'll equal a campfire."

Bread smiled at this wisdom and pressed the gray flint into the coin pocket of his jeans.

"This really is a good time," he said again, and then his smile straightened. "What do we do with the revolver?" he asked.

To be honest, Fish didn't want to see it, let alone carry it. When he took the thing out of its sack and placed it on the tarp, the weight of it in his hands went straight to his heart. He set it down quickly and didn't want to pick it up again. His grandpa's knife felt good. The dead man's revolver did not. It gleamed in the sun, the satin-finished steel soaking up the same placid warmth as the boys, but there was dread in that beautiful Smith & Wesson, a kind of darkness in all that daylight.

Fish shook his head. "You carry it," he said.

Bread picked it up and turned it over in his hands, and Fish could only imagine what he was thinking. The gun looked so massive in his hands, so out of place. Fish was surprised when a sort of brightness grew across Bread's face, as if he'd just had a pleasant thought. Bread used his thumb to push forward the cylinder catch on the revolver's side. He used his other hand to poke open the cylinder, and smacked his palm down on the ejector rod a few times. Fish knew the words for all the parts of guns from a book he got at the school library. He studied the history of firearms, the types of barrels, the locks and stocks. They seemed so wonderful then, the way it seemed wonderful the first time his dad went to war.

Bread shook the gun and six brass cartridges fell onto the tarp, one of them spent. He gathered up the five good ones and held them out to Fish with his palm facing downward. Fish tentatively held out his hand.

"Like the knife and the flint," said Bread.

Bread closed the revolver's cylinder and struggled to stuff the muzzle into his belt. Then he and Fish both looked down at the spent shell casing. Bread picked it up, held it in his palm. The casing was blackened where the bullet had been. Its primer was dented where the firing pin had struck it. It was no larger than a caterpillar. How could a thing so small send them out into the wild like this, into such exile? That's the word Fish's mom would use—exile— boys banished into the wild, to become wild themselves perhaps, like Ishmael, cut off from his father. Fish knew his mother would have insisted, of course, that Ishmael, despite his exile, wasn't truly fatherless, would have reminded him of the "Father of All," the miraculous springs of water in the desert. Fish wasn't so sure. There had been no miraculous spring after his dad died, only a folded flag delivered by a man in uniform he'd never met before. Fish hated him. He hated that folded flag. And right now Fish found himself hating that small piece of spent brass Bread held in his palm. It made the river ugly. Fish shifted on his wet knees. Doubt poured through his body.

Fish surprised himself and yelled at his friend, "Would you quit sitting there like a fool and get rid of it already?"

Bread's fist tightened on the spent shell casing.

"Why?" he said, menace creasing his forehead.

"Give it here, then, I'll throw it in the river."

Bread drew his fist away.

"I said give it here!" Fish was crying, and he hardly knew why. He lunged for Bread's hand, but Bread pulled it back even farther. Then Bread pushed him backward into the grass. Fish felt stupid for falling so easily, and then he just felt angry. As he rose to his hands and knees he heard Bread say, "It's mine, and I'll do what I want with it."

And then a thought came to Fish that felt cruel and logical. He stood up, brushed off his knees, and spoke it. He pointed a finger at Bread's face.

"You're right. It is your shell. And it's your fault. All of this is."

"What's my fault?" Bread's eyes widened and then narrowed into slits.

Fish's finger stayed pointed. Accusing his friend in this way felt like honing a knife too steeply. Knowing another stroke would ruin the edge, he finished the stroke anyway.

"It's because of you and your rotten old man that I'm even out here." The edge bit. Fish was ashamed the moment he said it. The men in his life, his grandpa, his dad, would never say such a thing and would be embarrassed of anyone who did.

It was too late. Bread lowered his head and charged. Fish took the hit in the stomach, and the breath was knocked from his lungs as they thumped to the ground. Bread kept his head down in Fish's chest and swung his fists into his rib cage. Fish retaliated, breathless, by driving the heel of his shoe into Bread's side. Neither boy was a very good fighter. The blows didn't do much damage. It was the shock of the thing that hurt. They'd never fought before. Not like this. Not with blows. Bread landed a good one into Fish's side. It hurt enough for Fish to grab his friend in a headlock, to try to stop the punches. He didn't know how to do anything but squeeze Bread's head. So he squeezed it as hard as he could. Bread kept swinging. Both boys were crying. Fish got his breath back.

"Get off me, Breadwin!"

Bread landed another hook into his side. "Take it back!" came his muffled cry.

Fish drove his heel into Bread's ribs, and Bread took another three or four swings. In the midst of it, Fish became aware of something. It was a sound. It sounded like a bird, a jingling of sorts. He remembered the finch, its watchful eye. But this was not a bird.

"Bread, stop hittin' me—Bread!"

Bread squirmed with all his might to get his head free. "Take it back!" he hissed.

"Bread, stop—I hear something." And he did hear something. He wasn't imagining it. It sent a bolt of fear through his body. Reflexively, he let go of Bread's head and tried to sit up.

"Bread, I hear—"

Free of Fish's grasp, Bread reared back and cocked Fish a round-house punch straight across the jaw. Fish saw stars in his eyes as his head landed back in the grass.

Bread cocked his arm for another swing, but suddenly froze and stared at the wood line behind him. "You hear that?" he asked in a hushed voice. "Fish, get up, it sounds like—"

Fish lifted his head and worked his jaw open. It hurt. "Horses" was all he could manage to say. He closed his mouth and swallowed. He tasted blood in his spit. And then he heard it again. It was the whinny of a horse, the jangling tack, up in the tree line. Then he heard the muffled sounds of men's voices.

Bread grabbed him and stood him on his feet. "It's the search party," he whispered. "Come on!"

Fish staggered after him, his hand on his jaw, and when he wasn't moving fast enough Bread grabbed him and pulled him along. Bread stooped to pick up the tarp as the two boys ran for the cleft of Lantern Rock. Fish dragged the backpacks and fish poles. The sun was higher in the sky now, but the cleft was still dark. They dove for it and lay down on their stomachs on the bed of brown cedar needles. Ferns blocked the entrance. The cedar blocked the sun. Bread balled up the tarp under himself and lay on it. His wide eyes looked out at the bright riverbank. His nostrils flared. Fish tried to meter his own breathing. It sounded very loud now that they were trying to hide. For a few breaths, he rested his forehead against the needles. They stuck to his lips as he panted. His jaw ached, and he knew he deserved every bit of it. He was the reason they were out here, not Bread. He was the killer, not Bread. Fish had a fleeting thought about how maybe he should walk out into the sunlight and turn himself in, hands in the air, confession on his bloody lips.

He nearly stood up when he felt Bread's hand press down against his back. "Shhh," whispered Bread, almost imperceptibly. When Fish raised his head, ever so slowly, the view of the riverbank was taken up almost entirely by a horse and half a rider standing not five paces from the entrance. Fish froze. He saw a brown boot in a silver stirrup. Jeans and horsehide. The cedar branches blocked the man's torso and face. Holstered to the horse's flank in a saddle scabbard sat a lever-action rifle. Fish swallowed blood again, and cursed himself for being so loud.

The horse stirred.

"They were here," said a man's voice, which Fish recognized as his grandfather's. "Horses smell 'em. Grass is flattened."

Indescribable hunger washed over Fish upon hearing his grandfather's voice. That voice promised competence, safety, rest. It seemed to remove all pain, even the pain in his jaw. Here was a man who could wash the world with his hands, wave them in the air and make it all ordered again. The urge to burst out of that cleft was overwhelming, and Fish nearly made up his mind to do so when he felt Bread's hand on his back.

"Wait." His friend mouthed the word.

Fish shook his head. "I want to go," he mouthed back.

Bread tightened his lips and shook his head. He pointed out farther into the sunlight.

Another horse and rider came into view, this one far enough off that Fish could make out the whole body. It was the sheriff. The man walked his horse up to where the tarp had flattened the grass. He studied the ground, looked out across the river, and back at the forest behind him. He had a shiny pistol on his belt. Unlike Fish's grandpa's rifle, with its hand-worn bluing and walnut stock, the sheriff's pistol shone in the sunlight like that revolver had only moments ago, majestic and terrible. Fish felt himself swallow again. He remembered the spotlight last night in the field, the sound of the bullets zipping overhead. Surely it hadn't been the sheriff who had fired on them. But then again, maybe it was. The sheriff had always been a bit of a mystery to the boys. He'd wave if he passed by in his truck, but there never seemed to be friendliness in it. He was a powerful man, Fish knew. But still, Fish's grandpa was here. What harm could come if his grandpa was here?

"You figure they crossed?" asked the sheriff. His voice sounded impatient, pained in some way. He adjusted himself in his saddle. Fish's grandpa pressed his heel gently into his horse's side. The stallion stepped away into the light. Fish felt the weight of Bread's hand again.

"Fish," whispered Bread.

Fish waited. His grandpa had pulled his horse alongside the sheriff's, looked down at the grass, and then across the river. The two men conferred in hushed tones. Fish couldn't make out the words.

"If you go out there," said Bread, "that sheriff is gonna take you away and put you straight in jail, or worse."

Fish's body tensed. He wanted so badly for his grandfather to take him up on that horse and ride him back home. He could imagine the warmth of the leather, the squeak of the tack, the smell of his grandpa's flannel jacket.

"Fish."

Fish looked at Bread. Bread's cheeks were red and mottled. He was clearly in distress, but he wasn't shaking. A sort of confidence shone through.

"I ain't gonna let my only friend go to jail. I ain't even gonna let you do it to yourself."

Fish didn't quite know how to respond to that, so he stayed silent for a time. They were boys. They didn't have horses or rifles. They couldn't face the forest as well as men, but something in Bread's eyes let him know they had to, that it was all or nothing, that a final decision had to be made right now.

Fish heard water splash and turned to see the two men lead their horses into the shallow rock beds upstream of the rapids, headed for the other shore. Soon they would be gone, as would Fish's chance to make up his mind. It was confess now or go deep into that forest, come what may. Fish lowered his face down to the cedar needles, let the earth into his lungs. He inhaled and exhaled. He felt as disoriented as he did when he tried to pray the way his mom had taught him. There was too much unknown, and he didn't know what he was allowed to ask for. He'd been told God was powerful, that he raised people from the dead, which only made Fish wonder why God couldn't raise his father from the dead, or worse, why he wouldn't. Fish's mom said he could ask God for anything, tell him anything, that he could just talk with him. She talked to God in silence, and in song, and in tongues, that quiet and lilting rhythm filling the hallways of his home at night. And when she prayed, God *did* seem to be there. Fish would feel calmed, protected, known. On the worst sort of nights, the approach of that comfort angered Fish. If God wanted to comfort him, he could give his dad back, a father Fish could touch, and see, and smell. But God didn't give his dad back, and Fish never asked the adults why not. It was too awful when they pretended to know the answers to such questions.

"Bread?" said Fish.

"Yeah?"

"I'm sorry for what I said. It's not true. All of this is my fault."

There was a pause.

"I'm sorry I cocked you. And no, it ain't your fault either."

Fish opened his sore jaw, lifted his head, and looked at the river. The men were out of sight. All Fish could hear was a bird in a tree, the sway of river grass in the breeze. Fish had decided. Bread had too. They were outcasts.

TIFFANY NEARLY BOUNDED WITH JACKS TOWARD THE SUNRISE CAFÉ. They walked on the sunny side of the street, and Tiffany inhaled deeply and looked up at the sky. The morning felt fresh, the air seemed excited. She already called in to work, took four days off. Jacks had a brand-new baby-blue leash from Briar's Feed and Tack, and Tiffany carried under her free arm a ten-pound sack of the most expensive dog food she could afford, a food and water bowl set, and a chew toy. The chew toy was a zebra-striped cat with crossed eyes and a bright pink tongue. Jacks seemed uninterested when she first waved it under his nose, but Tiffany knew he was just pretending. Jacks tried to seem standoffish—he even tried to bolt from her car, which was narrowly avoided by a lunging grab, which hurt Tiffany's knee and made her stifle a cuss—but he'd warmed up quickly enough, and Tiffany felt they were going to get along swimmingly.

Tiffany pushed her purple hair behind her ears and skipped up the curb with Jacks in tow. Claypot didn't have much of a downtown, but it did have one. There was the barbershop with a skull and crossbones in the window—which a few of the Baptists frowned upon—the public works department and firehall, which served as a bingo hall on Saturday nights, and the basement library, where Tiffany often scandalized Ms. Gart with her constant requests for poetry collections through interlibrary loan from the big city.

"These poems have cusses and sex in them," said Ms. Gart.

"So do you and I," said Tiffany, and Ms. Gart would go back to furiously stamping her due date cards.

The general disrepair of the brick buildings downtown suggested Claypot had known better times, but for Tiffany the town had remained unchanged since her childhood. It was home, equally dear and disappointing.

"Come on, Jackie boy," she said.

Jacks grumbled and walked at the far end of his outstretched leash.

There was a park bench outside the Sunrise Café. Tiffany's stomach growled. She usually spent her mornings off in the coffee shop, eating a piece of egg pie with a dill pickle, reading the paper, and pretending she lived somewhere else. Sometimes Burt Akinson would stop by on a feed run and the two would heckle each other, but otherwise Tiffany just stared out the window over a cup of coffee and hoped for something interesting to pass on the road. She once saw a pig trailer overturn on the corner of Walnut and Main—the pigs got free and stood in the road and destroyed some flowerpots—but that was a once-in-a-lifetime thrill. She often dreamed of the kind of café one would find near a college campus, with undergrads reading novellas and talking about big ideas, taking off mittens in winter, having friends. Tiffany already knew at twenty-five that she'd never leave. Lives like that were for other people, lucky people, worthy people. Sometimes she was sad about it. Sometimes she was not. Today was hopeful. She had Sheriff Cal's dog. She felt hungry. She'd grab a cup of coffee and a bagel to go.

She set the food and bowls on the sidewalk bench and stooped to tie Jacks' leash to it with three tight knots. She tested the leash with a tug. Jacks grumbled and diverted his blue and brown eyes. Tiffany set the chew toy at his feet and made him look at her.

"Don't mess this up for me, okay? I'll be gone just a sec." She smiled at him, at the sunshine surrounding her body. "I'm in love with your papa."

Jacks sighed and lay down with his chin on his toy cat.

Tiffany smiled and turned to go inside. "When I come back we'll go home and watch movies. I'll scratch your belly."

Tiffany was inside for less than five minutes. When she came out, her coffee hit the pavement and her eyes searched the streets. Tied securely to the bench was exactly half of a leash, chewed clean through in the middle. The food and bowls remained. The chew toy was gone.

Tiffany wrung her fists. "And he took his cat," she hissed.

"What's that, Tiff?" Burt Akinson stood on the sidewalk beside her. His big red truck was parked a few spots away, with one tire up on the curb.

"Oh, hey, Burt."

"Dropped your coffee there, Tiff?"

"Burt, you seen a dog?" Tiffany paced as she spoke, peeked down the gravel alley by the coffee shop, looked down Main Street toward the fields.

"You looking for a dog, Tiff?"

She bit her lip. "That's what I said, Burt."

"You dropped your coffee there."

"Forget the coffee, Burt!"

"Say, come inside and I'll buy you another so your face don't scrunch like that."

Tiffany ignored him now, and Burt didn't know what to do with that. Normally he'd say something about her sour face, or her dyed hair, and she'd question the status of his driver's license, and then they'd drink coffee together if Burt had time. Sometimes he'd grow serious and fatherly and ask her why she didn't have a man yet. He said she needed one. Told her she was too pretty and smart to be running around without a man, unless of course she was one of them new women he'd seen on the talk shows who don't want men in their lives.

"I seen a dog," he said, sensing she was in no mood to banter, "running just out of town, back that way."

She stopped in her tracks, turned, and grabbed Burt by the shoulders. "What'd it look like?"

"How should I know," he said. "I'm half blind."

"Burt, I'm begging you."

"Looked smallish, I guess, cattle dog maybe? Had something dangling from its mouth, caught a tabby cat or something."

Tiffany squeezed his shoulders and kissed his cheek. She grabbed the bag of dog food and bowls and ran back toward her car where it was parked in front of Briar's. Burt blushed, rubbed the lenses of his glasses on his shirt.

"See you, Tiff," he called out.

Gravel spun into the wheel wells as Tiffany sped down the road between the marsh and the cornfields. Her eyes were narrowed, scouring the shoulders and ditch grass for any sign of Jacks. Once or twice she thought she saw the dog in the plowed field, but it turned out to be a clod of dirt.

"Think think think," she said, drumming the wheel with her thumb. She'd screwed it up. Here was her chance to really know the sheriff, to get a dinner out of it, a firing range date—she could care less what it was—and she'd lost his dog within four hours. "Where are you, Jacks?" Tiffany bit her lip, made a decision, and then punched the accelerator. It was her only real hope, she thought, as she turned down a side road and headed for the driveway of the Branson farm. Cal said he'd spent the early hours at Teddy Branson's before he dropped the dog off. The dog tried to bolt. And where did it want to go? It wanted to go back to Teddy's place, to find Cal.

"Jacks?" she hollered out of the window as she pulled in beneath a maple tree. "Jacks?"

The Branson farm was a nice place with old but clean barns. The paint was fresh. The hay bales were neatly stacked. The order was amazing when she thought about it—the old man and his little grandson running the place by themselves. Whenever Tiffany saw a house with a well-kept lawn or a tidy garden, it gave her a pang of guilt. She'd missed out on college when she thought she'd done the right thing by staying in town with her abandoned mother. Five cool years passed, and then her mom remarried and moved to Tulsa, not a word about inviting Tiffany to join them. Tiffany tried to convince herself that she remained in Claypot so that her mother had a place to return to when her new marriage inevitably failed. It was a noble thought that bore much doubt, but the phone call never came. Once, a few months after her mom left, an envelope arrived from Tulsa with twenty-five dollars in it and no letter. After that—and it was three years now—silence. Except from the bank that held her mother's outstanding mortgage. Tiffany regularly received dunning letters until the day she had to pack her car with a camp stove and tent and embark on her hungry summer. So here she remained, with no boyfriend and purple hair, working at a gas station, renting a house without a garden and waiting for pig trailers to flip. She couldn't even keep her cupboards filled with staples. She often ran out of bathroom tissue. *When you gonna get a man?* Burt would ask, and it would stab her like a pin. Who would want her? Desirable women don't become homeless and sleep in the ditches of cornfields, or live off stolen eggs, or bathe in creeks at night, or shiver themselves to sleep beneath unwashed blankets. Not even the dog wanted to be with her.

She stepped from the car and walked toward the barn. The sheriff's truck was parked between the barn and the stable, as was

Teddy's. A small sedan Tiffany didn't recognize was parked in the driveway near the house. There was no sign of the dog. A cow looked at her from the stable, as if waiting for her to do something interesting, and then it scratched its forehead on a fence post.

Tiffany was losing steam. "You seen a dog?" she asked the cow in a quiet voice. The cow licked the post where it had scratched its head and stepped away toward its feed.

Tiffany began to cry. The wind out here in the farm fields felt cooler than it should have. It stripped the sunlight from her body. She folded her arms around herself as she walked to the house. Maybe she'd sit on the porch awhile, wait for the dog to show up, or for the sheriff to come back so she could tell him she failed. The sheriff would probably be nice about it, which would be the worst part, because she knew he'd never trust her again, and their relationship would forever be reduced to thirty-second conversations about the price of gas and empty coffee carafes. Tiffany's eyes blurred as she pulled herself up the front porch. She felt her throat tighten. She just couldn't hold it in.

As she turned to sit, the front door swung open. Tiffany stood and took a startled step backward. A tall woman with dark hair and reddened eyes stood in the doorway. She was holding a balled-up Kleenex in one hand and the box in the other.

"Who are you?" asked the woman. There was confusion in her eyes, as if she'd been woken from sleep, or hadn't slept at all. There was something familiar about those eyes too, their fierce competence, the way they were set in her face over that slim nose.

"My name's Tiffany," she said, wiping a tear from her face with the heel of her hand. She didn't like for strangers to see her cry. She didn't like for anyone to see her cry. The woman handed her a Kleenex. As Tiffany reached forward and begrudgingly took it, she realized who the woman must be.

"You're Teddy Branson's daughter, aren't you?" asked Tiffany, pressing the Kleenex against her cheekbones.

The woman nodded.

"I'm so sorry to—" Tiffany paused. She could hardly describe to herself what she was doing here. "I came out here looking for a dog, the sheriff's dog." Tiffany waved her crumpled Kleenex out at the fields and her eyes blurred over with tears again. "And I thought he liked me, and I bought his dog a stupid cat, and now he's not going to talk to me again." She felt miserable gushing like this, but it didn't matter. Not much did. All seemed lost in that bright morning light, those brown empty fields. "And you," she went on, feeling even lower, "you're here to find your boy." Tiffany's voice broke completely as she said it, guilt upon guilt, waves of it.

The woman stepped onto the porch and gave Tiffany another Kleenex. She looked out at the fields and the forest behind them. She looked at the young woman with purple hair crying on her dad's porch.

"Come inside," she said.

Tiffany let herself sob, feeling both pathetic and grateful.

"My name's Miranda," said the woman. "And I don't mind company."

SEVEN

"STILL TOO SHORT," SAID FISH. "WE NEED LONGER ONES."

Bread's shoulders dropped. He held in his hands a bouquet of spruce roots not much longer than flower stems. He dropped them on the moss, wiped his hands, and trudged back to the small grove of spruce trees to try again. "Longer roots, longer roots," he mumbled. "I can't find no longer roots."

Fish thought better of responding. After his grandpa and the sheriff crossed the river, the boys moved about a mile downstream, until they found a clearing in the cedars. Foot trails no longer existed, and they often had to force their way through brambles and tangles of pine. The woods left little sign of their passage. The wall of thorns and sap closed behind them, and they got to work on their raft.

Fish looked up at the sun. It was high in the sky now, well past noon. He'd busied himself for most of the morning trying to cut down a cedar tree with his grandfather's barlow knife. The cedar had soft wood, but it made for painstaking knife work. He was unsure if such labor was tenacious or just plain dumb. The tree was about a foot thick at its base, and Fish had to slice it away, strip by strip. He was thankful he remembered to bring the whetstone. After slicing for about ten minutes, the edge of the blade stopped biting, and he'd have to slice the whetstone for a while. It was a welcome break. The work made his hands cramp, and he couldn't get comfortable standing or kneeling. Fish stepped back to gauge his work. The progress was slow, but it was progress. He'd sliced away nearly one quarter of the tree's diameter. A pile of shavings covered the ground. If a beaver could do it with his front teeth, Fish told himself, he could do it with a barlow. They needed about ten or fifteen more trees for their raft. If this is what it took, he thought, then this is what he'd do.

Bread trudged back. "Maybe we could switch awhile," he said. "The roots keep breaking, and I'm getting sick and tired of it."

"Can't you just dig 'em out?"

"I got nothing to dig with."

Bread sat down heavily near his pack and pulled out a can of tuna. He wiped his dirty hands on his jeans, opened the top, scooped a bite into his mouth, and chewed without enthusiasm. Fish watched his friend looking out at the cool river sparkling through the gaps in the trees. The day had become hot, and mosquitoes rose from the ferns once the boys worked up a sweat. Bread swatted one.

"And these bugs," he said, his mouth full of tuna, "could drive a cow nuts."

Fish, too, was covered in welts and bites on his back and arms. Scratching them made it worse. Swatting them did nothing. Fish spat on the whetstone, scraped the blade along its length, and then folded the knife and sat down next to Bread in the musty cedar chaff. Bread handed him the tuna and scratched his arms. The boys looked at the small pile of failed roots, too short for rope. They silently stared at the chewed-up cedar tree.

"We're never gonna finish this raft," said Bread.

"We're making progress," said Fish.

Bread snorted. Fish handed the tuna can back to him. It was dry without mayonnaise. Fish felt a deep hunger for good-tasting food, for salt and sugar. He thought about a peanut butter and jelly with potato chips and cold milk in his favorite blue cup, but resisted the impulse to dwell on it. He had to be strong. They had to train themselves to go without.

"Behold the beaver," said Fish, swallowing.

"Behold what?" said Bread.

"We're in a new kind of life now, Bread. We're on woods time now, woods food. We are strong and we are good, and it doesn't matter if it takes ten years to build that raft."

"What's that got to do with beaver?" said Bread.

"What it's got to do with beaver is that beavers don't know about clocks. Or days or weeks. No bedtime. No lunchtime. No nothing."

Bread frowned and took another bite of the dry tuna.

"This tuna is awful," he said.

"I know," said Fish. "But what I'm saying is that no one can make us eat it, don't you see? No one can make us do anything anymore." Fish was thinking it through as he spoke, trying on the truthfulness of it.

Bread tried it out. "Beavers ain't got homework," he said, tuna flakes on his lips.

"They don't have to finish supper," said Fish.

"They ain't got to brush their teeth!"

"They only got two teeth to brush!"

"They ain't got to dig no more dang roots!" Bread stood as he said it and spiked his can of tuna against the cedar tree. He turned toward the river and lifted his fists above his head. Tuna bits spewed from his mouth as he yelled, "I am the beaver!"

"Behold the beaver!" yelled Fish.

The boys sprinted through the trees. The shade beneath the cedars was muggy, and ahead of them the river shone like a bright white field of snow. They ducked beneath branches and laughed while they ran. The footing was soft with needles. The heady musk of bark and moss and ferns filled their lungs.

Fish had his shirt off before he reached the water. He hopped on one foot to tear off his shoe, and when it was bare he hopped on the other. He bolted and leapt and splashed in feet-first. The water was clean and cold and amber-colored, steeped through the pines of its watershed like a glass of iced tea. Fish opened his eyes under-water, reached out, and felt along the cold gravel of the river bottom. Above him hung a ceiling of amber light. Fish arced upward and pushed off with his feet, the way he'd seen an otter do at the Milwaukee Zoo, blowing bubbles from his nose. This *was* right, he thought, this beaver freedom. They never *did* have to go back to the world, or answer to it. They were not of this world anymore. They could sleep until noon and howl until midnight. They could skip rocks and swim. They could live on fish and birds' eggs and cattail roots. They didn't even have to make fires. They could eat it all raw. Fish became aware of something that shocked him with its immensity. It was possible, he thought—he didn't yet know exactly how, but knew he was close to knowing—for a person to never again be afraid of anything.

Fish surfaced just in time to see Bread chuck himself off the riverbank. Bread lifted his knees into his chest, hugged them, and plunged beneath the water with a thump Fish felt in his neck. When Bread surfaced, he was smiling. He gave a hoot of satisfaction.

Fish looked upstream. The current wasn't very strong here. The river flowed through a series of oxbows and islands and sandbars. Some of the islands were thick with dogwood and picker bushes. The closest, about thirty yards across the river, was more open, with a canopy of cedars growing at its center. Fish started swimming for it.

"Last one there gets a leech in his wiener," howled Bread, div-

ing forward into his stroke. Bread was an incredible swimmer. Fish
was always surprised by his speed. It was as if the water carried him
along, parted for him, pulled and pushed him, his arms reaching, feet churning. Fish stretched out his body in his best stroke,
an elongated dog paddle, and kicked with all his might as Bread
pulled steadily away. When Fish finally felt the island under his
hands and lifted himself to wade in, Bread was already standing
on dry ground, grinning and shivering in his underpants. The interior of the island loomed behind him. Fish panted. Bread seemed
hardly winded. He looked happy, river water dripping from his
chin and nose. The sight of Bread so joyful confirmed the hope
that maybe they were real woodsmen. *Acquiescence* was a word Fish
learned in school. It meant to give in, to go along with, to accept
things the way they were. That seemed to fit what he was trying to
think through in his mind—a way to *leap*.

Fish reached down into the river, looking for mud. He found
two fistfuls of silt.

"What are you doing?" asked Bread.

"I'm going all beaver," said Fish.

Fish smeared a handful of river mud across his chest, and now
worked on his neck and face, like a warrior would. As Bread joined
him, the boys thought of new names for themselves, names like
Eagle Claw, Bear Claw, Coyote Fang, Beaver Tooth. Fully painted,
Fish walked up the riverbank, looked at his friend. "Let us explore
this new land," he proclaimed.

Bread nodded solemnly. He reached down for a final clod of
mulch, smeared it under his eyes, and pulled two cattail canes from
the water. He gave one to Fish.

"Spears," said Bread.

Fish grunted, and the two boys crept toward the island's interior, careful to not snap the twigs they felt beneath their bare feet,
moving like river water, like woodsmoke, hunters.

AS SOON AS CAL CROSSED THE RIVER ON HIS HORSE—WHICH WAS awful in itself for the way the frigid water soaked his jeans and filled his boots—the forest began closing in on him. The trails disappeared just like Teddy said they would, and they spent the day traversing cedar swamps and poplar stands on the far side of the river. The day grew hot and buggy, and Cal soon itched with sweat and fatigue. His legs burned. His back ached. He had no idea that merely sitting on a horse could be this tiring. He'd ridden a pony once as a kid, at a park in Wichita Falls, but that was a small horse tethered in a stable. This had been a full day's ride on an absurdly tall horse, picking its way over moss-covered stones and through cattail marshes, ducking between cedar and hemlock trees without concern for the rider dragging in the branches. At one point, while moving up the steep bank of a dry creek bed, Cal tried to urge his horse through a thick tangle of briars. The horse stood up on its hind legs, turned, and slid down the hill. With the horse on two legs, Cal got a good look at the creek bed, about fifteen feet below. Cal felt like he was falling from a ladder. He grabbed two fistfuls of the horse's mane and held on for his life. He hated ladders. He hated horses. When the horse found its footing again near the creek bed, Cal leapt off and jogged to a tree, shaking the adrenaline from his fingertips. He looked at the ground and spat in the leaves, wiped horsehair from his hands.

"You all right?" Teddy yelled down from the ridge above the creek bed.

"Yeah, I'm all right. Mr. Ed here ain't all right, though. He's trying to kill me!"

"For the fifth time, your horse is a mare. And don't push her into the brush like that and she won't stand up on you."

Cal stared at the ground. The morning had been filled with these little lessons. *Don't force the reins. Let the horse find its own way through the trees. Don't ride so far forward. Don't call the mare "Mr."* Cal stood and paced for a moment to try to wake his numb legs. He took his hat off, wiped his brow, and looked around at the forest. They were in hardwoods now, a bit more open than some pines they'd pushed through. Though they'd been riding since daybreak, it felt to Cal as if they hadn't moved more than twenty feet. The trees turned from thick to thicker, from green to gray and back again. There were no signs, no trails, nothing to distinguish one direction from another. The sheriff had been following Teddy's lead, trying to keep up. Teddy rode effortlessly and high in the saddle, ducking branches, eating on the go. The general strategy seemed to be to crisscross the opposing shoreline, ride a sort of grid across the land, look for any sign that the boys had been that way. At first they spent some time calling out to the boys, but then thought they might have a better chance of coming upon them if they stayed quiet. The boys were scared. The men didn't want to make them hide. Every now and then during their survey, the river would come back into sight, and that open sunlight called to Cal through the trees. He wanted so badly to be out of the woods. But he had to keep up, had to push through, just follow Ted through the forest. It made him feel like a child, this tagging along, which angered him. He was the sheriff, in charge of this search. Already his confidence in Teddy's approach was nearly exhausted. His comfort zone was in his truck, with his dog and his radio, on highways and freeways. That's where he felt he knew what to do. Out here, there was too much he couldn't control, his horse chief among them.

"Sun's getting low in the sky, Teddy. What do you say we head back? Think this thing through."

Teddy led his horse back down the ravine. The animal seemed hesitant, but it moved deftly under its rider's direction. Teddy opened a saddlebag as his horse came alongside Cal's mare. He reached inside and tossed his canteen to the sheriff. It was an old metal canteen, military issue. Cal opened the top and drank greedily. He'd already drank all of his own.

"We can't let up, Sheriff. We can't give up on the trail before nightfall."

Cal choked and wiped his mouth. "Trail? What trail?" he yelled, and felt his voice getting higher in pitch. "Can you show me the trail, 'cause I'd sure like to see it!"

Ted looked away for a moment, at the sky and the river.

"You ever stalk an animal, Sheriff?"

"Not much of a hunter, Ted." He felt silly for losing his temper. It made him feel even more like the boy in this pair. He capped the canteen.

"The trick to stalking, Sheriff, is staying stubborn."

Cal didn't feel up for another of Teddy's lessons. But if a story would keep him from having to ride that awful horse for another few minutes, so be it. He handed the canteen back to Teddy.

"How so?" he asked.

"I tracked a buck once for half a day through this woods. You can tell a buck track from a doe track 'cause of the way the hooves spread out in the mud." Ted held up two fingers and spread them apart. Cal nodded as if he was truly interested.

"Bucks' necks get thick when they rut," Teddy went on. "Makes 'em lean back when they walk, spreads their toes apart. I spotted a big set of tracks in the frost and spent the next five hours moving about two hundred yards until I lost them in a thicket. I backed out on my belly, made this wide circle downwind." Ted traced half a circle in the air with his finger. "And you know what happened, Sheriff?"

"Nope."

"I started thinking about the football game. About sitting in a warm kitchen. Started getting impatient, walked a little faster and noisier. Eventually the sun came up high enough to melt the frost and the hoofprints with it. I gave up and stood at the downwind edge of that thicket, and what bust up from the poplar slashing but a buck with antlers like this." Ted spread his arms wide, canteen in one hand. "Antlers thick as wrists, tearing off into the thicket again." Ted opened the canteen. "If I'd have spent five more minutes, just stayed stubborn, I'd have found him, bedded down with his nose facing the wind." He took a drink.

"There ain't no frost out here, Ted. There are no tracks. We're stomping around blind."

"The boys are out here. We just gotta keep at it."

The sun was well down in the trees now. The shadows were long on the forest floor. The sheriff cursed the shadows, and the trees. If he were back in Houston, they'd have a command set up by now. They'd have teams of men. They'd have coffee and maps and helicopters. They'd have a plan. Cal decided to put his foot down.

"We're going back, Teddy. We'll get some other departments involved. This ain't the right way to do this."

Teddy just looked at him.

Cal went on. "We had to come out here and try, but now it's time to get serious. Get some support. Teddy, my radio won't even reach town from out here. It's just you and me riding through the woods."

Teddy's face soured. "No offense, Sheriff," he said, "but I don't want more cops involved."

Cal cringed. Teddy sounded like Blind Burt Akinson, but Cal kept his cool. He needed Teddy to listen to him. "Why not?"

"Because more cops will turn this into a manhunt, and this ain't a manhunt."

"They're boys, Teddy. I know that. Everyone will know that. But we need dogs. We need eyes."

"I don't see it." Teddy waved his hands in the air, as if to wash his hands of the whole idea.

"Don't see what?" Cal was losing ground and patience. Teddy knew these woods, but he didn't know search work, and Cal didn't like being so much at the mercy of another man when the search was ultimately his responsibility.

"And speaking of dogs, where is that dog of yours, Sheriff?"

"He's in town."

"You come out to search for two boys and leave your dog? Could have used him out here. Could have used him back where we crossed that river. Could have given us a place to point. And now you think you're the one to go back and make the plan, the sheriff who fails to bring his dog to a search?"

Cal held up his hands to stop the comments. He spoke very slowly now. "I thought, Teddy, we'd be moving a little faster on horseback. I didn't think my dog would keep up."

"What do you mean, *faster*?"

Cal felt his face blush. "You know, like galloping or something. I thought horses galloped."

"Where do you think we are, Sheriff, the great plains of Texas?"

The sheriff bit his lip. How could he have known they'd be moving about as fast as a man on foot? How could he have known what it was like to ride through a brush pile of a forest?

"You think we're out here chasing buffaloes? Drinking whiskey for breakfast? The real Wild West, huh?" Teddy's voice quavered a bit as he spoke. His face had reddened. He waved his hands in the air again, as if to keep Cal's worthlessness from sticking to him.

Cal's face burned with shame. Teddy *had* smelled the whiskey on his breath in the kitchen. Cal was losing all leverage, and fast. He swallowed the accusation. "You've had your chance here, Teddy, and I went along with it. But now it's time to do it my way. We're going back. Now."

Ted brought the butt of his canteen down against the pommel of his saddle hard enough that both horses yanked their heads up. "My grandson killed a man, Sheriff, shot him in the head, and he took with him the pistol he used to do it!"

"Teddy—"

"And I'll be damned to hell, Sheriff, if I'll let a bunch of cops and newspeople out here in a woods they don't belong in, siccing their dogs and cameras on those boys!" Teddy tossed his canteen back in his saddlebag.

"Teddy—"

"To hell with it. To hell with you." Teddy took the reins in his hands.

"We can't do this ourselves."

"Maybe you can't, Sheriff," he said as he turned his horse to face the hill.

"Teddy, those boys are in danger out here. This ain't about what you want."

"They're smart boys. They'll make good choices until I find them." He snapped his reins and trotted up the hill.

Cal cursed under his breath. "Get back here, Teddy!"

Ted turned in his saddle and pointed a hand through the trees toward the river. "You'd better stick to the river after dark, Sheriff. The crossing is four miles upstream. Give my horse to my daughter. She'll be at my farm already, knowing her. I'm headed downriver."

"Teddy!"

His horse made the top of the hill. The light in the woods was bluish now. Cal hated the idea of heading back without Ted in tow. But he hated even more the idea of spending the night in these woods, only to spend another day aimlessly ducking pine branches. Ted was right about the stir the story of his grandson would cause. There would be news cameras. But that energy might help find the boys too, news helicopters or otherwise. That was the way things were done. But Cal still needed Teddy. The search, however complex it became, needed a man who knew these woods intimately.

Teddy's figure slipped in and out of sight between trees.

Cal cupped his hands to his mouth. "Teddy Branson," he yelled, "you are under arrest!"

No response came back through the forest. Teddy had disappeared from sight. Cal shifted his boots in the silent woods. The noise they made in the leaves seemed louder than it should have been. The forest at dusk tightened its grip. Cal tried to spit, but his mouth was too cottony. The mare looked at him with one large white eye.

"You're under arrest too," he told the horse.

There was no sense waiting around. Ted *was* stubborn, and Cal knew he wasn't coming back. He looked out toward the river. The light was still warm there, but was quickly giving way. He approached his horse, reached for the pommel, and put his foot in the stirrup.

When he tried to pull himself up, however, the horse trotted sideways and then bolted. Cal pulled himself toward the saddle, gripping the pommel with both hands, but was swatted from the horse's side by the branches of a scrub pine. Cal had the wind knocked out of him as he fell onto his back. He instinctively tried to sit up, but pain shot through his tailbone. He let his head fall back into the leaves, gasping. Above him, the branches wove a dark lattice across a purple sky with a streak of orange in it. The mare stood on top of the ridge, through the brambles where only minutes ago it had reared in defiance. It lowered its head now and calmly bit a mouthful of something sprouting through the forest floor, flicked its tail. Cal shut his eyes. His tailbone throbbed. Otherwise he seemed uninjured. He still had his hat. His flashlight. One of his boots was missing. He felt for the pistol in his holster. It was secured. He wondered how long it would take him to walk out of these woods once he caught his breath. He worried Teddy would find the boys without him and wondered what such a thought said about him as a sheriff. The mare whinnied on the ridge past the brambles. Cal wondered what horse tasted like, grilled over a cedar fire.

EIGHT

FISH WHISTLED QUIETLY, AND BREAD'S MUD-SMEARED FACE
emerged from behind a tree twenty yards away. It was becoming hard to see in the shadows. The sun was nearly gone. Only a backdrop of orange and red shone between the gaps in the forest. With Bread's attention, Fish pointed to his own eyes, then to a ledge of rock ahead, dotted on its top with baby spruce. He made a flapping motion with his elbow, and then a walking motion with two fingers. As his body moved, his mind whispered to his friend, *On ledge, a chickadee, I am closing in.*

Bread nodded, looked to the ledge, and began stalking forward with spear in hand.

The chickadee was distractedly preening its feathers, the bird's black and white head beating up and down. Fish slipped forward, stopping only when the bird stopped preening to look about. Fish felt every twig under his bare feet, every subtle shift of the air against his skin. He wondered why he had never tried this before—running away and swimming a river, getting muddied up and stalking birds on an island. The freedom thrilled him. He was a lone and painted warrior, cutting his teeth in the wild. He was

Adam, the world's first man, plus Bread. He had a cedar spear. A knife. A flint. He *was* good and strong, like his grandfather said.

Fish tried to keep cedar trunks between himself and the chickadee until he closed the distance to about ten feet. Bread worked into good position as well, crouching now behind a moss-covered stump.

The bird stopped preening its feathers.

Fish looked to his friend with his eyes only, his head unmoving. Bread's eyes seemed to nod, and his throwing arm moved slowly back behind his head. Fish readied his.

The chickadee cocked its head at the branch it stood on, the spruce ledge above it, the ground below.

In one fluid motion, a step and thrust, Fish launched his spear at the chickadee. The spear shot toward the bird and ricocheted from the stone ledge behind it. As the bird sprung into the air, another spear shot toward it, diverting its flight path. The spear buried itself on top of the ledge.

"Dang!" yelled Bread. He was grinning despite his disappointment. "Almost got that one!"

Fish frowned. Bread's playfulness seemed out of place. "No," Fish whispered to himself. "We did not."

The two boys walked out from their hiding places and retrieved their spears. Bread pulled himself up the ledge a bit to reach his. Fish stooped to inspect the tip. He'd make a better spear tomorrow, use the barlow to whittle a barbed point. He inhaled and smelled the earth beneath him, the river around him. He frowned at the spear tip. It was dirt-covered and blunted. This wasn't just about food. There was still a half can of tuna and a sausage stick across the river. They would eat tonight. But Fish felt dogged by something darker, some menacing doubt. He felt a pang of fear and loneliness. There was something very grave about missing throws at chickadees on islands in rivers. He wondered what Adam must have felt like that first night outside the garden.

"Fish!" Bread hissed, dropping to the ground beside the stone ledge, waving frantically for Fish to join him in hiding.

Fish crouched. Even in the fading light, Bread's muddied face had turned noticeably pale. Bread was not playing a game. Fish ducked closer to his friend.

"What is it?"

"I don't know."

"What do you mean, you don't know?"

"There's something up there."

"Where?"

"Shhh." Bread's eyes motioned upward. "Up the ledge. Some-one's up there. Or some*thing*. It was staring straight at me. He has horns."

Fish clutched his spear in both hands. Bread started to shake like he did around his dad. Fish got his feet beneath him and then peeked, ever so slightly, over the rise into the thicket of spruce. He came back down.

"Bread, I don't see anything up there."

Bread shook.

Fish breathed. "Do we run for it?" he asked. He didn't like the look of Bread balled up and trembling like this. He wanted the bold Bread back, shimmering and smiling on the riverbank. It bothered him like Adam bothered him, like missing throws at chickadees did. It just wasn't right.

"He'll get us if we run," said Bread. "He saw me."

Fish took a few more breaths, and then he got mad. "Then we fight him," he said.

Bread shook and breathed through his pursed lips.

"Bread, let's *fight him*." Fish nodded at him. "Okay?"

Bread nodded.

"On three."

Bread pulled himself up into a crouch, his head held low. Fish whispered—*one, two*—and the boys charged up the rise, screaming as loudly as they could, brandishing their spears. The spruce branches were thick atop the slope, and Fish yelled and thrashed as he pushed through their spiny grasp. He hacked the limbs with one hand and stabbed his spear blindly into the trees with the other. He pushed his shoulder through a tangle of branches and roared at the sky and the ground. His heart beat sloppily in his chest and ears. He found some good footing, drove his spear into a particularly thick bunch of pine, bellowed his battle cry, and ran smack into the immovable torso of a man, a *thing*, with a skull for a face. The thing wore ragged coveralls on its bony body and deer antlers on its head.

Fish's cry caught in his throat, and the last thing he remembered seeing was the intricate, lace-like hole of the beast's fleshless nasal socket, and then trees—pine branches spiraling upward as he fell beneath them into deep and lasting darkness.

SHERIFF CAL HOBBLED BENEATH A MOONLIT PINE BRANCH AND pulled the horse behind him. It was dark now, and he walked through the brush of the riverbank with his flashlight in hand. He knew his flashlight had a run time of about two hours, and he had about nine miles to get back to his truck—four to the crossing and five to the farm. He could do it in two hours if he walked at a fast pace, but there was no way to walk quickly in the waist-high ferns hiding stumps and rocks, the tangles of saplings. He never did find his other boot. He limped by moonlight whenever the terrain allowed it. His tailbone ached. He cursed the horse. The mare grumbled back if Cal pulled it after him between spruce trees.

"How do you like it?" he said to the horse. "It's called payback. Not that you would understand that." Cal found himself talking to the horse more often now that the sun had set. The woods were downright frightening at night, and Cal felt shamed enough to admit it. Every unseen noise, every snapped twig, every creak of a tree trunk put Cal on edge. Man was meant to sit by a fire at night, or inside a house with a TV on, not wander around a black forest filled with black bears, and coyotes, and marshy shorelines that filled his only boot with water when he got too close to the river.

Cal stood still a moment with the reins in his hand and took a drink from the small bottle of whiskey he'd tucked into his saddlebag. The moon, round and clear, watched him drink it. Cal saluted the moon's accusation, took another pull, capped the bottle, and tucked it back into his chest pocket. No sense trying to fake it, he thought.

"You couldn't understand payback, Mr. Horse, because you are a stupid animal, and I am a man. And when we get back I am going to hook you to a plow and make you drag a field." It was difficult walking. To the best of Cal's knowledge, he'd covered about three miles. The walking was even slower going now, because every hundred yards or so, Cal stepped as close as he could to shore, to try to spot the crossing. He remembered a small pebbled beach near a collapsed gravel embankment. He and Teddy had crossed near rapids, but Cal couldn't remember now if they'd crossed above or below them. No matter. He'd test the bottom before he crossed. He'd go by feel. The whiskey warmed his belly and reassured him.

Cal turned his flashlight on to step over a tangled shadow crossing his path. It was a fallen tree. He turned the light off again. "But you would probably like that," he went on, "plowing a field, because you are so stupid."

The horse stepped over the log and stood next to Cal. Cal could see its eye in the moonlight, looking back and forth, its ears pinned upright and turning toward night sounds. Cal thought about abandoning the horse after it bucked him, but in fact he was thankful for the company, and he brought it along because it was the right thing to do. He didn't know if the horse could find its way back the way a dog might, and he knew how much people have tied up, financially and emotionally, in their horses. Even though Ted abandoned him, Cal could not abandon the horse. He despised his loyalty with every step. He wished he could be a real sheriff, a Rooster Cogburn sort of sheriff, just eat the horse, avenge his honor, but Cal despised that thought as well. Minus the whiskey, he couldn't pull off the Wild West if he tried. He needed people too much. Typical, bleeding-heart Cal.

"Just think of it, Mr. Horse. You could walk back and forth with your plow. Eat your oats. Crap in the grass. That's all a horse needs, isn't it? Hey, maybe you could fix up an old cabin by a lake, get a dog, drink coffee in a pickup truck for the rest of your career." Cal raised his voice. "Well, life ain't that simple, Mr. Horse! No it ain't! Because life don't leave a man alone!"

Cal turned to walk again. The reins tightened and the horse plodded behind him. The grass parted as Cal stepped into it, mocking as he went. "You could move up into the Northwoods of beautiful Wes-consin. Land of the Beaver, they say. Well, I hate beavers. Hate 'em. Waterlogged sausages with their tree-chewing and tail-beating, as if anyone cares."

Wisconsin hadn't panned out as peacefully as Cal's chief suggested it would, but then again, Houston hadn't panned out either. Stress was constant in Houston. In Wisconsin, it was simply absent, or at least different in nature. In Houston he had reasons to be unhappy, circumstances to blame. Every night there were the same calls. Someone else shot, or shot at, or having heard a shot. Someone else getting bandaged up on a front porch, kids standing on couches and peering through windows while Cal tried to make some sense of what some grandmother told him. *It was a man. A young man. And he had a gun.* Cal could finish the story for any one of the witnesses on any night. *And then, Officer, my grandson, son, daddy, brother—who ain't done nothing—he got shot at right there under that streetlight.* There was a time in his career when Cal still believed the nobility and innocence. The older cops seemed callous. Eventually it began to blur, the testimonies became redundant, mundane. Life and death became like mail, or bills, or laundry. Cal worked at night and slept during the day. He had pancakes for dinner when he got off graves, because the regular people were having breakfast, and then he'd turn in for a few hours as the midmorning sun beat through the slits in his apartment blinds. Whiskey helped put him to sleep, but it made nights worse, the streetlights harsher, the voices louder. He ate and slept and took reports. Rarely was there any real resolution, any progress. And after about four years of it, Cal's life began to scare him. That he could feel this beaten, this numb, only a few years out of the academy was a startling revelation. The academy had been all green grass and firing ranges, drinks at the Foxhead. Cal had loved the idealism, the posturing, even though he recognized it as such. He was a fit young man with something to give to the world. But then a pain grew in his chest that wouldn't go away. A doc gave him pills for gastric reflux—which seemed pathetic this early in life—and the pills made his stomach feel like a gallon of milk sloshed inside it, so he threw the pills in a sock drawer and forgot them. After that, Cal had a patch of gray hair sprout above his right temple, and then he caught a head cold that left him deaf in one ear for a month. The same doctor asked him if the ear bothered him in any way, and Cal told him, "No, other than the fact that it doesn't work—it's a terrific ear." He went back to his apartment that day and drank until he fell asleep on the carpet. He woke shivering in the air-conditioned darkness, afraid.

"And *then*, Mr. Horse," Cal said with finality, "there was that kid and his mama."

Cal pulled the collar of his jacket up around his neck to ward off the cooling air. He and the horse stepped out of the river grass onto a higher bank covered in knee-high tangles of shrubs. White pines grew on the higher land, and the forest opened up beneath their massive trunks and branches. Cal remembered passing through white pines earlier in the day. As disorienting as the forest was, this rise in the land felt familiar. At least he hoped it did. Cal pointed his light into the shadows, turned it off again. He waded into the brambles.

It was getting harder to be a cop. Some of the old-timers who still came around the department talked about a time when a good guy could punch a bad guy and the crowd would cheer. But that hasn't been so since the sixties. Nowadays things were backward. Bad men were the victims. They had hard lives. They weren't fathered well. Who with half a heart could truly blame them for their choices? Well, Cal could. He'd seen fear in women's eyes. He'd seen, no, he'd *smelled* the kids with the bruises and swollen diapers. He'd seen the violence that can come out of men. And he'd seen time and again some abusive deadbeat *choose* to behave perfectly well when a cop is present, get all weepy and apologetic. But Cal didn't know how true that felt anymore either. There were some nights when everyone present—kids, mothers, old cops, young cops, deadbeats too—seemed to Cal to be a victim of something, which is part of what made him stop by that house that night in August with two sacks of McDonald's and a pack of diapers.

"Of course," Cal told the horse, "everyone said it's no good for a cop to get close. But I had to know. I had to see progress. I had to believe that just one mom and one kid were better off. Can you believe that? Well, it's the truth." Cal knew the story sounded so predictable, so typical, it embarrassed him to imagine other cops telling it in locker rooms. *So this young cop arrests this dirtbag father, checks in on the family, befriends the kid—stupid move—and then the husband starts coming back around and one thing leads to another.* But it wasn't a stupid move to befriend that kid. If it was, there was something wrong with the cosmos, not with Cal. Of that he was certain. The night Cal first arrested the kid's dad, the kid came out of the bedroom all sleepy-eyed, carrying a stained blanket and sucking on a pacifier. The kid looked to be too old for a pacifier, but what struck Cal most, what hurt him enough that he *had* to come back, was that the kid didn't seem startled by the commotion of it all. It seemed like just another night, Mom crying on the kitchen floor, cops around, Dad in cuffs. The kid smiled at Cal, and made a gun with his fingers, and shot it at him. Cal didn't know what to do with that, so he smiled and shot his fingers back, and walked the dad outside and started his cruiser with shaking hands.

"And do you see what happens, Mr. Horse, when someone tries to have a heart?" Cal held his arms wide. "Banishment, Mr. Horse, to the pine forest. That's what the good guy gets when he punches out the bad guy." Cal stopped walking, thought of the whiskey in his pocket, the moon overhead. He shook his head and walked.

"But talk is cheap, Mr. Horse. It's cheap."

The end of that story sounded typical too. The men telling it in locker rooms would never believe Cal *only* ate dinner with that mother, that he sat on the couch and ate chicken nuggets and watched TV while the kid played with blocks. But that's what he did. Cal tried to make the kid smile once or twice, but the kid seemed to smile as if to humor him, like he was the one who was older and wiser. *No matter,* the kid's eyes seemed to say. And then the night came when that proved true.

It was an hour after the bars closed on his night off, and Cal stumbled into his apartment to a ringing phone. It was the mother, frantic. The dad was out of jail. He was outside on the lawn, throwing rocks at the house, kicking the railing off the porch, all the typical stuff. Cal recalled only a handful of details about that night. He remembered spilling a bottle of whiskey in his lap as he fumbled to start his car. He remembered headlights lighting up the side of a white house. He remembered bending back the fingers of a man until the knuckles popped and the man squealed on the lawn. The rest of the story was recounted to him the next morning in the chief's office, with the oppressive aroma of cheap coffee filling the room while Cal learned his fate. *There's an interim position in Wisconsin, a snowy place of pine and forest, the kind of place a bleeding heart can relax and be forgotten.*

Cal often wondered if he would have done the same thing sober. It's not something he'd been able to fully answer yet. He was also still learning to navigate his new, northern life, this new solitude. But if he was being perfectly honest, Wisconsin wasn't entirely miserable. He did have a dog, and he did have a truck, and though he spent the first winter sitting on top of the heat register in his drafty cabin, there was hope here where there was none back home. The closest he'd come to an answer regarding his true motives that night on the lawn was that he didn't see any other way out. Cal could face down a grown man at three in the morning, but he was too afraid to leave a career he knew was killing him. Why? For the same reason those women stayed with bad men, he supposed. He lost his ability to believe. He befriended that kid and his mom to believe again. He beat that father into the grassy lawn to believe again. But Cal didn't know how true that sounded either.

Cal pulled his collar up more tightly around his neck. The river to his left shone like a polished stone, and the stars above were brilliant in a way they could never be in the city. There were times he stopped hating his drafty cabin here in the Land of the Beaver, even when he was cussing it all, up on a ladder, prying off rotten trim from around windows. It made him feel like a person with a life to live. He lived in daylight here, more or less called his own hours when duty allowed. Pancakes became a breakfast food again, and people did breakfast well in the North, kept a person warm. Cal took a deep breath of the night air. The pines reminded him of the smell of lavender, and Cal allowed himself to smile even though he was dragging a horse through a forest at night. Tiffany, he thought. Here in these lonely woods, banished forever, he had a house and a dog, and maybe, just maybe. What were the words she'd written down on those bills in her kitchen? It was poetry. Cal liked the idea of loving a woman who wrote poetry on bills. He couldn't remember the words, but he occupied himself with the thought of them, and of her.

The sound of water drew Cal's attention to the river. He and the horse had crossed over the pine-covered rise and were descending again toward berry bushes and river grass. At the bottom of the hill, Cal stepped to the edge of the riverbank. The ground was firmer here. Downstream, the black mirror of the river's surface parted around an island, broke into a million points of moonlight, and rushed over boulders and rocks. Cal stooped and dropped down the embankment to the water's edge. Firm gravel crunched beneath his boot.

"We made it, girl," he said, and the mare stood on the bank and tugged her reins, but Cal held her steady.

Across the river, Cal could make out the large rock outcropping they'd passed that morning, the one with the cedar tree growing out of it, where the trail had ended.

"I don't suppose you'll carry me across this?" Cal asked, turning to the horse.

The horse just stared at him with its big white eye.

"I didn't think so."

Cal removed his holster and belt and slung it over his shoulder. He thought of placing it in the saddlebag with the rest of his gear, but if the animal bolted for good, he'd be without a sidearm. *Gotta divvy it up,* Ted had told him. Cal was thankful for that lesson at least.

The water was terribly cold, waist-deep, and the current was strong enough that he had to lean into it, but Cal made it easily to where the river parted above the island. He remembered from the morning's crossing that the first channel had been deeper than the second. He paused a moment and studied the current. He couldn't remember the exact path they'd taken across. He'd just held on to the horse's mane and cursed the cold water when the horse stumbled and swam. Over the entire width of the far channel, the water fell through a shallow and glass-smooth depression about ten yards in length before rising again and breaking apart in the rapids. The horse now waded in upstream of the depression, and Cal figured it best to follow the horse's lead. The water seemed to come up only to the animal's thighs, which meant Cal's stomach or chest, but it would be manageable.

He waded into the channel and the current became immediately stronger. He leaned into its force when it got above his waist and chose his footing more carefully. He felt around with the toe of his boot for a stone or boulder, pressed his heel into the gravelly bottom, and then lunged forward to gain both feet again. He looked across the river. The shore was about twenty yards distant. The horse was nearly across. Cal placed his hands on the water's black surface and reached his toe out for another foothold. He felt a smooth rock about the size of a grapefruit, placed his foot there, and lunged. As he put his weight on the rock, it broke free from its gravelly hold, and in the moment it took for Cal to realize what was happening, he was up to his neck in water and moving rapidly downstream.

He felt his feet rake the river bottom. Cal used his hands to dig against the current, hoping to find a hold, and then the gravel bottom simply dropped away.

Cal felt water go up his nose as the river took him under. He opened his eyes to a complete absence of light. He felt himself get tumbled, his torso pushed downstream faster than his feet. He reached upward until he felt air on his hands and face, saw stars overhead. The current was so fast, so black. Cal spun and caught sight of the horse lifting its glistening body to shore in the moonlight. Cal slipped down the face of a glassy wave, the shoreline slipped from sight, and Cal heard rapids downstream. Dread leapt like water.

"Horse!" he yelled. "Horse!"

He kicked his legs and paddled with his hands. The first wave of whitewater broke over his head. The wave engulfed him in a vacuum of silence and night, sucked him down, released him again, sucked him down. He tried to take breaths between the succession of waves, but only managed to exhale and choke. No matter how hard he kicked, he sank lower in the water. Another wave hit him in the face. The water went into his throat, and he tasted the river as he shot beneath its surface.

He felt his body tumble along a gravel bed at the river bottom and felt as if he were watching himself go through the ordeal, coaching himself, giving himself advice. *Stay calm now. But I can't be calm! You'll get a breath soon. No I won't! Keep your head now.* And then he felt something hard hit his tailbone, and his world ignited in pain. It lifted him into the air again, and Cal tumbled over the hump of a giant boulder. Downstream of the boulder, a hole in the river glistened in the moonlight and opened its mouth. *Cal, do you see that hole coming? I see the hole! You're going to want to take a deep breath now.* Cal's throat opened just long enough to take one chestful of night air before he plunged back down into darkness and cold.

This hole was deep. Cal felt his hands dragging along a smooth rock bottom. He felt as if he was slipping down a wall, grasping for an exit in a pitch-black room. The smooth rock crumbled and turned to gravel, and Cal clawed his hands into it. Though underwater, Cal's only thought was to fight the current, to make it stop.

His lungs ached.

Water roared against his ears. His hands bit in the gravel for a moment. Darkness pressed in. Cal saw himself flapping like a flag in a stiff wind, like the one they'd flown the day he'd graduated from the academy. Guns saluting. Standing at attention. Sons given rare hugs by fathers.

This is a bad place to stay, Cal—Cal? What? Let go. I will not!

And then the river bottom crumbled in his grip.

Cal soon found himself washed up onto his hands and knees in a lapping pool of knee-deep water. Cal took in a warm breath of air. He looked down at the water, exhaled, panted. Water dripped from his hair and nose. He still held two handfuls of gravel in his fists. He smiled and dropped them in the water. And then he threw up.

When his stomach was emptied of river water, Cal crawled closer to shore where the water was only a few inches deep. He flopped onto his back and started to laugh. His senses felt intensely assaulted. It was as if he could smell the granite in the river, the tannins, the limestone. The air he breathed was filled with miles of dark forest and moss and oak, abandoned birds' nests, anthills. The stars were large in the sky, a terrifying map of blues and greens and yellows. And all of it rumbled through him, out of him. In the waning intensity, his body felt tired, so very tired. The exhaustion made him feel as if he might start crying right there in the water. Cal wasn't a crier. He used to be, as a boy, but he could still hear the words of his swim-coach father breaking him of the habit sometime about middle school, telling him to suck it up, keep it in, don't you dare let anyone see you cry. It was typical Coach. That's what he and his friends called his dad in the years following middle school. And he heard Coach's voice in his head all the way through his undergrad years, all the way through the academy, in all the alleys of Houston too. The voice always told him he didn't measure up, and that he needed to keep this truth about himself a secret, just keep it in. Fake it till you make it. Don't piss off Dad. Stop your crying. That voice made many decisions in Cal's life.

Out of habit, Cal damned the tears in his eyes, and then took his flashlight from his vest pocket. The light still worked. He lost his pistol, and he didn't even care. Somewhere back in those rapids, on that river bottom, a thought had come that terrified and thrilled him. He knew it now the way he knew he was lying in water. Something whispered during that black roar, *You never did want to be a cop.* Cal remembers the day he mentioned the possibility to his dad. They were driving back from a swim meet. His dad nodded approval, actual approval—*That's a man's job,* he said, turning the station on the radio—and something between them in the car seemed to lighten. So Cal pursued it, started telling himself and his friends and his teachers he was going to be a cop. But all he really wanted was his dad's nod, the way his dad's eyes seemed to say, if only for a moment, *You got this.* The thought hit him now with regret and sadness and anger all at once. The admission was terrifying, but hopeful too. He could actually quit this. And he could actually ask Tiffany Robins out on a date too. He could listen to her poems, fall in love, have babies. Cal's breath stopped with that thought. The image of Tiffany, pregnant and beautiful, stunned him to silence, and Cal felt an overwhelming and urgent need to paint the trim on his cabin, fix the screen door, mow the path to the river, make sure the front steps were tight and level. He felt keenly responsible for whatever happened next, as if he'd nearly stepped off the edge of something, was yanked back, and now must step very carefully. A new sort of eagerness filled him. He had to do something right now, choose something new right now. He took the whiskey bottle from his pocket, uncapped it, shook its contents into the river, and pitched it up at the moon. The bottle splashed in the river.

"Do you see that?" he said, holding his fist to the moon in the sky. He dared it to speak. "Do you see *that!*"

Exhaustion and nausea came upon him again, and he let his head fall back in the shallow water. He was beaten and wet and had lost his firearm. If there was ever a moment he hadn't measured up, this was it. But for some strange reason, he felt indescribably safe, free of condemnation. The moon hadn't spoken. Cal had spoken, and wept too, and he didn't care if anyone knew it. Just then, Cal heard footfalls in the water behind him, the jingle of tack. He felt warm breath against the side of his face, a wet muzzle. Cal closed his eyes and reached a tired arm toward the horse's face, but his hand met thick fur, and a collar with tags on it. When the horse whimpered the way a dog whimpers, Cal sat bolt upright on his aching tailbone, fumbled for his flashlight, and stared for what felt like a very long time at his dog.

There he stood in the bright light—Jacks—beaming, half a leash dangling from his neck, his tail wagging in river water, holding in his mouth what appeared to be a dead striped cat.

NINE

TIFFANY SAT WITH FOLDED LEGS ON THE LARGE SILL OF THE kitchen window. Her third cup of tea had long grown cold. The sky outside was black. It was past midnight, and there was nothing to do but lean against the window and wait. Wait for what exactly? She hardly knew. She spent some time thinking about the poem she was working on, about the coyote sprinting through a pine forest, but the poem felt aimless. Tiffany couldn't find the turn, and so the coyote just kept running, breathless, for line after line. But toward what? Tiffany sighed, folded her hands in her lap, and stared out at the darkness.

Miranda had temporarily busied herself upstairs, but Tiffany wasn't left without company. At the kitchen table sat the constable Sheriff Cal put in charge before leaving for the forest. His name was Bobby. Bobby was an old, red-faced man, kind, with an off-center bald spot that shone in the lamplight. He liked to talk.

"Now mind you," Bobby said, resting a cup of coffee on his large belly, "my ma wasn't much bigger than you are, but she could bale some hay." He nodded, and his bald spot caught the light again. "Oh yes, that woman could get right up there in that wagon en catch bales and stack 'em faster en you seen most boys do."

Tiffany exhaled and leaned into the coolness of the darkened windowpane. Miranda had excused herself from the room several minutes ago, and Tiffany hoped she wouldn't be much longer. They found they had to take turns listening to Bobby, nodding at him, raising their eyebrows in surprise during the more revealing moments in his stories, like the time his brother *did* find the possum under the steps. That was a hoot. *So,* he'd say. *Oh well.* Bobby showed up at the Branson ranch about twenty minutes after Tiffany did, to "stand by" like Cal asked and make sure all was well at home as the investigation unfolded.

"Oh well. That was before Ma passed, of course. The farm's sold now to folks who don't farm it, so the top fields ain't been baled in, well, let's see"—Bobby tapped out some arithmetic on his coffee cup with his shaky fingers—"several years now." Bobby then acted surprised by the package of Oreos Miranda set out for him earlier in the evening. He examined one and plucked it from its nest.

"So," he said, "of course I stop out there at the farm from time to time to see how things are going, only for an hour or two, mind you—new owners ain't much for conversation, always having someplace to get to." Bobby dunked the cookie in his coffee. "I always wonder what place could be worth getting to if a person's got a farm as fine as that farm is. If I'd of had the money to pay the banks, I'd live my life on that farm without leaving it. But all Ma had was that farm, and family farmin' ain't paid bills in, well, let's see." Bobby bobbed his cookie up and down in his coffee, stuffed it in his mouth.

Miranda strode back into the room. Tiffany lifted her head from the windowpane. Miranda didn't look refreshed despite her reprieve. The entire evening she had looked markedly tired, and afraid too. She had stopped asking the constable questions about the search once it became apparent he knew little about it. Cal had been out of radio contact since the search began. Bobby's only concern was that all was well and calm, and that they waited the thing out for word from the sheriff.

"There she is," said Bobby, swallowing his cookie. "Lady of the house. Yes sir, everyone here is staying nice en calm, en this is all going to work out in the end. Sheriff Cal will see to that. We have a fine sheriff in Sheriff Cal. County's been plenty impressed by him. Board's gonna vote to make him permanent this summer. I'm sure of it."

Miranda forced a smile and moved to the kitchen counter, where she wiped up a coffee spill with a rag. She put a few plates in the sink and turned on the hot water. There wasn't much to do that hadn't been done already.

"Just a sec, Miranda. I'll do those dishes," said Tiffany, hopping off the windowsill.

"No," said Miranda, a bit too abruptly, and caught herself. "I don't mind. Just keep the constable company if you would. Constable Bobby, could you use some more coffee?"

"Oh, that is nice of you, miss. Yes, I'll have some more coffee, just a spot."

"And how about more cookies?"

Bobby peered into the cookie package and gave Miranda a thumbs-up. "We're good on the cookies over here. Say, did I already ask you about what your pa still farmed out this way, acre-wise?"

Tiffany let out an exasperated smile and met Miranda's gaze. Miranda held back a pained grin as she lifted the coffee pot. "You did," she said, crossing the kitchen.

Bobby held out his cup and thanked her.

"Any word from that radio, Constable?" Miranda asked.

Bobby set his coffee on the table and checked the radio clipped to his belt. He squinted at it, fiddled with a knob, made sure it was on.

"Nope. Nothing yet, but try not to worry. We've got a good sheriff out there, and he'll bring your boy back." He looked at Tiffany. "And yours too, miss."

"My boy ain't out there, Bobby. I don't have a boy."

Bobby lifted a finger. "I knew that, of course, I knew that already. My apologies."

Something stirred in Tiffany at the mention of the Breadwin boy. She didn't know the boy well but had interacted with him a few times at the gas station. He was polite. He'd come in to buy a loaf of the cheapest white bread and a jar of peanut butter, and pay with a couple of oily bills and change from his dad's shop. Then she'd see him the next day, hiking toward the school in his sneakers, carrying only a paper sack. There was no doubt the boy had to make his own sad lunches. Tiffany knew what that was like, how lonesome it felt when the other kids unpacked perfectly cut sandwiches and handwritten notes with drawings of smiley faces on the napkins. Once, Tiffany wrote herself a note with a smiley face on a piece of paper towel, but the other kids could tell it was her writing, and they laughed at her. She ran to the bathroom, locked herself in a stall with her feet up on the toilet, flushed the note, and wept. The first time Tiffany ever saw the Breadwin boy was during the spring she finally lost the house. She was driving up Main Street and it was snowing hard, and there was this boy walking along a guardrail through the slush. He had no hat and his jacket was unzipped. Traffic slowed. A car stopped, and a woman got out and crouched next to the boy. As Tiffany drove past them at a crawl, she saw the woman ask him a question and the boy shake his head. Tiffany couldn't tell from his red face whether he was crying, or cold, or both. There was shame on his face. Thinking about that made her feel the way she did in that bathroom stall.

Against Miranda's will, Tiffany walked quickly to the sink. Miranda turned off the coffee pot and stood by her side.

"I'll wash, you rinse," Tiffany begged in a whisper. Miranda nodded and smiled.

"I'm glad you're here, Tiffany," she said.

Tiffany pushed the sleeves of her sweatshirt up to her elbows and swept her hair behind her ears. She was glad to be here too. She liked Miranda. She liked the farmhouse. And the thought of going back to her lonely rental seemed awful.

"So," said Bobby, "I expect to hear from the sheriff in no time at all." He leaned back in his chair and didn't face them as he spoke. He knew they were within earshot, and that was good enough. "In my experience that's how these things pan out. You just gotta wait for your radio here to light up, and it always does, and then it's over and everyone gets a little rest. The hard part's the vigil, is my experience of it. And a vigil is even harder when you're waiting on children. But they will come. Your boy will be found."

Miranda thanked him.

"And this is good coffee, thank you. Oh! And here's a cookie."

There was a window over the sink, and Tiffany looked out at her reflection as she scrubbed mindlessly at a dish. She couldn't see it now, but Tiffany knew that beyond the barn lay the field, and beyond that, the forest where Cal and the boys were.

"How far out do you think they are?" she asked quietly.

Miranda waited for the dish with her hands on the edge of the sink. She looked out into the night. Tiffany studied the woman's gaze in the windowpane. She was a pretty woman, Tiffany recognized that in her right away. She was older and taller than Tiffany, and had a darker complexion, darker hair, but also something more. There was something very dignified in the way Miranda carried herself, folded a rag, wiped up a spill, filled up coffee, held back tears. It wasn't feigned dignity either, like a person who bandied big words. It was genuine, deeper down, whatever it was. The woman made her own clothes from the looks of it, a flat-fronted denim dress of the sort Tiffany usually saw the wives of church people wearing. Tiffany hated those dresses. She hated watching women try to get into their husband's pickups with those things on, the way they restricted natural form. But something about Miranda's manner seemed incredibly noble, or hard-won, or both. The woman seemed to know who she was, which made her seem clothed in more than just denim and piety. Tiffany wished she had that kind of certainty. She wondered what Miranda thought of her purple bangs.

"They'd have made it past the islands by now," said Miranda. She straightened herself, took her hands off the sink. "It will be easier to find the boys at night anyway. They'll make a fire."

"So," said Bobby, speaking to no one in particular, "them boys is just having a bit of a run around in the forest, but they'll be fine, if I know anything about boys—"

"Do you think they'll make one, though," asked Tiffany, "if they're trying to hide?" She handed Miranda the dish to rinse. Miranda took it, and then surprised Tiffany with a broad smile.

"Fischer won't make anything but a bonfire so big we'll probably see it from here." She turned the faucet on. Her boy was there in her eyes, like fire itself. "I remember a time Fischer had a friend over and they slept in the yard in tents, had a campfire, told stories, that sort of thing."

"I did that sort of thing as a girl," said Tiffany, and she smiled to think of it as she scrubbed the next plate, and then she frowned. She'd slept in the yard in a tent, but never with friends. She never had any to come over. She had huge braces as a kid. And her green eyes were too bright for her skin. But she did love sleeping out in the yard, feeling so far away with her books and her flashlight, the stars and crickets and quiet. It didn't feel the same later in life. Tiffany didn't care for tents anymore.

"The last time Fischer had a campout, I woke up at three in the morning to a fire truck parked in my yard, lights blazing, blasting down Fischer's fire and knocking the door off my garden shed in the process." Miranda shook her head. "He and his friend stacked twelve pine pallets on the coals—twelve pallets, can you imagine?—*to keep it going through the night,* he said. Those flames were as high as the house. I'm just glad his father wasn't home. He wouldn't have been able to laugh at it, not then."

Tiffany noticed the woman's demeanor change at the mention of her husband. There was sadness there, and Tiffany wondered where the man was, who he was. Tiffany second-guessed the nobility of Miranda's denim dress and conservative hair. Maybe it was a carryover from a bad marriage, a thing the woman couldn't learn to shed. If that was the case, maybe Tiffany could help her loosen up, break a few rules.

"Of course," Bobby went on, "after the search is over, there's always plenty of paperwork to fill out for a situation like this. First the sheriff's department paperwork. County paperwork too. I've even seen paperwork from as far off as Washington!"

Tiffany admired the flame that grew in Miranda's eyes whenever she talked about Fischer. She'd seen tears threaten to choke that flame many times this evening, but the fire always won. There was a hunger in Miranda's eyes. That's what it was. And that hunger was fierce, and jealous, and consuming. Tiffany didn't recognize it right away. She'd never seen that look in her own mother's eyes, and certainly not in her dad's. She had a childhood memory of dancing on a coffee table in front of her dad, trying to get his attention. As she remembers it, she was four or five, and she put on her nicest dress and twirled and twirled, but he never even looked at her. He just watched the TV like she wasn't there.

"And that's Washington, *D.C.,* mind you," said Bobby. "Not the state. I've got a cousin out there in Washington State. Good berry farming out that way."

Tiffany stopped washing her plate and looked Miranda in the eyes. An idea had come. She desired more than anything to watch what happened to those eyes when they spotted Fischer again. Tiffany imagined an unapproachable fire of a woman, shreds of denim bursting into flame. And she wanted to go get that Breadwin boy, too, wipe the shame off his face, tell him he was good.

"Miranda," she said, "if you want to go out there and search, right now, I'll go with you, tonight."

"I thought of that," Miranda said. "Prayed about it. I know the woods pretty well, the river especially. I spent a lot of time out there when I was younger."

"Well, let's *go*, then." It made Tiffany feel strong to say it, though she knew nothing about the forest, or spending the night in it. Her camping excursions never made it past the backyard or Burt's fields. But standing next to Miranda, she felt brave. Here was this noble mother who loved her son, and here she was rinsing plates and feeding cookies to Bobby.

"God told me to wait here," said Miranda, taking the plate from Tiffany's hands.

"God told you that?" Tiffany asked.

Miranda nodded.

Tiffany felt instantly disappointed. In her brief experience with the church, when God spoke, he usually told people disappointing things, or convenient ones to suit their desires. That, or people became out-of-touch miracle seekers. Tiffany tried church once, about a week after she received the twenty-five dollars in the mail from her mother. She knew nothing of denominations, only that she felt very alone, and a group of people sounded comforting, particularly ones who were supposed to be nice. She made the mistake of walking into the sort of church where people moaned as they sang, and one of them fell down on the floor, and then two older women led her to the front during the worship service and shook her shoulders and spoke in tongues to "receive a word" from the Lord. It scared her so badly, she physically pulled away from them and ran for the door. She told Burt Akinson about it the next day at the Sunrise Café. He laughed, even though Tiffany still felt like crying.

"Pentecostals," said Burt knowingly. "The heck you go in *there* for?" But then Tiffany did start to cry, and Burt cleared his throat and became gentle. "Listen, Tiff, if you're gonna try church, listen, don't start off with the Pentecostals. Pentecostals is like the straight whiskey of church types. Start with something tamer. Take the Baptist church in town, for instance. Stacey used to drag me there on Easters. Let me tell you, the Baptists don't hardly do much of anything at all. They just sit there in their pretty clothes and take notes, pretend they're happy. If you're gonna do church, start there next time." There never was a next time. Tiffany had made her decisions about all of that. And she was particularly annoyed right now that God, or whatever it was people called God, was the one preventing her and Miranda from going to get the boys.

"And God will tell us when we might go, too, I suppose?" Tiffany regretted her tone and knew she'd apologize for it. She couldn't help it. She imagined Miranda's husband, a man like her own father, cold and absent, his beautiful wife tiptoeing around in silence and serving him.

"Yes, he will," and the certainty with which Miranda said the words made Tiffany regret her own. There was no retort in Miranda's tone, just a stated fact. Tiffany was so surprised, she forgot to apologize.

"And," said Bobby, "the state is going to want to have every detail in duplicate. But it shouldn't be too complicated really, not as bad as some cases—"

"But what about the note they left?" Tiffany asked. "They said they're going to the armory to see their dad. We know where they're headed." She wanted to do something. Anything.

"Paperwork is never too complicated when no harm's really done, as is the case here. First they'll want a statement from your son, to get the story straight."

"About that note, Tiffany." Miranda's eyes grew weary-looking.

"Then they'll take a statement from the other boy too, that Breadwin boy, and want to find another home for him most likely."

"What about the note?" asked Tiffany.

"I was going to tell you, but then the constable showed up. And we did just meet each other." Miranda picked up a plate and held it with both hands. "Fischer's dad isn't at the armory, Tiffany. My husband is—I'm a widow, Tiffany."

"And then," droned Bobby, "when he gets to feeling better in the hospital, they'll take down a statement from that Breadwin boy's father, though he ain't fit for fathering in my opinion. So. Oh well."

Tiffany and Miranda both spun at the sink. Bobby crunched a cookie.

"What did you say, Constable?"

Bobby turned in his chair, had to rock a bit on his haunches to do so.

"Say again, miss?"

"What did you say about the boy's father?" Miranda's voice was metered and quiet. She gripped the plate in both hands. Soap suds dropped to the floor.

"It's nothing out of the ordinary, miss. If his father is found to be unfit, as they say, the state will find the boy another place to live. But they'll find him a good home. Plenty of good foster families in the county. In fact, I remember—"

"The father, Bobby!" shouted Tiffany.

"Oh, now why are we getting upset?"

Miranda straightened herself to her full height. The fire was back in her eyes. She cut an imposing figure for such a slender woman. "Constable. The man my son shot. Jack Breadwin. Is he dead or isn't he?"

Bobby rocked in his seat. "Oh my word, no. You were thinking he was dead? He's a bit shook up, I'm sure, but he lives."

The constable grew uncomfortable under the women's glares,

rocked his weight in his seat again. He chuckled, and then he stopped, cleared his throat.

"Miss, that man they say your boy shot at was just grazed. Skimmed him right here—*zip*—over his left ear. Knocked him out cold as potatoes. He lost blood, but he'll come around." Bobby brightened. "And when he does come around, the county will take his statement and find that Breadwin boy a nice home."

"Tiffany," said Miranda, without removing her eyes from the man eating her father's cookies.

"Yes."

"Get your things."

"We can go now?"

"Immediately."

THE MARIGAMIE COUNTY HOSPITAL REMINDED TIFFANY OF HER high school. It was a multistory brick building with crumbling mortar. The lawn was mowed neatly enough, but the grass grew poorly under the pine trees, and the foundation hedges were overgrown and blocked some of the windows. She'd been there once for an appendectomy, and when she split a stitch from coughing, the doctor came in with what looked like a staple gun. She entered now with the additional trepidation of Miranda's unclear plan.

The smell of burnt coffee permeated the entranceway and lobby. A very tidy-looking nurse about twenty years old sat in a chair behind the information desk. She wore scrubs with kittens on them.

"And can you spell the last name for me, please?" she asked. Tiffany looked around. There was no one else there. The sound of the nurse's typing filled the quiet lobby. A clock on the wall read 4:35 a.m. It had taken them an hour and twenty minutes to drive here, despite the way Miranda pushed her father's truck down the highway at speeds that made the tires shake and pieces of hay straw roil in the cab.

"It's Breadwin," said Miranda, "just like it sounds."

The nurse mouthed the letters as she typed. "Relation?" she asked.

"I'm his wife," Miranda said without blinking.

Tiffany closed her eyes as Miranda said the words. Miranda hadn't said anything about that on the drive. The plan was to visit the front desk, confirm the man was living—to be *certain*—and then go after the boys. *I cannot allow,* Miranda said as they first climbed into Teddy's truck, *my son to spend another night in the forest thinking he has killed a man.* And when Tiffany asked her why they didn't just join the search right away—why go to the hospital at all?—Miranda told her that she needed to see for herself. *How did the sheriff and my father not know about this? Why was I not told about this? Why is this man not being questioned?* She slapped her hand on the steering wheel as she spoke. *Thank God my father is out there.* Tiffany felt the urge to defend Cal. To be fair, his only link to the world was the radio attached to Bobby's belt, which wasn't saying much. So he couldn't have been informed after the fact. But Miranda had a point. Why hadn't Cal known beforehand? Surely he felt for a pulse when he found the man lying in the kitchen, talked to the ambulance crew. Tiffany didn't know what to say, so she frowned at the mile markers speeding past in the darkness.

"Mrs. Breadwin, I can get you started with a bracelet. Your husband is in CC203. I will need identification."

"I didn't bring identification. And it's over an hour's drive home." Tiffany watched Miranda swallow between words.

"Mrs. Breadwin." The young nurse blushed slightly, opened her mouth before she spoke. "I can't let you visit without identification. However, general visitors are allowed on the second floor beginning at six a.m."

"Can't you let us up for a moment? We just need to see him, my daughter and I."

Tiffany tried to brighten her countenance and smiled at the

nurse without breathing. She feared she looked like a crazy person. Perhaps she was.

"Does your daughter have ID?" the nurse asked.

"I don't drive" was Tiffany's tight-lipped response.

The nurse looked at her and then at Miranda. Tiffany pretended not to see suspicion in her eyes. Certainly there was a page in the nurses' manual that said to be suspicious of people without identification, who claim not to drive, who have purple bangs. It was right next to the page about selecting kitten scrubs.

"You can wait in the lounge and can visit during breakfast. I am sorry for the inconvenience."

The nurse seemed to buckle a bit beneath Miranda's gaze. Miranda played the part well of a woman scorned. But then again, she wasn't playing it. Upstairs lay a man in a soft bed who had done something evil enough to make her boy shoot him, or at him, while Miranda's son was sleeping somewhere in a forest filled with coyotes. If that wasn't scorned, Tiffany didn't know what was.

"Come, Tiffany. We'll wait," she said.

"Let me know if I can get anything for you," said the nurse, and Miranda didn't respond as she turned away toward the chairs lined up in the lobby.

The lobby smelled like sweat and lemon Pledge. On the wall next to the restroom doors hung a framed picture of a beaver, swimming into current with a stick in its mouth. There was another photo of a sailboat with a blue and orange sail tacking into the wind. In the corner of the lobby sat a popcorn machine with the lights turned off, and a small table with a trash bin and a coffeemaker. Tiffany sat and watched Miranda pace the lobby. Miranda looked at the nurse, then at the clock on the wall, then at the nurse again. She folded her hands under her arms and turned toward the coffee pot. She spoke to herself in a whisper as she walked. But she did more than just speak. She was having a conversation. Agreeing. Arguing. Stating her case.

Could they not leave now? thought Tiffany. Was the fact that the nurse wouldn't let anyone up to see him not proof enough that the man was indeed alive? Tiffany was beginning to fear Miranda's lead in this. Tiffany hardly knew this woman. She hardly knew the family. What was she doing here in a hospital impersonating the daughter of a gunshot man she had never even met? She'd heard of him, of course. Breadwin was a name everyone knew in Claypot. It was synonymous with cheap auto work and the worst kind of man. She'd once seen Jack passed out in a lawn chair next to his shop, the sun burning his face, his work boots unlaced. He no doubt got what he deserved when that boy shot him, but this hospital business was going too far. Tiffany pulled her legs up under herself. And the pitiful constable, too, waddling out onto the porch the way he did, yelling for them to come back, spilling coffee on himself. She ran from a *deputy*. She ran from the *law*. And now she was here getting into who knows what kind of trouble. She thought of Cal then, his handsome face and his stupid dog. She had tried to do the right thing by Cal, by this woman, but now felt confused and fearful and very tired. Like she did with most things in life, she'd simply decided to go along with it all. When a door shut, she stayed put. When it opened, she walked through. She hated that about herself, and wished she could muster more direction, more backbone. She remembered walking into the bright kitchen when she was a little girl, rubbing her eyes in the morning light and hoping someone would put breakfast in front of her. Sometimes they did. Sometimes they didn't. She grew up knowing she wasn't worth the effort, and the world wasn't really worth hers. She thought about it specifically, in those very words.

Miranda stopped pacing in front of the coffee machine. With her arms folded and shoulders hunched like that, she didn't look as strong and certain as she did behind the wheel of her dad's truck. She looked wounded and afraid. Tiffany felt a pang of pity, and then guilt. She was here because of this woman's need, those hunched-up shoulders, this woman with fire kilns for eyes who was missing her son. That was reason enough to come along.

Miranda reached out toward the box of coffee filters. She lifted one filter partway out, then another, and then she reached inside and grabbed the rest and dropped them into the trash. Tiffany felt awake again. This beautiful denim woman was very odd. Empty box in hand, Miranda strode over to the information desk. Tiffany stayed put.

"I'm sorry," Miranda said, "for being rude earlier."

"I understand," said the nurse. "Family hardships are—"

"I haven't slept in some time, and—"

"I understand."

"I was wondering if you had more coffee filters hidden some place? I can't seem to find any. A cup of coffee would be a great comfort."

"Certainly," said the nurse. Tiffany heard the nurse's soft shoes squeak away down the corridor.

Miranda spun on her heel, pressed the front of her dress flat. "Do not follow me, Tiffany. Go to the truck and start it. I will meet you there in five minutes."

Tiffany swallowed and watched Miranda disappear through the double doors leading farther into the hospital. Without thinking, Tiffany was on her feet. She felt her heart in her neck as she sneaked toward the front desk. Each footstep seemed as if it might break glass, or make an alarm go off, even though she was tiptoeing through a lobby with no one in it.

"Miranda," she hissed. The double doors rocked to a stop on their hinges. "Miranda!"

When she heard footsteps squeaking back from the opposite corridor, Tiffany froze in midstep. It was now or never. Bolt for the swinging doors and find a stairwell, bolt for the exit, or be caught standing like a cat burglar in the middle of the hospital lobby.

She decided to bolt for the exit. She crouched low. The nurse's footsteps arrived in the lobby as her hand reached the door frame. Too late.

Tiffany stood up. "Hi!" she said.

The nurse gave a start to find Tiffany standing beside the information desk. She clutched a box of coffee filters to her chest, then looked around the room. "Where's your mother?"

"Restroom!" yelled Tiffany, plastering what must have been a frightening smile on her face. "She had to go very badly. She's in there now." Tiffany motioned toward the door near the pictures of the sailboat and beaver. Her arm felt artificial as she moved it. "Mmm, coffee filters! Sounds good!" Tiffany stepped toward the nurse and took the filters from her chest. She tried to rein in the enormity of her smile, but that made it feel even more insane, so she left it plastered there as she turned away.

She felt the nurse watching her walk across the room.

Tiffany turned back when she reached the table and shuffled the various grounds and flavored creamers. The nurse was still watching. "Mmm, hazelnut!" Tiffany declared, and cussed under her breath as she hastily pulled filters from the box. The nurse sat slowly down behind her desk.

"Would you like a cup?" Tiffany asked, not turning around.

"No, thank you," said the nurse. "I'm off at six."

The nurse's keyboard started up. And then it stopped.

Tiffany yanked open a package of grounds and spooned the contents into a filter. She heard squeaking shoes and froze.

"Mrs. Breadwin?"

The nurse stood next to the restroom door, tapping her knuckle on it. Tiffany could only smile as the nurse narrowed her eyes at her. The nurse pushed through the door, and Tiffany could hear her walking on the tiles inside, checking the stalls. For some reason, Tiffany was still spooning coffee. This was it, she thought. This was the end of the road. Not only would Sheriff Cal come home to a lost dog, but Tiffany could tell him all about it when he transported her to the county jail for impersonating a hospital-ized man's daughter and helping a madwoman break into intensive care.

"Your mother is not in the restroom."

The nurse stood in the lobby between Tiffany and the double doors. Tiffany tried not to look at them, but the nurse followed her gaze. The nurse was sharp and on her game. Her ponytail flashed in the fluorescent light. Her cheeks flushed red and her mouth opened. Tiffany felt hunted.

"I'm calling security," said the nurse, and moved quickly be-hind the desk.

Tiffany made a rush for the exit doors. "What? Security?" she heard herself saying, and she feigned laughter. The last thing Tiffany saw as she turned to push through the glass doors was the nurse with a phone to her ear, drilling her finger into a keypad. Tiffany couldn't breathe. She banged through one set of doors and then another, and as she bolted out into the parking lot beneath the purple dawn, she turned to see the nurse speed-walking into the double-doored corridor where Miranda had gone. Tiffany aimed for the red truck parked beneath a streetlamp and sprinted with all she had. Were there sirens going off? Tiffany couldn't tell. She could only feel the pavement beating her feet. The cool air in her throat. There probably would be sirens soon, and lights, and then handcuffs and fingerprints and Sheriff Cal.

TEN

FISH DREAMT OF A MAN WITH HORNS PUSHING TOWARD HIM through a hedge of briars. The man, or beast, snapped branches with cloven fists. It wore shreds of coveralls dripping with gasoline. When the beast became entangled in the hedge, it dropped to all fours and raked its antlers in a rage. And then it roared the way a river or a train can roar, and the hedge burst into flame.

Fish cried out, sat up, and brushed frantically at his body. The fire wasn't there. His clothes sat in a pile on his backpack. He was in a dark place lit by firelight, with pine branches reaching in from the shadows. To his left sat a boy hunched over a hot fire. Fish could feel its heat. The fire snapped and popped in the darkness.

"I wondered how long you'd sleep," said the other boy, turning from the fire. He held a stick in his hand and held its tip in the coals. Fish became aware of the smell of food cooking. He remembered he was in a forest, on an island.

"Bread?" Fish asked.

"You slept like a log. Breakfast is cooking."

Fish felt cold and pulled a flannel over himself. He remembered stalking chickadees. He remembered Lantern Rock. And he remembered the reason they were out here, felt again the silence of Bread's house.

The fire was almost too bright to look at. Overhead, Fish could see purple light slipping through branches. It was dawn. Fish buttoned the flannel shirt and shimmied into his jeans. He felt the barlow knife in his pocket, the wad of chew in his flannel. Everything seemed to be as it was. Fish still felt caught in the dream, that beast tangled in brush, roar, and fire. Fish's head ached. He was thirsty. He remembered the man with horns on his head, in the spruce trees. But that hadn't been a dream. Fear rose to his throat.

"Bread," Fish whispered. He stood and discovered his left leg had fallen asleep. He limped toward his friend. As he got closer to the fire, he noticed all of their gear lying beside it. The packs. The fish poles. And some things he didn't remember bringing. Cast-iron cook pots and some cans of beans. Two spoons gleamed on the stone edge of the firepit. Bread lowered the lid back onto the pot. The smell that rose from it made Fish's stomach feel incredibly empty.

"Are we back at our camp? How'd you get me across the river?"

Bread lifted the stick from the coals. It was attached to a pot lid. Steam rose up in the firelight.

"We got a new camp," said Bread. "And guess what else?"

Fish didn't want to guess about things. He felt too foggy.

"The man on the island, with the horns?" he asked. "Where is he? And what is all of this? How long have I been asleep?"

Bread grinned at him. The food smelled excellent.

"You slept all night. And there's your antler man right there," said Bread. "And guess what else?"

Bread had motioned to a deer skull lying in the shadows near the fire. It came from a large buck, and the skull was picked clean of all its flesh. The intricate gaps in its nose and eye sockets flickered in the firelight. A cross of wood draped with a pair of rotten coveralls lay beside it.

"Scarecrow," said Bread, pushing some coals nearer to the cooking pot. "Fish, this island. It's some kind of abandoned camp. I think it was a poachers' camp. There's some old stuff around, pans and such, a lot of rope. I found three cans of beans."

"A scarecrow?" Fish closed his eyes. He was so thirsty. His throat seemed to catch on his words. Why was there a scarecrow in the forest?

"Did its job, too. Fish, you hit the deck so hard I thought you died. I couldn't wake you up, but I heard you breathing, so I swam the river and fetched our stuff. I figure whoever abandoned this camp was poaching deer. Just wait till you see all the skulls! But guess what else, Fish."

"Do you have water?"

Bread handed Fish a mess tin. "It's river water," he said.

Fish drank it greedily. It tasted like silt.

"Fish, guess what else I found?"

"Did you swim our bikes across too? I don't see our bikes."

Bread took the mess tin away from Fish. "Fish," he said, and his eyes lit up. "That's what I've been trying to tell you. We don't need bikes anymore."

Fish wanted more water.

"Fish, we found our raft."

Bread motioned past the fire, deep into the shadows. There looked to be a large boulder hulking in the darkness, but it was far too square to be natural rock. Fish stared at it for a moment. It was a small cabin, the roof caved in and the whole thing leaning into the dirt.

"We found the makings of our raft, anyway," said Bread. "That old cabin is a pile of cedar." He lifted the lid of the pot away, inhaled deeply through his nose. Fish's stomach growled, and he forgot all about rafts and dreams and scarecrows.

"Mm-mm," said Bread. "*Beans.*"

"WE KNEE MARE ROWF," SAID BREAD. HIS WORDS WERE MUFFLED BY the manila rope he held in his mouth. Bread needed both hands to straddle and muscle the log in place. Fish hurried over to the long coil of rope Bread had found in the cabin, and used his barlow to slice through another length of it. The rope was dry and coarse, the kind that burns your hands if it slips. When he returned to the build site, Fish took the other rope from Bread's mouth and tied the two together with a double fisherman's knot his grandpa taught him.

The boys had a plan again. This was progress.

The project moved quickly now that they didn't need to cut their own trees and dig their own rope. The abandoned cabin made a perfect lumberyard. It was a twelve-by-twelve-foot structure that once stood about six feet tall before the roof and doorway collapsed. The logs were big cedars about as thick as Fish's waist, and only the very bottom row showed any sign of rot. The rest were dry and gray and solid as bones. The boys knocked away mud chinking using river rocks for hammers.

"Got it?" Fish asked.

"Go ahead," said Bread.

Fish wrapped the rope around the end of a log Bread held in place. This had been their pattern of labor for the majority of the morning, setting the logs together with tight S-curves of rope, lashing the logs to ridgepoles in a continuous weave.

The boys stepped back to admire their work. Only feet from the water's edge lay a nearly finished platform of a raft. At twelve feet wide by twelve feet long, the raft would prove stable enough. The sun was high in the sky again, and the weather warm. A stiff breeze kept the bugs at bay, and overall this day in the forest was shaping up to be much better than the first. Fish's jaw still ached, but he couldn't help smiling at the job being done. Bread had a big smear of sweat and dirt across his forehead. He smiled back.

"How many more, you figure?" asked Fish.

"I'd say the ridgepoles can fit two more logs," said Bread.

Fish nodded.

The boys weren't sure how the raft would handle in the water, or which way to point it once they got it floating—with the length of the logs running with or across the current. Either way, they were certain it would float. Cedar this dry was as buoyant as cork, and it wouldn't become waterlogged either. Fish's grandpa shingled his porch in cedar. The stuff shed water like a duck.

It was Bread's idea to construct the raft on top of roller logs. When they first started binding the logs in place on the gravel shore, Bread stopped them. *We're not going to be able to move this once we finish it, Fish,* he said. For a moment the two boys stared at it and the lapping riverbank. Fish gave a fruitless shrug. Then Bread remembered a picture book he'd read where the ancient Egyptians used logs as wheels to move huge stones for the pyramids. The boys placed two of the roundest logs near shore. It was a good thing Bread realized the problem when he did. Even with only three poles lashed together, the boys could hardly lift the raft onto the pair of rollers.

"You getting hungry?" Bread asked.

Fish nodded, brushed the fine gravel and cedar chaff from the front of his shirt. Fish's muscles trembled with fatigue, but this progress was irresistible. "I'd finish the base of the raft first," he said. "If you're up for it."

Bread nodded and wiped his forehead and smeared the dirt to his ear. Adding the final logs went quickly, and when they were finished the boys sat in the shade and leaned against tree trunks while they ate and gazed at their creation. They both pretended not to be too proud.

"It's a little crooked on that far end," said Bread. His comment was the pure false modesty of a true craftsman. Fish was proud as punch of the thing, and he knew Bread was too.

"It'll do," said Fish, nodding severely. "The *Hope of Lantern Rock*."

"I been thinking about that name," said Bread. "We ain't on Lantern Rock anymore. We should name it something about the island, or beavers maybe."

Fish thought about this. It was a good idea. After all, the beaver freedom and the island were what gave them the boat.

"How about *Beaver's Hope of Lantern Rock*."

Bread wrinkled his brow. "I'm not sure that has the right ring to it. Not dangerous enough."

Fish agreed. There was something a bit too soft about their patron animal. He and Bread were warriors too, after all, braving rivers and hunting with spears and raiding poaching camps as they pleased. After breakfast, Bread had given Fish the grand tour of the poachers' camp he had explored while Fish had slept through the night. There was the cabin and its half-buried pots and pans, a chest filled with rope. Outside the cabin were some old saws and kettles and a stack of deer skulls. Bread figured the kettles were used to boil the fat off the skulls before selling them to bankers and judges and other city people who wanted to put some horns on their walls. Except for the scarecrow head, the other skulls left behind didn't have antlers. And there were hundreds of them, some on the ground and chewed up by mice, some tacked to tree trunks with rusted nails, others hung on old wire strung through their nose and eye sockets. Interspersed were a few coyote skulls, with canine teeth protruding from their weathered snouts. Fish touched one of the teeth with the tip of his finger. It was dull and pointed like the tip of a rifle round. The poachers must have sold hides too. How Bread could have explored this place at night, alone in the dark and shadows, was beyond Fish. Fish was glad he'd passed out. It was Bread who faced down the scarecrow while his friend lay collapsed in the spruce trees. Bread swam the river and collected the gear. Bread took the lead on the construction of the raft, ordering Fish back and forth for rope, coming up with the good ideas.

"You should name it," Fish told him. "What do you think it should be named?"

Bread popped the last of his Slim Jim in his mouth, squinted out at the raft and the water.

"*Poachers' Hope of Lantern Rock.*"

Fish liked it immediately.

"I was thinking we could dress it out with some skulls before we push off," said Bread. "Make it fearsome, you know?"

Fish liked the idea even more.

"Only thing, though," Bread added, "is that we ain't really poachers. Not really."

Fish felt the disappointment, but then nodded at the empty Slim Jim wrapper in Bread's hand. "You got any more of those?" he asked.

Bread shook his head.

"Me neither. And we only got one can of beans, Bread."

Bread looked at his friend. "Tuna's gone too."

"So starting tomorrow," Fish explained, "we gotta kill what we eat, or we don't eat."

A light dawned in Bread's eyes.

"So tomorrow we'll be poachers," he said.

"Tomorrow we'll be poachers."

"Come on," said Bread, standing and wiping his hands on his jeans. "Let me show you what I was thinking with them skulls."

It took until dusk for the boys to finish and outfit the raft. It was what Fish's grandpa used to call rough work, as opposed to fine—more like sinking fence posts or slapping boards onto a chicken coop than carefully squaring a window or trimming a door with oak. It was the kind of work that needed little precision, so it went quickly and was deeply satisfying. Carry the log, lash the log, carry the skull, lash the skull. The boys were crafts-men, creators. They even had enough poles to lash together an A-frame they could throw the tarp over when the weather turned sour. They exhumed from the camp a box of old nails and a black-powder rifle with rye grass growing out of its barrel. They used the nails and river rocks to tack a railing of branches in place around the bow end of the boat, and they wove deer and coyote skulls onto it so any would-be boarders would see the gaping snouts and eye sockets as they approached. The bow end would be the galley and storehouse. They brought the old rifle on board to use as an an-chor pike they could pound into sandbars. They lashed their bags to the posts of the A-frame to keep them high and dry, and hung three cast-iron pots from nails. Fish imagined drifting through the sunshine a few days from now, miles away, the pots clanging lazily with the breeze and the rocking of the ship. Maybe they could just keep going, rivers to lakes, lakes to oceans, the tropics, the desert. Fish thought of sand dunes, but decided to back up and think again about tropics instead.

At the stern they made loops of rope to hold their fish poles, so they could let out line and drift for pike and catfish in the day-time and walleye at night. They brought aboard five flat pieces of limestone from the riverbed to make a fireproof base in the galley. The poachers' old boiling kettle would sit on top. They could boil crayfish and pike without leaving ship. The finishing touch was the antlered skull of the scarecrow.

Bread straddled the top pole of the A-frame. The sun was still large but beginning to set. The first streaks of orange and red shot across the horizon. Fish shielded his eyes and watched the silhou-ette of his friend lash the antlered skull to the pole. It reminded him of a picture he'd seen in school of American soldiers hoisting a flag after winning some hill. The antlers reached up like the fingers of a strong hand, grabbing a fistful of sky. There were no limits out here. Fish had never been prouder.

Bread wiggled the antlers to make sure they'd hold, then dangled his legs and dropped to the floor of the raft. He stomped his foot against the deck for good measure.

"Pretty sturdy," he said.

Fish couldn't feign indifference any longer. "It's perfect!" he exclaimed, and Bread beamed.

The boys planned to spend the night on the raft on dry land, to try it out before setting sail. They figured they could make beds from green cedar branches stacked a few inches thick. They could make one bed on either side of the river rock and kettle, under the tarp in the galley. The railings would keep them from snoring off into the river, and they'd keep coals in the kettle at night for warmth.

Bread exhaled through pursed lips. He looked at his hands and winced as he picked at a blister. "Let's eat some supper," he said. "I am about to keel over I'm so hungry."

Fish got the can of beans from the galley while Bread waded into the river and washed the spoons and mess tins. They decided to eat them cold. The two boys sat on the edge of their raft and watched the sun set on the river, ate beans in the quiet. A grasshopper clicked and fell in the river. Currents carried it downstream. A fish rose and snatched it under. The whole world was hungry, and the whole world was fed. Fish's back ached from the work. The hand that held his spoon had a blister on it the size of a nickel. Rough work was rough, but it was good. Fish used to love putting in fence posts with his grandpa. He loved most how that sort of work ended, letting his sweat dry and his muscles stiffen up while he ate a meal, drank water from a jug. It was the most serene thing to look out across several acres of land with fresh fence stakes pounded into the dirt, the swallows picking off bugs in the field. The summer after his father died in the desert, Fish's grandpa decided it was time to fence in an additional forty acres. Another fence didn't seem necessary to Fish, but he remembered how, as work progressed and days passed, the world became more stable and ordered again. *It's what man was meant to do,* his grandpa told him when he commented on how he enjoyed the work. *Build something. Then look at it. It makes food taste better.*

Viewed from where Fish sat, the river ran straight and then disappeared around a bend about a quarter mile distant. Poachers Island was the final island in the group, and the river converged once more downstream of it, creating a void filled with confused eddy water, which lapped at stones near the raft. The sky above the eddy had turned a vivid red, and the water caught and played with the light in its peaks and troughs. Soon Bread and Fish would leave the eddy. They'd point downstream and go.

Fish thought of his grandfather, who was out in this forest someplace, looking for him, looking at the same sky perhaps. He wished he could send his grandpa a message. Let him know he was okay. Fish felt more in command of things now that they had built the raft. Maybe that's why adults sought busyness. Busyness solved fear and silence and hurt. Maybe that's why his grandpa always waved his hands in the air and got back to work.

Your mom wants you to learn Jesus was all his grandfather said when Fish asked why they needed to start going to church. So they put on clean clothes and Grandpa shaved his silver neck and they drove to sit quietly through the morning in wooden pews. Fish got the sense that all of the adults there didn't know what to do with him. They knew his grandfather from when his grandmother was still alive. Fish had only fragments of memories of the woman on Sundays—an apron with flowers on it, a hand with blue veins, a jar of pickles spooned out on a rose-colored dish, a black Bible with writing in the margins. This was Fish's first time visiting her old church. The adults folded their hands in the foyer and smiled at him, curiosity in their eyes. They'd say things like, *Oh, and that's a good young man you got there, Teddy,* and they'd continue to glance at Fish and his grandfather while they pretended to talk to each other about the weather or farming. It went on this way for several Sundays. The pastor had a sheepdog who sat on the porch during services, and Fish usually looked around for the dog when the adults talked afterward, raked his fingers through the matted white hair. Once, when he was near enough to hear the conversation, a woman used the phrase *that poor fatherless thing,* and something rose up in Fish that made him leave the dog and turn toward the road so that no one would see him crying. Then he heard his grandpa take the Lord's name in vain, call the woman a fool, and then felt his grandfather's hand firmly clasp his shoulder and guide him to the truck.

Fischer, his grandpa said, gripping the wheel when he got inside and shut the door. He stared through the windshield. Fish couldn't be sure if his grandpa's eyes were angry or just very tired. *That woman back there,* he said, gripping the wheel harder. *Fischer, your dad loved you more than you could know. And if he'd have heard what that old bat*—he clenched his jaw and struck the steering wheel, hard, with the butt of his hand. Fish began to cry again. He was unsure what had happened between the adults, or what this all meant for his grandpa, but he understood that some important line had been crossed and that what was said next would be important and grave and perilous. His grandpa breathed through his nose awhile. *I know I don't talk about it, Fischer, because I don't know if I should or shouldn't,* said his grandpa. *I'm just an old man. And I know that life is both good and cruel.* He released his grip on the wheel a bit. *And it's been cruel to you, Fischer. But listen to me now, hear this—it also gave you your dad, and your dad was good. When you were real little your dad used to scoop you up and tell you he loved you from your heart to the sun.* Fish couldn't remember it, but he could see it somehow, and when he did, he saw sunlight. *He'd point to your heart, and then he'd point at the sun, and you'd smile and laugh and make him say it again. And he always would, as many times as you asked him.* Bread's grandfather looked out at the road. He took his hands off the wheel and rubbed his palms on his jeans. Fish felt a tear roll down his cheek. *And just because he's not with us doesn't mean you don't have him. You have a father. Do you understand?* Fish nodded. His grandpa wiped his eyes, and then he sighed. Minuscule particles of hay dust floated and sparkled inside the silent cab. *I gotta go back inside. I have to apologize to that woman. I'll be back.* He started the motor so the heater would run, and after a few moments of profound absence, he drove Fischer home and made him pancakes. They did no work that afternoon. Fish's grandpa slept upstairs the remainder of the day, his work boots unlaced in the kitchen. That was their last Sunday at church. From then on they stayed busy on Sundays instead.

Bread snorted and startled himself awake. Fish hadn't noticed his friend had nodded off. Without comment, Bread smacked his lips, took another bite of beans, and stared at his mess tin until his head slowly dropped again. Fish was tired too, tired of remembering. He was tired of thinking about his dad and grandfather, and what it meant to lie to his friend about his father's life, ask him to run toward something that wasn't there. He liked the beaver life better. Out here with the trees and rocks for fathers. But when he looked at Bread, he couldn't help wondering if his dad ever told him he loved him, ever pointed at his heart. Fish felt again the awful weightlessness of raising the revolver, that shattering report that filled the room with smoke and deafness. Fish's tired mind swam between visions of his father's hand pointing from his heart to sunlight and of Bread's father choking his son on a linoleum floor. Fish felt accusation rise in his heart, guilt, shame. He closed his eyes and opened them. Forget it, he told himself. At least for now. That's something his mom used to tell him when he couldn't sleep and worried about not sleeping. *You have permission to forget it,* she'd tell him. *Just for a minute, just enjoy your pillow, just rest, let it go. Close your eyes and sail away from troubles on a raft made of stars.* And then she'd pray and hum.

Fish looked out at the bending river grass. He didn't need to cut cedar branches for beds tonight. The wilderness was soft enough. They could cut down some push poles tomorrow before shoving off. Tomorrow would be perfect. Just like everything else. Just like the sunset. Like the river. Just like the raft and the crickets. Fish closed his eyes. Bending down and down, he thought, like river grass. Like cattails.

"Boys!"

Fish spilled his bean tin from his lap with a clatter. He looked out at the river. The far bank stood quiet with its reeds and brush. The shadows sat still. The air didn't stir. He spun where he sat to look back at the interior of the island. Bread slept soundly. Had Fish dreamed the voice?

"Boys!"

He heard it this time. It was a man's voice, off to his right, not very distant. Fish crouched and clawed through the river grass to where he could get a good view of the opposing shoreline. The first thing he saw was a riderless horse standing on the riverbank, eating grass. And then he saw a black and white dog sniffing along the mud. Fish crouched behind a windfallen tree, peeking over the stump. He didn't see the sheriff until the man moved. The man appeared like a deer appears, seemingly from nowhere despite its lack of camouflage. The sheriff moved through chest-high grass. Fish's hands felt numb. The sheriff looked right at him.

The two locked eyes for what seemed to be minutes. Fish couldn't tell if the sheriff could see him or not, but it sure felt like he did. Fish felt the same way when he stumbled across a wild animal in the woods. He could remember it happening only a handful of times, but when he'd come upon a fox or a deer, it made him feel like a creature too, the surprise of it, not knowing at all what to do and certainly unwilling to make a move to find out.

The sheriff moved first, and Fish let out a rattling breath. The sheriff looked up and down the length of the island. He took off his hat and wiped his forehead with his sleeve. He slapped his hat against his leg. He now stood in the exact place where the boys had crossed, where they jumped in like cannonballs and swam. How did that already seem so long ago, tramping in there with their packs and bikes, cutting down trees with pocketknives, like children. Fish didn't feel like a child anymore. The raft was finished, and that made him feel capable. But that was all in danger now. Fish remembered the bikes—Bread had left them behind. The sheriff had to have found them. The dog sniffed for tracks, whined at the river.

"No," Fish whispered under his breath, willing the man with his words. "Do not come across. We are not here." And then he tried it like his mom would do it, except she would raise her voice and her hands when she spoke, as if gathering electricity. "In the name of Jesus Christ," whispered Fish, "I forbid you to cross."

Fish heard the sheriff saying something, but it came over the water as a mumble. The sheriff was talking to the horse. He pointed his hat at the ground on the riverbank and then pointed it across the river. The dog paced back and forth, its nose to the ground. The sheriff spoke to the horse once more. It looked to Fish like he was trying to convince it of something.

"You shall not cross," whispered Fish, and the sheriff looked right at his hiding place again, dropped his hat, and started to unbutton his shirt.

Fish's heart beat faster. The sheriff removed his jacket and shirt, then his boot and socks and pants. He left them in a pile and waded into the water. The dog joined him, its bushy tail floating on the surface.

"He is coming across," Fish said, openmouthed, and watched the sheriff lower himself into the water and begin to swim.

There was no time for stealth. Fish sprang from his hiding place and bolted through the grass toward the raft.

"Hey!" yelled the sheriff. He'd spotted him. Fish broke branches as he ran between cedars. "Hey!" the sheriff yelled again. The voice seemed farther away now, but it wouldn't stay that way for long.

"Bread!" Fish shouted as he burst into the campsite. Bread shot awake and tossed his bean tin in the air.

Fish started pushing the raft toward the water with Bread still sitting on it. He rammed his shoulder into one of the A-frame posts and dug his shoes into the gravel.

"Bread! The sheriff!"

Bread was on his feet, a confused look in his eyes.

"The sheriff's swimmin' at us!"

Bread crouched where he stood. He'd been sleeping soundly.

"Bread, push the dang raft!"

Bread scurried around to the back side of the raft, put both hands on a post, and pushed. The raft didn't move.

"Fish," he asked, "are you sure you seen the—"

"Boys!" came the sheriff's call through the trees. It sounded much closer now. The sheriff was nearly across the channel.

Bread's eyes grew wide with fear and he punched his shoulder into the raft and began driving his feet. The raft swayed, rolled an inch, and stopped again. The boys planned to launch it using their push poles as levers. But they hadn't cut any poles. They'd fallen asleep.

Fish's feet slipped out from under him. Pain shot through his knee. He cussed and regained his footing. They only needed to push the raft a few feet to get it floating. Bread frantically pushed and winced in pain as his shoulder and neck pressed against the cedar log. His feet slipped on the gravel and bedrock beneath it. Fish's hurt knee made him angry. Being chased like this made him angry.

"Boys!" came the call again, which made Bread's efforts become even more frantic and fruitless. Fish envisioned the sheriff pulling himself onto shore, winded, rising to his feet now.

"Bread," said Fish. The forest seemed to disappear as he spoke, as did the pain and panic. There was just the raft now, the river, and five feet to freedom.

"Bread!" he said again.

Bread stopped and stared at him. His face was pale and his cheeks were mottled. The sheriff's voice made him shake.

"Bread, we have to push together, at the same time and in the same way, or we're not going to make it."

Bread took a rattling breath. Shook his head adamantly. "I can't," he said. "I can't." Bread put his neck into the post again and beat against it until his feet slipped out from under him and he fell on his stomach. He lay there a moment, huffing in the dirt, blowing a tuft of grass with his mouth. "Fish, I can't go back. I can't. They'll send me off. I—"

Fish watched his friend, his open mouth, pleading, blowing grass. And then he remembered the half-buried rifle they'd found. He bolted to the galley of the raft. Bread stayed in the dirt, dread on his face.

Fish came back with the old and long black-powder rifle. Bread's face looked more desperate when he saw it, until he saw what Fish was doing with it. Fish held the rifle like a spear over his head and drove the muzzle into the gravel beneath the edge of the raft. He then pushed up against the lever with all his might. Even by himself, he moved the raft about six inches on its rollers.

Bread was back on his feet.

"Boys!" the sheriff called. A dog barked.

"You push, I'll lever," Fish said. "Last chance!"

Bread had his neck and shoulder down again, driving his feet with all he had. Fish levered, repositioned, and levered again. The raft was rolling. With each heave it moved about a foot, and Bread could keep the momentum going for another foot with his driving legs.

"Push!" yelled Fish. The front of the raft gained water, nosing beneath the surface. "Push!" This time it kept moving. Slowly but certainly, the front of the raft began to rise back up out of the water, floating. Fish tossed the rifle aboard and put his shoulder into a post. The raft gained momentum. Fish felt water on his ankles, then his shins, his hips. The raft was free.

"You boys stop right where you are!" There was anger in the sheriff's voice, and it came from directly behind them.

Bread and Fish jerked their heads around to see the sheriff standing atop the small rise above the riverbank. The dog growled and barked at his side. The sheriff was in his boxer shorts, soaking wet, his chest huffing. He began picking his way down, barefoot, through the pine needles and stones.

"Keep pushing," said Bread.

Fish put his head down and pushed even harder. His foot slipped on algae-covered rocks, but he was in deep enough water that he didn't fall. The raft was in the eddy now. The boys were chest-deep. Soon the current would catch it.

"I said stop!"

Fish glanced back. Ignoring the sharp stones, the sheriff sprinted into the water. A few steps in, he slipped on a rock and crashed beneath the surface. His dog swam in a circle and barked. The sheriff came up gasping and facing the wrong direction. He turned, wiped water from his face, and started staggering toward the boys.

"Fish, get on!"

The raft was in the current and pulling away. Bread was on board already, crouched and waving him up, reaching out his hand. Fish swam a few strokes, but the raft pulled away from him. He put his head down and kicked as hard as he could but couldn't catch it. Behind him, he heard the sheriff swimming with powerful strokes.

"Fish, rope!"

Fish looked up to see a coil of rope unfold in the sky. It landed on top of him and Fish grabbed an armful of it. He was turned onto his back as Bread pulled the rope in, which gave him an upriver view of the approaching sheriff. The raft was moving fast now, but the sheriff was keeping up, gaining even. He swam even better than Bread. The dog trailed behind with wide eyes. Fish felt Bread's hands grip his armpits, and he was dragged on board across the cedar. Panting and wet in the pile of rope, his hair dripping in his eyes, Fish watched helplessly as the sheriff came closer. He was in the current now too, and about twenty feet from the raft. He looked like a machine, like he had his own motor. The sheriff would catch them.

"*You*," Bread yelled, so loudly it startled Fish, "are not taking us in!"

The sheriff kept swimming. Fish watched with wide eyes. He heard Bread behind him, rustling around in one of the packs. The sheriff was only fifteen feet away now. Fish could hear the man's breathing. Then he saw Bread's shoes appear next to the piled rope and looked up to see Bread holding the revolver into the orange and purple sky.

Bread's chest thumped with his breath. His jaw was tight. He had power in his eyes.

"This is the *Poachers' Hope of Lantern Rock*!" he shouted, so loudly that his voice cracked with the effort.

Fish looked back at the sheriff and saw the man's expression of surprise when he raised his face for a breath. He'd spotted the revolver.

"And you will *not*," yelled Bread, "take this ship!"

Bread cocked the hammer of the giant revolver, squinted his eyes, and unleashed a thunderous blast overhead. The muzzle whipped backward, and Bread fell onto the deck.

The sheriff stopped swimming, and his head rose higher as he treaded water. The shot echoed through the river valley, through the forest and sky. A flock of birds lifted from a tree. Bread cocked the revolver again, and the sheriff drifted. As the raft peeled slowly away, Fish locked eyes with the man. The sheriff glared at him from beneath plastered wet hair. His eyes looked as black as the river. Fish wasn't sure what he saw there, but he had the distinct feeling he got when he knew he'd screwed up badly. It summoned in his mind the look his dad could give him when angered. It was a look that stopped the earth from spinning. And all Fish could do now was stare back into those eyes, as if he'd come across some animal in a forest. Fish heard Bread catch his breath on the deck behind him. Fish was still too winded to speak. His knee hurt. He held it, and let his head fall onto the wet pile of rope as the sheriff waded to shore with his dog, and then Fish closed his eyes.

ELEVEN

TIFFANY STAGGERED DOWNHILL, STRUGGLING TO HOLD HER HALF of the canoe and a flashlight at the same time. Her arms ached. The grass on the riverbank was slippery, wet with evening dew.

"Okay," said Miranda, nosing the front of the canoe into the water. "We made it."

Tiffany dropped the back end of the overloaded canoe onto the grass, and it landed with a muffled thump. She worried that she should have set it down gently, but Miranda didn't seem to notice, and Tiffany was nearly too bug-bitten and winded to care. She wasn't good at this sort of thing, carrying canoes, running from law enforcement, breaking into hospitals. Ever since she found herself relying on Miranda as a guide, her reservations about the woman grew. The more she trusted her, the more dangerous she seemed to become. Tiffany stretched her back and arms. Blood flowed back like needles into her forearms. The stars shone brightly across the full breadth of the sky. Tiffany recognized Ursa Major and Minor, the Great Bear and Little Bear, the mother and son circling each other in all that darkness and light. *We're on our way,* she thought.

She caught her breath and closed her eyes and rubbed the cramps from her hands.

Tiffany felt she had to prove something to Miranda, though what that was, exactly, she didn't know. The widowed woman was stoic and fiercely attached to her son, and these were admirable qualities. But why Tiffany felt so obliged to stand by her in all of this was a mystery. It wasn't like her to attach herself to others. She'd been alone a long time, and her own troubles were plenty. But here she was, on the lam and about to push a canoe into a black river with a woman she'd known for a night and a day. Tiffany smiled in the darkness. Despite the reckless abandon of it all, or perhaps because of it, she felt more alive than she had in a very long time.

Tiffany could hardly believe she'd taken part in their actions at the hospital. It seemed like a scene from someone else's life, certainly not from hers. After sprinting across the parking lot and slamming herself shut in the cab of Teddy's truck, she gathered the courage to peek over the dashboard. She spotted security guards running around inside the lit corridors of the hospital, black jackets whizzing past windows, through lobbies. *Come on, Miranda, come on,* she whispered. When she heard sirens coming from the streets behind her, she ducked to the floorboards. She closed her eyes as the red and blue lights passed, breathing as steadily as she could on the sandy floor mats. Did the police know which truck was theirs? They'd search the parking lot for sure. Tiffany swallowed. When the passenger door of the cab burst open, she couldn't bear to look at her accusers. She just held her breath, waiting for a voice to command her to stay down, to move out of the cab, to read her her rights or whatever else it was police say when they arrest people. But it was Miranda's voice that broke the silence. *Tiffany, let's go,* Miranda hissed, slipping into the cab. Tiffany snapped back up into the driver's seat, glanced at the empty cop cars blocking the hospital entrance, and then at Miranda, who was panting and untangling a small tuft of cedar needles from her hair. She had dirt on her face. *Start the truck!* All Tiffany could do was gape. Miranda stopped untangling her hair, placed a hand gently on Tiffany's shoulder, spoke into her eyes. *Tiffany, I did not just leap from a window to a pine tree to be arrested in the parking lot. In Jesus' name, fly!* The next part made Tiffany smile most, the way she turned the key and pumped the sloppy pedal all the way to the floor, the engine igniting and roaring to life. With her foot on both gas and brake, she yanked the truck in gear, popped the brake pedal, and fishtailed that big red pickup right across the median. She could still hear the squealing tires and see the empty cop cars in her rearview mirror, their turning lights drifting from sight.

Tiffany grinned at the stars. Madness, she thought.

"Okay," said Miranda, "I think we're ready."

Miranda stooped over the canoe, touching the various packs and pieces of gear, tugging straps. They'd spent the morning packing for the trip—bedrolls and pillows, lighters, batteries, saltine crackers and peanut butter, cans of tuna, a hunting knife, and a twelve-gauge pump gun from Teddy's cabinet. Constable Bobby, thankfully, had run out of cookies and left the farm. They spent the afternoon and early evening dragging the loaded canoe through fields and forests, miles of pines and brambles and boulders. Miranda didn't want to leave the truck parked at any boat landings. If they hiked to the river, they could disappear. Tiffany cursed the branches and bugs. Miranda prayed out loud for a better path, and protection from mosquitoes. Then she took a shortcut, which proved to be even worse, dusk and mud and marsh, more bugs than before. But Tiffany was committed and irate by that point, and would have dragged the boat through a grass fire if it meant getting to the river any sooner.

"Water. Food. Extra blankets." Miranda stood up. "We're ready. Are we ready?"

"Just a sec," said Tiffany. With all the gear in the canoe, there was only room left for two paddlers, bow and stern. It'd be a cramped ride, and no telling how long. They'd packed enough food and water for five days, but Tiffany drank four glasses of water to fully hydrate before leaving the farm. It made her nervous being away from amenities again. She ducked into the jack pines, found a place devoid of briars, and turned off her light as she squatted down in the grass. She became aware that now was her chance to turn back, but already knew she couldn't. The thought of doing so seemed far worse than the bugs and mud and discomfort. She knew she'd stay with this woman, unreasonable as it seemed. When she returned to the riverbank, Miranda had set the paddles in place, bow and stern, and stood by the back of the canoe.

"Do you mind letting me steer?" Miranda asked. "I never asked how much paddling experience you had."

"Very little, and no, just tell me what to do."

"Hop in front, then. I'll push us off. Wait. Do you want to pray?"

Tiffany shook her head.

"I'll pray," said Miranda, and folded her hands over her heart. "God," she said, "be with us."

"That's it?" Tiffany expected something with a bit more gravity, given the seriousness of the endeavor, and given the way she'd already heard Miranda pray in the truck on the way back from the hospital. The woman was flighty.

Miranda nodded. "Hop in."

Tiffany had no fear of water. She could swim fairly well, but the river was cold, and black, and the canoe felt awfully unsteady as it glided out into the current and nosed downstream. Tiffany clutched at the gunwales. The world was dark and fluid. She heard Miranda's paddle stir the water, turning the canoe, and it felt to Tiffany as if they were tipping.

"Relax," Miranda said. "Just let your hips absorb the roll. Don't fight it." The paddle stirred the water again, and the boat rocked again, and Tiffany deliberately forced herself to relax and loosen her grip on the sides of the canoe.

"That's it," said Miranda. "One with the water."

"I have canoed before," said Tiffany, "at a girls' camp." She looked out at the shoreline. Its shadows passed by very quickly. Already, the place where they'd put in was out of sight. The current pulled powerfully into the wilderness.

"Did you like it?" Miranda asked.

"We flipped."

There was silence for a moment. Tiffany thought she heard Miranda smiling. "Tell you what," Miranda said, "don't paddle for a while."

Tiffany wasn't planning on it.

"Just sit and get used to it," said Miranda. "Enjoy the stars."

The river drifted on, and the stars—once Tiffany allowed herself to notice them—were indeed beautiful out here. The sky had a curve to it, an overturned bowl cupping the earth and pricked with light. Again, there crouched the Great Bear. They made their way past one bend and then another. Tiffany realized how in control of the canoe Miranda really was. With only the smallest stir of her paddle, she'd turn the boat sideways in the stream and glide it back toward the river's center, then back off the momentum and angle downstream again. Tiffany turned around and realized Miranda rarely took her paddle out of the water. She left it there, stirring, stirring, back and forth, feathering the blade as she moved it, prying and drawing. The woman was a boater. After a half hour or so, Tiffany grew accustomed to the motions and began to truly relax. The air was cool. Tiffany rummaged for the scarf she'd packed in her bag. With the warmth of the scarf around her neck, and stars drifting through the branches, Tiffany recalled that she hadn't slept for a long time. The rhythmic stirring of the water seemed to bring order to it all, and Tiffany was struck by the odd sense that she was exactly where she was meant to be at that moment, floating down a river filled with stars on a planet floating in space. It made her feel childish, wonderstruck in a dreamy campfire sort of way. She thought about Cal, too. He was out here somewhere, and she couldn't help but imagine he was searching for her, and she for him, like a story she'd read long ago.

"Do you ever think about boys?" Tiffany asked, breaking the long silence. Her voice seemed contained in the darkness, as if the words she spoke were for the darkness and Miranda alone. It reminded her of whispering secrets to imagined friends under a blanket, and she felt again the weight of her old loneliness. It comforted and hurt all at once. It was a place she'd trained herself not to go.

Miranda's paddle stopped its stirring, and suddenly Tiffany realized how cruel her words could seem to a widow searching for her son. She'd been too caught up in the sight of the stars. Too tired and dreamy. She'd forgotten where she was, whom she was with, what had been lost.

"Forgive me," she said.

The paddle stirred the water. "No, I understand what you meant."

They drifted past a half-sunken tree.

"Tell me," said Miranda.

"When I was in middle school, boys wouldn't talk to me, but that didn't stop me from hoping." She stopped. "This is silly, though. I should be quiet."

"It's not silly. Please, talk."

"I used to imagine a boyfriend who could see me, you know? It was more than attention. I wanted to be *known*. I imagined us parking a car out by the river, hidden by the tall grass, fireflies everywhere, and I could talk and he would listen and nod, his eyes wide in the dark. And the way I imagined it, he would want to listen. He would want to see me. And he'd listen until he knew everything there was to know." Tiffany laughed at herself. "There were times I imagined it so long, I ran out of things to tell him, and we'd just look at each other. In a way, that was the best part."

The shadow of an owl passed overhead, tipping its wings through the cosmos. Miranda stopped paddling and Tiffany sensed that the woman was actually listening to her. She felt both grateful and ashamed. The owl lifted up out of sight, and Tiffany had a realization that Miranda could become an actual friend. That's who this madwoman was. That's why Tiffany felt so deeply for the fire in her eyes. It's why she played getaway driver in her dad's pickup. It's why she was here in a canoe, floating a dark river and searching for sons. Miranda could be a friend. Tiffany looked at the mirrored river in front of her, the stars in it. The thought of friendship warmed her, but she didn't trust it. She'd trusted that warmth before and been burned by it. It reminded her of lunchrooms.

Miranda lifted her paddle from the water and balanced it across the gunwales. She reached down by her feet and picked up a milk jug filled with tap water. She took a small drink, capped it again.

"I once heard a woman describe marriage," she said. "At my old church, before my husband died. She said when you first meet your lover, there is nothing but romance. We're blind to flaws." The paddle skimmed the water, bit again. "And then one morning— this takes about six months, sometimes much less—you wake up next to a man who groans when he gets out of bed, and limps off to the kitchen and then the bathroom, in his boxers, so he can drink coffee while he poops."

Tiffany snorted, and then covered her face because of how loud it sounded. "So, that's the truth of the fairy tale, then."

"No, it's not," said Miranda. "It's not the truth, even if it seems that way. I think about my husband, how the deployments were exciting at first—the distance it created—because when he came home we were new again for a time." Miranda pried against the water, and the canoe nosed toward a right-hand bend in the river. "My husband used to get lost, distracted. And I found I could never talk him out of that, but I could summon him, offer him a palace, gates wide open. Don't laugh, this is about more than what it seems. Everything is. That's what I'm trying to say. Everything is spirit. It's hard to remember, but when he and I knew it—*my God*—that man would kill lions on my behalf. Call me old-fashioned. I know what is good."

Tiffany liked this woman very much. And she liked the idea of Cal wrestling a lion, and then walking toward her with hunger in his eyes and sweat on his neck. Her old imagined boyfriends seemed totally insufficient.

"And then we forget again!" Miranda went on, like she was trying to describe some wonderful and elusive flavor. "It's a mystery how beautiful we can be, and how terrible too. We catch glimpses only. But it's there. We're not just poor damn things. Even if it feels true, it's not the truth. There's more to us, more for us, right now, right here, in *this*."

Tiffany sat quietly a moment. She didn't know what to do with all of that, but she had always felt, from her anonymous youth through her hungry summer, that she was worth more than the world suggested she was. She once sat in a moonlit tent, eating a stolen hard-boiled egg, and found herself marveling at the sight of her hand lifting the thing to her mouth. There seemed something miraculous about it, about just existing, that demanded to be acknowledged, celebrated even.

"I've heard your dad say that," she said. "*Poor damn things*. He seems like a good man. People like him."

"He is hard, but yes, he is good. Mom said it was Korea. I wish I'd known him before. I saw pictures. His smiles were bigger then. For as long as I knew him, though, he demanded peace and quiet. He loved us and was good to us. I never doubted his goodness. But there was distance. We could never rock the boat. It was hard to be a teenage girl and never rock the boat."

"Yes."

"But I knew he'd be good for Fischer. I knew the farm and barns and fields would be good for Fischer, for his heart, and maybe Fischer would be good for my dad. After my husband died, I watched my son wilt. I barely caught it in time. This *quietness* came over him. This fear of things. I knew I had to get him out into something bigger than himself, bigger than his mom. Boys need to shake their manes, as my dad used to put it. He was right. It's been good for Fischer, this place. Do you know, he came back so changed after that first summer, so much like his dad, smiling again, proud too."

Tiffany sensed a change in Miranda's voice. She'd struggled with the last few words, brought back no doubt into the present, her boy lost in a forest. He was probably cold and hungry and scared. He'd *shot* a man. During their ride back to Claypot, Miranda described her encounter with Jack Breadwin in the hospital. His scalp was shaved and bandaged, and the left side of his face was bruised all the way down to his jaw. But that wasn't the ugly part. The ugly part was his eye. Only one red eye looked out from the bandages, the other was covered with a patch. He was awake enough to know who she was and who her son was, and she saw fear and hate fill that eye. She rebuked him there in that hospital bed. Shouted down whatever "foul thing" lived inside him, pleaded with the humanity in him to pity his son, who was now fleeing down a river. *Shame on you,* she shouted. *Shame! Ashes!* She used these exact words as she recounted the story, which made Tiffany grow quiet. She tried to imagine Miranda saying such things at Jack's bedside, and then leaping from a window. Miranda wept for most of the ride home, praying softly, sometimes loudly, tears streaming down her face.

"Come on," said Tiffany, picking up her paddle. "You better teach me how to use this thing." She dipped the blade into the black water.

Miranda remained quiet.

"Miranda," declared Tiffany, "I give you my word that we are not stopping this canoe, not for sleep, not for food, until we have your son."

Miranda nodded, wiped her eye, looked at the riverbanks. She inhaled and exhaled forcefully. "We'll have to stop in a few miles," she said, "before the rapids by the islands."

"Before the what?"

"I feel like praying," Miranda said. "Yes, let's pray." She lifted her paddle over her head with both arms outstretched. She took a massive breath.

Tiffany bit her lip. Here came the gravity.

Miranda raised her voice and called on the Father to place a hedge of protection, his own spirit hand, around the boys. She declared the canoe and the river anointed in the divine presence of the Holy Ghost. She invited Jesus, high priest, to intercede on their behalf, to bring the full work of his cross between them and any evil thing coming against them. She reminded the devil of God's terrifying majesty, his ferocious power. She reminded the darkness that she and Tiffany were God's daughters, loved and guarded with insatiable jealousy. She shook her paddle at the stars as she spoke, at the forest, as if power flowed from its shaft. The river trembled with her voice, and Tiffany couldn't tell if the woman was frightening or beautiful. It felt like watching a storm approach, roll in, bend the trees in half. It really was a thing to behold.

"King Jesus!" Miranda yelled into the forest, beating her paddle skyward, and Tiffany worried she might upset the canoe. She worried about what kind of church Miranda went to. She worried about why she didn't want it to stop.

"*King Jesus!*" Miranda cried. "*Yes, King Jesus!*"

As if in response, howls erupted from the river's edge. Not far beyond the bank in the darkness of the cedars, the wailing of a pack of coyotes pierced the night. Their yips and cries filled the forest and then fled, tumbling away like demons downriver. Miranda lowered her paddle. Smoothed her denim dress across her lap. She let out a contented sigh.

"Yes," she said. "That is better."

CAL LOOKED UP FROM THE PILE OF TINDER HE'D BEEN ATTEMPTING to light. Jacks looked up too, cocked his head toward the sound. Coyotes, Cal thought. They were far off. The sound might carry for miles on a night this still. The forest seemed quiet tonight, calmer somehow, and Cal was growing accustomed to it. If he had heard coyotes the night before, he would have lit up the shadows with his flashlight. But even after these short two days in the wild, he'd become accustomed to the sounds, or lack of sounds, the loneliness. He had braved a rushing river, been bucked from a horse, made a decision to ask Tiffany on a date, and nearly had the boys. It was amazing what a man could sort out in the woods. Besides, he thought, turning back to the task at hand of starting a fire, he had Jacks with him now, Jacks' keen eyes and ears, and nose, too, which had led him to the boys' bikes and a chewed-up cedar tree. He imagined a man could sleep more soundly in a forest while a dog kept vigil at his side. He smiled at his dog, shook his head. How did Jacks get out here, anyway? Was Tiffany here somewhere? Cal thought it over and decided she couldn't be. Jacks must have run away. Sniffed him out. Cal couldn't begrudge that kind of loyalty, yet he felt sorry for Tiffany's sake—she'd worry—but all would be well very soon. Just another day or two, and then Cal would walk out of the forest with the boys, and Jacks, and he would stride up to Tiffany and scoop her waist and take her out to dinner.

Cal became aware he was smiling dreamily at his dog, alone in the dark, and the fire hadn't been started. He shivered and resumed his work. Fire was becoming increasingly important. The night would have been cool even if he had stayed dry, but the swim at dusk had chilled him to the bone. After letting the boys slip, Cal waded to shore through the muck and cattails, and pushed his way slowly through the thick brush of the riverbank. Thorns stuck in his feet, and after picking them out and dressing again Cal had to warm his hands in his pockets for a few minutes before peeling some bark and rummaging through the horse's saddlebags. His matches had been ruined in his swim down the rapids the previous evening, and he found himself muttering, "Come on, come on, please be there," as he searched blindly through the depths of the saddlebags. Eventually he felt what he was looking for—a two-inch-long rod of ferrous metal tied to a sharp-edged rectangle of steel. The whole unit was no larger than a nail clipper, but it was all-important. His early faith in Teddy was vindicated. The man had placed a flint and steel in both their saddlebags. Cal smiled when he found it. "Divvy the gear," he said to no one in particular. The horse shifted its weight, blinked its giant eye.

Cal studied his little pile of cedar bark. The moon was up now, and nearly full, and it provided enough light to work. He'd been on a few Boy Scout trips as a kid, but he hadn't really been into earning merit badges, and he usually opted for a lighter or match when it was his turn to start the fire. Once, when it became apparent that his scout leader wouldn't remain quiet about his need to learn the flint, a young Cal secreted a Bic lighter in the folds of his uniform. He made a big show of wanting to work alone, and after a few feigned strikes of the flint, he reached down and lit a thread of birch bark with the Bic. He remembered cupping the tiny flame with his hands and blowing on it until the smoke rose into his face and the fire grew hot. His scout leader was proud.

"What kind of scout cheats at fire-making?" Cal asked himself. He shook his head and laughed. "A scout who wants to eat hot dogs already," he answered. Cal's stomach growled. There were two cans of tuna and four cans of beans in the horse's pack. Cold tuna would work, but after that swim, with the ache and chill of the river still in the knuckles of his hands, a hot can of brown beans next to a fire sounded a whole lot better.

Cal bunched up the cedar bark again so it made a little pile next to a tepee of twigs. The dried twigs looked white and brittle in the moonlight, like chicken ribs. He was so hungry. Cal held the ferrous rod in his left hand, with the rod's tip buried in the cedar bark. With his right hand he pressed the sharp edge of the steel against the rod and prepared to strike it toward the tinder. He'd experimented with the thing a few times to get the hang of it. With the right amount of pressure and speed, the steel's edge threw an impressive shower of yellow sparks from the rod, but he couldn't figure out how to keep from knocking over his tinder pile in the process. He'd make sparks, knock over the tinder. He'd regather the tinder and strike at it harder, and then knock over the tepee of twigs as well. This time he stroked more gently, and a few yellow sparks landed on the tinder pile. He watched the silvery bark for any sign of a glow. One of the sparks seemed hopeful. It landed in a successful position and glowed for a moment, just the smallest pinprick of orange. Cal's eyes grew wide and ravenous, but then everything faded again to moonlight. Cal, impatient, stroked the rod again and knocked over his tinder pile.

"Son of a—" He stopped himself. Jacks looked at him with a question in the tilt of his head. "No need to get upset, Jacks. Getting upset won't help." The horse gave a slight whinny from the shadows and sounded like it was chuckling. Cal sat up on his haunches and turned toward the noise. "Well," he said, "I don't have to talk to you anymore, do I?" He paused for effect. "No, I do not. I got Jacks now, and Jacks ain't rude." Cal turned back to the fire, the lack of fire, and sighed. Cold tuna sounded brutally unsatisfying. It didn't seem right, lying out under the stars with a dog and a horse, eating a cold can of tuna.

Cal heard the coyotes again. Jacks' head perked up. The coyotes yipped and yipped, noisy as blackbirds, their yips breaking into howls and ending in prolonged silence. Cal had heard that when coyotes rally and howl and then go suddenly quiet, that's when they begin to hunt. He pictured them now, out in the brush and the moonlight, their noses to the ground, rooting out mice and rabbits. Cal thought of the boys. He was glad they had the raft. They would be safe if they just stayed on the river.

The sight of the Breadwin boy firing that revolver played again in Cal's mind—the ferocity in his eyes when he touched that thing off, the surprise when the recoil knocked him back. Cal knew the boy didn't fire at him. It was a warning shot, plain and simple. And Cal took the warning. The boys were scared and running, and Cal wasn't going to push that fear to a more dangerous level. He thought it best to back off, to regroup, to follow them from a distance until he knew what to do. In hindsight, Cal cursed himself for chasing them into the river like that. He should have stood onshore, reassured them, told them it was okay, told them he knew they were the good guys in all of this. Cal now questioned whether it was Teddy's grandson who had shot Jack Breadwin after all, even if that was what the note said. The Breadwin boy looked bold enough, but Teddy's grandson just looked scared. Cal stared right into that boy's eyes. Poor kid. Cal wanted so badly to scoop those boys up and get them into the warm cab of a pickup, get a meal in their bellies, some burgers and fries and Cokes. It was wrong for boys to be out in the wild like this, running like criminals. In this case it was clear they were the victims. There was no doubt in his mind that Jack Breadwin, lying in a morgue somewhere, deserved exactly what he got. Cal remembered something his old police chief once said about men who hurt children, how it'd be better for them to have millstones hung around their necks and be cast into the sea. Well, Jack Breadwin would know, wouldn't he. Poor Jack, too.

Cal couldn't tell anymore who deserved what. Some people in town said Jack wasn't always so much of a bastard. They said that before his wife died in a wreck, leaving him alone with a crying nine-month-old and a floundering business, that Jack may have been a screw-up but he wasn't mean. They said he liked duck hunting in that boat of his, that he knew the river and marshes better than anybody. They said he was a fun sort of drunk, played a lot of softball. And then his wife died in the fall, and winter came, and Jack never really came out of it.

Cal looked at the pathetic, tangled pile of tinder. Cursed it. He should have gotten involved in that Breadwin kid's life. He *knew* what Jack was like. But he couldn't get involved. Cops respond to the calls. Fill out the papers. That's how it worked.

Cal rebuilt the tinder pile as neatly as he could.

"Well," he said to Jacks, "to hell with this job."

He smiled to think of the Breadwin boy shooting that revolver into the air. He was proud of him in an odd sort of way. What a little man. He'll really be something when he's grown. Both those boys will, out here building rafts, fending off sheriffs. *Damn.* Cal was glad the boys had each other. It's good to run in a pack. In Houston, Cal had a few guys in the department he could gripe to, drink beer with, but in the end they were all in it alone. They were too grown up, too busy. Every guy had his own shift, his own family, his own bills to pay. Boyhood was better. Cal remembered what it was like. Riding bikes. Building jumps. Playing outside until the dark came and the grass got cold.

"Worthless," Cal said.

Jacks rested his chin on his paws. The dog had grown bored. The horse whinnied.

"I wasn't talking to you, horse," said Cal.

Cal assembled the tinder a final time. This was it. All or nothing. It was beans or tuna, but either way it was time for supper and sleep. His plan was to get after the boys in the morning. The woods were too thick to move through with any speed at nighttime. And he didn't want to spook the boys into moving any faster than they already were. He knew where they were. They were on the river. And even if they started off onshore again, Cal would see their raft moored to the bank. It was only a matter of time. And this time he'd have a plan in place to bring them peacefully in. He'd just talk to them, tell them they were good, drop his badge in the water, tell them—and himself—he wasn't sheriff anymore.

Cal positioned the rod, positioned the steel, and forcefully struck a spray of sparks that made Jacks lift his head from his paws. When the sparks died out, the tinder and tepee lay scattered on the ground. Cal dropped the rod and steel next to the pile. He thought about trying it one more time, but then again, he could do this all night, knocking over tinder piles.

He was about to stand up when a voice filled the darkness.

"You ain't gonna get it started like that," it said.

Cal spun so fast he fell back onto the twigs and tinder. His bruised tailbone shot pain through his spine. Jacks was on his feet, barking fiercely at a shadow standing several yards away in the moonlight. The man was tall. He held the reins of a horse.

"Who's there?" Cal said. On his feet, he reached for his pistol, then remembered he'd lost it. He couldn't find his flashlight, so he just balled up his fists, pathetic.

"It's just me." The figure took a few steps closer, which made Jacks bark even more. The figure stopped. Jacks wasn't a big dog, but he could still bark in a way that made a person think twice.

Something calmed in Cal's gut. He recognized the voice.

"Teddy? That you?" Cal reached down to calm his dog. He felt hackles raised on Jacks' back and smoothed them with his hand.

"It's me."

"How long you been standing there?" Cal felt his face flush with shame. He turned to his dog, doubting the faith he placed in the animal's eyes and ears. "Where were you on that one, buddy?" he whispered.

"I've come to turn myself in," Teddy said.

Cal remembered how he tried to arrest Teddy when he'd walked his horse up that creek bed. He felt embarrassed now, partly because he'd tried to do such a foolish thing, but mostly because it didn't work. There wasn't much in the world more pathetic than a sheriff who couldn't arrest a man.

"Well," said Cal. Jacks grumbled, still unsure of the man in the shadows. Cal rubbed the back of his neck, then said the thing he'd been thinking through since his swim in the rapids. "I ain't a sheriff anymore, Teddy, so that arrest doesn't count."

"Since when?"

"Since last night, and today mostly."

Teddy tied his horse to a tree limb and walked to where the other horse was tied. He ran his hand along the animal's neck.

"You brought my horse."

Cal felt suddenly like a boy waiting for praise from a father, or a good grade from a teacher. There was an authority about Teddy that made a person want to please him. Teddy should be sheriff. He knew the county. He was tough. People liked him. Cal could paint houses for a living. He'd be good at painting houses. Fill all the cracks, dream about Tiffany.

Teddy turned back toward the failed fire. "Thank you," he said.

Cal nodded.

"I'm sorry I walked off," Teddy said. "I mean it when I say that if I'm under arrest, you can arrest me."

"And I mean it when I say I'm not sheriff anymore." Jacks left Cal's side and crept up to sniff Teddy's boots. When Teddy reached down to pet him, Jacks wagged his tail.

"Well, you still got your badge on."

Cal looked down at his vest. The silver star held the moonlight in its crevices and crest. That star had become like a wallet or a watch. He could forget about its presence but felt unclothed without it. It made life different for a person, wearing such a thing. Cal reached up to pluck it off.

"How'd you get your dog?"

Cal fiddled with the pin clasp, but his hands were cold.

"He showed up last night." Cal spoke into the sheriff's star like a microphone, prying at it. "Found me washed up after I swam the rapids," he said.

"Swam the rapids?" asked Teddy, mirth in his voice.

Cal gave up on the star for the moment. He was hungry. He was dead tired. He could deal with only so much right now. "Yes, Teddy, after I was abandoned by my guide in this black woods— which I'm getting used to, by the way—I was clipped from that mare of yours by a pine tree, crushed my tailbone, lost my boot, got dragged along a river bottom, lost my gun, and been shot at by a boy. I been pretty busy, if you care to know!"

Teddy had been trying not to laugh, but at the mention of the boys, his head snapped up in the moonlight.

"You seen the boys?" he asked. There was that urgency in his voice again. "Where? When?"

"They're in the river. They built a raft. I almost had 'em."

"They shot at you? That was them? I heard the shot. I portaged at the islands."

"They didn't shoot at me, exactly. The Breadwin boy touched one off when I got too close." Cal looked at Teddy's dry clothes. "And that's some great portage by the way. It's a real treat to cross without a guide."

Teddy looked at the ground and rubbed his chin. "Sheriff, how long ago did those boys put in with the raft?"

"I don't know, Teddy."

"How long!"

"Couple hours, maybe? Sunset. Why?"

Ted moved immediately toward his horse.

"We've got to move," he said. "We can catch them by tomorrow if we move." Ted was lifting a foot into the stirrup when the sheriff stopped him.

"Teddy, I know you want to get after them. I do too. But racing off is not the way to do it."

Teddy pulled himself up into his saddle.

"Teddy, do not get all cowboy again! You chase them and they're going to run even faster. There's only one river. We know where they are."

Teddy ignored him and fastened something on his saddlebag, turned his horse to point downstream.

"Teddy! I will arrest you again if I have to!"

Jacks barked.

Ted moved the reins in his hands. "You don't understand, Sheriff."

"Yes I do. Everything in me wants them back too. But thrashing through the woods at night is only going to keep that from happening. I'm with you, Ted. I'm all in. But we gotta do this calm, and in daylight."

Teddy stopped his horse from moving side to side. "Sheriff, I hear you, and I thank you for it. But there are things you don't know about this river."

"There's a lot I don't know about this river."

"Sheriff, there are rapids."

"I swam the rapids."

Teddy shook his head and said, "What you swam ain't rapids, Sheriff."

"What do you mean?"

"How fast do you think the water's flowing?"

Cal opened his hands in frustration. He was at a loss.

"That's a real important question right now, Sheriff. How fast?"

Cal gave up. He'd have to get used to it when he quit police work, he reminded himself. "I don't know. Water's high. Maybe two, three miles per hour."

Teddy nodded. "Let's go with three to be safe."

"Ted, you gotta let me know what you're thinking."

"Less than one hundred miles north of here, the river drops through the Ironsford Gorge. I know a hundred miles sounds like a long ways off, but if they drift the whole time—"

"How bad's the gorge?" Cal asked. He knew it existed, but he'd never seen it. Most of the land belonged to the National Guard armory. They used it for training. Trespassing teenagers used it for beer parties.

"It's a half mile of river canyon that drops a quarter mile in that same length. It's all ledge rock and falls. I don't think the boys know it's there. If they go in, they die."

Cal tapped his fingers together. "If they drift, we have about thirty hours."

Teddy nodded. "We gotta move."

Cal looked reluctantly at his mare. He cringed to think of placing his tailbone back in that saddle, his socked foot in the stirrup. The horse eyed him in the moonlight, hateful.

"We'll be moving slower than they will at first," said Teddy, "but we can make up time in the daylight. We don't stop."

Cal stepped over his attempted fire. He was thankful, at least, to leave that failure behind. "Lead on," he said.

TWELVE

FISH STIRRED TO THE SOUND OF BIRDS. THE FIRST THING HE SAW when he opened his eyes was the limb of a birch tree, moving overhead through a purple sky. In its branches, finches and chickadees preened their feathers and flitted and sang. Fish blinked and took a deep breath and smelled river, and then heard it lapping against the logs of the raft. He sat up from the wet pile of rope where he'd slept. He was chilled, damp.

"Hey," whispered Bread.

Bread sat cross-legged near the edge of the raft, just aft of the wicker railing. He was turning something small and metallic over in his hands, looking out at the riverbank where the white trunks of birch trees reached over the water from hedges of cedar. River grass and cattails drifted past. The river was narrow here, maybe thirty yards at its widest. Fish closed his eyes and stretched his arms overhead, wrapped his flannel more tightly around himself, and walked tentatively to where Bread sat. Fish bounced his weight on the edge of the raft once or twice. It was a stable craft.

"I'm surprised the raft didn't get hung up during the night," Fish said.

"It did," said Bread. "I pushed us off a sandbar a while ago."

Fish noticed his friend's jeans were wet up to the hips.

"Why didn't you wake me up? I would have helped."

"You were snoring," Bread said, and tried to smile. His face looked pale beneath his matted hair. Fish squatted down next to him.

"Bread?" he asked. "You slept at all?"

"A little," he said, and he fidgeted a bit, opened his hand to look in it, and closed it again.

"We're out of food, I guess," said Fish, trying to see if he could cheer him. "We're poachers now." Maybe it was the quiet of the woods, the cold air and dark cedars, but Fish felt something too, some kind of darkness. With the busyness of boatbuilding completed, they now just drifted through a silent forest. Fish looked up at the orange and purple sky. The sun would rise over the trees soon, and then Bread would perk up. Darkness would lift.

Bread forced a grin, swallowed it, and nodded. He bit his lip and looked out at the trees.

"Fish," he said, and then tears fell from his eyes as if they'd been dammed there. A whole river let loose. Bread wiped his face with his shirtsleeve, but more tears came. Fish leaned forward, then waited a moment, and he saw what Bread held in his hand. It was an empty brass shell casing, the Magnum cartridge that killed his father.

Bread's face twisted up, and his body shook when he tried to speak. His voice came out in a squeal. "My dad," he said, and shook some more. "I'm all alone."

Fish moved toward him and patted his back, but that felt wrong, so he put his arms around him instead. What else could he do? It was the first time he'd ever hugged his friend, but Bread leaned into it and accepted it, and Fish was glad he did it. Bread felt heavy in his arms, limp, and he sobbed and sobbed, and Fish felt his shirt get wet from it all. Fish remembered how he wept when he lost his dad. It didn't come right away. It waited. But when it came he had his mom, and she knew what to say, knew *something* to say. Fish didn't. So he just held his shuddering friend in a stiff embrace and looked out at the dark trees. The woods and river, so quiet a moment ago, were filled now with Bread's sobbing. It sounded eerie out here in the wild, louder, sadder somehow. It went on for a long time, and then it stopped. Bread wiped his mottled face.

"Sorry," he said.

Fish shook his head. He *knew*. Then he said what his grandpa had told him in the parking lot of that church. "Just because he's not with us doesn't mean you don't have him. You have a father."

Bread's eyes widened in pain, and Fish figured he'd said the wrong thing. In Bread's face flashed guilt and fear, even anger, all balled into one frown. The tears welled up, but this time Bread choked them back with great effort.

"I don't want him with me, Fish. I'm glad he's dead. I prayed he'd die." The tears broke loose again. "And I know what that means about me, how bad I am."

Fish sat quietly on the cedar logs, folded his legs like Bread's. He didn't know Bread's trouble. Another branch filled with noisy finches passed overhead. The sky turned from dark purple to blue.

Bread closed his eyes. "I used to sit out behind my house," he said, "and ask God to kill my dad. That's true about me, just so you know."

Fish sat entirely still.

"And when he didn't die, I dared God to kill me if that's what he'd rather do." Bread exhaled heavily through his nose. "You know what God did?"

Fish shook his head. Bread looked away from Fish and held up the bullet casing between his fingers. He turned over the blackened brass husk once or twice in the early-morning light, and then he flicked it into the river. It made the smallest noise when it broke the surface, tiny as a frog slipping off a rock.

"God didn't do nothing, Fish. *Nothing.*"

Fish did know what it felt like to think that. He remembered the silent ceiling of his bedroom that first winter, the way blankets hid him, silence answering silence. But he remembered, too, his mom's prayers, the strange comfort that came when she laid her hands on him, murmured bubblings of the spirit, deep calling to deep. He was always reluctant to accept it. It was a warmth from outside him. That's all Fish could call it if asked to describe it—in the middle of a cold, dark river, *warmth.* Fish would pray for Bread right now if he knew he could give him that feeling, but he didn't know how to, or if he should. Fish couldn't untangle this sort of knot. Instead, he was struck again by his friend's strength, and shame fell on him, and he suddenly needed to tell Bread the truth about his own dad. He wanted to confess he was a liar, that there was no father waiting at the armory, that they were drifting toward something that didn't exist, that they were more alone than Bread even knew. Tears rose in Fish's eyes. The raft turned in the current. All was a tangle of trees and cattails and wilderness. It all looked the same. Fish felt the rising terror of lost hope.

"Bread," he said quietly, "I'm sorry."

Bread shook his head.

This made Fish's chest tighten. He had to whisper as he spoke. "You don't understand."

Bread looked at him, stubbornness in his eyes. "Fish, if you didn't come back when you did, and done what you did—" He stopped. "It was different this time. Worse."

Fish's vision blurred.

"Bread. There's something you don't know. My dad—"

As he opened his mouth to confess, the shoreline broke open with noise. Branches cracked. River grass fell down in heaps. There was the sound of something yelling, or screaming. It filled the forest and sent Bread and Fish scrambling to their feet. The closest thing to it that Fish ever heard was the baying of a calf, but there weren't any calves in the woods, not this far out. The river grass thrashed again and moved in waves, along with that awful baying. It sounded tortured, whatever it was.

And then the boys saw it, saw *them*.

A black bear cub bounded onto the shoreline near the trees. It scrambled and fell and turned onto its back and kicked its legs at four attacking coyotes. The coyotes took turns lunging at the cub, distracting it, dividing its defenses.

Fish glanced over at Bread, who was staring openmouthed at the cruelty of the scene unfolding before them. The cub bayed and lashed out at one of the coyotes' snouts, gained its feet again, and bolted twenty yards farther downstream. The coyotes sprinted and caught it easily, nipping at the cub's haunches. The cub fell again and lifted its paws. The coyotes circled, and the cub twisted and lashed out as each one came in snapping and growling. The coyotes moved so quickly and with such precision, and the cub so comparatively slowly and with such panic, that it was clear who would eventually win.

Fish saw Bread rustling around in his pack. When Bread stood up, he was holding the revolver.

"Gimme the rest of them shells, Fish!"

Fish dug into the chest pocket of his flannel. He scooped out the four remaining cartridges and handed them to Bread.

"What are you gonna do?" Fish asked. He found himself short of breath. He knew things had to kill to eat. He and his grandfather killed to eat. But to watch it like this, coyotes taking out a cub with their teeth, was horrible to witness.

"I'm gonna shoot off them coyotes," said Bread, fitting the thick cartridges into the massive cylinder. His hands shook as he did it, but he managed to close the thing and cocked the hammer and took aim.

Fish, seeing it coming this time, covered his ears. Bread narrowed his eyes at the coyotes, and the barrel drifted a bit as it found a mark. Bread's hands tightened on the grip and his finger began to squeeze. Even with his ears covered, Fish could still hear the awful baying of the cub, but when he turned toward the revolver's point of aim, squinting in anticipation of the muzzle blast, the cedars behind the coyotes exploded, and it wasn't from a gunshot. Bread never fired. The trees shook to their tops. A strange blackness shot forward, quick as an owl's shadow. The coyote nearest the shadow yelped, cartwheeled, and landed, still as a stone, in the mud.

Fish took his hands from his ears. And then he heard it, and then he saw it, the massive shadow spiked with black hackles, raging through the underbrush, attacking the coyotes, moaning with wrath so great it shook the river and made Fish's knees go weak. It was a black bear, a very big one. The remaining coyotes recoiled in panic. The cub regained its footing and scrambled up the nearest birch tree. The cub reached a fork in the trunk and sat baying into the morning sky as its mother killed. One coyote spun just in time to see the sow come down on it from behind. It tried to retreat by jumping backward, but it was too late. The sow grabbed the coyote's hunched back with its forepaws and crushed it, followed up immediately with moaning jaws—silent for the split second they clamped the coyote's skull.

Bread lowered the revolver. An openmouthed grin formed on his face. Fish met his grin and nodded.

"Mama came" was all he could say. And it sounded so silly to say it, but he said it again as he watched, to affirm in some way the miracle. "That's mama bear!"

The cub bayed and the sow bellowed as the other two coyotes circled a moment more. They were overwhelmed by ferocity. They circled once or twice, defensively, no longer hungry. The bear turned toward whichever was closer, rocking back and forth in the cattails on her massive paws, popping her lips in menace.

The coyotes lowered their tails and fled inland. The cub bayed in its tree. The sow watched the coyotes run off, huffed, circled, and then answered her cub. Bread and Fish, caught up in it, cheered.

They hooted and howled, unable to resist celebrating such a triumph. And then they realized their mistake. When the boys made
their noise, the distracted sow spun and rose up on its haunches.
She popped her lips and exposed her gums and teeth. She was still
primed for battle. Fish realized then what she must have seen—a
raft covered in skulls and snouts and glaring eye sockets, yipping
like coyotes. The boys were silenced.

When she charged at them through the river grass, Fish fell
backward. The grass parted like fire. It was amazing the speed at
which so large an animal could move, and all Fish could do was
stare, raise his hands, fingers outstretched as if to hold the bear
at bay. The sow crashed into the river muck and sent waves toward the raft. Bread still held the pistol in his hand, seemed to remember it was there, and took aim. As Bread's knuckle tightened
on the trigger, Fish was met by an overwhelming certainty that
something irrevocable was about to be broken. Some set order,
some good plan, was about to shatter if Bread pulled that trigger.
Fish had recognized something in the bellow of that sow that he
couldn't put his finger on. It was the same noise he'd heard in his
dream, the sort of roar that sets the briars on fire.

"Stop!" yelled Fish, surprised to hear the roar in his own voice,
and more surprised by its effect.

Everything but the raft froze in place. The sow stopped in her
tracks, huffed through her nose, muddied ripples emanating from
her legs. Bread sat with the revolver's muzzle outstretched, shaking, knuckle tight. And then the sow reared up on her hind legs
and let out a baleful noise that rose from her bowels and made
Fish cover his ears. The bear had to be eight or nine feet tall. Her
muddy forepaws stirred the air. Her jowls shook as she moaned.
The sound was so similar to the sound in his dream that he feared
he might be dreaming now, that the cattails might erupt. When
the roar ceased, the forest grew silent. The sow watched the raft,
let herself down onto her forelegs. Fish heard the revolver rattling

against the wooden railing where Bread still steadied it. And with all held just so, the raft drifted away in the black water. The sow stood. The cub watched, blinked its shiny black eyes. And all remained that way for a long time, until the raft drifted downriver and the bear out of sight and the sky turned white overhead. For the next ten miles, still cold, still damp, Fish could feel the sow's bellow in his mind, in his bones. He thought of his own mother, her talk of visions and dreams. He felt as if the wilderness was trying to answer a question he couldn't remember asking.

"THERE. NOW YOU KNOW," MIRANDA SAID, THREADING THE BRUSH A final time through Tiffany's hair. Tiffany ran her hand experimentally through the tangles she'd been trying to tease out by the campfire. She laughed out loud when Miranda first produced a hairbrush from her pack. The woman was prepared. And Tiffany felt awkward at first when Miranda offered to brush it out for her. She sat rigidly on the tree stump near the fire, letting the older woman smooth and tame her hair. But it felt good, and Tiffany eventually relaxed into it, ridiculous as it was.

Tiffany remained quiet for a time. The sky was pink and blue and orange overhead, the first sign of true daylight. Soon it would be time to get back on the river. "Thank you," Tiffany said, nearly a whisper.

They stopped at this place an hour or so before first light. When Miranda had edged the canoe toward shore, tied off, and grabbed her pack, Tiffany was confused.

"What are we stopping for?" she asked.

"We need to wait for daylight before running the rapids."

"About that," Tiffany began, climbing out of the canoe—she'd just gotten the knack of paddling in flat water—but Miranda was already striding away in the darkness to a promontory downstream. Tiffany heard the river before she saw it, the rumble of water, a soft hum in the rocks she walked on. When she reached the shore-line, she reeled. There in the starlight churned a raging stretch of whitewater, shining its way downriver as far as she could see. She could make out an island in the river, whitewater in both chan-nels. Boulders poked through the froth in places, creating pillows of water and churning pools. Tiffany closed her eyes. She felt her throat become very dry.

"Couldn't we just go around it, you know, carry the canoe? What's the word?"

"Portage," Miranda said, her eyes not leaving the river.

"Yes," said Tiffany, forcing a smile in the darkness, "let's defi-nitely portage."

Miranda shook her head. "We could, but it will take us two or three hours to drag the gear and canoe. If we run the rapids, it will take us about two or three minutes. Besides, I ran this stretch when I was younger. It's not as bad as it looks."

"I think I'm for dragging," Tiffany said. "Dragging is good. I like dragging canoes."

Miranda touched Tiffany's elbow and smiled. "We'll use the time until daylight to warm up and eat. When the sun rises, if you still don't like the look of it, you can hike down and I'll run the canoe myself."

This denim-clad woman was filled with power. Tiffany felt both inspired and inadequate in her presence. Miranda was like a poem. The inertia, the turn, the confidence. Great poems inspired Tiffany to write as often as they discouraged her. Who could write like Dick-inson? Like Whitman? There was something supernatural about a great poem, and there was something supernatural about Miranda too. Tiffany once came across a word in her reading that described the sensation—*numinous*. It meant to be marked by the presence of divinity, to be more than met the eye, things and words and people indwelt with a larger heartbeat, a larger breath. Once again, all Tiffany felt she could do was totter along behind this woman.

They dropped their gear on a flattened grassy area near a large split stone with a cedar growing from its center. Tiffany watched as Miranda prepared to start a fire. Miranda made a small nest of cedar twigs and birch bark, collected some larger pieces of wood, then crouched with her flint and knife. Tiffany knelt to watch more closely.

"I've never seen it done like this," she said.

Miranda smiled and then paused, appearing to realize she was being asked for more than a mere demonstration. "So most people, if you hand them a rod and a knife, tend to go at it something like this." Miranda held the tip of the flint into the nest of fibers and feigned a stroke or two along the stationary flint with the spine of her knife blade. "The problem with that is you'll knock over your tinder in the process. You'll get sparks, but they'll scatter. They won't catch."

"So what's the right way?"

"Hold the blade real still near the tinder and pull the flint *away* from the pile—like this." Miranda made a fist around the handle of her knife, placed the flint beneath it, and scraped the flint sharply away from the tinder. The knife blade and tinder remained unmoved, and a shower of bright sparks accumulated in the same concentrated spot. They glowed for a moment, then went out.

"Neat, isn't it?" she said.

"Yes, it is."

"Here, you can try it."

Tiffany pushed back, shaking her head.

"There's nothing to it," Miranda said, placing the flint in her hand. "And it'd be good for you to practice in case we get separated out here."

The word *separated* tumbled along Tiffany's spine, and Tiffany couldn't tell if it was fear or excitement. After only a few hours in the canoe, she felt more competent. She laughed at herself—Tiffany, the frontier woman. She pictured herself in a jerkin and coon cap, the desirable mountain woman from a Zane Grey novel, seductive and capable of skinning her own deer. But the thing was, those women all had stables of cowboys pining after them, men they could send outside for more firewood when the weather turned cold. Tiffany had never seduced a man or skinned a deer. Not in real life.

Tiffany took a tentative practice stroke with the flint and was pleased to see a few sparks spray onto the dirt.

"A little more pressure," said Miranda. "And remember, the flint moves, not the knife."

Tiffany braced the knife over the tinder pile, wiggled her flint in beneath it, and then, increasing the pressure between blade and flint, drew the flint away from the tinder. An intense shower of sparks piled up on the birch bark. The glow worked its way along the papery tendrils.

"Okay, quickly now, but gently—give it some air."

"What?"

"Breathe on it."

Tiffany had seen this in movies, a cowboy blowing on a fire. So she knelt down and nudged air through her pursed lips, as if whispering to it. The glow became brighter and consumed more of the birch bark. She took in another breath and blew again, whispering louder, and the glow found a twig and leapt into flame with a nearly inaudible *whoof.*

Tiffany sat up, thrilled with herself. The smaller twigs caught and consumed themselves. Miranda showed her how to place larger and larger twigs onto the fire, then sticks, then branches from a white pine, which burned hot and noisily. The flames lit up the darkness, warmed it, tamed and softened it. Tiffany felt less forlorn.

"Nice fire," said Miranda.

"It is."

Miranda stepped away while Tiffany admired the flames. She looked at the knife and flint. "Would have been handy last summer," she said to herself. She'd never allowed herself a large campfire while homeless and squatting in cornfields. She boiled her eggs in creek water over a small camp stove until the stove ran out of gas. By that time, fall had come, and Burt Akinson came out because of the stolen chicken, and after that she started small fires with her Bic, and stole chickens from other farmers. But there was something beautiful, something numinous, about starting a fire with sparks. She could have used that, all of that.

"Say again?" said Miranda, rooting through a pack.

Tiffany shook her head.

After the fire had burned for some time, Miranda raked aside a few coals and set two opened cans of chicken soup on top of them. When the soup was hot, they ate it hungrily, blowing on each spoonful. They added more wood to the fire and watched the sky for any sign of daylight. It wasn't until Tiffany started toying a few knots from her tangled hair that Miranda disappeared into the darkness and reappeared with the brush.

"I thought we were roughing it," said Tiffany, reaching out for it.

Miranda drew it back to her chest. "May I?" she asked.

"Oh," Tiffany said, biting her lip for the briefest moment. "Okay."

Miranda smiled, sat next to her on the cedar log, and motioned for Tiffany to turn her back toward her. Tiffany complied. The brush pulled deftly along her temples and the back of her neck before working upward from the tips of her hair. It felt wonderful. Tiffany laughed out loud.

"I've never had my hair brushed before," she said.

The brushing stopped abruptly, then resumed. "What do you mean?" Miranda asked.

"I mean, no one's ever brushed my hair. I didn't even brush it myself until first grade. The school nurse taught me."

The brushing stopped again. Miranda's voice was cautious now. "Your mom never brushed it?"

Tiffany shook her head.

"Friends?"

No.

"Well," Miranda said, running her hands through it to gauge her progress. "It is lovely hair. It deserves to be brushed. It is worthy of brushing."

"Please don't say that."

"Say what?"

"What you just said."

Miranda paused again. Tiffany sat forward a bit. It was difficult being spoken to that way when she'd grown so accustomed to its absence. She had a grandmother who called her *pretty girl* a few times, but it always sounded as if she was speaking to a parrot. And there was that boy with cigarette breath who called her pretty once, but he said it so he could kiss her, and when he tried to do more than kiss her she kicked him in the stomach, and that was the last boyfriend she ever had. That was in seventh grade, after which the decent boys wouldn't talk to her, and none of the girls. She wanted to tell her mother about it, but the woman had a way of playing solitaire in front of the TV that walled the world off, and little girls too. Tiffany wasn't worth the time. She'd gotten used to it.

"I think the sun's coming up now, Miranda," said Tiffany in far too quiet a voice.

There were indeed the slightest purple hints of dawn behind the tops of the cedar trees. To Tiffany the cedars looked like torn construction paper pasted against the stars. She inhaled.

"The sun is not up yet," Miranda said in a voice that seemed both gentle and fierce. "And the sun is not allowed to come up until I finish brushing your hair. Okay?"

"Okay," whispered Tiffany.

After Miranda put out the fire they loaded the canoe. The sky was orange and red and blue now, and Tiffany's hair felt as light on her neck as the wisps of clouds overhead. Something had occurred in the darkness of the previous hour that didn't need to be spoken of in the light—like a gift or secret that can be received in silence. That's all she could call it. And she accepted the warmth of it, which both frightened and thrilled her. As she stowed her gear quietly in the canoe, a new thought came to mind. The problem with her poem wasn't that the coyote had no aim. The problem was that the coyote ran alone. Coyotes have packs. They have tribes. Her coyote needed a pack. Tiffany would write in a pack somehow. She tugged a tight knot into her gear rope and made note of the revision in her mind.

They hadn't worn the life vests before, but now Miranda insisted they put them on. Tiffany tugged the straps of hers more tightly around her torso, while Miranda secured a few lines that held a tarp over the gunwales, to keep out as much water as possible. Satisfied, she removed the mooring line she'd tied to a birch tree.

"You're sure you're up for this?" Miranda asked before completely loosening the knot.

Tiffany nodded and clutched her paddle across the gunwales. She trusted this woman, frightening as she was. Her time with Miranda had been a time of firsts. She looked downstream where the river bent sharply to the right, beyond which it would begin its run downhill to the whitewater. Her stomach filled with knots.

"It's really okay if you want to hike down, you know. I'm pretty sure I can make it without you. It doesn't mean anything if you change your mind."

Tiffany rapped her paddle against the gunwales. It made an impatient thump.

"Miranda," she said, "if you ask me again, I will push off with this paddle and run these rapids myself. Now let's go." Tiffany's voice was firmer than she meant it to be. Miranda smiled, let the mooring rope drag in the water, and pushed off into the current with a smooth, one-footed glide. She sat and pointed the canoe downstream.

"Now listen to my paddle calls," she said. "There will be times we need to be sideways in the current. Just let that happen. Don't try to straighten the boat."

"Okay," said Tiffany. The canoe picked up speed toward the bend in the river. The flat surface began to hint of the disturbance that lay ahead.

"And if I ask you to lean in a certain direction, do so without hesitation."

"Okay."

Tiffany could start to see around the bend. There was a definitive horizon to the river, a glassy ledge with whitewater licking up like flames beyond it. The flames grew larger. The cutbank drifted past, and the rapids opened up to full view. Tiffany forgot what it was she was supposed to do. The horizon of river drew them in and Tiffany could see over the edge of it now. Whitewater churned and dropped, leapt up in peaks, smashed against the black hulls of boulders. The canoe accelerated into a glassy depression and then lifted along a rise before dropping steeply into what could only be described as a hole in the river. Tiffany froze as the maw opened up to swallow them.

"Tiffany, paddle forward! *Now!*"

Miranda's voice got lost in the water as the bow of the canoe smashed downward and disappeared beneath the surface. It was like an ocean wave about to wash ashore. But it didn't wash ashore, it just churned in place, forever breaking over itself. Tiffany was hit in the chest and face, submerged in the frigid wall of water. The tarp did its job. The bow punched and dove and then resurfaced, shedding its water and riding high over the peak of the wave. Tiffany wiped the water from her eyes. Explosions of white rose to her right and left, behind and in front of her.

Somewhere within the roar of the water, Tiffany heard Miranda's voice calling commands, and she did her best to follow them. The voice went silent as a wave washed over it, and then it reemerged.

"Back on the right!" she yelled. "Back on the right!"

Tiffany, remembering the paddle in her hands, stuffed the blade into the whitewater. She braced it forward for a moment, as Miranda had taught her, and then lifted the blade and braced again. The effect wasn't immediate, but with Miranda drawstroking on the left, the bow began to point toward the right shoreline. The canoe weathered another wave, smaller than the first, but the boat's new angle made the impact seem far more precarious. Tiffany lifted her paddle, dug in, and braced it forward again. She looked downstream and saw the peak of a hidden boulder, revealing itself between surges of whitewater.

"Now forward, Tiffany! Forward! Make this boat move!"

Frightened, Tiffany reached and pulled with everything she had, leaning out with the paddle, grabbing a bladeful of water, and sitting up with it. The canoe slid across the current, avoided the boulder, bumped sideways down a shallow ledge of rock, and fell into another hole in the river.

"Lean downriver—*lean!* Lean left—*left!*"

Tiffany did as she was told just in time. When the canoe reached the bottom of the hole, it slammed into the wave face, and the canoe's momentum was stopped in its tracks. Tiffany felt the force of the hit in her knees and back.

The canoe stalled sideways in the bottom of the river hole, surfing in place. Tiffany crouched forward on her knees, trying to stay low and left. The current leading into the hole rushed beneath the right side of the canoe in streaks of black and green and white. A pile of froth rose to her left. The canoe shuddered and bucked as it tried to climb out of the hole. Water flooded across Tiffany's lap. The canoe wallowed.

"Brace downstream!"

Tiffany had no idea what that meant. She was busy clutching

the gunwales and trying not to lose her paddle. She glanced backward and saw Miranda leaning out over the downstream side, her paddle buried vertically in the white curl of the wave. Tiffany was struck by the sight of her, Miranda leaning out of the canoe in her wet denim, her sinewed arms buried in a pile of leaping water, wet hair wrapped around her face and neck, teeth bared. And then the realization struck her in that compressed and precarious moment: *Tiffany was in the boat too, alongside that fierce woman.* It was *her* clothing wet and plastered, her strong arms, her wet and worthy hair.

Tiffany released a battle cry, leaned out, and jammed her paddle down to shovel the whitewater. At first the blade just fluttered in the wave. But when she pressed it down deeper, as Miranda had done, her whole arm in the water, the blade seemed to catch against a firmer current that pulled downstream. Tiffany pushed her blade deeply into that hard water, pulled against it, and the canoe lifted and broke free of the hole.

The boat rose into the sun, and Tiffany unleashed another howl into the blue sky.

But the celebration was short-lived, because Miranda started cussing. Loudly. And it was bad cussing, too, the kind even Tiffany rarely let fly.

"Back left! Back on the left!" boomed Miranda.

The canoe felt much heavier and cumbersome now that it was half filled with water. It wasn't as responsive as before. Tiffany glanced downstream as she pulled back against her paddle. There was another drop ahead. And downstream of that, a massive boulder arched its back into the morning sunlight. The river formed a pillow of water against the rock, and then shattered down either side of it.

Tiffany cussed too.

"Back left! Back left!" Miranda hadn't stopped yelling.

Tiffany paddled with everything she had, but the sodden canoe wouldn't respond. They were headed right for the boulder, dead center, broadside. The canoe sped down the face of the wave toward the hissing pillow of water. For a split second, as they crashed into the spray, Tiffany felt as if the canoe might be buoyant enough to rise and spin off, but as they rose, the upstream gunwale slipped just beneath the surface, and instantly—Tiffany actually thought about this as it happened, how *instantly* the craft seemed swallowed— the canoe disappeared from beneath her. Tiffany's world became white. The froth rose to her neck. She saw the black gleam of a wet boulder, reached out for it, and then everything in her field of vision became tea-colored. Sound stopped. Water rushed into her throat and nose, pressed on her ears. She felt tangled in some- thing, the canoe or her paddle, and she kicked away from it. She felt herself being dragged along something hard and smooth. She closed her eyes and opened them. She saw darkness and light. Her outstretched arms raked glass-smooth river rock, pockets of gravel. And just when she began to be really afraid, she was carried up- ward, burst into air and light. She gasped, wiped her eyes, and found herself riding the peak of a high white wave. She held her breath as another came. All was tea again. She held her breath. And then all was light. The cycle repeated until the river calmed and Tiffany drifted along gentle black waves washing toward a shoreline.

She pulled herself to her knees in the gravel, took two deep breaths, and blinked. She flexed her hands, her toes. She was okay. She made it. She was alive.

"Tiffany!"

Tiffany turned to see Miranda floating along downstream of the boulder. Beyond her the overturned canoe bobbed heavily in the water. Tiffany saw a paddle near the far shore.

"Are you okay?" Tiffany called, shielding her eyes from the glare on the water.

Miranda coughed as she swam. Tiffany hauled her in. Miranda

collapsed on her back in the shallow water, winced. The two women just breathed for a moment. They made it. The angle of the sun made the water they sat in a pool of light.

Tiffany couldn't remain quiet any longer. "I've never experienced anything like that," she exclaimed. "When that boat went under? *Whoosh!* I mean—the power of it!" Part of her felt like doing it again. Everything seemed to be so bright right now. The trees were extra golden and green. The river shone like the sun itself, the rapids spraying sparkles of fire and ice. The air smelled so good she could taste it. She could taste rocks and river. She could feel her heart in her chest, the blood in her veins. She took a deep breath and held it in so the oxygen could spin around in her body awhile. "And you," she said, "you were amazing out there! I didn't know church girls could cuss like that!"

A red grin crept onto Miranda's face as she tried to push herself up. She winced and clasped her wrist to her stomach. "I'm a Pentecostal," she said. "People say we're enthusiastic."

Just then the canoe floated past their little pool of light, its bulbous hull floating belly-up in the water. Like an exhausted carp, it nosed onto a rock and lay there. Laughter rose into Miranda's eyes and mouth. She bowled over and cackled. Tiffany laughed too. It felt wonderful to laugh. It gave the adrenaline a place to go. Tiffany remembered what Burt had said about Pentecostals, but the word seemed less frightening out here, amid the roar of the river, the tall cedars, the expanse of things.

Tiffany watched Miranda wipe her eyes and lift her face to the sunlight. She was praying, Tiffany knew, speaking a silent poem to it all. After a time, a lone cloud passed. Miranda cradled her wrist against her stomach and frowned downriver, and Tiffany knew the woman was thinking about her son again.

THIRTEEN

CAL'S SORE TAILBONE FORCED HIM TO STAND MORE HEAVILY IN the stirrups, which helped him move as one with the horse rather than as an accessory to it. In all, he began to feel less like a saddlebag, physically at least. They had moved slowly during the night, and Teddy had been good enough to take the reins of Cal's horse and lead it directly behind his own through the dark. For the first several hours, Cal rode in a ducked position and felt the branches brush over his back. It made him feel like a child being led on a pony ride, but the maintenance of his tailbone mattered much more than his pride at the moment. One more fall on that thing and he would be thoroughly out of commission. Eventually—lost in the darkness and branches and sound of hooves—Cal closed his eyes and dozed.

When dawn arrived, the air was cool and the sky vivid. Cal opened his eyes to horsehide, and lifted them toward orange spires shooting up and breaking apart the purple sky. To his left, the river ran like a sliver of light through the trees. The conifers awoke and filled the forest with musk. Cal smacked his lips and wanted water. He had horsehair on his tongue. Teddy rode ahead of him, still holding the reins.

"How long was I sleeping?" Cal asked, slightly embarrassed. He reached for his canteen.

"Didn't know you were" came the reply. Ted turned and smiled, bags under his red eyes, and tossed Cal's reins back to him. As the morning turned to day, they were able to spur the horses into a canter from time to time. When the shoreline grew too thick, they followed deer trails and creek beds. They weaved between white pines. Cal noticed the landscape begin to change. The thick underbrush and river marshes opened into meadows that grew wider and larger, the edges bordered with wild blueberries and poplar slashings.

Jacks jogged wildly along with the horses, bolting now and again after a squirrel or rabbit. The dog had refused to leave his toy cat behind, so Cal stuffed it into his saddlebag so Jacks could run and breathe without his mouth stuffed. He smiled at the thought, and then smiled at his smiling. Cal hated to admit it, but he was beginning to enjoy being out in this forest, up here in the Northwoods, in the Land of the Beaver. It smelled good. It filled the lungs with pine and river. The forest itself seemed to breathe. Cal exhaled. He still had to concentrate on riding, but he could see himself getting into this woodsman's life, maybe learning to hunt with a bow, one of those recurve jobs with cedar arrows and feathers hanging from the quiver. He could wear moccasins, carry a bowie knife. He shook his head. That was too much. But there was grace out here, a mercy of sorts. Being led on the horse made him feel like a child, but being led by Teddy allowed him to accept it in some new way. The whole forest seemed to be giving Cal a nod, telling him he was *okay,* where he was, as he was, a sheriff without a gun, missing a boot. It was enough. It was plenty.

The sun rose high overhead, and the day grew warm. They emerged from beneath a canopy of hemlock into a sun-filled meadow bordered by immature hardwoods. Teddy drew his horse to a slow walk. It shivered its hide at a mosquito, switched its tail.

"You hungry?" Teddy asked, stepping down from his horse in one smooth movement.

"I could eat." Cal closed his eyes and tilted his head up at the sun. After missing last night's supper, now even cold tuna sounded good. Cal let himself down from his horse, yanked his boot from the stirrup.

"We're making good time," said Ted, loosening his saddlebags.

"How close are we to the gorge?"

"We've covered maybe thirty miles. I figure we can make another forty before nightfall. More if we push 'em," he said, nodding to the horses. "If we have to." Ted reached into the saddlebag and pulled out a map. Cal looked around the meadow. He noticed a few bald spots in the grass, weathered slabs of granite emerging from the earth and soaking up the sun. The closest slab was twenty feet wide, its cracks sprouting lichen and moss. An ancient-looking apple tree grew near its edge. Teddy crouched on the rock and unfolded the map. Cal joined him, wondered at the apple tree, how it got there. He walked to it and ran his hand against its scaly trunk.

"That radio in your saddlebag been making any noise, Teddy?" Cal asked. During the ride, Cal had spent about five minutes second-guessing his decision to follow the older man again. Maybe it would have been better to hustle back to town, call in reinforcements to meet at the gorge. But the boys were so close, and Teddy seemed confident they could beat them to the falls. And besides, surely the boys would see the gorge, or hear it, and get out of the river. Cal was committed to Teddy's course.

Teddy shook his head. "We're too far from town." He pointed to a place on the map where the river bent its way through a blank green patch encompassing half the county. "By my reckoning, we're within a mile of this bend." He slid his finger north along the river for an inch or two. It wound to the northwest before spilling into the plains and lakes of Ironsford, where the map turned tan. "The gorge is here, before the town." Teddy stared at the map, then lifted his hand to his face and rubbed his eyes.

"You all right, Teddy?"

"I'm fine. Need some coffee is all."

"You sleep since we left town?"

"No."

Cal bit his tongue and shook his head. He admired the man. Teddy had the kind of grit Cal knew he did not possess, which was why Cal also knew he needed to seriously rethink this sheriff business. Maybe growing vegetables was more his speed. Corn farming, maybe. He pictured himself on a tractor, digging furrows through a field. Back and forth, the dirt overturned, the world turning around. Cal liked that image of himself riding a tractor. It felt peaceful like the forest felt peaceful. Lonely and quiet and good-smelling.

"If we keep at it, we should make the gorge a little before the boys do." Teddy tapped his finger on a line in the map, nodded to himself as if making a decision. "Or," he said.

"Or what?"

"I've been thinking how if we left the river entirely, we could travel along an old logging road that runs through here."

Cal studied the map.

"There's no road there."

"It's there. I drove skidder for the guy who logged it. About eight or nine years ago, but it's there, and it's long and it's straight."

"If we leave the river, we also leave our chance of spotting the boys."

"We've been weaving in and out pretty regularly. There's a good chance we'd miss them anyway, if we haven't already. We know where they're headed, and if we take the logging cut, we can make a beeline for about twenty miles, then cut back in. That should do it."

"You're the boss, Teddy."

Teddy looked at him. There was immense exhaustion in the older man's eyes, but there was fire there too. The old rancher had reserves. Cal knew that Teddy had served in Korea but used to have a hard time picturing it. He could see it now, though—a younger Ted with those same gray-blue eyes, humping a pack along some steep Korean hillside, a pouch of Red Man tucked in his helmet band, pure severity.

Ted looked back at the map.

"I'm lost out here, Ted. I mean it. Just tell me what to do."

Ted nodded, softened a moment. "You could get us a fire going," he said quietly. "I'm going to water the horses. I'll get some water for coffee too." Ted rubbed his eyes again.

Cal swallowed at the prospect of having to try to make a fire again. "Teddy, how about you hang back and make the fire and rest up. I don't mind walking the horses down and fetching water."

Teddy was already on his feet, however, unbuckling packs from the horses. "I'll water 'em," he said, dropping a heavy saddlebag onto the bedrock. "You don't know how much to let them drink."

Cal nodded, pushed out his lip, feigned confidence. The slab of bedrock nearest the apple tree was littered with dry sticks of various sizes. The lichen and moss, some of which looked dead and dry, seemed like it would make decent tinder.

"No problem," he lied.

While Teddy continued to unburden the horses, Cal set to work assembling a small tepee of twigs and sticks atop a nest of moss and lichen. He then rummaged in his pack for the flint and striker. He knew right where they were, but didn't want to take them out. He felt self-conscious about using them in front of Teddy.

"Need a hand?" Teddy stood behind him, holding the reins of the horses in one hand and a tin pot in the other.

"Nope. Got it," said Cal. He pulled the flint and striker from the bag and gave them a happy practice spark in the air. "Got my old flint here," Cal said, standing up. "I'll have it going."

Ted looked at the tepee and frowned. "Hang on," he said, and started to move toward the tinder and saddlebags. Cal winced at the thought that Ted found fault with his tinder pile, and was going to fix it for him like a father would fix a boy's necktie. But Cal surprised himself and accepted the idea. He was simply less bothered out here about who he really was. There was a freedom in that sort of acceptance he'd never really known. But Teddy stopped short of the tinder pile and stooped to retrieve something from his own kit.

"Here," he said. "Might as well use these up."

He tossed a small box of matches to Cal. Mercy spilled through Cal's body. He pocketed the flint and shook the box. The matches rattled happily.

"Why not?" Cal said as nonchalantly as he could. "Might as well."

Cal watched Ted lead the horses through the meadow. Jacks bounded along beside them. In the distance, the river sparkled through a line of trees, and Teddy became a dark and wavering silhouette. The old man walked lightly out there in the high grass. The oddest thing about Teddy, Cal thought, was the way he seemed somehow *filled* by all of this. If it wasn't his own grandson they were searching for, Cal could almost be convinced that Teddy was enjoying himself amid the sleeplessness and hard riding. Teddy wasn't known for being overly cheerful, and Cal had seen the flash-pan of anger or frustration ignite the man. But out here he seemed eager, awakened. The old man had a vigor in his step Cal had never seen.

Cal crouched by the tinder pile and struck a match. The lichen caught easily. He smiled as the yellow flame licked its way up the twigs and caught hold of the larger sticks. By the time Teddy returned, Cal had managed to make a nice bed of coals. The horses stood under the shade of the apple tree and nipped at the grass where Teddy spilled a few handfuls of oats from a pouch. Jacks rested his head on Cal's lap while Cal raked the dog's neck. They all sat in silence, watching the coffee percolate alongside two opened cans of beans. The smell of food and woodsmoke filled the air. The plan was to leave after breakfast. The logging road would easily make up lost time.

"Ted?" Cal asked. "You like farming?"

Ted looked at him, lifted an eyebrow.

"It seems like a nice life," Cal said. "Seems peaceful."

Ted looked back at the coals. A thoughtful frown grew on his face.

"It's peaceful," he said.

Cal nodded, frowned at the fire himself. He pictured the tractor and fields again. No more people problems. No more radio calls. Just him and his dog and a list of chores. And a wife, if she'd have him.

Ted leaned back on his saddlebag and sighed. "I've had my share of peace. Damn near a lifetime of peace." Cal nodded in agreement, but then noticed something about the way Ted spoke the word *peace,* like it was a hair he spat from his mouth.

"You can get tangled in that much peace. Get caught up in keeping it going. And then one day you realize peace and quiet was never what you wanted." Ted glanced at him, grinned, and turned back to the coals. "No, I don't like farming. I never did. It bores the living hell out of me."

Cal thought of his own work, his attempt to find himself in it, and how Houston had worn him so thin, just keeping on where his heart never was.

"But what did you want to do instead of farm?" Cal ventured. If the man had wisdom on how to live, or how not to, Cal would take it. He was lost in the woods.

Teddy leaned toward the coffee pot, pulled on a leather glove, and poured two cups. He handed one to Cal and leaned back on his saddlebag.

"When I was just out of high school, I worked for cash at a feed mill. I helped Dad on the farm." Teddy sipped his coffee and nodded appreciatively. "When I turned nineteen, I took out a loan for nineteen hundred and seventy-eight dollars, plus tax, and bought a brand-new, chariot-red Oldsmobile 88 Rocket." Ted blew on his coffee. "My old man was hot when I drove it up the driveway. Loans were for tractors and land, he said, not race coupes. My dad and I already knew we didn't see eye to eye. I had slicked hair and a leather jacket back then like all the other idiots."

Cal tried to not spit his coffee back in his cup. "You were a greaser, Ted?"

Ted smiled. "No, I wasn't no damn greaser. I was just a kid. And I had a *car*." He said the word in so different a way than he said the word *peace,* like it was rich food, dark coffee. "Gas was cheap. The car was fast. I can still feel that 88's pedals, smell the motor, feel the way it crouched through corners. Sometimes I'd go driving alone, but most nights I'd have Becky with me—that's Fischer's grandma." Teddy's eyes narrowed in a mischievous grin. "She had long hair then too. This one night Becky and me got some bottles of beer and had it in our heads to drive to Chicago. She had her bare legs draped out that window, sipping beer, the big moon lit up over the coast of Lake Michigan. We didn't stop until Navy Pier, and I remember sitting on that 88's hot hood, watching stars drop in the water, Becky dancing on the beach, spinning and spinning. I can still see her, hear her even, howling at all them buildings and stars with her hair going round. Prettiest woman I ever seen in my life."

Teddy took another swig of his coffee.

"A month or two later I was in Korea. After my tour, I came back to a baby girl, and my father's loans, tractors and land, calving seasons. You asked what I wanted to do instead of farming." He looked at Cal and then back at the coals. They glowed white. "That night I roared down the lake coast in too fast a car with too beautiful a woman. I can't name it and ain't gonna try. I suppose there was something of it in war too. All I've ever wanted was to do that night again and again. Beats the hell out of peace and quiet."

Cal sat for a moment. "Can I ask you one more thing?"

Teddy looked at him.

"How'd you keep going?"

"Same as anybody else," Teddy said. "I had a wife and daughter. People needed me." He looked into his cup. "So you make a decision to give things up instead of burning the whole thing down. You just don't light the match. You don't make life even worse. You suffer when you need to. Sometimes that's as good as it gets."

Cal watched the man drink the rest of his cup in silence. Ted looked up at the sun, tucked a shred of tobacco into his cheek, and tossed the dregs of his coffee on the hissing coals. He hesitated a moment, spat, then stood and grabbed his kit and hefted it toward his horse.

"That Breadwin boy," he said, "he's a good boy. I should have killed his old man myself."

THE BOYS HAD BEEN DRIFTING FOR A FISH ALL DAY, HUNGRY, WAIT-ing, poling the raft into the center of the stream whenever it drifted too close to the bank. They stopped once to dig worms from the riverbank. They pinched lead sinkers onto the lines with their teeth to keep the worms on the bottom. The hooks kept snagging on rocks and sunk logs, so the boys attached red-and-white bobbers the size of nickels to the lines. Ever hopeful, they watched the bobbers trail in their wake. They even started a small fire atop their rock oven and dipped the kettle full of river water to set it boiling. Around noon, Fish caught a floating pine branch, and then both boys turned their attention to other things—the emptiness in their stomachs, an eagle overhead, Ninja Turtles, a distant bank of dark clouds to the north. They let the fire die out and the smell of woodsmoke filled the air. Hunger smells like woodsmoke, thought Fish, turning to lie flat on his belly and twirling Michelangelo's nunchucks in the river water.

Then one of the rods twitched, and Bread scrambled to it, and Fish knelt at the edge of the raft and told him, "Easy, easy."

The line became taut and lifted from the water. Bread set the hook. "We got one!" he cried. "Here it comes!"

Fish put his arms through the sleeves of his flannel and held the tails of it in his fists. He reached his net down into the tea-colored water. He saw something flash that looked like the belly of a fish, something orange or yellow or white. And then he saw the fish's dark back as it rolled into the cradle. He sprung his trap and grasped the fish as tightly as he could. He felt something alive in the flannel, something kicking and bony, and he clutched it against his shoulder and rolled onto the deck.

He and Bread crouched near the balled shirt, instinctively corralling their catch so it wouldn't flop back into the river. Both boys grinned. Fish, panting, untangled himself from the line that had wrapped around his back.

"Got him." He smiled. The wilderness was blessing their exile. First the sow bear. And now a fish.

Bread lifted the corner of the flannel. Fish watched expectantly, wiped his hands on his jeans.

"What is it, a pike?" Fish asked, and then saw Bread's face contort into a frown. He lowered his expectations. "A carp?" he asked. Bread lifted the flannel completely away, and Fish frowned too. The thing lay on its back, its belly sunward—hard-shelled and glistening—four webbed feet pawing furiously at the air.

"It's a turtle," said Bread, and picked it up by its shell. Fish noticed the bright markings on its legs. It was large enough that Bread had to use both hands to grasp the girth of its shell.

"It's a painter," Bread said, worry in his voice, holding it up at eye level.

Fish had caught painter turtles in the past when fishing—they liked worms too—and he always felt awful when he caught one. Pike and carp didn't seem to have feelings like turtles. Turtles had hearts. Some had angry hearts. Some were cheerful. Painters were the cheerful ones, the friend turtles.

Bread grasped the hook in his fingers. The turtle recoiled and pulled its head in, but it hadn't been hooked deeply at all, so Bread was able to wiggle the hook free of the turtle's beak. Bread apologized to the turtle while he did it, and put it down on the flannel again, on its back. It pawed the air, trying to swim down into the mud and away from this new and awful predicament.

"So what do we do with it?" Bread asked.

Fish shrugged. The smell of woodsmoke lifted from the ashes and hit his stomach. The water in the kettle was probably still pretty hot. It wouldn't take much to bring it to a boil again. He knew people ate snapping turtles sometimes, although he'd never done it, or seen it done.

"I suppose we eat it," said Fish. "Don't we have to?"

Bread shrugged, grave doubt in his eyes. He lifted his hand to his face and rubbed his mouth, as if there were stubble there to think about. He looked at Fish. "I guess so," he said.

Fish removed the barlow knife from his jeans and unfolded the blade. He rubbed his thumb across the edge to test the sharpness, frowned at the turtle.

"How do you cut into these things?" Fish asked, and Bread just shook his head, tight-lipped.

Fish couldn't fight away the thought of the bear cub, the way it bayed and bayed, the way those coyotes snapped at it. This world was all wrong, the way everything had to eat each other. He looked at Bread, who seemed a bit ashen-faced. The world was not pure blessing. There was a sense of betrayal in it all too. Fish looked up at the sky, downriver. The dark clouds seemed much closer now. There was menace in them, rising up in front of that blue sky. The knot in Fish's stomach turned to hunger again. Fish looked back at the turtle. If it was a snapper instead of a painter, this would be easier.

Fish reached forward with the knife, pinned the turtle on its back, and placed the well-honed blade against the turtle's belly shell. He gave it an exploratory tap. The shell felt leathery beneath the hardness of the steel, and Fish knew it would be easy enough to plunge the knife in. Bread shifted where he sat. Woodsmoke filled the air with emptiness. Fish tightened his grip on the knife, took in a deep breath—and then folded it closed and put it in his pocket.

"I ain't doing it," he said.

Bread coughed. "Yeah, me neither," he said, more quickly than he probably intended. There was relief on his face.

Fish flipped the turtle onto its belly and sat back in the sunshine. He'd rather stay hungry, he decided. The turtle sat with its legs drawn inside itself, unsure if the ordeal was over.

"Go on, turtle," said Fish, disappointment in his voice. "We ain't gonna eat you. We ain't gonna eat nothing."

Fish saw disappointment in Bread's eyes, too. Bread reached back onto the deck of the raft, fetched his Ninja Turtle. He held Donatello by the legs and poked his face down near the painter's.

"Hey turtle turtle, you got a name?" He knocked gently on the turtle's shell with Donatello's plastic bō staff. The painter didn't respond. "My name's Donatello. You hungry too?"

Fish felt confused. He was ashamed of himself for not being able to kill the turtle and eat it, but he was proud for bearing the hunger rather than giving in to it. They'd find another way to eat.

"You want to eat some worms, turtle turtle?" asked Donatello.

Bread looked at Fish, and Fish looked at Bread. Fish knew what he was thinking. Both boys looked at the empty bean tin that still held half a dozen night crawlers. The worms were all over six inches long, real whoppers, as Bread called them.

Fish sighed. Beaver life was hard.

"Well, I ain't eating them raw," said Fish, and Bread agreed to stoke the fire.

Ten minutes later, the boys sat over the boiling kettle of water in the galley. The worms had died instantly, and now roiled around in the bubbles like pale white noodles.

"Wish we had some salt," said Bread, apprehension in his eyes.

Fish's stomach growled angrily at the sight of the boiling worms.

"I'm just worried about the flavor is all," said Bread. "I mean, I'm gonna eat 'em, but I just don't know about the flavor." Bread went on and on as the worms continued to stew.

The soup wasn't promising. The river water was tannin-stained, and the worms were bloated. The whole brew smelled like pee and river bottom. It needed *something*. Bread turned to rummage through his pack, drew out a white and green pouch twisted up in his fist. He unfurled it. The pouch had bright red letters—*Red Man. America's Best Chew.*

"What do you think if we add some of this?" Bread asked, teasing open the pouch with his thumbs. Fish looked on uncertainly. He'd forgotten about the tobacco. The wad he'd placed in the chest pocket of his flannel had grown sticky and lint-covered. He'd dropped it in the river.

"Your grandpa eats this stuff," Bread proclaimed, and then frowned as he lifted a pinch of it out of the bag with his fingers. "It must taste all right." Bread dropped the shreds of black tobacco back into the pouch. He lifted the bag to his nose and smelled it. He tasted the tips of his fingers. His face brightened.

"Smells like raisins," he said.

He passed the pouch to Fish, who smelled it. It did smell like raisins. He lifted a small piece of the tobacco to his lips, touched it with his tongue. It was sweet and then spicy in a way he couldn't describe. He looked back at the soup they had made. A waft of steam rose from the pot and hit him in the face.

"Dump it in," said Fish, handing it back, and Bread complied.

The boys watched the pot for another minute, stirred it with a cattail cane. While the water continued to simmer, Bread checked on the painter turtle. It remained where they'd left it, out in the sunlight near Donatello. Bread had placed half a night crawler near the opening of its shell to try to coax it out.

Satisfied that the tobacco had stewed enough, Fish removed the kettle from the coals and brought it out onto the deck of the raft. The water had turned from yellow to dark brown. The worms, too, had soaked in the darker color and looked much more wholesome for doing so. The raisin smell of tobacco came up from the steam, which was promising. Fish got two spoons from a poacher's mess kit. The boys settled themselves on their knees near the pot. The turtle stayed in its shell.

"Well," Fish said, "dig in."

Fish took the first taste, slurping a spoonful of broth into his mouth. The heat of it was enough to make his stomach turn over, but not in an altogether bad way. The first thing Fish tasted was sugar, from the tobacco, no doubt, followed by a deep earthiness, not unlike the earthiness in a garden carrot or a pickled beet. After the sweetness and earthiness came the odd, spicy sensation. It filled Fish's mouth and throat. He could feel it in his stomach. Its warmth was different from the heat of the broth.

Bread slurped in a spoonful too. The boys watched each other. Downstream, the bank of dark clouds covered the sun. Rain would come soon. But they could ignore that because they had food, and they didn't kill a painter to get it. They were making it in the wild, on their own terms.

"Not bad!" Bread exclaimed, and dipped two more spoonfuls into his mouth. "Red Man stew!"

Fish joined him, spooning the broth greedily into his mouth. It felt so wonderful to have something in his stomach. He wiped juice from his chin and laughed. "Red *worm* stew!" he said proudly.

In a few minutes, the boys became bolder and started cutting into pieces of the worms and tobacco. The warmth radiated from Fish's belly. He felt as if he were bursting with it. He felt the odd spiciness of the tobacco in his neck and face. He laughed as he spooned a worm into his mouth, slurping it noisily. His face felt numb. Why did his face feel numb? And his fingertips?

He looked at Bread, whose eyes seemed a bit glassy. The sensation of numbness reminded Fish of the time he and his grandfather varnished a gun cabinet in the corner of the basement. The fumes made them dizzy, and they had to step outside until the dizziness left.

And now the warmth in Fish's stomach turned hot, uncomfortable, and he wanted it out of there.

"Hey turtle turtle," Bread said, talking to the painter and giggling with his spoon in his hand.

"Bread, I don't feel good," Fish said, and put his spoon down and moved instinctively toward the side of the raft. He was so lightheaded he needed to place a hand on the deck to steady himself. He crawled to the edge. Overhead, the sky had turned a deep gray. Fish felt a prick of rain on his neck.

Bread's giggling stopped. "Fish?" he asked. There was uncertainty in Bread's voice. Something bad was happening in his stomach too.

A stiff breeze rose up and rippled the water, spun the raft. The heat in Fish's stomach moved higher, into his throat, until he couldn't hold it any longer. His vomit splashed in the river. He heaved until his stomach was empty, and when he heard Bread being sick off the other side of the raft, he got sick some more himself.

Fish stared at his reflection in the rippled water as the first crack of lightning ripped overhead. Fat raindrops began to fall. Fish washed his face with a handful of river water, rinsed his mouth, and spat. Bread lay with his head draped over the far side of the raft. The rain darkened the cedar logs and made the boys' shirts stick to their backs. They were too sick to pitch the tarp. The coals in the galley hissed. Fish heard Bread groan through the heavy patter of rain and thought again of that baying bear cub. Fish thought of his mom, too, making him a sandwich in the kitchen. He missed her fiercely. Fear came. He felt something awfully bad was coming. Where was he? No one knew where he was.

On the sodden deck, the painter turtle emerged from its shell just long enough to paddle toward the edge of the raft. It dropped into the water like a gently kicked stone, wildness and loneliness in the ripple it left. Fish crouched in the raindrops and shivered. He knew it somehow—things were about to get worse.

FOURTEEN

TIFFANY PADDLED THE CANOE BY HERSELF NOW. SHE PAUSED and let it glide through the black water for a stroke as she zipped the collar of her rain jacket to her chin. It was midday, but the sun had disappeared behind a thick bank of slate-colored clouds. A cool breeze came from the north, where the clouds looked darkest. Tiffany heard thunder downriver.

"How am I doing?" she asked.

Miranda smiled from where she reclined against the bow, facing backward. "You're an old salt," she said.

Tiffany didn't feel like an old salt, but after the rapids, this smooth water winding through cedar forest and cattails was cake. Miranda's wrist was in bad shape. It had swollen as thick as her forearm. She winced if she tried to make a fist. When it first became clear it would be up to Tiffany to paddle them out, she wondered aloud if they should portage back upstream instead. She was pretty confident she could drag the canoe above the rapids by herself if it was emptied of gear. Miranda shook her head at the idea, said the easiest way was to go downstream to Ironsford, even though it was farther away. Tiffany hesitated. She recalled a line from Robert Frost, *the best way out is always through.* True enough, but there was a lot of talk about madness in that poem too. Tiffany relented. They'd been back in the canoe for five or six hours now.

Tiffany put her blade in the water and pulled. She was learning to feather it, keep it in the river, which was a whole lot better than constantly switching sides and dripping water across all of the gear. They were wet enough from the rapids.

"How's your wrist?" Tiffany asked.

Miranda had elevated her arm on the gunwale and wrapped her wrist in a wet handkerchief. Tiffany didn't know how often she should ask about it. Miranda lifted the handkerchief and peeked at her wrist. It was bruising. She tested her fingers, made a loose claw of a fist. "The same," she said. She dipped the handkerchief in the water, squeezed out the excess, and reapplied the cold compress.

"Do you want to stop awhile?" Tiffany's back was fatigued from paddling and sitting. Her clothes were still very damp from their swim. During the past half hour, she'd daydreamed about standing next to a warm fire with a warm tin of food to eat, some coffee perhaps. And she wanted Miranda to stop and eat too. Her face had grown pale. She had darkening circles beneath her eyes, the fire in them smothered by restlessness.

Miranda sat up slowly, held her wrist in her lap. She looked downstream, at the river and then up at the sky. The headwind from the north had picked up, but it wasn't yet strong enough to make the paddling impossible.

"I hate to lose time," Miranda said, turning back toward Tiffany. "It looks like we'll run into that storm within an hour. We could take out then."

Tiffany nodded and repositioned herself on the stern seat. She found that by shifting her weight every so often, she could convince her legs they weren't completely numb.

"Sure," she said, though she wasn't, "but maybe—"

Miranda waited for the rest of the sentence. "Maybe what?" she asked, a bit too tersely.

Tiffany shook her head. She eyed the storm clouds. They'd been rising into the sky pretty steadily. She didn't make a habit of watching storms roll in, but her gut told her the storm would be upon them soon. She wondered about Miranda's judgment. The woman had great reason to make rash decisions. Tiffany took another stroke, and knew she might need to take the lead in other ways too. She felt it.

"I was just thinking it'd be good to have a camp already set up before the rain hits—pitch a tarp or something, get some dry wood." Her damp jeans made her legs itch. The thought of getting drenched again in a rainstorm sounded downright awful.

Miranda looked downstream at the clouds again, careful of her wrist as she turned. "Just a shower at worst," she said. "We'll have time."

They rounded a bend, and the river opened up into a web of broad channels separated by low-lying islands. Cattails and red dogwood rose up in mounds. Here and there, an island was marked by a sickly tree doing its best to grow between floods and droughts. Tiffany steered them into a center channel, which seemed the most reasonable choice, though they were soon separated from the mainland by sloughs and islands. She looked at the clouds, paddled in silence for ten or fifteen minutes. Already the clouds had doubled in height. They didn't look like a featureless bank of gray anymore. Tiffany watched the greenish wall of thundercloud roll over itself like a wheel. It filled the horizon, its uppermost regions shaved off and smeared southward by wind. Tiffany cringed as the clouds lit up in a crash of thunder.

"Miranda, I'm taking us out of the river." The breeze grew stiff, making it difficult to keep the canoe on center. Tiffany had to point the bow directly into it or be pushed off course. It took a lot of muscle to bring it back to midchannel.

Miranda sat up straighter in the canoe, and Tiffany noticed impatience in her eyes as she looked at the clouds, the islands. "There's no shelter here," Miranda said. "Let's get through this."

Tiffany bit her tongue. They could have sheltered in that nice stand of cedar a mile back when she first suggested it. About a half mile farther on, forest rose up on the far side of the floodplain. That meant higher ground, drier land, something to hide beneath. Tiffany took an angry stroke in its direction, but a stiff wind swept the river before her and swung the bow of the canoe askew. Tiffany pried hard against the water and managed to nose the boat back. The surface rippled in swaths. The wind blew the canoe upriver about as forcefully as the current pushed it down. Even with the canoe pointed into the wind, their forward progress was next to nothing. Cattails rattled. A lightning bolt cracked across the face of the thundercloud. The canoe rumbled. Tiffany felt a raindrop hit her eye.

"I'm turning back to the woods," she said.

Miranda shook her head in disgust. "It's more than twice the distance. It's best to keep going."

"Miranda, I cannot paddle into this wind! Have you noticed we're not moving anymore?"

"I can help," Miranda said, and turned awkwardly in her seat to face downriver. To avoid using her bad hand, she leaned on her forearm as she turned and nearly tipped the canoe. Tiffany pried the water to keep the bow facing straight, cussed under her breath. Lightning struck, and the report of thunder was so loud, she nearly lost her grip on her paddle. It was like a cannon blast. More rain hit Tiffany's face now. She squinted at the mountains of thunderclouds. Framed beneath them lay the whipping cattails and the figure of Miranda in the bow, digging fruitlessly at the rippled water with a paddle she held in one hand, her other hand clutched against her stomach. She didn't look strong anymore. Not here. Not crippled like that with the storm so large before her. Miranda looked desperate, pathetic even. The wind blew harder. Tiffany braced and pried. Another lightning bolt shot across the face of the cloud. She pulled hard against the water with a few forward strokes. The canoe made no progress at all.

"Miranda, I'm turning back!" she said, more forcefully than she meant to.

"We can't turn," Miranda huffed. She looked doglike, wounded and mean, digging against the water, her hair tangled in the wind.

"We can't go forward either, Miranda!"

There was no answer.

"Miranda!"

Miranda stopped paddling, gripped the gunwale, and faced Tiffany. She had fire in her eyes, but of a different sort. It wasn't confidence. It was terror, anger, wildness. "My son," she bellowed, "is not back in that tree line. He is forward, through that storm. And I will have my son and will have him now!"

Tiffany stopped paddling. A gust of wind whipped Miranda's hair across her wild eyes, her panting breast. This was a different woman from the one she knew the previous night, who paddled in moonlight and spoke of walking in step with the spirit of God. Today Miranda's sunken eyes had a demand in them. They were red and panicked. Tiffany felt a wave of fear move through the canoe and wash over her body. It felt physical, like a third presence, like the air had changed.

A bolt of lightning struck one of the forsaken trees on a nearby island, and the tree exploded in flame. Black branches shot into the river. Tiffany cowered, and even Miranda was jolted from her adamance. The air felt filled with static, and as both women ducked low in the boat, Tiffany watched the flames of the tree grow white and hot as they were breathed on by a wall of wind. Other trees on other islands bent in the same gust, the cattails flattened, and with the wind came a wall of rain that obscured the land and river like a curtain dragged across the earth. The curtain swallowed the burning tree. It swallowed the island. It swallowed the river between the island and the canoe, and like a horrible wet maw, it swallowed them as well.

"Hang on!" yelled Tiffany. Her voice was lost in the downpour.

The rain filled the air with the smell of mud and water. The bow of the canoe swung violently toward the left bank, nearly swamped as it spun and pitched back upstream. The canoe pushed broadside through the water. The rain stung, and the water around the canoe erupted with it. Tiffany pulled her hood tightly around her head. Around her knees in the bottom of the canoe, little white balls the size of dimes began to gather. She studied them a moment, confused. They stung her hands and pelted her jacket. They sounded like stones hitting the canoe. The wind wailed and the stones drummed. A hailstorm. One of the stones stung her squarely on her right hand, and she drew it in quickly toward her chest.

It was as if night had come in a moment. Peering out from beneath her hood, Tiffany could no longer see the river and islands upwind. Downwind, she could still make out fifty or sixty yards of water and a bit of sky beyond it. She made up her mind to try to work with the wind, to go with it and back to the trees. It wasn't Miranda's choice or her own anymore. The wind decided.

"Hang on!" she yelled again. Miranda sat on her knees, folded forward, her wrist cradled against her stomach. It was hard to discern, but Miranda's back shuddered as if she was weeping. What surprised Tiffany most was the complete lack of pity she felt at that moment. She felt anger. Anger at the storm. Anger at Miranda. Anger at being out here at all on this rotten river.

Tiffany channeled it. She rose onto her knees, grasped her paddle, and pried hard on the left side of the canoe to point it straight downwind. She then pulled against the water with forward strokes, and the canoe sprang to life. The speed surprised her. The canoe skimmed upstream with the wind. Tiffany discovered it was her job to drag her paddle more often than to paddle forward. She didn't need to propel the canoe. She only needed to attempt to steer it, like sledding as a kid, dragging this hand or that to keep straight. The wind pushed even harder. The water boiled with hailstones. A bright crack of lightning—the flash and the report were inseparable—filled the storm's night. As it flashed, the cattails to Tiffany's right and left were illuminated so brightly they looked made of paper, the color bleached from the world. Tiffany squinted beneath her hood. As fully as the lightning illuminated the river, the darkness overtook it, plunging the canoe into blackness and noise, leaving only the wind to give any sense of direction.

Tiffany clenched her teeth. She knew the tree line was there somewhere ahead of them, at the end of the marsh. Just keep it straight, blow with the wind, rudder it straight, rudder again. Eventually they'd blow out of the islands and hit a shoreline blanketed in cedar. Her only fear was being blown into one of the islands first and having to weather the entirety of this storm in a cattail marsh. She feared, too, being struck by lightning, but then reasoned that given the circumstances, it was up to the lightning to strike her dead if it wished to. She had no say in it. All but her paddle was out of her hands.

Lightning filled the air again, and Tiffany noticed how the channel narrowed, which meant they were making it out of the islands and back toward the woods. She pried angrily at the river. There were only a few hundred yards of open water, if she remembered correctly, and then they'd be back in the trees. The world snapped black again. Hail pounded. When the lightning came the next time, Tiffany saw no cattails at all. They were making progress. It wasn't far now.

Tiffany nearly gave a yell of triumph, but the yell caught in her throat when two things happened simultaneously that she could hardly comprehend. First, she saw something approaching through the wall of rain. Second, Miranda was trying to stand in the boat.

The thing in the water looked square and low. It was too angular to be natural, and she'd seen no boulders before. The river here was just silt and shoreline. Lightning flashed and she saw it again, closer now, about fifteen yards away and blurred by hail. It appeared to be moving, not that Tiffany could gauge its progress, but she could clearly see what appeared to be a wake pushed in front of its bow. It looked like a whale, wide and square-lipped and rising to meet them. And before the approaching whale rose Miranda's slim figure. Miranda stood to her full height, lifted her arms into the hail, and began rebuking the storm, rebuking everything.

"Miranda!" Tiffany cried, prying at the water.

There was no response, at least not to her, but then in the briefest pause of thunder, the words drifted back, terrifying in the blue and white flashes of light. The lonesome screams swirled like wind, lightning, hail. Miranda screamed again and again, her back curling with effort. She was a woman up against it, against forests and storms and rivers, and dead husbands and lost sons and a whole host of other demons and devils. Miranda damned all of it. She damned cattails, and hospital beds, and deserts, and flags. She damned herself. Maybe God too. Tiffany had it in her own heart before. Forsakenness. It comes from the deepest deep. Forsakenness is a woman standing in a hailstorm, or a tent at night, forsaking everything back.

And now this whale. Tiffany became aware of a different sort of noise in the wind. A growling or moaning. It immediately grew louder until the moan and growl overtook the sound of the storm and Miranda. Tiffany braced herself, clutched her paddle in the darkness and the noise. Whatever was coming, it was upon them. Miranda raged in the bow of the boat, her hands purple fists.

"Miranda, get down!"

Lightning cracked again as a realization crystallized in Tiffany's mind: the moan was a motor. The whale was a boat. And in

the space of that realization all hope shattered in fear. There was
no way the boat would see them in this downpour. Lightning illuminated the scene in a maze of flashes, and everything froze in
strobes, still-frames. Within arm's reach, a flat-bottomed boat raced
into the wind. Its motor howled and warbled with strain. A bright
white wake of water hung suspended in an arc over the gunwale of
the canoe. A lone figure sat in the back of the boat, one hand pin-
ning the throttle of the outboard motor, the other holding the hood
of a rain poncho down over his eyes and face. The boatman didn't
even see them.

The world snapped black again, the canoe rolled across the wake,
and Miranda went overboard with a percussive splash. The wave of
river water, as cold as it was, felt warm in Tiffany's lap. The growl
of the motor swept past and filled the sodden air with the smell
of hot exhaust. Without thinking, Tiffany found herself bailing
the canoe with her paddle blade, shoveling water and hailstones
out into the darkness. The canoe wallowed but was still floating.
About three inches of gunwale remained above the surface.

"Help us!" she yelled to the boatman as loudly as she could.
Hailstones stung her face, and she had to turn away from the wind.
"Jerk!" she yelled into the sky, but it was no use. The boat was already out of sight, its wake of froth and exhaust winding away into
the storm. Tiffany heard Miranda sputter and cough several yards
off in the darkness, beating her way back to the canoe in her denim
dress.

Not pausing, still shoveling, Tiffany had a thought, and was
struck by the peculiarity and clarity of such a thought during
this sort of moment. As she reached out and stroked toward Miranda, she felt something very odd, some warm presence, some sort
of charm in the storm. As she paddled, she felt as if she was gathering blessing unto herself, like the coyote in her poem, stretched out
in a desperate run toward its tribe, toward abundance, and pain

too, and she felt that the more she paddled, the more she would gather. And she wanted to gather it, pull it all into her lap like the river and embrace it.

The hail fell. The wind pushed. Miranda called out to Jesus in the water. Tiffany felt blessed.

CAL SPENT THE PAST HOUR SLAPPING MOSQUITOES AND WATCHING Teddy cuss and slash his way through spruce trees. The constant drizzle wasn't enough to keep off the bugs. If anything, it seemed to enliven them, prod them to feast. The rain was just enough to soak everything slowly. First the foliage, then Cal's jacket, and then his jeans and boot. Cal heard thunder far off to the west, back where the river was, and couldn't decide which would be worse, to be caught in that storm or in these clouds of mosquitoes. Right now, damp as a rag, with itchy welts on his neck and hands, sweating but unable to remove his coat for fear of the swarm, Cal voted for thunderstorm, hands down. A tree-bending wind would do these bugs in nicely. There was another itch too. Cal wanted a drink. And he wanted one badly enough that it scared him, threatened all the hope of newness he'd found in this forest.

Cal walked slowly behind Ted, who hacked and hacked. Cal held the reins of both horses. Jacks fell in behind, constantly whining and grumbling and shaking his ears. It would be Cal's turn to slash through the undergrowth soon, and he'd welcome it. They'd already traded off about four times.

Hours ago, when they first approached the stretch of forest that held Teddy's logging road, Cal felt in his gut that it was a bad idea. As they moved farther inland, the open hardwoods and clearings gave way to cedar and pine and spruce. Every so often they'd come across a small stand of white pine that made for easier walking, the massive trees keeping the ground clear of undergrowth. But then the men had to plunge once again into thickets and branches so tangled a person couldn't see more than ten or fifteen feet. It was just pine. An endless hedge of pine. When the woods became so thick that they had trouble leading the horses, Teddy took out his map. Pine boughs looked on over both of his shoulders. Cal held one away from his face, swatted bugs with his free hand.

"Shouldn't be much farther now, and we'll make the road." He ran his finger along the map while Cal eyed the woods suspiciously. They should have stayed by the river. This was misery.

Teddy rolled up the map and retrieved a long canvas sheath from his saddlebag. The sheath was matte green and faded, with a military designator printed along one side like an old tattoo. It held a machete. Teddy grinned a bit as he slid the machete free.

"We weren't supposed to keep these," he said. "But I figured they wouldn't miss it. Some guys kept more." He turned the blade over in his hand, brushed his thumb against the edge, held it up into a patch of gray light. "Come on," he said, "less than a mile now and we'll make the cut."

And with that, Cal led both horses as Teddy swiped and slashed his way through the hedge of pine boughs. The mile was a slow one, and when they made the road, or what used to be the road, Ted took his map out again. He studied it, put it away, rubbed his eyes, and kept them closed.

"Where's the road, Ted?" Cal asked. His mare whinnied. "I wasn't talking to you, horse," he said, and reached toward the horse's face to wipe a blot of mosquitoes away from the corners of its eyes.

Ted lifted his arms. Eyes still closed, he tilted his head up to the rain.

"You're standing in the road," he said.

It was hard to discern, but once Cal took his bearings via the treetops, he could make out the cut clear as day. A few paces to his right and left, pines rose to their adult height. Between them, where the men stood, younger pines not quite as tall marked a thirty-foot swath where the cut had been. The road hadn't been kept up. Cal knew from his interactions with game wardens that most state logging projects around here were plagued by budget shortfalls and politics. This one had been abandoned. But the forest paid no mind. When the trucks and saws left a path of sunlight behind, the woods wasted no time filling itself back in.

"We could go back," said Cal.

Ted opened his eyes, gave a laugh without humor in it. "To think I drove a skidder right through here." He looked around at the tangle of trunks. "Can't say I thought of this."

"Well, you didn't, and that's that, so let's go," said Cal, wiping rain and mosquitoes and thoughts of whiskey from his neck. The forest dripped in the humid quiet.

"We ain't going back," Teddy said, and spat.

Cal dropped the reins. This again. "We're not going to chop our way to Ironsford. Let's go back to the river and get on with it."

"It's too late for that. We've wasted too much time just getting here."

"So let's waste even more by staying? I didn't come out here to prune trees, Teddy. I came out here to find those boys."

Teddy glared at him. It was icy, but Cal challenged it and glared back. He was hot from walking. The mosquitoes had doubled their efforts since they stopped. His tailbone still ached. And they now stood in the middle of a pine forest so thick a person couldn't see over his own shoulder. If they kept it up, they'd be the ones needing a search party. At least the boys had the presence of mind to stick to the river.

"I know where the forest opens up again," said Ted. "If we keep going, we can push to the river without backtracking."

"Opens up? Opens up! We've been headed for miles through one big bush!" Cal slapped a hand against the buzzing at his ear. He looked at it, the small blotch of blood on his palm, the crumpled smear of wing and leg. "And if I get bit by one more mosquito," he yelled up at the trees, "I'm going to burn this bush down!"

Teddy exhaled through his nose. He stared at the ground and his face got red. He kept staring at the ground until the color left it a bit.

"Cal, we can go back if you want," he said. "You're the sheriff."

"No, I am not," Cal snarled.

"But we're not going to make up any time. This road's a bust, and it's my fault, but I know where these pines turn to hardwood that reaches clear to the river, and we can use that as a road out."

"How far?" Cal asked. He was aware that his tone wasn't helping, but he wasn't in the mood to reel it in.

"We didn't cut it. We wanted to, but the foresters marked only the pine. The hardwood is five miles down this road, give or take."

"Give or take." Cal spat on the ground. Jacks whined and shook his ears. "May as well be fifty."

To his credit, Teddy kept his cool. Cal knew it.

"Look, we can backtrack to the south," Ted said, "and then head north." He traced a wide loop in the air. "Or, we can cut through this road and keep going north through the hardwoods." His finger cut a much tighter, straighter path.

Cal spat again. He'd rarely been so mad. These woods had pressed in on him. Cal no longer feared it as he did in the past. But it had found a way of making him terribly angry. These bugs. This damp. This heat in his coat. The prick and slap of pine branches. As a cop, he'd seen plenty of men lose their lids over less—some call about a guy out in his yard beating a lawn mower to death with the whole neighborhood watching, or the guy he once saw kicking in the quarter panel of his minivan because his spare was flat, with the wife and kids standing out by the highway, vacation just beginning. Cal felt it in himself more often than he'd want to confess, that awful draw to boil over.

"Give me that machete," Cal said.

Ted held it out, and Cal snatched it from his hand.

"I'm mad at you, Ted!"

"I know you are."

"I'm mad at all this pine, Ted!"

"I know."

Cal took the lead, or what he thought was the lead. He looked to his left and right and gave a practice swipe at a sapling. In a spray of raindrops, he clipped it clean in two. That felt good. He looked back at Ted for direction. He widened his eyes at him.

"Well," he said, "are you going to tell me which way to go, or are we going to sit around and scratch?"

Ted tried not to smile, and pointed into the trees, north, and Cal attacked the wall of pine, putting his whole back into his swings, cutting upward and downward, throwing sidearms from time to time.

"Careful," said Ted, behind him.

"Don't tell me how to cut pine branches, Ted."

"I ain't. I'm just saying to be careful is all."

"I know how to cut off pine branches, Ted," said Cal, and as he said it, a particularly stubborn branch failed to sever, so Cal kicked it free and stomped it flat with his boot for good measure. He slashed and cut for the better part of an hour. They made decent progress. If they could push through it, they pushed through it. If they couldn't, Cal cut it down. Both men were covered with welts and scratches. The sweat stung their necks. Every now and then, Cal had to stop to pull his sodden sock back onto his foot. It was rotten work, but at least a man with a machete had a way of fighting it out. To hell with pine. To hell with whiskey. Cal had a machete! What Cal didn't know was that during the hour he was blowing off steam, Teddy was building it. Toward the end of his shift, when Cal was beginning to feel pretty emotionally stable again, pretty pleased with himself, he was startled by Ted's enraged voice.

"Would you give over that damn chopper already!" Ted bellowed. Jacks, who had been walking at Teddy's side, bolted into the underbrush.

Cal stood straight up. "Yeah," he said, as calmly as a man rising from a chair. "I didn't know you wanted it."

Teddy strode forward and smeared bugs from his forehead, yanking the machete from Cal's hand. His face was red and his lips were clenched. He didn't stop walking when he grabbed the blade either. He just snatched the thing and bullied his way into the nearest tangle of pine, beating it to pieces.

Cal, who by now felt at peace with everything, empathized with Ted's plight but couldn't help himself from egging him on, seeing how hot the old man could get.

"Careful," he called out. "Just be careful chopping there, Teddy."

Ted was too angry to see the joke. He spun away from his work and shook the machete at Cal and the horses. "Don't tell me what to do, Sheriff! Don't you tell me how to cut trail!"

Cal stifled a smile and raised his hands in the air. Teddy turned and resumed his violence.

This pattern repeated itself a number of times, one man getting frustrated enough with the bugs and horses to steal back the hateful pleasures of the machete. Eventually, Cal knew, they'd cuss and beat their way out of this forest. And as they rode the ebb and tide of their anger, Cal couldn't help thinking about their conversation that morning, the way he really did hate police work, the way Teddy hated his quiet life of farming. He felt that beating their way out of the forest was a continuation of that conversation, like something was being hashed out between each man and his life.

After several hours, Cal still felt the heat rising in him, but to be honest, it rose a little less. They'd made good progress, but they were also running out of steam. Cal looked forward to riding again. A breeze and passivity was what he craved now. The sky overhead was gray and framed on all sides by the spires of spruce and hemlock. Nothing but pine and drizzle and bugs and sky. Ted, it was clear now, was running on fumes. His slashes with the machete grew less adamant, halfhearted. Despite the mosquitoes, he removed his coat, and sweat and dirt stained his entire back. The neck of his shirt hung loose with rain. Eventually, he stopped and stood, stretched his back.

"Can you cut awhile?" he asked, breathing through pursed lips.

"Sure," Cal said, dropping the reins. He wasn't angry enough to attack the forest, but he'd do it. They weren't fighting anymore. They were searching again. Keeping on. Finding the boys.

"Want some water?" Cal extended his canteen out to Ted.

Ted nodded, exhaled. He dumped some of the cool water on his neck, rubbed the dirt and bug bites. Then he lifted the canteen skyward and drank, his eyes closed.

Cal's eyes followed the mist upward. He hadn't immediately realized that there was something different about the forest's canopy ahead of them, about twenty yards off, a new kind of green rising among the spires of the pines.

"Ted," Cal said.

Teddy kept drinking noisily before lowering the canteen and wiping his mouth with his arm. He capped it and panted, looked at Cal.

Cal nodded up at the treetops, grinning, the broad-leafed canopy dangling over what was no doubt much more open ground.

Ted saw it and nodded, nearly too winded to smile. He stretched his back. "Hardwoods," he said.

As the men mounted and rode out of the pine into open, moving air, Cal looked back at the path they'd carved, the cut and snapped branches, the carpet of needles and mud. It felt good to look at it. It felt like clarity. Cal wiped the welts on his neck and spurred his horse forward.

FIFTEEN

"**A**ND WE ARE NOT QUITTING," SAID BREAD. "NOW GET UP!"

Fish didn't move. He lay on his stomach on the giant sandbar. The sand beneath him was saturated in rain and leaf litter. River water dripped from his clothes. Falling rain soaked him. After the worst of the storm, the rain didn't quit. It fell and fell, windless now, but heavy, the occasional rumble of thunder encircling their ruin. Fish's stomach growled. His head ached. He lowered his forehead to the cool sand. It felt fine there, just being still. This is how it ends for beavers, hungry and dying on the sand, as wet and quiet as driftwood. The storm had ruined them.

Bread glared, his hair plastered against his forehead. He had welts on his face and hands from the hailstones. Water dripped from his nose. He blew it away and started pacing, kicked sand at the river. Beyond him, closer to the vast expanse of cattails, lay the pieces that were left of the raft. The boys were still on board when the raft broke up in the storm, spinning and tilting, water washing up on the deck, the boys shielding their faces from the wind and noise. Fish had never seen a storm like that. Wrath was real. Bread had been wrong about God not doing anything. He could do something, all right. And it made Fish lie down on the sand to die. The image of the raft spinning and reeling beneath that terrible funnel cloud played again and again in Fish's mind. It felt like judgment, and it didn't matter if they were strong or good. They were fatherless. They were lost.

When the storm came, the raft drifted into a part of the river that was wide and flat. Sandbars and cattails reached out into the channel. And then the rain got heavier. And then came wind and hail. And when the boys picked up their poles to try to push their way into the cattails, the hail and lightning became so fierce they were forced to take cover in their flannels and wait. Blind to the storm, Fish thought the wind sounded very much like a train, distant at first, and then rumbling up from downstream. He'd heard of a storm sounding like a train. The hum became feverish, whistling on its tracks until it shook the river in ways wind shouldn't be able to.

He and Bread clutched the ropes holding the deck together. The first thing to give was the wicker railing. The branches and skulls rattled and splashed, and then they stopped splashing. They tore off and flew, coyote skulls and deer skulls lifting off into the green and black. And when the ropes securing the A-frame broke, they snapped so sharply Fish thought the raft was lightning struck. He tore back his flannel hood and looked up just in time to see the cedar logs lift into the air, unfolding like the hind legs of a giant locust. After the legs tore away, the ribs broke. It wasn't until he was neck-deep in water, holding on to a cedar log under each armpit, that he realized the deck had broken apart. He was too stunned by the sight he saw in that strobe of lightning. There on the riverbank—he could have thrown a stone to it—stood the heart of the storm, churning and booming, the engine itself. Lightning flashed white and black. The thundercloud had an arm. It was black and dangling. And that arm reached down to the earth and did violence to it, searched the ground for whatever it was it wanted.

In the space of two or three flashes of lightning, Fish watched the arm grab hold of a grove of cedar trees. As easily as a hand pulling weeds, the funnel cloud twisted them in a knot and tore them free. The arm whipped itself farther inland and made a crackling knot of a stand of pines. Lightning flashed again. Fish closed his eyes and clutched his logs. Hail beat his face. Somewhere in all of that light and darkness and noise he heard Bread's yell. *Fish! Fish! Fish!* But Fish felt too choked by the storm and river to answer. There seemed so little air in all that wind. He just held to his logs until the funnel cloud broke apart, dropped its debris, and he felt river bottom with his toes. He let himself down from his logs, parted the stew of broken cattails, and fell upon the shore.

Now lying on the sandbar was all there was left to do.

Bread came back from kicking sand.

"You're a liar, Fish, for everything you've ever said," Bread shouted, and it stung worse than Fish's welts. Bread seemed switched on. He paced and spat, wrung out the sleeves of his shirt. "If you weren't all I got, I'd leave you here for the coyotes! But you are all I got, and I'm gonna fix this dang raft and drag you on it, and we are going to make it to that armory! Now give me that barlow knife."

Fish winced when Bread mentioned the armory. *Liar,* he thought. *I am a liar. I am not good.* There was nothing for them at the armory. Fish opened his mouth to confess, and he knew that when he did the destruction would be like that storm, his tongue a hand reaching down to wring life from the earth. It would wreck the past. It would wreck the future. Bread would abandon him, stalk off into the woods. But Bread had to know. It was too cruel to let him hope anymore. They were not warriors. They were not beavers. They would never become tankers like Fish's dad, because Fish's dad was dead. There was nowhere left to go. They were without food. The river claimed all their gear except what they carried in their pockets or belts. They were finished.

"Bread, I—"

"I don't want to hear it," said Bread.

Fish lifted his head from the sand, his mouth open.

"I said shut up, Fish!" Anger flashed in Bread's eyes, righteous anger, and yet there was kindness in it somehow. "The knife!" Bread yelled. "Give it over so I can do what you won't!"

Fish caved. Tears welled up in his eyes. He didn't have the courage to tell Bread the truth. Fish was too much of a coward to face any more wrath today. His throat clamped shut. He'd just lie there and die. Hide and wait, cling to the sand. He reached into his wet pocket and pulled out the barlow. Bread snatched it away. The revolver still sat in his belt. Bread adjusted it, shook his head at the sand, and walked back toward the remains of the raft.

Fish let his head hit the sand and stared out at the river. The storm had blown the raft into a side channel, and the slower water was littered with cattails and branches, tufts of grass, peppered with raindrops. Mats of pine needles collected like puddles. The river seemed not to care where the raft went, or why it was going where it did. The image of Bread's dad hitting the floor came back to Fish, the way that blast filled the room like lightning, left it ringing and silent. The man crumpled forward so easily. It was as if there hadn't been anything in him in the first place that kept him standing. But there had been something in him, and the bullet ripped it out of him, and it had mattered. The world had spirits in it. When that sow bear came, Fish had rarely felt such triumph. Something good *is*. Something evil *is*, too. It mattered that that sow saved her cub. It mattered that Fish killed a man. It mattered that Fish was a liar. But what mattered most right now to Fish was that Bread stay alive, that he keep inside of him whatever it was that bullet tore out of his dad. It mattered to Fish that Bread keep going, even if he didn't know why, or to where.

Fish rose to his knees and looked at his friend. Bread was hip-deep in water, pushing a section of the raft to shore that hadn't been completely wrecked. It looked to be about five or six logs wide. It floated, sort of. They could ride it. Between the two of them, they still had a flint, a knife, a gun, and four rounds. They could keep going.

Fish stood and made his way toward Bread. He stumbled. His stomach hurt and his legs tingled, but he found a way to totter forward and splashed into the water beside Bread. Without speaking, Fish leaned into the raft with both hands and pushed it. With both boys pushing, the raft moved easily. The logs were still bound together loosely, waterlogged but floating.

"We got more rope?" Fish asked. On the beach lay a pile of logs Bread had already collected.

Bread nodded, looked at Fish warily. "There's some tangled rope on them logs. There's no way to rebuild it like it was."

"This will do," said Fish.

The boys stooped lower to push the raft up to the beach. As the raft nudged onto the sand, Bread shook his head in disbelief. Then a grin broke through.

"What?" said Fish.

Bread rolled his eyes. "*What,* he says."

Fish brushed sand from his hands, worried that he was no longer welcome in this.

"You're a yo-yo, Fish," said Bread.

"You're a yo-yo," said Fish. "I'm a beaver."

Bread grinned, handed the barlow knife back to Fish.

It was good to see Bread smile. It made the world feel less wrong. Fish unfolded the blade and wiped it on his jeans. He decided to wait until the raft was rebuilt to tell Bread the truth about his dad. That way, if Bread abandoned him, at least Bread would have a boat, a way to get out of the woods. Fish moved toward a tangle of logs and began freeing rope.

The boys worked in the steady rain for a couple of hours. The time went quickly. They had only seven logs to tie together, and the waterlogged rope, though it was heavy, was more limp and easier to work than when it was dry. While they heaved and tugged and sliced, Bread talked about whether he'd rather be a tank driver or a tank gunner when they got to the armory, and Fish let him dream. This might be the last day on earth Fish knew the joy of a friend. And if he was going to lose it soon, he wanted this moment to take with him into exile. Bread went on and on. Firing the gun had its obvious merits, but so did running the tracks. Both boys knew how tank treads worked independently of each other, how tanks could spin on a dime, crush bunkers, jump trenches. Eventually Bread decided that he'd like that best, having those giant treads in his hands.

"Giant robot feet," he said. "That's what driving that tank will be like."

While he talked about it, Fish got the sense that Bread *knew* they weren't actually going to drive any tanks, that he *knew* he was running toward a lie. At first the thought scared Fish. How much did Bread know? Fish stood still in the rain and watched Bread out of the corner of his eye. Did he know his dad was dead, all the stories Fish had made up for all these summers, all the excuses about his dad having another deployment? Bread *had* to know. But then, why was he here? With that thought a new hope dawned in Fish's mind. Of course Bread knew. Only a fool would believe otherwise. Which meant Bread, too, was fighting some vague fight for something unseen, unknown.

Bread stopped working. "What?" he asked.

Fish bit his lip and then scowled at the ground. He felt tears coming into his eyes. If Bread did know about his dad all this time, then his silence was too great a kindness. Bread stood there dripping wet, concern on his brow, already great. He had a bad father and was still this good. Fish's grandpa was right about him.

"What?" Bread asked again.

"I just—" said Fish. "I'd love to be the tank gunner, if you want to run the tracks."

The concern fled from Bread's face and he nodded, as if a solemn decision had finally been sorted out. Fish wiped his eye on his soaked shoulder, folded his knife into his pocket, turned his attention to the diminished but completed raft.

"What do you think of her?" asked Bread.

The raft was about ten feet long and six feet wide. It looked tippy compared to the prior craft. It also looked tired. The ropes were soggy and frayed. Strips of cedar bark hung like a wet beard in the water. Fish stepped on it with his foot. The whole thing wavered a bit. They hadn't secured a ridgepole this time. It was just seven logs woven alongside one another. Near its bow, if it could be called that, lay a coil of about forty feet of spare rope. Two muddy push poles lay in the sand beside it.

"Well, it needs a name again," said Fish.

"The *Poachers' Hope of Lantern Rock* is still a good name," said Bread.

"Needs more now," said Fish. He looked downriver. They couldn't be that far from Ironsford now. This was their final stretch, and then, who knows? The river was so wide here, and the sandbars so numerous, it hardly looked like a river at all. But because of the debris marking the nearly imperceptible flow, all they'd have to do to make their way through is choose the channel where the leaves and logs flowed fastest. The realization made Fish feel like crying again. Here was this river rooting for them, saying in a voice so much quieter than the storm—*Come this way. There is more.* Fish felt the same odd comfort he felt when his mom prayed, a warmth within the cold. He didn't want to trust it. But maybe that storm wasn't God after all. Maybe God was in this whisper. Maybe God was in the river. It was a miracle they still had a raft and a place to take it.

Bread broke the silence. He held up his hands as he spoke, as if offering a blessing to the boat and a challenge to the sky. "Here floats," he said, and then spoke slowly, "*The Last Stand of the Poachers' Hope of Lantern Rock.*"

"You're getting good at that," said Fish.

Bread smiled. "It's good, right?"

"It is."

"Beaver warriors," said Bread.

Fish nodded. "Beaver warriors," he said.

The boys basked in the rain until they heard something in the air. At first it reminded Fish of the storm, and a lump formed in his throat. He didn't know if he could bear another. But when he listened more closely, and assured himself that the wind hadn't stirred, he thought it sounded more like a whine, a hum, a moaning from upriver.

"Boat!" shouted Bread, ducking and pointing as he said it. Fish saw it at once. Several hundred yards distant, a boat crossed a channel between sandbars and cattails. Bread and Fish bolted toward the shoreline and crouched in the reeds. The boat disappeared behind an island, then reappeared, its motor grating and popping and leaving a blue trail of smoke on the black water.

"I don't like this," said Bread. "Who is that?"

"He won't see us," said Fish. The boat was in the channel along the opposite shore. It disappeared and reappeared, moving quickly. "From where he is, our raft's just gonna look like a log. There's lots of logs."

"I don't like it is all. I don't like someone being out here." Bread drew a sharp breath, blew it back out between his lips.

Fish studied the boat as it crossed an open section of water. It was a flat-bottomed duckboat, the same kind everyone else used on this river, the same kind Fish's grandpa had, and Bread's dad. Fish didn't know of any major boat landings, but there were plenty of backwoods paths that led into the river at various places. A person had to drag his boat in through muck and briars. Duck hunters came out here. Muskrat trappers. Fish squinted. The boatman rode with a rain hood pulled over his eyes. The hood stayed facing forward, and then it turned, slowly, and that dark mask seemed to stare right at him. Fish couldn't explain why, but the dream he had of the antlered man, the scarecrow on the poachers' island, came back to him as he stared into that black hood. It sent a shiver up his spine and he found himself holding his breath. Slowly, the hood turned back downstream, and the motor sputtered on, and soon all that was left of the boat was a disturbed wake of water and smoke. The boatman hadn't spotted them. The dread of Fish's dream hung in the cattails.

"I think it's a trapper," said Fish. "Ironsford must be closer than we think."

Bread trembled. "I can't breathe," he said. His back twitched like a horse's hide.

"What's wrong?"

"I just got"—he tried to smile—"really cold, you know? Got cold all of a sudden." Bread tried to shrug, but the movement was muted by his shaking. A memory came to Fish's mind of a time the two boys hid in the garage rafters while Bread's dad tore through it, stone drunk, tripping over tool chests and smashing bottles.

"It's all right, Bread. The boat's gone. He's gone."

Bread folded his arms more tightly around his chest. He nodded. Swallowed.

"I think we shouldn't wait to shove off," said Fish. "It's getting dark out."

Bread nodded.

"Beaver warriors," Fish reminded him.

Bread nodded again, cow-eyed, sitting in the cattails.

AFTER TIFFANY EMERGED FROM THE CEDAR FOREST AND BAILED THE remainder of rain and river from their canoe, she tightened the ropes on their gear. Miranda sat silently near the riverbank, her arms hugging her knees. Tiffany asked if she was ready to go and saw in Miranda's eyes the weight of shame and condemnation, a flash of spite too: *Go where?* they seemed to say. But Miranda just swallowed, nodded nearly imperceptibly, looked out at the rain-pocked water, and stepped into the bow lightly and silently, giving Tiffany's arm the weakest squeeze as she passed.

Paddling through the aftermath of the storm made Tiffany grow quiet as well, out of awe and fear amid the greenish calm. Thunder still pealed in the distance, and the rain fell, but there was no more breeze, and Tiffany soon became lost in the spell of paddle strokes and undulating river grass. The air felt cooler than the river, and the river carried a thick litter of leaves and branches. The world seemed somehow both broken and refreshed. Tiffany filled her lungs. Looked downstream. She felt hope. The air felt hopeful. The canoe still floated. They were underway, her paddle clunking against the gunwale with each brace stroke like a slowly beaten drum.

They crossed the open water and reentered the marsh plain from where they turned back. It would be dark soon, and their progress was slow, but for an hour or more Tiffany followed the bright green constellations of floating maple leaves down the black water, moving with the candied current through the greater channels. Their way was hidden by the surface of things, guided by deeper currents. The channels looked identical, they all had the same stands of cattails growing at their edges. But some channels moved the leaves and some did not, and so Tiffany found the way through.

"Can we stop?"

The sound of Miranda's voice surprised Tiffany.

"If you need to," she answered. In the distance, Tiffany could see the forest rising up on the far side of the marsh plain. She'd prefer to keep going, to exit the marsh and arrive at a single channel again.

But Miranda nodded. There was grave tiredness in her body. "Okay," said Tiffany. "I'll find a spot."

Tiffany glided the canoe around a bend of cattails where the river split in three. In the distance, on the right side of the river, Tiffany made out what looked to be large sandbars, and when her eyes moved to the shoreline, her paddle stopped midstroke. Miranda saw it too. Her good hand tightened on the gunwale.

Opening before them in the growing dusk lay a half-mile-wide stretch of shore that had been ravaged in ways Tiffany had only seen in newspapers. Pine trees were snapped and stripped of their needles—some treetops were missing, others dangled in the rain at awkward angles. Some trees lay flat against the ground, their rooted skirts revealed. The scene reminded Tiffany of the time a classmate broke his shinbone clean in half on the playground, how she and all the other kids gawked at the foot, the way it dangled from the boy at so unnatural an angle.

Tiffany paddled forward into the slough. The leaves didn't move on the water here, and in places pine needles floated in mats so thick the water looked like solid ground. Tiffany aimed the canoe toward a large sandbar and cut a path through the debris. She spotted a stand of hardwoods set well back from the shore. The branches were bare as winter. In some places the cattails had been stirred to mud. In others they stood erect. A cedar grove was pressed flat, all except a single younger tree. Tiffany had heard of tornadoes behaving like this, selective almost, flattening every home in a trailer park but leaving a glass case filled with knick-knacks untouched.

Miranda faced forward. Her shoulders shook. There was nothing Tiffany could say. Miranda's son was out here, somewhere, in this devastation. Or was he? Was it possible the boys were already back in Claypot, eating cookies with Constable Bobby? She could almost see it, Bobby with cookie crumbs on his lips, poking a radio's transmitter again and again—*Sheriff? Sheriff? Bobby to Rover.*

And for that matter, was the sheriff even out here anymore? Tiffany took one or two more paddle strokes, too tired to consider at length the thought that she and Miranda were floating around out here for no reason, everyone else back in town. She shook it from her mind. The possibility was real, but her gut told her otherwise. There was something odd about that storm, the way it rose up and broke over them so violently—and the near miss with the boatman too—and the way Miranda's spirit seemed pushed so hard it'd been hushed. Tiffany felt they were in the right place.

When the canoe grated against the sandbar, Miranda let out what sounded like pain.

"Are you okay?" Tiffany asked. She told herself she should have beached more gently. She'd forgotten about Miranda's injured wrist.

Miranda gasped again, clutched both gunwales, and moaned, staring down at the loosely packed sand of the beach. She scrambled out of the boat, and on her hands and knees started patting the sand. Then she pressed her sandy fingers to her lips, her hair dragging. Tiffany couldn't tell if she was laughing or crying, and the scene raised the hair on her neck. She stowed her paddle and rustled through the bag near her feet for a flashlight. Dusk had come. She didn't want to be alone in this darkness. Miranda had been through a lot. Too much maybe. Thunder pealed in the distance. Tiffany was alone with a madwoman.

She felt the smooth heft of the C-cell Maglite, removed it from the bag, and aimed it at Miranda. In a snap of white light, the world grew small. What was left of the sky and the broken trees disappeared. Tiffany saw only the pointed bow of the red canoe, a sandbar strewn with leaves, and a weeping woman sitting on her denim hip, lifting and dropping fistfuls of muddy sand. Tiffany felt fear, and then noticed something odd about the sandbar. Surrounding Miranda in the sand, everywhere, were the shadowed rims of hundreds of small indentations, like crescent moons in negative, like heels and toes.

Heels.

And toes.

Tiffany shouted aloud, "Footprints!"

She sprang from the canoe, forgetting the stern was still afloat, and plunged down into waist-deep water.

"Footprints!" she yelled again, wading for shore. She fell to her knees next to Miranda and studied one of the indentations with her flashlight. Sure enough, there was a boy-sized footprint, and as she ran her light a few yards up the beach, she saw more and more of them. Despite the rain, the prints seemed fresh, and upon closer inspection there were clearly two different pairs of shoes, one with a deep zigzag pattern running from instep to heel, and the other flat-bottomed and worn.

A triumph rose in her body that felt physical, in the same way that running those rapids felt physical, the way that strange warmth arrived in that storm. Tiffany didn't feel chilled now, or even wet. Her body hummed. She felt like leaping. She looked to Miranda, who was too overcome to smile or speak, just patting one of the footprints with the zigzag in it.

"It's Fischer," Tiffany said.

Miranda could only lift her head enough to nod.

"They're here, Miranda, we found them." Tiffany laughed. "We *found* them!"

Miranda closed her eyes and exhaled rattling breaths through her lips. She patted the sand, lowered her forehead to it.

Tiffany couldn't wait, but as she stood to search the beach, Miranda reached out and grabbed her ankle. She swallowed heavily before she could speak. "Forgive me," she whispered, and it was all she could manage to say or do.

Tiffany grinned and clasped Miranda's hand.

"You stay here," she said. "We found them. We found them."

Miranda released her grip, and Tiffany was gone like a shot. The excitement of a search fulfilled, the joy of getting to see that mother wrap her boy in her arms, was too great to contain. Tiffany smiled as she jogged up the sandbar, laughing to herself. Those boys had no idea of the smothering that lay in store for them.

She noticed the tracks led in and out of the water at times, but always moved farther toward shore and a hedge of cattails.

"Fischer!" Tiffany yelled into the night. She ran the beam of her flashlight toward the cattails, out into the water, and back toward the other end of the sandbar. "Fischer! Your mom's here! Fischer!"

Tiffany jogged again and came across a pile of three or four stacked logs. Amid the logs, the footprints intensified. Bits of rope were strewn about. Tiffany picked up one of the bits and studied it in her light. It'd been cut with a sharp knife. She followed the footprints beyond the pile of logs and noticed that the toes of the shoes faced both ways. The footprints went into the cattails, and while Tiffany shone her light into the shadows and stalks, she could see very clearly where the footprints came back out and headed to the log pile.

She returned, called Fischer's name again, and then she realized what the boys had done, what they'd built. On a path leading toward the water, the toes of the boys' shoes dug heavily into the drag marks of logs. In the water itself, the floating mat of pine needles remained parted. Tiffany followed the path with her light. It cut a weaving arc through the slough toward the main channel and disappeared beyond the reaches of her light.

Tiffany pinched the flashlight in her armpit and cupped her hands around her mouth.

"Fischer!" she bellowed into the wet blackness. She inhaled deeply and yelled again, sustaining his name for the entirety of her breath. They're gone, she thought. Her heart fell, but she knew they were close, and she was determined now to paddle all night, all morning, for the rest of her life if needed.

She heard footfalls approaching her, a panting breath. She

turned toward the canoe. "We've got to get back in the river, Miranda." She lifted the light toward where Miranda's footfalls jogged to a stop. "The boys aren't here. The*eeeaaahhhhhhhhh! Eeeaaahahhh!*"

Tiffany's mouth screamed. It could do no other. There in the sickening light of her flashlight stood a winded man, hunched over and panting, soaked to the core and filthy. His face was mottled and scratched. A string of red welts ran from his cheek to his ear. Mud was smeared from his forehead to his open mouth. Between panting breaths, he grinned at her, and then lifted his hand and stepped toward her.

Tiffany was done screaming. She gripped the end of the heavy Maglite like a baton and brought an overhand swing down hard on the man's hat. She felt it connect with a crack and the man stumbled backward. She attacked again, terrified as the whipping baton met the man's neck and hands and then his huddled spine.

"Tiff, stop!" the man cried out, which for some reason made Tiffany more afraid and hit him even harder.

"How do you know my name!" She landed another crack near his tailbone, and the man howled in untold agony and rage.

He caught the next blow with his hand and wrenched the flashlight free, catching Tiffany by her wrist with his other hand, which pulled her down on top of him. She fought and kicked. She bit a mouthful of shirt.

"Tiff! It's me—*it's me!*"

Tiffany froze. Her breaths came as fast as her heartbeat. She realized she was gripping the man's shirt with both hands, still biting it too. It smelled of pine and horse and sweat. She looked up at the face in front of her, caught squarely in the beam of the light. Through mud and welts and days of stubble, there was Sheriff Cal, grimacing at her.

"It's me," he said.

She held tight to his shirt and felt lost for a moment. There was too much happening. Miranda weeping in the sand, the footprints, and then this attacker—*Cal?*—this man panting beneath her. She felt the rise and fall of his ribs.

"Oh!" she said. She was trembling. "Cal?" She released his shirt and flattened it against his chest. "Are you hurt?"

Cal winced. "Yes. I am."

Tiffany remembered she was lying on top of him and scrambled off.

"Cal, I—" She collected his hands in hers and began to help him to his feet. He groaned and she dropped him on the sand, which made him groan even more, for which she apologized.

He sat himself up, looked around for his hat, not yet ready to rise to his feet. Tiffany knelt alongside him.

"Tiffany," he said, "what are you doing out here?"

"I came with Miranda. We brought a canoe. To look for the boys. And to find your—" She stopped, remembering the bad news she had to tell him about Jacks, which seemed so distant and insignificant now. Nevertheless, she did have to tell him, and had thought through about fifteen different ways to break the news, and now she had to tell him after beating him with a flashlight. And that *face* of his, that beautiful square face. This forest had been bad to him. But good too. She couldn't make sense of things.

"Sheriff, I lost your dog."

Cal shook his head, and Tiffany's heart sank.

"Cal, I'm sorry."

He kept shaking his head and rubbing his neck as she apologized. "No," he said. "You didn't. I mean you did, but you didn't."

With a spray of sand, Miranda burst into the orb of light, racking a pump shotgun as she did so. She leveled it at Cal's chest.

"Back off, pervert!" she said, ferocity in her voice.

Miranda raised the muzzle up into the night sky and loosed a deafening round of twelve-gauge buckshot. Spark and flame erupted from the muzzle. Cal hit the dirt. Tiffany sprang from where she knelt. Miranda racked the pump gun again and leveled it at Cal, who was very nearly burying himself in the sand, yelling, "No, no, no, no, no!"

Tiffany leapt between Miranda and Cal.

"Don't! It's the sheriff, Miranda! It's the sheriff."

It took a moment for Miranda to lower the muzzle. Her eyes flicked from Tiffany to Cal and back. The three remained in deafened silence for a time.

"Miranda," said Tiffany, "meet Sheriff Cal."

Cal got up, painfully, to his feet. He stooped, painfully, and picked up his hat and used it to slap the sand from his jeans.

"What is *wrong* with you two?" he said. "Beat me down. Blow my ear out. *Damn it!*"

"Cal, she didn't know who you were."

"I know that." He spat.

Miranda held out her good hand and cradled the shotgun with the other. Cal shook it.

"Nice to meet you, Sheriff," she said, wincing.

He nodded and released her hand and then punched his fist into his squashed hat and put it on his head. "You're injured," he said. "Are you okay?"

"I am, and I'm sorry for shooting," said Miranda. "I just thought—"

"I know what you thought, and you had every right to think it. I was just excited to see somebody, anybody, to see you," he said, glancing at Tiffany when he said it. He seemed to catch on the words a bit as he said them, so he waved his hand in the air to clear it. "I was glad to see you all brought a boat."

Tiffany looked into his eyes when he spoke of her, and looked away when he said he was glad she brought a boat. It was ridiculous. She'd just pummeled the man with a flashlight, and now she worried whether he loved her. It was foolish, but she didn't care. He looked even more handsome muddy and bug-bitten, like he'd been fighting bears. She wasn't afraid of how she felt anymore. She wasn't afraid to trust the warmth, to gather it along with all the fear. She wanted her weed-patch rental in Claypot. She wanted her poems and small kitchen table. And she wanted him.

"Do you know where my father is?" Miranda asked, tucking the shotgun under her arm. "And have you seen Fischer or his friend? They were here. We found footprints."

Cal nodded. "Yes, and yes, and yes. Look, I still don't understand what—"

"And what were you saying about the dog? Sheriff, I lost your dog," said Tiffany.

Cal rubbed the back of his neck again, tried to roll it and test it a bit. "We just saw the boys. They left here less than an hour ago. And you didn't lose my dog."

"Where, Sheriff? Which direction!" demanded Miranda.

Cal nodded at the river, but held his hands out when Miranda took a step toward the water, as if she were about to drop the shotgun and swim for them. "Everyone hang on just a second. I'm trying—"

"Did they swim?" Miranda asked.

Tiffany spoke up. "They took a raft."

"A raft!" said Miranda. "What raft?"

"They built one," Tiffany informed her.

"How?" said Miranda, and then, turning to Cal, "Sheriff, I demand answers."

"Now everyone hang on a second," Cal said. "I've been out here for days, and I'm tired, and hungry, and I lost my pistol, and found my dog, and got bucked from a horse—and by the way, I had to arrest your father and then unarrest him because it did me no good. And before we go any further, you both may as well know that the second we get out of these woods I'm not sheriff anymore, so please stop calling me—"

"You found Jacks!" Tiffany exclaimed. "And what do you mean you're not sheriff anymore?"

Cal opened his mouth and closed it.

"You arrested my father? What for? And what horse, Sheriff? I don't see any horse."

"Yes, and yes, and no. Would everyone just—dang it, my neck hurts!"

Everyone stopped talking. Cal's yell echoed. Miranda shifted uneasily, until a mare whinnied from beyond the riverbank, near the broken stand of hardwood.

Cal took a breath. "First, Miranda, do you think you can still ride?"

Miranda nodded. "Better than I can paddle."

"As I was saying, the boys headed downstream. Teddy took off after them onshore and asked me to stay here. That's when you showed up."

"Why did you stay?"

Cal took a breath, let it out. "Teddy said I'd slow him down, and if I never ride a horse again it's too soon. Also, if the boys hit a dead end in this slough and circle back, I'll be here. It's less than ten miles between here and the gorge, and Teddy's headed down-river where he can cross over to the left bank. I sent Jacks with him, in case his nose becomes useful."

At the mention of the gorge, Miranda took one step back from the circle of light.

"That horse, Sheriff. Is it tied in those trees?" she asked, moving away into the shadows.

"What? No, that horse ain't tied."

Miranda let out a piercing whistle.

Cal took a step toward her. "So now that you're here, I'm thinking the plan might be for you to ride on and join your dad, and Tiff and I could paddle downriver. We'd be able to get on both sides of the boys, upstream and down. Miranda?"

There was no reply. Miranda was gone.

Cal took off his hat and slapped his leg with it. "Wow—if that woman isn't *just* like her father." Cal spat the words. "Get on the horse. Get on the horse. Logging road my ass!" Cal gave up and sighed. "Tiffany, how are you? It's good to see you. Really good. I'm glad you're okay. Are you okay? I'm sorry I scared you."

"You saw the boys? You really saw them?"

Cal rubbed his neck and pointed with his hat. "Teddy and I came bursting out of those cattails as the boys were pushing out into the main channel. We yelled. They saw us and pushed on even harder."

"I don't understand."

"They think they're on the run, Tiff."

"From whom?"

"From me." The sheriff looked at the ground for a moment, at the hundreds of little footprints. Tiffany saw fear in his face, and sadness too. She took a step toward him.

"Are you okay—Cal?"

His eyes met hers.

"Yeah."

"You look tired."

"I am. I am very tired."

Tiffany placed a tentative hand on his wet jacket. He looked at it, and at her. She wanted to tell him everything, about herself, her youth and her poems, last summer, about all she'd been thinking about him. But she realized that he hadn't known any of her thoughts. He hadn't been with her in any of her daydreams. To him, she was just the woman who worked at the gas station, the one who lost his dog, or didn't lose it. She had lived out the entire romance in her mind, and he wasn't there for a moment of it, and now she realized she didn't know who he was either. The thought caught in her throat. They were strangers.

"Cal," she asked, "what did you mean when you said you weren't going to be sheriff anymore?"

"I want a different life, Tiff."

The way he answered, so quickly and harshly, made Tiffany's heart fall.

"Oh," she said.

The sound of hooves pounded to a stop behind them. Tiffany turned the flashlight and saw Miranda, high and wild-looking atop a horse, the shotgun slung across her back, reins held in her good hand. In order to ride, she'd hiked her denim skirt all the way above her hips. Long, shining legs stood powerfully in the stirrups. The horse seemed enlivened to have a good rider on it again. It huffed and paced back and forth in Miranda's hands, eager to find its direction and run. The fire was back.

"Sheriff, here is the plan," said Miranda. "You and Tiffany will follow the boys down in the canoe. I'll catch up with my father. We can get on both sides of them before the falls."

Cal shut his eyes and mouth, and then opened his hands in acquiescence. "That sounds like a really good plan."

"You said they'd left about half an hour ago?"

"About that."

Miranda nodded. Her eyes were already downriver. Tiffany knew that if Miranda could get to the boys, they'd stop running.

The horse paced and stomped its feet. Miranda turned it. "Tiffany, give me that light, there's another in the boat."

Tiffany handed it over, and Miranda wound the reins around it so she could hold both with one hand.

"Listen closely," Miranda said. "When you get to the gorge, there will be a thick rope strung across the river. It marks the first falls. It floats on red buoys from the right shoreline to the main island. Do not cross it. There is no surviving that gorge in a canoe or in anything else."

The horse turned and stomped again and Miranda corrected it.

"Go, Miranda," said Tiffany, and Miranda's face tightened in pain.

"Sheriff, did they look okay?" Miranda asked. "Did the boys look hurt?"

"The boys were fine," he said.

Miranda shut her eyes and opened them. She was giving thanks, Tiffany knew. "I will meet you both at the gorge," said Miranda. "Do not cross the rope."

And with that, she turned the mare and kicked her heels into its side.

"*Hyahh! Hyahh!*" she yelled—leaving Cal and Tiffany standing together in the drizzle and darkness, watching the beam of the Maglite race ahead of the galloping horse, over the sandbar, through the cattails, amid the trees and forest downstream. Miranda sped through the trees like a flying spirit, spurring and shouting—"*Hyahh! Hyahh!*"—a mother after her boy, majestic and terrifying.

"Jesus," Cal said, still watching her.

"You have no idea," Tiffany said, and turned her back on Cal and walked to the canoe alone. A different life, she thought. She had no need of a man desiring a different life.

SIXTEEN

"**T**HIS ROPE IS TOUGH!" IN THE DARK AND RAIN, BREAD STOOD in the water and sawed at a wrist-thick rope strung across the river. The rope floated on buoys between the mainland and a rock island dotted with cedars growing from its plateau top. A new wave of thunderstorm had come, less violent but hotter somehow, more lightning in it—and as the storm came on and the rain began pocking the river, the raft ran afoul of a buoy in the dark. The buoys were red and oval and the size of bathtubs. Each was painted with bold white letters the boys could read in the lightning strikes: *Danger—Dam 100 Feet—Do Not Cross.* The buoys were arranged in such a way that the rope draped between them at water level, too high to cross over and too heavy to lift to get under. Fish was thankful for it, as it gave them an excuse to shelter for the night and plan their next leg. He was wet and sore, and the relative dryness of an island of cedar trees beckoned. But after the boys pulled their way along the rope to land and climbed to the downstream peak of the island where sheer cliffs fell away into whitewater, Fish realized there was no next leg of the journey, at least not by river. The boys sat for a time on that peak, stunned by what the rope had spared them. Fish felt sick to his stomach. The sound of the roaring river mixed so thoroughly with the sound of thunder, he was sure they wouldn't have heard the rapids at all. The first drop was fierce, vertical. It made the rocks hum.

The island they stood on was twenty yards wide. To his right, the lip of the falls stretched several hundred feet from the island to the mainland, its whitewater interrupted by an outcropping of rock. The falls fell about fifty feet. Tongues of whitewater lashed upward and outward, all of them boiling at the bottom before surging downriver. From the left side of the island spilled a second channel through a series of sieves and logjams. Downstream of the convergence, the water remained white and thunderous. Lightning flashed, and Fish saw a stretch of river the length and width of a football field, marked by vertical cliffs on either side, with two or three craggy islands dividing explosive currents. The water seemed to fight itself. It tumbled into pits. It bellowed. It hissed and leapt. It beat against the faces of the islands in giant, upswept pillows of water. Downstream of the islands, the entire river disappeared again, presumably over another falls, sprays of water rising into the lightning.

Fish's knees trembled up on that peak. And he knew it wasn't only because he was wet and cold. The rapids spoke of something great and terrible, a storm of water that had churned for ages. The boys sat silently for a few minutes more, then walked in silence back to the rope and raft, wiping water from their faces. When Bread first asked for the barlow knife, Fish assumed his friend wanted to shave some bark or make a feather stick for a fire. Cutting the buoy rope was beyond reason. Bread's pretense in doing so, that some possibility still existed downstream, was infuriating to behold.

"Would you just knock it off?" said Fish.

Bread looked up from his work. He stood knee-deep in the eddy of a small ledge, atop which Fish perched on his heels. Lightning illuminated the sky, and the barlow knife in Bread's hand flashed as white as the gun in his belt. The rainwater plastered his shirt to his chest and stomach. Thunder filled the air with noise. Now that he knew to listen for it, Fish could more easily discern the low thrum of the rapids beneath the pops of thunder.

Bread challenged him. "Why don't you knock off doing nothing? I'm trying to get us moving."

"Bread, we can't get through that!" Fish had pulled his shirttail up over his head. It didn't matter that the rain ran down his back and into his shoes. At least the hood kept it out of his eyes.

"Yes we can. I cut through about an inch of it already. This rope is like wood. But it cuts."

"Rope? You think I'm talking about rope! Bread, did you see the same rapids I saw? We're done. Don't you get it?"

"I'm not done," said Bread, and he turned back to his work, sawing and sawing the massive braid with the small knife.

This was suicide. Fish jumped from the rock and splashed in the water. The rocks under his feet were round and smooth, the size of melons. Even here, the river ran fast enough to polish the stones, suck the silt off the river bottom. It was unthinkable, the power of the river past those falls. Fish waded forward and grabbed Bread's shoulder.

Bread whipped around, anger in his eyes, and shook his shoulder free. Fish couldn't tell if Bread meant to brandish the knife when he spoke, but it was in his hand when he waved it.

"Don't you try to stop me, Fish. You hear me? Don't you try to stop me!"

"Bread, you can't run these rapids. You'll die!"

"All you've wanted to do from the beginning of this is give up. Don't lie, Fish. You've been running scared this whole time. And now you want to run away again."

Fish fumed. "The way I see it, I'm only out here because of you!"

Bread stopped sawing, clenched his fists. "You killed him, Fish! And we're out here because of you!"

Rain fell between them, shot the river full of holes.

Fish felt spite rise up in the shame. It ran thick from his tongue. "I saved your life."

Bread shot back, "You ruined my life!" His chest heaved. As wet as he was, tears were in his eyes. "He's dead! And there's nowhere else for me to go, Fish!" Bread's eyes flared. He clenched his jaw and looked out at the water. When he spoke again it was filled with a malice nearly too dark to hear in the storm. "But what would you know about it, your perfect life with your mom and your dad. You never been alone for a day."

"You're running scared too, Bread."

Bread shook his head in disgust, looked downriver at the falls.

"That's the difference between us, Fish. You run away. I'm running forward. And you, and this rope, and those rapids, none of it's going to stop me. I'm going, Fish."

"Toward what? Look at the river. There is no forward." Fish watched Bread's puffed-up chest, his tiny knife, and hated the strength he saw there, the tenacity. If Fish knew what to say to wound him, he would. Out here in this miserable forest, knee-deep in river water, hungry and wet and cold as he'd ever been, Fish wanted to ruin him and silence him.

"I'm sticking with the plan, Fish. I'm making it to the armory. I'm finding your dad."

Raindrops fell in sheets. Lightning lit them like sparks. Astonishment dawned in Fish's mind. Bread didn't know. He really didn't know. And this was Fish's opportunity to crush the life out of Bread, to stop this whole game. Once spoken, there would be nothing left to do, for both of them, but lie down and die. Fish's teeth clenched. Rainwater dripped from his eyes and nose. The words rose up in him like bile, bitter, and sweet to be free of.

Fish looked Bread right in his eyes.

"My dad is dead," he said.

The pounding of the falls coursed through the river bottom,

the rocks and pebbles, the bones and silence beneath it all. Thunder crackled through a cloud.

"What did you say?" asked Bread.

Fish laughed through his nose, felt fire in his throat. "You didn't know, did you?" He felt powerful and awful. He felt as if he were watching himself say the words, twist them up and wring them out, pour them on Bread. This was too much power, and Fish hated himself for possessing it, for freeing it. "My dad's been dead for as long as you've known me, and you didn't know it. You're too stupid to know."

"Are you telling the truth?" Bread trembled.

Fish trembled too. The river trembled.

"There's nothing out here, Bread. There never was. There is nowhere to run."

Bread swayed in the rain. He tucked his chin in toward his neck and closed his eyes. He clenched the barlow in his fist. Fish didn't know if he was going to fight, but it didn't matter. Nothing mattered. It was over. They'd reached the end, standing in a river above a falls in a storm, alone.

"Go away from me, Fischer."

Rain fell and filled the river. Fish imagined the water rising, the dark current filling his legs and arms. It filled his eyes and mouth and ears with silence, his stomach like handfuls of lead shot. He felt the way he did the night he learned his dad had died, the chasm opening underfoot.

"Bread," he whispered.

Bread's eyes stayed closed.

"Bread."

"Go away from me, Fischer. Or I will kill you."

Fish felt dizzy in the current, and he wished at that moment that Bread would kill him, just take it out of him and let the husk of his body breach the falls, whatever it was Bread needed to take to make himself whole again. But Bread just stood in the rain, breathing it in, swaying there in the lapping waves, the trees and cliffs pasted to the sky.

Fish left him.

He stumbled alone, uphill, into the interior of the island. He looked back at the river only once before entering the tree line, and saw Bread unmoved in the water, staring up into the rain, the knife in his hand, the gun in his belt, frozen in so much shimmering ice. Fish was too tired to cry. He didn't even know if he wanted to cry—his body, his cold hands, everything was numb. He walked beneath cedars and over carpets of needles. He crawled up and over moss-covered rocks. He emerged and sat in the rain at the edge of the rock cliff above the rapids, crossed his legs, and let the rain soak him. He put his hands on the lip of the rock, felt the grit on his palms. He stared out at the horrible, watery divide that cut the earth, all of that aimless moaning and hissing. He wondered what it would be like to be in it, to just lean out a little farther, a little more. The thought made him reel and allowed his body to weep.

He wept over the lies he'd told. He wept over his killing hands. He wept over the tangles in it all, how the lies he'd told allowed him to live, allowed his father to live. What choice did he have? Fish leaned nearer to the edge. He let a small stone fall over, watched it swallowed by violence. Gone. Fish, in the space of a breath, had crushed all pretense by speaking into the air the ugly truth. And he didn't wave his hands and wash it away like his grandpa did. He spoke it over them and let it stay. *Your dad is dead. And so is mine. And no one is coming to save us.*

Fish imagined his father watching him across the chasm of water. The eyes hovered, sad and ashamed, and then they turned away. Fish looked up into the rain and thunder at the mottled, lamplit clouds. He didn't know if he was praying, but it felt like prayer. He didn't know what to ask for, even as he pleaded, word-lessly, without meaning or direction. His heart simply moaned like the river, murmured like the sky. A single word eventually escaped his mouth. *Help,* he asked, sitting with his hands planted on that humming rock, eyes filling with black and white rain. *Help.*

An answer came from the water. It sounded like the thump of a car door, a dropped pail. Fish heard it again. It sounded less metallic this time, more plastic or wooden. It sounded hollow. He looked down into the river, but all he saw was white. He heard it again, this time to his right, and looked toward the main race of the falls. Something dark and round fled with the water, on top of the water. The object fell toward that churning hole, encountered a rock. *Thunk.* Lightning flashed. The river was white and the object red. Fish's chest tightened. He looked to the top of the falls and saw a line of buoys floating free of their tether toward the gorge chasm.

Bread, thought Fish, and then he said it aloud.

Still tied to the mainland, the line of buoys spilled toward the falls in a giant sweeping arc. When it reached the precipice, the cable snagged at its middle on the rock outcropping. The line to the mainland snapped taut as the free end was claimed by the falls. *Thunk. Thunk. Thunk.* The torrent stripped the buoys from the line. One, two, three, four, five. The buoys rocketed downward, bounding, springing, then devoured.

Fish watched, frozen.

"Bread," he said again, rising from his hands and knees at the cliff's edge. Downriver, only two buoys reappeared, bounding toward islands.

"Bread!" Fish yelled. He ran back over rocks and through trees, wet branches tangling his arms and neck. "Bread, don't do it! *Bread!* I'm coming with you if you go!"

FISH SPUN THROUGH A TANGLE OF PINE AND EMERGED BREATHLESS in the clearing lower down the island. He could make out the raft about twenty yards away, still tethered to the rock point. But where was Bread? Fish could still talk him out of it, or go with him, it didn't matter which. There was still a thread of light in Fish's heart. There was still something out here amid so much darkness, something worth running toward. There was still hope, and it astounded Fish. He would throw himself at Bread's feet and beg forgiveness, and Bread would forgive him, and they would keep going as before, reconciled, together.

Crossing the clearing, lightning flashed, and Fish saw something dark and round out of the corner of his eye. He turned in the darkness and made out a silhouette near the edge of the island, where the land fell off into the river.

"Bread?" Fish took a slow step across the pine needles. His pulse rose. Between two cedars, something shook in the brush. It looked hunched over, like a bear's back, and suddenly Fish got the uncanny feeling that he was in the presence of evil. Wet hair stood on his neck. His dream came back to him, the man with horns on his head, shaking and writhing. Fish didn't know if he should speak, but he tried.

"Bread?" he said, more loudly this time.

The form stopped wrestling itself and stood up to a ghostly man-sized height. As it did, lightning flashed and lit the clearing.

Fish's stomach balled in a knot. Air stopped in his lungs. The trees reeled and spun. A flood of river water rose through their branches. All was dark water.

The man wore thick, mud-smeared boots. His rain poncho lay open and waving. At his feet knelt Bread, eyes wide and terrified, a blackened claw of a hand holding Bread's collar. Bread struggled against it, beat his arms and fists. The man held the revolver in his other hand and struggled to tuck it into his belt. But upon hearing Fish's voice, his body froze. His face was half shaven, from jaw to scalp. A thick white bandage crossed his forehead and covered one eye. A bruise enveloped his nose and cheekbone and jaw.

Bread dropped free of the astonished man's grasp.

"Fish, *go!*" he yelled.

Fish couldn't move. The man's stare bore through Fish's middle, stole his breath, pinned him in place against the trunk of a pine. Fish felt more air leave him, as if he'd never taste it again. Before him, on this island in this wilderness, stood the man he'd killed. Muddied and wet, bandaged and startled, Bread's father stood, grave-filthy. Fish watched confusion rise in the man's face, in his eye. And then he saw the revolver twitch. A soiled thumb rested on the hammer. The man squared his stance, gained purchase on the revolver with both hands, and aimed it at Fish's face. Fish gazed into the revolver's bore, the honeycomb of the cylinder, the man's dark eye plumb and still behind the sights.

Fish felt spit rise in his mouth.

"Both of youse," spoke the man, nodding as he spoke, "are in trouble, and coming home right now." It was the first time Fish heard the man speak rather than shout. His voice sounded like any man's voice he ever heard, like it might be trusted, or might have been. Fish took a step forward, hesitated, felt a stone with his toe. Something inside him told him to pick it up. It was a small stone, the size of an orange. Fish stood with it in the rain, held it in his fist, which brought a dark change to the man's face. He lowered the revolver a bit. Looked at Bread, then back at Fish, spoke to both of them.

"Neither one of youse is good for anything. No thanks in youse at all. No gratitude." The man shifted his weight, nervous almost, confused. "You think you're special, like someone owes you something special. And you've caused trouble you can't fix. Well, I'm fixing it. I am! And I came all this way. I brought a boat, see? To bring you boys home."

He paused, and nothing moved. Bread's body shook. Fish held his rock. Heat rose in the man's voice as he spoke. Heat and then severe quiet, in conflict with itself. Fish couldn't tell if the man was there to save him or hurt him.

"Don't you see there is no one else came to get you? Don't you see I came! I'm the one out here with you." He laughed through his nose, spit on the ground. "I am! No one is coming. Nothing ever comes. There's only you and me."

Something in those last lines made Fish lift his rock in the air. He lifted it against some darkness he couldn't explain.

The man's face went sour and tight.

"You son of—" The man didn't finish. Three things happened all at once. Bread tried to scramble, his dad stooped to snatch his collar, and the revolver went off.

Fish ducked. Heard the bullet rip through the trees to his left. The shot surprised Bread's dad enough that he missed his grab at his son. As Bread scurried into the shadows, his dad gritted his teeth and raised the revolver at Fish. He crushed it in his grip, put his finger on the trigger, but then spiked it into the dirt with an exasperated cry and came at Fish like fire. The man took three or four steps, and then reeled backward and howled in pain. Fish watched as Bread drove a dead branch into the backs of the man's knees. The man's hands went instinctively to the pain. He crouched and stumbled backward, toward the cliff. Bread swung again, caught him on the neck, and Bread's father tumbled off the island.

Bread stared over the edge of the cliff. He lowered the branch, lifted it. There was panic and indecision in his movement, and then Bread dropped the branch and bolted upriver toward the raft.

"Dad!" he screamed. "*Dad!*"

Fish raced to the island's edge. In the water leading to the falls, Bread's dad slapped at the surface, his poncho over his eyes. Fish picked up the revolver at his feet and tucked it into his belt, looked upstream. Bread had made it to the raft and gathered in his arms the coil of rope from its deck. Turning downstream, he began to splash along the edge of the cliff face through knee-deep water. It was deeper where his father had fallen in, up to his waist, but Bread charged through it.

"Dad! Rope!" he yelled, holding the rope high overhead.

Bread's dad struggled to keep afloat in his poncho and boots but had managed to uncover his face. He dipped and bobbed toward the lip of the falls, his bandaged head and hands flailing. He spotted his son.

"Dale!" his father yelled, dipping into the water and spitting it out. "Help me! *Dale!*"

Dale Breadwin launched the rope to his father. It uncoiled through the lightning flashes and landed like a fly line. Bread's dad took three panicked strokes and clutched the rope against his chest. The rope lost slack and lifted from the water, a taut line between father and son.

Bread slipped and went under. The rope slackened. He came back up on new footing, and the rope tightened again. Bread's dad dangled and spun. Bread leaned back and screamed from the effort.

"Dale!" His dad spat water from his mouth.

"*Swim!*" yelled Bread.

"Dale!" shouted his dad.

Bread was underwater again. And when he came up the rope stayed slack, and both Bread and his dad were in deep water now, drifting toward the falls. To their left rose the cliff. To their right, the outcropping of rock where the buoy rope snagged.

Fish was already running. He leapt into the water, untethered the raft, and pushed it into the current. He was no swimmer, but he might be able to reach them with the raft. He rolled aboard, grabbed a pole, and started pushing the rocky river bottom as hard as he could. Under power, he moved faster toward the falls than the swimmers.

"Bread!" Fish yelled. "Swim for the rock!"

Bread turned in the water, keeping himself untangled from the rope as best he could. His eyes grew wide when he saw Fish coming down with the raft. Bread backstroked against the current with one arm to slow their progress. Downstream, Bread's dad sank and resurfaced, attached to the rope.

"Bread, the rock," yelled Fish. "Swim for the rock!"

Bread lifted the rope in his hands. "My dad!"

Fish looked at the outcropping. He could make out the buoy rope much better now. It was wrapped tightly across the back of the boulder, held by the force of the falls. Bread could make it there if he let go. If he didn't, they'd all die. Fish made a decision.

"I'll get him!" he shouted, and Bread stared back from the water. "I'll get to him!" Fish repeated. "I promise! Now swim! *Swim!*"

A bolt of lightning shot directly overhead. It made the water crackle.

Bread released the rope that tied him to his father and swam hard for the outcropping. Head down, his flattened body glided smoothly across the troughs and peaks of rolling black swells. He swam as fast as Fish had ever seen him.

Fish looked back downstream. He judged he was about twenty feet from Bread's dad, maybe sixty from the falls. He narrowed his eyes in the rain and jammed his pole against the river bottom. He felt it connect with the rocks and pushed the raft downriver with all his might. He lifted it and found bottom and pushed again, accelerating the raft toward the falls and Bread's dad. He knew what lay ahead. It was death. The falls roared. The lightning crackled so brilliantly it illuminated the river bottom, the rocks and boulders, the clinging crayfish. Fish saw clearly. This act, he knew, would release him. He promised he'd get to Bread's dad, and he would. Bread would keep swimming and live on, knowing he tried to save his father, knowing he was good even if his father was not. And Fish would go over the falls, having kept a promise, having offered life to his friend with his own. Fish was not a poor damned thing. Bread was not a poor damned thing. They were not forsaken. Fish gave himself over to it, the abandon of it. There was nothing left to fear. Fish pushed even harder against the river stones.

The man's boots rose to the surface, kicked, then disappeared again. He faced the falls, backpaddling, panicked, his left arm a tangle of rope. Fish was ten feet away from him, the falls thirty. The depth of the canyon gaped before them. The river rose and fell through glass black waves.

Fish repositioned his pole. The pole found bottom. Lightning illuminated stones. Fish yelled for Bread's dad to turn around, leaned into the pole with his full weight, then leapt toward the front of the deck. Fish landed hard on his stomach and reached out into the water. Bread's dad turned upriver, went underwater, lifted his hands. Fish grasped his wrists, and the man grasped his.

Fish had him.

The man's face emerged in the darkness. The water had washed the bandage free, and the bloody gauze hung loosely across his nose and mouth. The uncovered eye was blood red, cut through with river channels and lightning bolts. And just where the crease of his eye met his temple, the stitched and bleeding track of a wound ran back toward a torn ear. The cut followed the arc of his skull, a vein pounding next to the wound. The bullet had only grazed him, Fish knew, and with it knew he never was a killer.

Five feet from the lip of Ironsford Gorge, the weight of the man dangling from the raft spun it just enough for Fish to glance upstream. Equidistant from the falls and the rock—ten feet from death and ten feet from life—Bread's body still sliced across the surface like a streak of light. He kicked and reached. Kicked and reached. As Fish watched Bread's hand plant itself firmly on solid rock, he felt the raft roll to his left. It spun. Its bow faced upstream and then pitched up toward the thunderclouds.

The last thing Fish saw before blackness was a blue and slate thundercloud shaped like a beautiful mountain, a bolt ripping through it, and then Bread's dad stretched prone, his poncho and boots waving skyward, his arms clasped to Fish's arms, that dreadful eye wild and startled, flying like a beautiful bird.

SEVENTEEN

TIFFANY HURLED HER PADDLE INTO THE DARKNESS. "THERE!" SHE said, folding her arms before the paddle even hit the water. "Maybe *that* will make it easier for you."

Cal's jaw dropped as he watched the paddle dart off into the rain. Now what's this about? Cal realized how little he knew this woman, how much of a stranger she was. It was an odd realization. During the countless hours of sitting horseback and staring at stars and wading through brambles, he'd imagined himself married to her, and all the way through their honeymoon, their first house with a dock, their third or fourth child. But now he remembered he hadn't so much as asked her on a date. He only knew where she lived and worked because he was a sheriff living in a very small town. And now she'd thrown one of their two paddles into the darkness.

"Tiffany—what on earth, woman!" He knew it was a mistake when it came out of his mouth.

"Woman? Woman!" she retorted, astonished. "I am not going to sit up here—*man*—and listen to you tell me how to paddle any-more." She mocked his voice—*Tiff, left side. No, right side. No, left.*

"I paddled this canoe through a tornado, Cal, and a rapids. Nearly eighty miles of river. And all of it went pretty smooth until you pretended to take over!"

Her tone was dark as river water. Cal reeled.

"Tiff, you never said you wanted to steer. And the person in the back does the steering. And I'm in the back."

"I know who does the steering! And it sure isn't you! Back and forth. Back and forth. I've never been so seasick."

Cal paused, thought a moment. "What is wrong with you? Is this really about steering? You can steer, okay? You steer."

"Oh, please," she said, which made Cal drop his jaw at the night sky. He bit his knuckle.

It was raining hard again. Thunder rumbled around them. They'd made good distance, or at least Cal thought they'd made good distance. It was hard to tell. For the past half hour, Cal had been looking in earnest for the buoys and gorge. The river narrowed to one channel again, and the pines and cedars grew thick amid rock outcroppings. The lightning was such that finding the buoys should be easy enough, if they could focus for a moment. Why was Tiff like this? First the silence, then this anger, and for what? Cal was no boatman, but he knew his steering was not as bad as Tiffany claimed.

So he tried again. "No, really, you can steer. We'll spin around. I'm glad to let you have the rudder." Cal turned the canoe with a few drawstrokes, but Tiffany just sat in the bow with her arms crossed, facing upstream.

"I don't have a paddle, *Cal.*"

"Well." He paused, careful now of his next words. He was playing with fire here, and he knew it. "You can have mine."

"Oh, you'd like that, wouldn't you? A woman paddling you around while you lounge in the bow and play captain. I watched your dog for you, Cal. How could you?"

Cal froze. He remembered once getting a call to a backyard in Houston where a pit bull was tangled in a neighbor's garden hose. It snarled whenever he moved. He didn't know how to approach it.

"How could I *what?*" he asked, in as monotone a voice as he could muster.

Tiffany growled and beat her fist on the gunwale. "You just paddle this canoe! Do you understand? Just get us downriver!"

Cal dipped his paddle experimentally in the water, turned the boat again. They floated around a left-hand bend where the river widened. Cal made out what looked to be a slough leading off to the left of a rocky peninsula, and a few rock outcroppings to the right. A vertical rock face rose from the peninsula and seemed to indicate the main channel. He applied enough pressure to the paddle to nose toward it. No island yet. No buoys. He was tired of this river, this rain. He wanted his warm truck and his dog and a cup of coffee. Maybe a stiff drink. He shook his head at the thought. No drink. That's going away, along with this badge. And as long as he was shedding old comforts, he decided his daydreams about Tiffany might as well go too. She wasn't for him. He wasn't for her. No use pretending anymore.

"We'd go faster if we had two paddles," he said.

Tiffany spun in her seat and nearly capsized the canoe. She stared him down in the lightning flashes. She was so beautiful, so exasperating.

"Don't you mock me, Sheriff. Don't you dare mock me!"

"I'm not mocking you. I just don't understand why you tossed your paddle. I wasn't bossing you."

"Bossing me? Bossing me. Do you think I threw my paddle because you were bossing me, Sheriff?"

Cal let his eyes glare back. "That's what you said!"

"I did not say that, and you know it, Sheriff."

Thunder bellowed overhead.

"You said I was telling you how to paddle, and you were seasick, and then you whipped your paddle off into the night, Tiff. And I told you before to stop calling me Sheriff!"

"I said your steering made me seasick, not your bossing, Sheriff. There's a difference."

"What the hell are we even talking about?" Cal beat the gunwales with his paddle more loudly than he hoped to. "And *stop* calling me Sheriff!"

The cliff face rose to their left, up to a high plateau covered in cedar. The current seemed to quicken.

"We are talking," said Tiffany, "about you and your *different life.*" She lifted her hands from the gunwales and made air quotes with her fingers. Then she gripped the canoe and leaned forward. "And how stupid am I to get steered around by a man and babysit his dog and chase it through the wilderness while he dreams of going back to Houston or Dallas or from wherever else some syrupy blonde writes him letters?" Then her voice changed. The sarcasm left it. "Can you not see me sitting here, Cal? Can you not see me at all?"

"Who said anything about Houston or another woman?" The words she just spoke, the way she spoke them, seemed to push aside the rain and thunder. A fresh wind of realization, pure and light, rose in Cal's heart. She was yelling at him because she was jealous. Cal felt a dumb grin spread on his face.

"Don't smile at me, Cal. I can't bear it."

"No," Cal said, softly now. "You don't understand, Tiff. I thought you were mad at me."

"I *am* mad at you!"

"Well, I know, but for the wrong reason. Listen, Tiff, when I was talking about wanting a new life, I wasn't talking about leaving here."

Tiffany sat very still. She inclined her head, as if waiting for the rest of his thought, and then she followed Cal's gaze.

Cal had stopped paddling. He'd seen something onshore.

"Tiff, are those buoys?"

Lightning crackled and illuminated the right shoreline. The canoe seemed to be drifting beside a string of large floating orbs, like calf tanks, Cal thought, but red. Cal had envisioned arriving perpendicular to the line of buoys, not alongside it. Lightning flashed again, and the line of buoys arced out into the center of the river, where they seemed to attach themselves to a rock outcropping. To the outcropping's left, where the canoe was headed, lay the channel, and beyond the channel rose the high rock face of the peninsula.

"That's the island?" asked Cal, nodding toward the small outcropping. He had a sinking feeling in his stomach. He didn't like the thought of being confused by buoys that were supposed to warn him of a killer waterfall. He began looking around for the boys and their raft.

"Cal!" Tiffany pointed toward the far left shore. A post emerged from the shallows, with a slack cable dragging a single buoy that bumped against the rocks. Cal looked back at the rock outcropping, where the line of buoys now clearly clung, snagged because the rope was cut. He started backpaddling furiously.

"Cal?"

"That outcropping is not the island," he said, nodding at the rock, now twenty yards downstream to their right. "That's the island!" he said, jerking his head toward the cliff face. Directly ahead of them, the horizon of the falls became clear. Cal could hear the rumble of it now and cursed himself for missing it. He leaned into his paddle strokes. It was too late to make it to the main island, or the mainland. It was either make the outcropping or go over the falls.

Tiffany didn't need prompting. She knelt in the bottom of the canoe, faced upstream, and dug the water with both hands. It was too late to try to turn the canoe. Their only hope of making the rock was to beat upstream at an angle, try to ferry over to the rock.

Cal pushed and pushed, leaned and sat up, felt his blade thrum with each stroke. They were ten yards off the falls now, and the river thundered more loudly than the sky. The gorge boomed and hummed. This was no small hole in the river.

"Keep paddling!" Cal yelled. He glanced at Tiffany. She wasn't looking back at the falls. She was all in, digging forward, upstream, for her life.

"Keep paddling!" Cal yelled again, if only to himself. In a moment he'd be able to reach out and touch the outcropping with his paddle. They were that close. He focused on a few more strokes. He pushed down. He sat up. He wrenched the water. He spotted a handhold, a crack in the rock. He dropped his paddle and slapped both hands against the wet rock, curling his fingers into the fissure. Knees hooked inside the stern of the canoe, he felt the force of the river stretch his arms and back. The bow, with Tiffany, pointed itself toward the lip of the falls. The canoe banged against the rock, Cal's body its only tether. Beneath his armpit, Cal could see Tiffany grasping the gunwales, reaching out toward the rock, jounced by the current.

"Jump!" Cal shouted. The force of the water wracked his joints. His shoulders and torso burned. "Jump now!" he screamed in desperation. He felt his strength fading fast.

The canoe swayed out from the rock when she leapt. The canoe felt lighter, and the current swung its empty hull back into the rock again. Cal looked down to see the empty bow dangling over the void. A sickening feeling came. He couldn't see her. His own grip was about to fail. He was about to call out when he saw movement, a white and green running shoe scratching its way up to safety. I am going up, he thought. One chance.

Cal dug his fingers into the fissure as deeply as he could. He let his knees unfold, and as soon as he did, the canoe shot out from beneath him, leaving his legs skimming on the black water. Cal was startled by how quickly the canoe rocketed into oblivion.

Now he dangled in that same thrum of current, trying to pull himself up onto the rock. He tucked his knees. His hard boot slipped against the wall. His legs plunged back into the current, and he thought for an instant that he'd lose his grip. Pain seared his shoulders. He looked at his hands. He looked at the falls. He had only a few seconds more, he knew, and then he'd have to let go. He lifted his socked foot this time. It gained purchase, enough to help him cling a moment longer.

He rested his forehead against the rock, bellowed for help, lifted his knees a final time, and then felt hands on his wrists. And he felt himself being slowly hoisted, like a wet rag, higher up the flat of the rock. He dug the toe of his boot and his knees into the rock, to give any boost he could, but he knew he was mostly dead weight. He heard Tiffany scream with effort, and felt his chest lifted up near the flat surface of the rock, and then saw something that confused him: Tiffany's hands wrapped around his right wrist—both of them. On his left wrist, a slightly smaller set of hands clamped firm.

One more pull and Cal was up on the rock, flattened and spent. Rain pelted the side of his face. In his immediate field of vision, he saw Tiffany, legs folded, her palms flat on the wet rock, too winded to speak. To her left knelt a boy in a wet flannel shirt, looking at Cal with astonished eyes.

"Dale Breadwin," panted the sheriff. He rolled painfully to his side and placed a heavy hand on the boy's knee, patted it. "You okay?" he asked.

The boy nodded, and Cal tried to smile at him.

"Your bud here?"

The boy shook his head, and Cal frowned, looked at the rock. The scene took no great sheriff to discern. Two boys on a raft. One boy left on a rock near a falls. Cal felt exhaustion take his body, his mind too. There was nothing to say. Nothing could be done. It was over. Cal felt a knot rise in his throat. He rolled onto his back and hid his eyes with his forearm. He found Tiffany's lap with his free hand, began to quietly weep. He wept for the past few days of briars and rivers and horses. He wept for the sight of that boy Fischer, and Dale, pushing off with that raft, how he'd *seen* that boy's eyes. He wept for Houston and all its wasted time and hope. Tiffany took his hand and held on to it. Her fingers were soft and cold. Cal let out a slow, shuddering breath, let his head rest on that humming rock, and fell asleep in the roar and rain.

FISH RESTED HIS FOREHEAD ON THE BACK OF HIS HAND, UNABLE TO lift himself. He threw up river water. The air burned in his lungs. He didn't know how long he'd been here, or how he got here from the bottom of that river, or where *here* even was. His heart banged in his chest and neck. He couldn't tell what was hurt. He was just throb and puddle and fire. He tried to lift his head again, but it was still too heavy.

When he first hit the base of the falls, he thought he had died, so absolute was the darkness and weightlessness and breathlessness. His limbs freewheeled. His body spun through the hiss, pricked full of holes like the universe itself. Dying felt like the cosmos, some part of him thought, the cosmos at the beginning of things, only darkness and light and water. It wasn't until Fish hit the river bottom, hit it hard on his right hip, that he remembered he was underwater, that he'd gone over the falls, and that he wanted to live. He tried to swim, but his arms and legs seemed wrenched in every direction. He opened his eyes, but there was no light. He opened his mouth to scream, but it filled with water. The desire to inhale was terrifying. Fish fought it and fought it, tumbled on in the gravel and stones. And just when he thought he could fight no longer, when his lungs seemed physically unable to remain so empty, he felt himself borne by a strange and powerful current. It boiled up from beneath him and lifted him like a leaf in a gust of wind. Fish bent and spun upward through the water column. He saw flashing lights, dappled and amber-colored. He saw froth and foam. Then he felt air rush in, heard his own breath as the river surged and spat him onto a smooth stone surface.

Fish found himself lying flat on his stomach, above water, hugging the flat curve of a massive stone rising from the river. Stunned and panicked, Fish dragged himself along the stone, scraping his nails against the marbled surface, his knees and toes propelling him forward. A few yards onto the stone, he looked back and saw a giant pillow of whitewater churning near the rock face like a fountain, a miraculous spring.

Fish waited for his heart to slow. He could still feel its pulse knocking in the back of his throat. He moved his arms and legs experimentally, flexed his fingers. They worked. He drew another rattling breath. How long had he been under? He had no way of knowing. He rolled on his side and looked up at the sky. Lightning shot through it, slowly somehow, and Fish felt as if he could see individual raindrops spinning and throbbing as they fell, blackened and jeweled in so much light and darkness.

Fish drew his knees under himself and rose to his feet. His hip hurt, and he felt as if he had a cut on his face, but everything was too wet to tell if it was bleeding very badly. He took his bearings. Whitewater charged down either side of the island. This part of the island was low in the water, sloping downward until tucking itself back into the current. Upstream, Fish saw where the two main channels of the falls converged, the smaller cutting into the larger before colliding with the island.

The island had the footprint of a large house. Fish followed its shoreline. Near its center rose the island's highest point, a fifteen-foot ledge of rock. The face of the ledge revealed rounded-out hollows and bends where the river had carved it long ago. Some looked large enough to provide shelter, and Fish took a step toward them. He stumbled. He held his hip and rubbed it with his hands. As he rubbed his leg he was surprised to find the revolver still tucked in his belt. The sight of it startled him. Fish had forgotten about Bread's dad. He frowned at the thought of that man's eye, the way it stared into him as he dropped down the falls, the way it seemed to plead with him. Fish looked around the island. From what he could tell, he was alone. He looked up, beyond the island, and in the distance could see the sheet of the falls plummeting down. He could make out the black ribbon of the gap formed by the outcropping. Bread was up there somewhere. Fish could only attend to himself now. He took a few more hobbling steps toward the craggy face of the rock wall. The air smelled musty here, like river bottom. The hollows in the ledge seemed deeply cut, and Fish hoped they would be dry. But any sort of roof was welcome. It would be important to try to stay warm. Fish felt waves of exhaustion. He knew as soon as he hit the hollows of that ledge, he would curl up in a ball and sleep.

And then Fish stopped walking.

Something caught his eye, a sort of glistening amid the whitewater. He didn't step toward it immediately. He didn't even want to look directly at it. He knew in his gut what it was. Near the shore, an old pine was pinned against the ledge, its branches polished smooth by the water. Caught in the branches was a work boot, sole up, with a leg in it. The boot belonged to Bread's dad. The rest of his body dangled beneath the whitewater.

Fish stumbled toward the edge and got down on his hands and knees. He reached out for the boot. His instinct was to save the man, but a deeper instinct told him it was already too late. The boot moved ever so slightly, like the rocking of a tied-up boat. The man was dead and Fish knew it.

"Why did you do this?" Fish whispered to the dead man. His voice didn't sound like his own. It sounded younger, higher. He felt afraid. His body shivered in the cold. Whatever dark spirits lived in this wild had gathered here, in this one man, but now they were gone and there was only a shell. The man was gone, but Fish didn't want to let him dangle like that. He reached out to the boot again. It was just beyond his reach. Fish tested the log with his foot, to see if he might shimmy out. His foot slipped and he clung to the rock. He shivered. Stared at the boot. He stared and he waited. He couldn't leave his friend's father like this, no matter how bad he was, but Fish knew he was too weak to get him. Minutes passed. Fish listened to the river whisper and hiss, to the rain fall on his back, until his body started to shiver less. He began to feel the cold a little less. Some part deep in his mind felt already home in his bed, his mom praying over him the way she prays. Another part of him, a more frantic part, knew he needed to get into the shelter of the island's ledge if he was to survive the night. He remembered one of his grandfather's lessons: *If you're cold enough to stop shivering, you're in a bad way.* The thoughts wrestled in his mind, in the river mist, his eyes opening and closing. A lightning bolt crawled very slowly across the sky, and Fish became certain he could sleep in the cold rain, if only for a few moments.

And then he felt a warmth that came from outside himself. He heard it, too, a warm breath exhaled on his back and neck. His eyes opened wide as a giant shadow stepped over the top of him. Fish's heart pounded in his neck. He lay perfectly still. It was a bear. A bear stood over the top of him.

The bear blocked the rain, and Fish could feel the heat of the animal's stomach, like a humid tent. This bear was much larger than the sow they'd seen save her cub. This was a male, a bruin. Fish watched the animal reach its muzzle out toward the log that trapped Bread's dad. The bear sniffed, and then huffed, and then it bellowed.

The sound was like a giant drum. Fish's body shook. The rock he lay on shook. And Fish took the opportunity to scramble out from under the bear. He rose to his feet and ran toward the ledge. His legs gave way and he fell.

The bruin took another breath and bellowed at the dead man again. It seemed ecstatic, as if a fire was loosed inside of it. The bruin's hide shivered as it screamed. Its hair stood along its back in tall, wet spikes. Fish waited for the river to burst into flame, and felt like throwing up. The river basin echoed when it stopped. Rain fell against the rock. The bear looked out at the water. It popped its big jaws. *Snap, snap.* It lowered its muzzle to the man's boot, nudged it sharply, and the body of Bread's dad snaked into the current. *Gone.*

The bear watched the river. Fish watched the bear. It seemed made of the stone it stood on. The animal's majesty was terrifying. Fish knew there was nothing in the wilderness this bear feared. There was nothing in the night that could touch it. Fish had heard of black bears getting old and big. His grandfather told him they could sometimes live for twenty years, the rarest of the rare reaching a quarter ton. This bear was the size of a steer, higher somehow, thicker, a mass of rump and shoulder and jaw.

Fish hadn't waited to pull the revolver. He tried to open the cylinder to see if he had a round ready, but the latch proved too heavy for his wet and trembling hands. He pulled the hammer back with both thumbs. Fish's hands shook as he tried to get a better grip on the revolver. His whole body shook, and as it did, he inadvertently squeezed the trigger. The muzzle blast erupted at his feet, and Fish heard the buzzing zip of the bullet ricochet into the night. The bruin bayed and its body shook as it spun toward him. Without hesitation the bear lumbered toward Fish, who was trapped with his back to the rock ledge several yards behind him. The bruin licked its nose as it walked. It towered over Fish.

Fish took a step back. The bear swayed on its paws. Fish fumbled with the hot cylinder. He didn't know if he had another round. He thought about leaping into the river, but he was too weak to leap. His hands shook so badly that he couldn't cock the hammer. He tightened his grip on the gun and tried again. But then he stopped trying. The revolver seemed so small, so impotent. And

Fish did too. But what surprised him most, staring into the wide, black and brown face of wildness itself, was the knowledge that he wouldn't shoot the bear even if he could. He didn't want to shoot it. The bear was close enough to smell now, its powerful odor of mud and musk, honey and heat. The bear alone was justified in being out here. There were spirits in this world, and the bruin was among their chiefs. Fish had no ability to change its course.

"Leave me alone!" Fish said, his voice rattling.

The bear licked its nose. Moaned a little.

"I said, leave me alone!"

The bear took a step forward.

Fish's fear allowed him to cock the hammer, and so Fish aimed the revolver at the bear's giant eye. But as he straightened his grip, he saw something about to erupt from that eye, and from the rest of that massive body. It came from its mouth, through its teeth, and across its piebald gums. The bear bellowed. Fish felt heat on his face.

The revolver clattered at Fish's feet.

The bear stared at him. Fish stared back. The bear huffed, blew rain from its nose. Fish felt his lungs filling and emptying. The bear came face-to-face with him, and Fish could see the grain of hairs on its nose, the stippled texture of its black nostrils, the river gleaming in its marbled eyes. Fish had fought one too many times, and he couldn't anymore. His body was numb with fear and exhaustion. He'd been wet and cold for far too long. He had no food in his stomach. He felt dizzy. The world could have its way now. Tears came to Fish's eyes, staring at that bear, the musk coming out of its nostrils. And Fish suddenly felt as if he was outside of himself, watching himself stare at the bear. Lightning flashed. The bear's eyes flashed. Fish saw a boy weeping silently in the rain, his hands at his sides. Very hungry and alone. And tired too, he thought, so tired. It was okay that this was the end of things, because then he'd finally get to sleep. And after a long sleep, if it was true, the boy would wake in a field of light, and his dad would be there, smiling at his handsome son, scooping him up in his big arms. And for eternity, the boy would be six years old, and his dad would hug him to his shoulder, and carry him around, and show him beautiful things.

"Dad," whispered Fish to the lonely darkness, to the face of the bear. "Dad."

The bruin came so close that Fish could hear the rumble of its lungs. The sound wasn't menacing. It rolled around like distant thunder, the sound of so massive a force moving and living, breathing. The bear dipped its head down and gave Fish a push in the belly with its massive snout. The bear's head, from forehead to lower lip, was larger than Fish's torso.

Fish stumbled back a step. He wept out of fear and acquiescence, and thought to lift his hands in defense, but then thought better of it. The bear came at him again, and there was no fighting it. It stepped forward and nosed him again. Fish stepped back again. Fish felt as if this back-and-forth went on for a very long time, the bear nosing him backward, but then Fish bumped his head on something hard. He turned to see that he'd run into the overhang of one of the hollows carved in the cliff face. The bear stood guard, lungs thumping. Fish had nowhere to go but in. The bear huffed, stepped closer. Fish backed up against the interior wall, crouched, and looked out from an opening not much larger than his body.

The bear stared at him a moment, then looked up at the rain and grumbled. It turned a half circle in front of the entrance, like a giant dog about to bed down, and then it lowered its generous body onto its haunches and foreleg, slumping across the entrance to the cave.

Fish crouched in absolute darkness. The sound of splattering rain and thunder became muffled. The air in the small space filled with the musk of bear and river rock. Fish listened. He could hear the sound of the bruin's lungs. He remained perfectly still for what must have been minutes. When the bear grumbled, Fish sank to his knees, inches away from the bear's wide back.

The ground beneath him sloped outward. It was dry. The stone was cold, but the bear gave off incredible warmth. Fish raised his hands tentatively to the bear's back, touched the tips of the wet spikes of hair. The hide twitched, and Fish withdrew his fingers. He kneeled in silence, listening to his breath and the bear's breath. Everything was dark and quiet and warm. Fish had never felt so great a need for warmth, nor had he ever been so tired. The bear breathed in and out, its giant lungs lulling the storm outside. Fish was sealed in. His head began to drop and nod, lower and lower, until he lay on the rock floor and curled his body. On the furthest edges of consciousness, Fish inched toward the warmth, closer and closer, until he felt his knees bury themselves in coarse, wet hair, his fingers and face entangled in it, rumbling breath and unspeakable quiet.

That night Fish dreamed of his mother on horseback, racing across frozen dunes, his father sitting atop one of them, smiling, whispers of tongues in the breathing sand.

EIGHTEEN

CAL SAT IN THE MORNING SUNLIGHT WITH HIS ARMS FOLDED over his knees. The sun warmed his face and dried his clothing. He'd removed his boot, setting his one good sock out on the rock to dry. Before him stretched the open air of the gorge, the river rumbling below, and beyond the gorge and forest stretched the tilled plains of Ironsford, a blue horizon. The armory owned most of these woods, Cal knew, used the river and cliffs for training, but today the river was quiet, nothing in sight but the gorge and the sky. There was nothing to do but wait. The falls roared at Cal's feet, fanning out to tumble to the river bottom. The spray that hung in the air was shot through with sparks of light. Gone were the rain and thunder. Gone was the drizzle that lasted the entire evening while Cal sat his vigil. Gone were the dark and damp. All was black rock and gold sun and green trees now. The sunlight lifted puddles from rocks. It dried the cedars, and the gorge became filled with the smell of rocks and trees. Below him in the gorge, a pack of hungry swallows swooped for bugs. Above the swallows, rainbows formed in the mist.

Cal heard stirring by his side. Tiffany lifted herself onto an elbow, then onto her hip. She discovered Cal's jacket then, wrapped around her waist and still half draped over the sleeping boy. Bread slept with his head on his arm, his mouth open and huffing against the rock. The boy had huddled close to Tiffany during the night, and Cal had taken off his canvas coat and placed it over the pair of them. Tiffany pulled it off her waist now, tucked it back up to Bread's chin. He didn't stir.

Cal looked at her. Her eyes were puffy and her hair was tangled. Her jeans were muddied. Cal, too, was dirty and scraped up from head to foot. His face, he knew, was sunburned and bug-bitten. The two adventurers smiled sad smiles at each other. Tiffany moved to sit close to him.

"Hi," he said.

She smiled and looked out at the gorge. "It's pretty," she said.

The sparrows charged down the river valley, swooping over and between islands, dipping defiantly close to the torrent of waves.

Cal looked at the boy. "He's tired."

Tiffany smiled at Bread. "He didn't move all night. Did you sleep?"

Cal shook his head. "Not since we heard that shot. I keep waiting for him to poke his head up from some rock. I haven't seen him."

Bread told them what had happened, how Fish had gone over the falls, how they'd tried to save Bread's dad, the mention of whom startled Cal into abject silence. He'd thought the man dead, remembered the man's slick blood on his hands when he slipped in it. Cal remembered the way he tried to lift his hand to the man's neck to feel for a pulse, and how his hand shook so badly he cursed it and pulled it back and went for the sink and the whiskey. He had no excuse. He was too embarrassed to speak. Bread finished recounting the night, and when tears welled up in his eyes, Tiffany beckoned him sit near to her. *You look cold,* she said. Bread sniffed and said, *I ain't cold.* But Tiffany said, *Yes you are, now come here,* and pulled him in to her and wrapped him in her arms. It wasn't more than two minutes before Bread's head dropped and he nuzzled in, unconscious against her chest.

Tiffany looked at the gorge, the rapids, and the falls, and at Bread. All that beauty, she thought, all this light, and they still had to steel themselves to face the gravest kind of news.

"Tell me it's possible," she said.

Cal paused a moment.

"It has to be," he said.

Tiffany leaned toward him, and Cal felt the slow sway of her breathing body.

"Do you think I should wake Dale?" she asked after a time. "We still need to get off this rock."

"No," Cal answered quietly. "Let him sleep."

A voice from the island cut through the rush of the gorge. A dog barked.

"Cal!"

Cal knew it was Teddy's voice before he even turned his head. On the low bank of the main island, Teddy stood with his hands cupped around his mouth. He was wet to the hips, and so was Miranda, who arrived beside him by stepping lightly down a stone ledge. The pair stood next to the buoy post. Miranda lifted her hand to her eyes and peered across the bright water. Jacks shook water from his neck and tail, stooped for a drink of river water.

Cal waved his hat. He and Tiffany stood.

"Do you have the boys?" Teddy called, and a bit of hope dropped from Cal's heart. He had really hoped Ted would bear good news, say he had Fischer, and Cal could tell him he had Dale, and then everyone could rejoice.

Cal cupped his hands to his mouth. "We have Dale!"

"Where's Fischer?" returned the call.

Cal didn't know how to respond, particularly with Miranda staring at him. He couldn't very well yell out that Fish had gone over the falls, dragging with him Bread's dad, who Teddy thought was dead back in Claypot. It was too much bad news to shout across a river. Teddy seemed to sense Cal's hesitation.

"We found a boat!" Teddy yelled. "It's got a motor! I'll come out for you!"

Cal nodded in an exaggerated way, gave a thumbs-up, and watched Ted turn back toward the trees, Miranda speaking excitedly to him, Teddy patting her hand. Before they made the wood line, an older, heavyset man hobbled out of the brush, clearly winded. The crossing apparently went less smoothly for him. He was wet up to the shoulders of his blue coat. Spotting Ted and Miranda, the man stopped and panted, leaned over with his hand on a tree to catch his breath. Cal watched a brief exchange among the trio, the winded man pointing downstream. Miranda put her hand on her mouth and ran into the trees. Ted followed her. Cal heard the distant thrum of a helicopter. The armory, he thought. Thank God. And then the winded man stood up and peered out at the river. It took a moment for the man to locate Cal in all that brightness, but when he did, he waved furiously and happily.

Cal laughed quietly, then heard a boy's voice behind him.

"Who's that?" Bread sat up on the rock, squinting one eye in the bright sunlight, the wet jacket atop his lap.

"Fish's grandpa and mom are here," said Cal. "They're coming out in a boat."

"But who's that?" Bread asked again. The man had stopped waving now, and leaned on his tree again, wiping his brow with a handkerchief.

Tiffany answered him this time, and Cal gave her a look, which she waved off. "That," she said, "is Constable Bobby."

FISH HEARD SINGING BIRDS, LILTING AND MELODIOUS, BEFORE HE opened his eyes. The rock felt gritty against his head. His mouth was dry. His body, when he began to move it, seemed incredibly stiff, so he lay still another moment, peering through scratchy eyelids.

The sunshine flooded his vision with yellow light, warmth. He could make out trees and rocks and sprays of water, and then he noticed two trees growing up right in front of him, from the rock itself. The trees wore one boot each. They were a soldier's boots, high and laced and polished. Camouflage fatigues were bloused neatly above the leather uppers. Odd trees, Fish thought, still unable to wake. And then he heard voices, men's voices, and all of this seemed to muddle in the memory of rain and lightning and rafts and waterfalls. Fish closed his eyes, reopened them. The boots were still there. They were attached to a tall silhouette of a man surrounded by a halo of light.

Fish lifted his head. His body was terribly sore. He looked at the boots again, the light again.

"Dad?" he asked. The boots pivoted on the rock.

"Lieutenant," said the man. "Lieutenant—Reach Two."

Fish sat upright. His eyes began to adjust to the enormity of the sunshine, and he shaded his eyes with his hand. The man standing before him was definitely a soldier, but he wasn't his father. Fish wasn't dreaming and he wasn't dead. The soldier was a man about the sheriff's age, with a helmet pulled low over his eyes. He spoke into the radio in his hand. Farther down the island, Fish watched another soldier making his way across the dome of rock, holding a yellow drybox in his hand.

"Reach, go ahead."

"We found him, sir. He's on island three. He's conscious. I'll have Grady assess and we'll prepare to evac."

"Copy that."

The soldier looked at his wristwatch and secured the radio to his vest. Fish noticed that the man was wearing webbing and harnesses that looked like some sort of rock-climbing gear. He had a coil of rope over his shoulder, a black sidearm fastened in a hip holster. Fish looked around. On the ground between him and the soldier, the revolver still lay on the rock. He remembered where he was now, and how he got here, and the great weight and enormity of the previous evening rushed upon his consciousness like a river. He remembered firing one shot, or maybe it was two. The details swam, but he saw again a wild and pleading eye, an upturned boot, a man's body slithering into water. But something critical seemed missing. The pieces fell into place slowly, murkily, but lacked a cornerstone. Fish's stomach churned. He felt weak, like he'd throw up if he tried to stand.

The soldier with the radio squatted low on the toes of his boots. He had a friendly face. He didn't say anything right away, but just smiled at the boy, and Fish felt strangely comforted by the man. He knew, down to his empty stomach, that this man meant help. The other soldier, the one carrying the yellow case, placed it on the ground next to Fish, knelt before it, unlatched its top. They looked at the boy.

The soldier with the radio spoke first. "I'm Sergeant Blake," he said. "This is Specialist Grady. He's going to ask you a few questions and then we'll all get off this island. Sound good?"

Fish nodded.

The medic knelt closer and placed his left hand on Fish's back. With his right, he gently squeezed Fish's wrist between his thumb and fingers. The man looked at his watch. "When's the last time you ate or drank anything, buddy?" he asked.

Fish stared at him. "Who are you?" he said.

The two men glanced at each other.

The medic looked at Fish, then back at his watch. "Can you tell me your name?" he asked.

"Fish."

"Good. Can you tell me your birthday?"

"September tenth."

Grady let go of Fish's wrist and felt along the boy's neck and shoulders, asked him if he had any pain. He shone a light in his eyes, made him wiggle his toes and fingers. Fish did what the man asked him to do, told him where it hurt. Grady asked him again when he last ate or drank, while carefully placing a small gauze pad against Fish's right temple. He secured it in place with white tape he snipped with crooked scissors. Fish couldn't answer him. His mind was still too foggy. He still had too many questions of his own.

"Where's the bear?" Fish asked.

The men looked at each other again. Sergeant Blake tilted his head in question.

"The bear," said Fish. "The big bear that was here all night. Where did the bear go?"

The two men hesitated.

"There's no bear out here, bud," said Blake, who then looked around at the island, at the enormity of the whitewater surrounding it. "Bears can't get past the whitewater. You just had a dream."

Fish shook his head. "There was a bear here. He kept my hands warm."

Sergeant Blake opened his mouth to speak, but the medic shook his head, so Blake dropped the conversation.

"All right, big guy," said the medic, shaking a crinkled metallic blanket out of his pack and wrapping it gently around Fish's shoulders, "you rest right here and we'll get you home real soon." He rummaged deftly in his kit. "I have some crackers for you to eat, and water. You rest up and try to eat and drink and let us take care of things."

"Where's the bear!" demanded Fish.

The medic smiled. "We'll take care of things. You eat."

The soldiers smiled, the medic patted his knee, and they stood and began uncoiling ropes and repacking kits and looking up at the bluffs onshore.

The strangers' kindness, the bruin bear, and the thought of home brought tears to Fish's eyes. Home again. Grandpa's farm. His mom's kitchen. What would his mom say to him? What would his grandpa say to him? It all swirled in his mind, but there was only one comfort, one thing that Fish knew for certain in all that fog: he was done running. And he didn't have to run. Fish looked down at the opened package of oyster crackers in his lap, and his stomach growled in ways he didn't know it could. He took a sip of the clean water, bit the corner from a cracker. The salt dissolved in waves. He ate the whole bag, drank the whole bottle.

The soldier's radio crackled to life, and a jovial and fuzzy sort of voice came over the airwaves.

"Okay there now, you soldiers down on them rocks. Soldiers down on them rocks, come in. This here is—say what? Oh."

The soldier unclipped his radio and frowned at it, then looked up at the lip of the falls. Specialist Grady stopped packing up his kit.

The voice came again. "Lieutenant here says I gotta say *Reach Two*. Reach Two, come in down there. Calling Reach Two."

Sergeant Blake grinned at Specialist Grady as he lifted the radio to his mouth.

"This is Reach, go ahead."

"So, there he is. This is Constable Bobby. You say you got that young man down there on them rocks?"

"That's affirmative," Blake answered.

A chuckle came through the radio. "Well then, soldier, put that young man on the horn! We got his mama up here wants to talk to him. Here you go, missus."

Fish's throat caught. His eyes blurred.

"Lieutenant?" Blake queried into his radio.

There was a pause, then, "Reach, Lieutenant. It's fine if the boy is able."

There was a pause, and then a quavering female voice. "Fischer, are you there? Fischer?"

Blake offered the radio to Fish, and Fish nodded and swallowed, and then the soldier showed him the button to push to speak and went back to his work. Fish held the radio in his lap, his mom's voice coming through it. Her voice was so beautiful to hear, even through the static of that tiny speaker. It was a voice that made the world okay, the voice that calmed him in the night. She said his name three or four more times before Fish was able to answer.

"Mom," he said.

There was a long pause. "Talk again, Fischer. Tell me it's you."

"It's me," he said, tears completely stealing his vision.

"It's you," she said.

"It's me," he said.

"It's you," she said.

IN LESS THAN AN HOUR, FISH WAS IN HER ARMS. SHE WOULDN'T LET him go. She wouldn't let anyone come near them. She scooped him up in that crinkly blanket and carried him into the trees on the island, pacing back and forth in the cedars, weeping on him and rocking him as if he were younger than he was. Fish didn't resist. He just lay with his head on her shoulder, smelling her neck. From time to time Miranda would stop walking, and they'd pull their heads apart to look at each other, and then Fish would bury his face again and Miranda would rock and sway with her eyes closed tight, whispering praise and prayers.

Scattered around the base of the island remained a handful of guardsmen in uniform, and Cal and Tiffany, and Bread, and Teddy, and Constable Bobby. Cal stood by the shoreline and conversed with the deputy and one of the guardsmen. Tiffany sat on a rock. Bread leaned back against her and she wrapped him in her arms, a blanket around them both. She liked the way the boy's dirty hair smelled, liked the warmth of his bony back against her stomach. Teddy lay on his back beneath a pine tree, his legs splayed flat, sleeping with his green cap pulled over his eyes.

Constable Bobby's voice rose up from the small group of men. Tiffany watched as he hiked his belt up on his waist.

"Like I says, when Jack bust out and hitched his duckboat, I knew he was headed downriver, and I knew them women was headed downriver, and I knew downriver don't go farther than here, so I figured I'd get us a spot of help." Bobby finished the sentence with a proud grin and gave the lieutenant too hearty a clap on the shoulder. "Yes sir," he said, "got me some Army on the horn and all is nice and calm again. So."

Tiffany grinned and shook her head, and then watched Miranda and her boy in the trees. The mother and son sat cliffside now, looking off at the river. Miranda turned to talk to him, and Fish turned and smiled, and the two would look out to the river again, Fischer melting into his mom.

Tiffany noticed Bread watching too. He sat very still, so she squeezed his shoulders a little, and he looked up at her. He seemed on the edge of tears, and that was to be expected given all that had happened. He didn't have a parent to meet him. Tiffany felt her throat get tight, but decided to swallow it back and straighten herself up a bit.

"What's your favorite kind of food?" she asked him.

Bread thought for a moment. "I like spaghetti," he said.

"Me too," she said. "And what about dessert?"

"I like pie."

"What kind of pie?"

"Apple."

Tiffany nodded knowingly, as if apple was a very wise choice.

"What do you say, when we get back to town, I take you to the Sunrise Café and you and I absolutely stuff ourselves with spaghetti and apple pie."

Bread smiled at the thought. "They have malts there too," he said, a little embarrassed.

Tiffany wiped the embarrassment and a tear right off his face. Smoothed his hair in her hand. "I wouldn't have it any other way," she said. "Malts are a given."

Bread beamed, and his eye caught Teddy, sleeping under the tree. Bread felt for something in his pocket.

"Tiffany, would you excuse me?"

She released him, surprised by his formality, and nodded accordingly.

She watched Bread walk over to where Teddy dozed. Bread spoke and Teddy lifted his cap and smiled tiredly at the boy. He leaned up on his elbow and patted the ground by his side. He stifled a yawn and wiped his eyes while Bread shifted in place. The boy held out something small and metallic in his hands.

Tiffany watched this as Cal sat down at her side.

"We'll get moving upriver in a few minutes," he said. "More boats are on the way. It will be easier than the hike down to Ironsford."

"Good," said Tiff distractedly, and then nodded toward Teddy and the boy. Teddy had sat upright and accepted the offering. He turned the barlow knife in his hands and then unfolded it. He wiped the blade a few times between his fingers. Held the edge up to the sunlight, tested its sharpness with his thumb. He stared at it for a moment, nodded, folded the blade, and handed it back to Bread. Teddy said a few words, and Bread's face brightened, and Teddy patted the boy on the hip. Bread turned and bounded back toward Tiffany. Teddy fell back on the pine needles, hat back over his eyes and a grin on his face. She was amazed at the way the youth seemed capable of rallying so fast. And she was humbled by it too. For a boy to be so good-hearted after surviving so awful a father was a testament to his strength and spirit. Bread's smile brought tears to her eyes. Made her sit up straighter.

"Are you going to take me shooting now?" Tiffany asked.

Cal smirked. "I lost my gun," he said, and shook his head, but then he took a deep breath, looked at the sky. "I'm thinking of farming, Tiffany. I am thinking of buying a farm."

"Farming," Tiffany said, with a bit more surprise than she intended.

Cal winced, looked at his boot.

Tiffany put a hand on his arm. She imagined him strolling up some gravel drive with a rake or a bucket in his hand, a rag in his pocket, suntanned, dusty.

"Cal, it's good," she said. "I can really see it, and it's good."

He looked at her and smiled.

"Can I come over to your farm?" she asked.

"That's all I want," he said very quickly, which made Tiffany stare right into his eyes, and her face colored. She was still looking at him when Constable Bobby strode up to them, hiked his pant leg, and put one foot up on the rock.

"Well, Sheriff, not much to do but get back and start the paperwork." Bobby sighed heavily at the thought. "Gonna be plenty of that. And that Breadwin boy." Bobby clicked his tongue. "Gonna have some extra work there getting some fosters lined up. Oh well, plenty of good fosters in the county, a mama and a papa and maybe a dog too."

"Bobby," said Cal.

"But then, of course, you got to do the state's paper—"

"Bobby," said Cal, more curtly this time. Bread was approaching the group, still wearing a smile. He rubbed the barlow knife with his thumbs.

"We'll sort that out later," Cal said.

Tiffany looked at Cal's eyes. The thought of Bread going to live with strangers set an unbearable pang in her chest. She envisioned him walking through the slush in his sneakers, same as before, saw his face with all that shame and pride in it. She felt all of her own lonely years pile up inside her. Never again, she thought, and knew it like she knew she had bones. She was not going to let that happen to this boy. She gripped Cal's hand and stared at him until he recognized the fire in her eyes. She would not, under any circumstances, let that boy be taken away. She'd pitch a tent outside the courthouse and live in it all summer if she had to. She'd work double shifts, buy a house, plant a garden, fill her cupboards to overflowing, to prove she was worthy of him. Tiffany was adopting a little brother, and there was no height or depth or power that could stop her. He was now part of her tribe.

Cal seemed to see it in her, and he put his hand on her hand and held it tight, gave her a nod. He felt it too.

Bobby turned and pulled up his belt when Bread arrived. "Say, this young man has got himself a real fine pocketknife."

Bread sat between Tiffany's legs, lifted his trophy up to her. She smiled at it.

"He said I took good care of it and I can hold it for him until we get back. And *then* he said he's gonna take me and Fish to Briar's and buy us our own barlows, might even get 'em engraved!"

Bobby blew air through his lips. "Well!" he said. "Your own barlow is a special thing. Yes indeed. I remember when my papa got me my first barlow. Had a spring-steel sheepfoot blade, nickel bolsters en handle scales made out of a rhino's horn. Of course, you can't get rhino horn these days. At least that's what they say on the TV. Not a bad thing, mind you, letting rhinos alone, but a body's gotta wonder if you lay off 'em too long they don't become as much a menace as 'em packs of coyotes we got around here. Imagine *that,* young man! *Packs* of rhinos!"

Bread looked at Tiffany and saw in her eyes that he should just listen politely, so he did. And Bobby went on about how he heard a good many of them bushranger fellers still made good livings letting rich folk shoot crocodiles on safari, but Bobby couldn't see why anyone wanted to shoot a crocodile in the first place. They didn't have no horns to speak of for making good barlows, and they had to smell something awful muddy. At least with turtles a person can rustle some soup, maybe make a pair of earrings for a girl from the bits of shell. Oh well.

EPILOGUE

THREE FLAT-BOTTOMED BOATS SMOKED AND HUMMED THEIR WAY upriver through the black water. The breeze felt cool and good on Fish's forehead. He sat on the rumbling aluminum floor, leaned back against his mom, who leaned back against the bench. Cattails and marsh grass scrolled past. The river bent west into the sunset, and Fish let the trees and sky and light wash over him.

Up ahead, Fish could see the silhouette of his grandfather in the first boat, kneeling in the prow and shielding his eyes from the sun, pointing out channels. Constable Bobby sat behind him, huddled in a blanket, while two of the soldiers looked at maps and steered and spoke into radios. As the boats banked, Fish turned for a moment to look back. In the last boat sat Bread, between Tiffany and Cal, all three wrapped up. Bread's face was angled up into the orange light, his hair ruffled in the wind, his eyes closed, still and calm. Jacks stood in front of them all, with his paws up on the gunwale, his fur ruffled too, his tongue wagging.

Fish had already finished telling his mom how the river spit him up, how Bread's dad came at them, how the bruin bear came. He told her everything—about how they ran and swam, about how cold the rain was. He told her about his grandfather astride a horse, peering out over a river. He told her about Bread facing down the sheriff, and the man with antlers, and the belly of the turtle he didn't eat. He told her what it felt like to go over the falls, tumble through all that darkness and thunder. He told her what the trees sounded like in that storm. He told her about their raft. And then he said something that made her weep and smile and hug him to her chest.

"Dad's not gone, Mom," he told her. "We can't see him, but he's not gone."

His mom trembled. "You're right," she said, smiling through her tears. She kissed his head, smelled his hair, rubbed the bones and muscles in his back and shoulders. "He's still here," she whispered. "I can feel him."

THE BOAT PITCHED. ITS SQUARE BOW LEAPT AND SLAPPED THE WA-
ter. The sun was lower in the sky now, orange and red, and darkness would come soon. The moon rose. The soldiers tightened clamps of spotlights to gunwales. The breeze felt colder. Something about the air felt like heaviness, something about the transition of light, or the smell of the boat exhaust. The boats hummed, and Fish couldn't put his finger on it. And then it struck him. It was the weight of a dead man, still buried in the river. They hadn't found him. The soldiers talked to Cal about it in hushed tones, turned their backs to Fish and Bread. Fish tried to picture Bread's dad down there, waving in some dark current, pinned in the rocks, but when he did, it mixed together in his tired mind with all the other ways the boys imagined saving Bread from his father. There was the time they buried him in the anthill. There was the time they ran him down with tractors. And now there was the time they went over a waterfall, and the bruin bear came, and how it all buried the man for good. Fish couldn't hold it all in his mind.

The river spread out into a tangled maze of marshes and channels now. Fish's grandpa pointed, then held up his hand. As they passed the bay where the storm had hit, all of the boats slowed down and gathered together. The trees were all topped off, the water still strewn with debris. Everyone watched the bay as it passed. There was silence and stillness except for the low thrum and pop of idling motors. Bread and Cal and Tiffany stared together at the wreckage. Fish stared at them and at it, and then looked upriver toward his grandfather. His grandpa was already looking back at him, and he gave Fish a nod. It was a slow nod, quiet, and Fish knew what it meant. It made something cold and brave rise inside him. Fish stirred in his seat. He and Bread were alive, but the darkness had come too close. It had come with so much force. And part of the heaviness Fish felt—and there was something of this in his grandfather's nod, too—was the realization that the darkness would come again. He and Bread would grow up. They'd learn to drive cars. They'd become men like the sheriff and Fish's grandpa, and the darkness would come for them again.

Fish scooted back more fully into his mother's arms until the warmth returned. As the boats sped up, Fish's mom pulled him into herself, her wrapped wrist over his chest, and Fish knew he didn't have to face anything right now, not right here, not yet. The sound of the motors sang bright songs. The boats ran together in a tight pack. Fish closed his eyes and looked up into the setting sun, let the shadows of branches pass through it. The bow of the boat leapt and sprayed, the wake hissed like sand spilling across a wilderness, and Fish imagined his dad sitting on top of a bright dune, smiling back at him. And Fish knew, leaning on his mom, looking up at his dad, that when the darkness came again, he would beat it again. And so would Bread. They would beat it because they would just keep going, like his grandfather said. Fish opened his eyes and watched Bread across the water. The river shone. Bread's face shone. Bread rested against Tiffany with his eyes closed, with Jacks draped across his lap. Tiffany's eyes were closed too, her purple hair waving. Cal had his arm around them both.

And then Bread opened his eyes without stirring, looked right at Fish for the space of a breath or two. The air filled with the smell of river and cedar and dusk. And the two boys smiled at each other, with the sun and moon above them and the river beneath them, and the smile wasn't joyful and it wasn't sad. But it spoke. It said, *I see you, Bread.* It said, *I see you, Fish.* It said, *You are strong and you are good, and you are not alone.*

ACKNOWLEDGMENTS

MANY THANKS TO THE TEAM AT ECCO, WITH SPECIAL THANKS TO my editor, Helen Atsma, for loving these characters as much as I do, and for guiding the book toward a wonderful fruition. Many thanks to Janet Silver and Maggie Cooper of Aevitas. Thank you, Janet, for your guidance and kindness and investment in my work. Thank you, Maggie, for your phenomenal reading and energy and belief, and for bringing so much life and precision to this story. Many thanks to my colleagues and friends in the ELML department, present and past—you are a noble lot. Many thanks to the Iowa Writers' Workshop, with special thanks to Sam Chang, Marilynne Robinson, and James McPherson, who provided opportunity and wisdom for which I will always be grateful. Many thanks to the English department at Lawrence University, who taught me to love good books, with special thanks to author and mentor David McGlynn, who has always been there when the answers mattered most, and who first taught me how to sit in the chair and do the work of writing. Many thanks to my family, to my brothers for being the best sort of men, and to my parents, who gave much to provide a home in the Northwoods where their sons could holler and dream and sit in trees and swim in creeks and rivers. And many thanks to my wife, Heidi, for all the days and nights—you are strong and you are good, and you are not alone.

ONE PLACE. MANY STORIES

Bold, innovative and
empowering publishing.

FOLLOW US ON:

@HQStories